MALFEASANCE

Running Bull Publishing

Los Angeles, California

All of the characters in this book are fictitious, and any resemblance to actual persons, living or dead, is purely coincidental.

ISBN: 978–1–7364527–3–8

Printed in the United States of America

PART 1

"If you want to know your past – look into your present conditions. If you want to know your future – look into your present actions."

Ekhart Tolle

1

As the city lights claim the view, Senator George Claxton sits up in his chair and turns his attention from the window to the papers on his large antique desk. His is one of the more spacious and imposing Senate offices with a wall upon which hang an impressive array of framed awards and photographs of him with famous philanthropists, international figures, and high–ranking politicians. Among the display is a photo of a young George Claxton with his wife, Cynthia, and her father, the intimidating K–Street player, Jacob Windsor.

Claxton's aide, Joel, hovers near the desk as the Senator comfortably reviews the document in front of him. Joel's been with George nearly a year and does a fine job and without the usual whining or novice mistakes. Tall, slight and a bit baby–faced, but not entirely unattractive, Joel always stays late and seems eager to learn the games of the Hill. Learn in a real way, George thinks, not in the typical entitled, *my father was so–and–so, therefore because I breathe I should be allowed to be a moron and still jump ahead* way. In Washington, setting out for a career in politics is no small ambition, or one without a minefield of potential pitfalls. George has certainly encountered his share of idiots with more power than good sense. He's been surprisingly pleased with Joel. Joel is the type of young person that can be guided and can understand the requirements necessary in DC political life.

The faint echoes of conversation in the hallways drift in through the open doors of his office. This is the time of year, so close to the holidays, the building begins thinning out earlier and earlier. George finishes reading and looks up.

"Have a seat," the Senator instructs the well–groomed young man, who does as he's told.

"Is everything alright with the brief?" Joel inquires.

"Yes. Fine." Claxton leans back in his chair and studies his disciple. "Do you think the Abramson bill is going to pass?"

"Well, they're twelve votes short and have only three days left, but Charlotte Jameson is surprising people. Her staff is setting up back-to-back meetings all over town, so I wouldn't doubt if she might get it over the line," Joel offers.

"She's a beast, that one. That's what it takes – guts, manipulation, grabbing the bull by the balls – to make anything happen around here. There are a lot of people in this building with a title or a position, but they're ineffective." Claxton's mind wanders off for a moment.

"Yes sir."

"Sadly, that number seems to be growing." Claxton pushes his chair back and stands. Joel studies his boss and mentor as Claxton walks over to the small bar and pours himself a scotch. "Want one?"

"Oh...no. No thank you," Joel manages, delighted that he's finally being offered.

"The focus of the Abramson Bill is to nationally legalize pot and loosen the penalties for use on other illegal drugs to help alleviate our overburdened prisons and so on, yes?" Claxton begins and downs his scotch.

"Yes," Joel responds.

"Some states have already done this, so it seems possible. Right?"

"Right."

"Wrong. The bill won't pass. Mark my words." Claxton sits back down and leans in toward Joel, fingering his glass. He studies Joel and leans back. "Number one, the more you strip people of self–responsibility and impede their thinking for themselves, the more control you have over them. We need them to feel they are not capable of being responsible to make their own decisions. Number two and most important in this fight is that the needed votes are from people whose jobs, hell, their very existence, is too dependent on the war on drugs. The primary reason we don't legalize drugs is not because of their dangers, hell, prescription drugs are just as dangerous and ruin more lives, but because prisons, the war against drugs, and the whole system is a multi–billion–dollar business. Too many of the smaller states depend on it. It's always about the money, Joel. You want to know what's at the core of an issue? Follow the money."

Claxton smiles at the fascinated young man who delights in being brought into his confidence. Joel's eager face urges the Senator on. Claxton is usually stiff and curt and certainly doesn't go on about his views with low–level staff, but tonight he's in a good mood, having heard a whisper that he's up for Majority Whip.

"We need the problems, so we have something to fix. Think about..." Claxton's cell phone, sitting in the middle of his desk between the two men, suddenly rings. The Senator looks at the caller ID and immediately snatches up the phone and stands, "I've got to take this outside. Make copies of the brief and put them on my desk and you can get out of here." With a growing scowl, the Senator is out the door leaving Joel perplexed at the abrupt shift in his mood.

Joel reaches across the desk for the brief just as the desk phone next to his arm lights up and rings. He jumps and his hand jerks and hits the Senator's open briefcase off of the desk, spilling its contents. Thankful the Senator is out of view, Joel scrambles to clean up the mess. He glances at one of the documents as he picks it up and it stops him cold.

* * *

Confident that the Senate building is now empty, George puts the invitation down and steadies his hand. The embossed parchment stares up at him. Another political schmooze fest and he's late. Very late. But he can catch the last hour or so. Not showing up is not an option. Especially now. He has work to do, on more than a few fronts. He can't risk anything going wrong.

He takes a deep breath, finishes tying his bow tie, and adjusts his tuxedo. He looks around the office, then closes the door to his private bathroom, puts a last sheet of paper in the shredder and reaches for his black cashmere coat, catching his reflection in the mirror. Still fit, in his fifties, with only a slight greying in the temples. His looks have always been an asset–never had any trouble attracting women. He must focus on summoning all his charm for the evening.

His recent divorce from Cynthia, the shrew as he likes to call her, doesn't seem to be hurting him too much with his constituents and it surely makes him a catch on the Hill. Cynthia made the mistake of equating money with power. A common misperception.

Why that woman had insisted on knowing his every move was beyond him. Didn't she know that suffocation was a key relationship destroyer? What did she expect? He's a young enough U.S. Senator, and events, late nights, and impromptu business trips, come with the territory. Routine and ennui are not part of a powerful Senator's life. Cynthia knows this; after all, her family name went a long way in getting him in the right social circles and helping him win elections. George isn't sure what it was that had set her off in the extreme last year. She must've been bored, especially with both girls off to college. He wished she had found a hobby. Instead, the woman tried for months to prove he was having an affair. Her father, the great Jacob Windsor, had an affair or two and no one went ballistic on him. Claxton must concede that at least Cynthia had the decency to wait until their youngest daughter moved into the dorms before filing the papers. But nothing about their divorce has been kind to his pocketbook. Cynthia hardly needs the money. Her trust fund alone can feed a small country for a decade. No, it's not about the money. She wants him to feel the sting. That's why this next year is so critical.

The Senator grabs his scarf and keys. Opening the door, he looks back at the paper shredder next to his desk. The final sheet makes its way through the blades, then shuts off.

"On your way home, Senator? It sure is a cold one out there," a voice startles Claxton as he closes his office door. He catches himself, locks the door and takes another deep breath before turning to face the old janitor, right on time, making his rounds.

"No, Frank. Got a fundraiser tonight. The tail end anyway," Claxton says as he walks several steps down the hallway to the elevator bay. Frank accompanies him, pushing his supply cart along.

"The election comes up for you this year, don't it? Hope it goes well for you, sir."

Claxton pushes the down arrow and notices that Frank doesn't seem to be moving on. The far–right elevator door opens. Claxton looks inside the empty cab, then instead of entering, he pulls a fifty–dollar bill from his pocket, turns back to Frank and hands him the money. The elevator door closes. "Thank you, Frank. Buy your wife some flowers," he says, then pushes the button again.

Frank grins from ear to ear. He likes the Senator, always has. Claxton always remembers his name. This man is nice to the help, not demeaning like many of the others. "Thank you, sir." Frank gives Claxton an approving nod, then moves down the hall to continue his rounds.

The middle elevator door opens. Claxton enters, selects the Lobby button and checks his watch. He'll just get there before the early birds begin leaving. As the elevator starts its descent, he begins to feel overly warm and constricted. He should've waited to put on his coat, and the scarf. He pulls the bulk loose from around his neck. A strange noise intrudes from somewhere, but he's alone in the cab. *What can that be?* He wonders and loosens his bow tie. The noise gets louder. *What is that?* A grating or a scratching, then a bumping. The elevator moves along smoothly. Another scraping sound. From above.

As he looks up, the top of the cab breaks open and a large mass descends from its darkness. Before he can think, it hits him with full force, causing his knees to buckle, and sends him to the floor. A weight, a stickiness, and heavy breathing is on him.

Something envelops him. *What the...?!* He fights to break loose but there are arms clinging around his neck. A body. And... blood...and more blood. He pushes the torso away far enough to see that it belongs to Joel, his aide, pale and struggling to remain conscious. A gasp escapes George's lips. *How can this be?* Joel's hair, wet with brownish red ooze, sticks to the side of his face.

Joel's head goes limp, but his pleading eyes fight to stay open. George panics. He pants and flails, trying to get Joel off him. The blood is thick and slippery, and he can't get any traction. The more he tries to wedge himself away, the more entangled he becomes. His heart nearly pounds out of his chest. Joel can't weigh more than one hundred sixty pounds, but gravity along with the descending elevator's motion prevent him from pushing Joel off. Joel's arm remains wrapped around his neck. So much blood. George feels his chest constricting. He must find a way to breathe. The elevator reaches the lobby, and the doors open. He needs to get out of there. "Good God! Somebody please...help me!"

2

In the pre–dawn light, the charming neighborhoods of Georgetown are still dark and undisturbed. March is the time of year when it can feel like winter one day and the promise of spring the next. The Reeve's home is silent, in harmony with its neighbors.

Stephen's eyes open, looking at the ceiling. Instantly he's awake, as if sleep is a distant memory rather than something he is just waking from. A strange eagerness seizes him, and he feels more energized than usual. The past year has brought Stephen a strange insomnia. One where falling asleep takes longer and waking occurs before dawn. He started working sixty to seventy hours a week at the office about the same time the insomnia began.

In the gray light, Stephen turns to look at his sleeping wife. Janet's long, dark hair flows around her magnificently pretty face as if staged. With her lips slightly parted and eyes gently closed, Stephen is reminded of the first time he watched her sleep in her dorm room bed. The serenity of her expression exposes the vulnerability of the woman who needs stability, gentleness and reassurance when the lights go out. A contrast to the displays of strength and fire of her waking self. As he watches her, she twitches and flings her arm away from him, turning onto her side, still in a deep sleep. He takes this opportunity to slide out of bed without rousing her.

Stephen enjoys getting up before Janet and the kids during the week. The morning quiet allows him the opportunity to slip into himself, go into his workshop and sketch out new ideas or work on old projects. It's the time before other people's demands come calling. Today, he doesn't have to get to the office. Jury duty. He'd debated throwing out the summons as he did the last time, but instead he filled it out, sent it in and forgot about it thinking he wouldn't be needed. His understanding was that most people just call in daily for the five days and are done. But he was told to show up at the courthouse. His first impulse was to get out of it due to work, but the heavy lifting for the design on the Kairos Tower is finished and he needs to regroup, refresh his perspective and get his mind out of the usual routine. Thinking about the day ahead, he looks forward to something different.

He quietly makes his way downstairs and flicks on the coffee pot. Its familiar gurgles fill the kitchen. Coffee and peace constitute the first two hours of his weekdays. Once Emily and Mark wake up, the house will turn into a tornado as nine–year–old Mark has a way of annoying his older sister from the minute he gets up. The Reeves have a rugged handsomeness in their lineage and Stephen is no exception. His looks are more refined, but still notable, whereas his brother Rob always got the immediate attention of the ladies with his strong nose and impressive beard. Stephen suspects Mark will grow into resembling his uncle Rob's ruggedness. As the liquid finishes brewing, he pulls on a sweater and grabs a large mug. Pouring himself the first cup, Stephen inhales the sweet aroma and looks out into the small yard at the breaking light as it reflects off the workshop. He designed and built the workshop to maximize usable space while preserving enough of a yard for the kids.

Every time he looks at the structure, a glint of pride surfaces and he's reminded of his architectural talent large windows facing the house to augment light, high ceilings and walls with angles and protrusions to make it much more than just a box. The small building is an artistic and well–crafted vision worthy of comment. There were times Stephen craved working in other cities – Singapore, London or Paris – but living in Georgetown would be tough to give up.

Stephen steps outside. A damp chill envelopes him. The moisture–laden air is thick, familiar, and fills him with a sense of home. He enters his workshop. The space soothes him. A large desk inhabits the center of the room. On one side sits a computer with a few papers next to it, on the other is an abstract multi–faceted steel sculpture and some drawing supplies with the center of the desk surface devoid of any clutter. A smaller table, with lower shelves, is positioned at an angle to the side, supporting both a laser printer and a 3D printer, a variety of colored plastic printer filament and paper.

Opposite the desk is a couch with a small coffee table in front. The wall behind Stephen's desk consists of a built–in bookcase filled with a variety of well–worn titles such as *The Elements of Style*, *How Buildings Learn*, *Architectural Lighting Design*, along with numerous books on art including Phaidon's *The 20th Century Art Book*, *Masterworks of Modern Art* and *Stark*.

Stephen sees the CAD file of the tiny chair next to his keyboard. For Emily. He had promised to finish the furniture for her dollhouse last year, but life and work got in the way. She turned twelve this year and he's noticed more of an edge to her. That edge doesn't seem to be going away. Girls. He knows that he can't expect her to stay the same sweet little girl forever, but maybe just a little sweeter for a while longer. He's not so sure he's ready for full on teenage–dom. One of his favorite projects has been designing and building the dollhouse for her. He relishes taking an idea from his head, putting those concepts into a structure on paper and then turning it into something real.

With the dollhouse he had complete autonomy. He didn't intend this small project to take so long, but with all the kids' sports and school functions, he and Janet barely have time to themselves let alone time for extra projects like this. And when the 3D printer came along, he was like a kid in a candy store. This was the toy he needed to create the kind of furniture he envisioned. It took time to master the printer before the miniature pieces started to turn out right. This chair is the last of the set for the dining room. Stephen pulls out the red filament and measures it. Janet suggested that maybe he was making this furniture more for himself than for Emily. He thinks that's ridiculous. He cuts the piece and begins programing the printer.

* * *

Through the upstairs bedroom window, Janet sees that Stephen is in his workshop and smiles to herself. The house is still quiet, but only for the next few minutes. She goes into the bathroom and as she turns on the shower, something about her reflection causes her to move to the mirror and look closer. Under her eyes there's a puffiness. She squints and looks closer. She notices new lines etch themselves toward the edges to create definitive crow's feet. *Ugh! So, this is what over forty has to offer.* Overall, she's been lucky. Turning thirty hadn't fazed her like it did some of her girlfriends. She relished each age of her life. At least up to now. It felt natural to her and, as her friends point out, she's genetically fortunate, has a great husband, the requisite two kids, her career of choice, and lives in a beautiful house in an enviable area of town. Lately, however, small things have begun to bother her. She would notice a new spot on her arm or face, a slight droop in her jaw from a certain angle, and her desire to work out has given in to her desire to have a glass of wine and crap out more often than it should.

Agingsucks. Shetakesoffhernightshirtandturnsawayfrom themirror. The lastthingshewantstoseenowisherchildbearing breasts. She wants to start her day off focusing on the positive.

Today, she's pitching a new client – Adele and Mark Winston. Her biggest job yet. The Winston's are throwing a gala for the opening fundraiser for the new Museum of Contemporary Art and have asked Janet's company to submit a bid for the contract to plan and manage the event. Her company, Ellis Events (EE), consistsofherselfandKathy,herassistant,butshehaslearnedto hire subcontractors in growing numbers to give the impression that no event is too large. She chose the company name after her maidenname,Ellis,whenshewasincollege,whenthecompany was just an idea and a concept for a paper, and before Stephen entered the picture. Stephen, the handsome, sweet and shy, architectural student, always trying to keep up, and to outdo his friends.

The first time she saw him, she knew her life was about to change. She never would have believed a person could feel that kind of knowing if it hadn't happened to her. As a young girl she used to love watching reruns of the old television series *Hart to Hart* with Robert Wagner. Janet's mother, Michelle, would say how she refused to believe that Wagner could be suspected of foul play over the death of his real wife, Natalie Wood, who died during a couples' outing on a boat when she was forty–three. Janet's mother insisted that Wagner and Wood were the perfect couple. She told Janet the story of when Natalie was just a young girl and was with her own mother when she first saw Robert Wagner. Natalie stopped dead in her tracks and told her mother, "I'm going to marry him." It was a preposterous statement at the time, and she was just a child, but even then Natalie knew – their fates were inexorably linked. Janet considered it a fantasy and brushed it off, but her own experience hadn't been that different. Something about Stephen jolted her the moment she saw him. An inexplicable recognition and at the same time a strange comfort. It seems as if their fates, too, are inexorably linked.

After they were married and in a position for Janet to start her event planning enterprise, Stephen encouraged her to keep the company name she created, as a reminder of a dream fulfilled. EE had been the perfect solution for a working mother. Janet set her own hours and took or rejected jobs around her schedule with the kids, especially when they were younger. In the past two years, she kicked the business into higher gear, taking on more and larger clients, and it's starting to pay off. After Janet's father died, her mother, Michelle, moved close by and still delights in picking up the kids from school and watching them until Janet or Stephen arrive home. Stephen is still the primary bread winner, but now Janet is able to make more than a small, arguably negligible, contribution. Stephen's work hours have been outrageous this past year, but he assured her that he would make more time for family now that his design proposal on the Tower is complete.

Janet dresses in her dark navy Armani suit just as she hears Mark burst into the room yelling, "Mo–om! Emily is still in the bathroom!"

"Good morning to you too, little gremlin."

"I can't be late today! It's early lab!" Mark stands firm, fully dressed and ready for school.

Janet flinches as she looks at the time. She had forgotten that his school schedule shifts this week to accommodate his early science lab. She throws some things into her purse and grabs her shoes. "We're still okay. We'll get there on time. Go downstairs and grab some granola bars. You guys can eat in the car on the way, and I'll get Emily going."

Mark shakes his head in dismay and heads downstairs as Janet makes her way to Emily's room.

* * *

As the tiny chair completes its form and Stephen pulls it out of the printer, Emily plows through the door.

"Mom says you need to come in," she announces briskly, then is gone. "And good morning to you," Stephen responds.

The door slams behind her and Stephen shakes his head, "Hey!" Chair in hand, he follows Emily into the kitchen.

"Em, hey, manners are helpful. I got something for you," Stephen says.

"Good morning dad. Stephen holds out the chair to his daughter who is dressed in jeans and a t–shirt with her hair pulled back in a ponytail.

"For my dollhouse?" she grimaces.

"What's with the face? I thought you wanted a complete set."

Emily sighs the sign of impending adolescence as she informs her father, "That was eons ago, Dad. I'm not really into dolls anymore."

"That was barely a couple of weeks ago."

Seeing Stephen's disconcerted face, Emily adds, "It's a great chair though. Thanks."

Janet walks over to her husband and gives him a kiss. "Deep down she appreciates it."

"Unbelievable. What time is it?"

"Not even seven. I completely forgot Mark has early period today, so no time for a real breakfast. Sorry. I pulled out bran muffins and blueberries for you."

"Thanks. I might be home early. Depending."

After a moment, Janet registers that he's referring to jury duty. "Try to get dismissed, will you?"

"Mommm." Exasperated, Mark stands by the door, backpack in hand, tapping his foot.

"I'm serious," Janet says to Stephen. "We need you here more not less."

Stephen nods.

"Mooommmm!" Emily grabs her lunch and turns for her brother.

"Stop," Stephen orders. "Where're my kisses?"

Mark runs up to Stephen and quickly plants one on him, then turns and dashes, while Emily blows him a kiss on the way to the door.

"Love you. Always have," Stephen says to Janet.

"Always will," she adds in their customary repartee, then to the kids, "Alright, move it," and follows them out of the house.

With the house empty, Stephen observes the bowl of berries and bran muffins on the counter. He sniffs the muffins, puts them away, then steps into the large walk–in pantry. He searches amidst an array of health food and pokes around until he finds the box of Cap'n Crunch. He pours himself a bowl, opts to sprinkle a few blueberries on top before adding milk, and digs in as he clicks on the morning news.

3

An obnoxious buzzing of the phone alarm fills the room. "Shit!" Terry's arm shoots out and flails about, grabbing for his cell. As he shuts it off, his still sleep– deprived brain informs him that at seven fifteen he has little time to shower and get himself together in time to meet Stephen for coffee before needing to be at the office and prepare for the morning rounds in court. Having coffee together is a rare opportunity for them.

He sees Stephen and Janet together at their house for dinner a few times a month.

A tradition that began years ago, after the Elise incident and after it became clear that Terry wasn't inclined to settle down anytime soon as a result. Right after the demise of his relationship with Elise, it had been difficult to be around Stephen and Janet. A reminder of what would never be his – love, marriage, and constant companionship.

Stephen's been his best friend since college freshman year, and he can't imagine Stephen without Janet. It did't take long for Terry to slip into a comfortable accceptance and admiration of them. Terry became an extended part of the Reeves' family. To Mark and Emily, he is Uncle Terry.

Terry rolls out of his rumpled bed, stumbles to the kitchen for coffee and turns on the TV. Two used wine glasses and an empty wine bottle litter the counter. His foot catches on something on the kitchen floor. He looks down at the smooth turquoise woman's thong and vaguely remembers the late–night romp with Brigitte, thankful that she didn't stay the night. She stopped by for a couple of hours during her pass–through flight to Florida. He loves flight attendants. Especially the ones who aren't based in D.C. Terry understands that being over forty and still single isn't especially encouraging to women seeking a long–term relationship and it makes others wonder about you, but that works well for him. He'd decided long ago, no more long–term relationships.

Elise had ripped that idea from his head right about the time she ripped out his heart. Terry proposed to Elise, and they got engaged two years after Stephen married Janet, nearly fourteen years ago. At that time, Terry saw himself as a budding young attorney who could easily fill the role of family man with a woman who excited and intrigued him as much as Elise did. Also an attorney, Elise was smart, ambitious and a golden–haired knockout. Terry felt like the luckiest man in the world. Elise wanted a spring wedding, so they set a date and began putting plans in motion. Terry thought everything was heading toward the perfect life, until March. Elise had gone to New York on a case, and when she returned, nothing was the same. She stopped kissing him or touching him or running her fingers through his hair as they sat side by side. Her work hours seemed to increase, and he could swear that she avoided looking him in the eye. He tried to talk to her about it, asking if anything were wrong, but she wouldn't admit that anything had changed. That went on for nearly a month, then one Friday afternoon, before they were scheduled to leave for dinner, she placed her engagement ring in Terry's hand and said, "I'm sorry." That was her only explanation. Nothing more. Terry tried fighting with her, but she wouldn't engage. She turned away from him and walked out. It was the most surreal moment of his life. He hasn't seen her since, and the notion of marriage became a thing of his past. He heard she moved to New York.

Feeling the silk thong between his fingers brings up memories of Brigitte's smooth skin and Terry smiles. He knows Brigitte thinks of him as too old for her and that's good. Keeps the distance in place. He slips the panties into a random drawer as the morning news fills the kitchen.

"Since current Majority Leader Bob Elwell announced his retirement with the upcoming election, rumors were that George Claxton would be named Majority Whip. Since the Senator's arrest, the decision was put on hold, confident the Senator will be acquitted," news anchor Janie Holland reports.

Terry looks at the screen. He had an encounter or two with Janie, but it didn't end well. She wanted him to escort her to several highly visible functions and when he explained his position on dating, she threw her food at him and walked out. *Crap.* He forgot that the Senator's trial is about to start any day, if they ever get through jury selection. The huge crowds at the courthouse have been increasing daily. Senator Claxton's supporters continue to challenge his arrest. As a Public Defender, Terry's office is in the building near the swarm. The good news is that it's likely that several judges will again be late on their dockets today. If he meets Stephen at Peet's Coffee around the corner, they can walk to the courthouse after they finish, and both still make it on time.

4

In the sunshine, Stephen drives his Volvo sedan into the heart of the nation's capital, situated along the majestic Potomac River. The monuments of a great nation and its elegant and imperial white buildings litter the skyline. Buildings that were built with vision and pride. Beautiful and affecting on a clear day, the cherry blossoms are early this year and fill his view with pink and white splotches along the river. Led Zeppelin's *Whole Lotta Love* fills the air, "...Um baby I been learning; All them good times baby, baby; I've been year–yearning; A–way, way down inside; A–honey you need–ah..."

Stephen jams along to the music and feels strangely excited to have a few days away from the office. This jury duty thing could prove to be opportune. It'll be good to get his mind into a different space and out of the box – out of his office. Larry Simms has no balls and he kept taming Stephen's designs on the K Tower. Because Simms is a partner, Stephen's team has had to go along. Even so, the clients asked Stephen to be the lead and come up with a proposed building plan. The project depends on him, not on Simms. Stephen has been with Graeber, Fike and Simms since right after he married Janet. After graduating from Georgetown University, he hadn't looked elsewhere for work. Now he sees that he probably could have advanced quicker or set up his own architectural firm had he considered it. He needs to formulate a plan, if he's ever going to have his own practice. The music cuts out, interrupted by the ring of his phone.

"Hello!"

"Hey, man. You here yet?" Terry asks from the other end of the line.

"No. Not even close. I forgot how miserable traffic can get this time of day going in this direction. Sorry. I was about to give you a call. Coffee's out. Can you do lunch?"

"No, I can't predict the timing. But, come find me after you're done and let's grab a drink."

"I'm not sure what that is."

"Come on family man. Pretend we're back in college for a minute. See how the other side lives. I'm sure Janet won't mind. She likes me, remember. Besides, that way you can avoid traffic on the way back."

"Sometimes. She likes you sometimes."

"Whatever you gotta tell yourself, man."

"Alright. I'll pop in when I'm done." Stephen grins, looking forward to hanging out with Terry.

The imposing E. Barrett Prettyman Courthouse grounds are swarming with press vans and a curious public. The triangular 24–foot–high granite monument, called the Trylon of Freedom, depicts scenes and excerpts from the nation's founding documents and stands in front of the entrance as a reminder to all that justice intends to be meted out here. Two sides of the sculpture represent guarantees offered by the U.S. Constitution and the Bill of Rights. The third side exhibits the seal of the United States, inscribed with portions of the Preamble of the Constitution and the Declaration of Independence.

Stephen makes his way toward the entrance. The security line coils like a discordant snake out of the front of the building as the colorful masses arrive in all their divergent forms. Mid–century modernism in government buildings is difficult for Stephen to get excited about, but the Bryant Annex is an exception and although constructed in the new millennium, its attempt to create harmony with the old courthouse works well. He had studied the building on paper and from the exterior, but now hopes to see the courtrooms firsthand. Stephen glances at his watch and falls in line. He makes it through security quickly and receives instructions on where to report for duty – the Annex.

After sitting in a waiting room with other potential jurors, he, along with three others, are summoned by a bailiff and led into a large, curved and impressive wood paneled courtroom filled with press and security. He is seated in one of the only three empty seats in the jury box. The low din of murmuring and the absence of the judge suggests that this court is on a break and obviously the full jury still hasn't been selected. Two lawyers confer at the counsel tables. At the defense table, a group of attorneys stand around a tall, well–dressed man who, upon closer look, Stephen recognizes as Senator George Claxton. The man is fit, in his fifties, with only slight greying in the temples. He can't believe that the jury selection for this is still going on. He'd heard snippets on the news about the uproar around the Senator's arrest but hadn't paid much attention. All he remembers is that Senator Claxton was alone in an elevator when a body fell on him from the hatch above. The next thing he knew, the Senator was arrested for murder.

The majority of the jurors, spectators, and press are on their electronic devices, either cell phones or tablets. Feeling tempted, Stephen refuses the urge to pull out his phone and tap into a game of Solitaire. In recent years, he's felt a low, but ever–present and growing hum of anxiety with the news, the Internet, and all the new tech gadgets that he's expected to keep up with, except for the 3D printer and things associated with his work. That kind of useful technology excites him, but the social media stuff leaves him blank. Stephen's level of tech savvy rates a five on a scale of one to ten, and his lack of patience with new programs and apps grows with the addition of each one. His kids can figure anything out on his computer, his phone or his tablet, but he prefers the tangible.

Things that result in something he can touch and build.

After sending another text, the man next to Stephen leans over and, as if conspiring, sneers, "Well, we sure landed the big one." Then gesturing toward Claxton, adds, "I think these guys are all shysters." His large head bobs on a neck that appears inadequate to support it and a bit of spittle on his chin catches the light and shines. In his head, Stephen names the man "Bob."

Unsure of how to respond to "Bob," Stephen is saved by the judge's entrance. For guys like Claxton, managing exposure must be a nightmare. Judge Judith Cohen, with her beautiful mane of chestnut hair, carries herself with poise as she takes her post. Her demeanor reflects her impatience, and the attorneys seem well aware of the need to move things along. Court resumes immediately once Judge Cohen is seated and proceeds briskly.

The jury selection resembles a casting call for a bizarre theater production. "Bob" is immediately dismissed after commenting, "To tell the truth, I don't know how anyone can think that the high and mighty government halls aren't filled with corruption. They know all the shady things they're doing, but the people are kept in the dark." Some qualified and articulate candidates are also dismissed. As one is taken out of a seat another body fills it. So far Stephen can't make out what constitutes an acceptable juror over one that wouldn't be allowed to sit. Janet warned him that based on her jury experiences, most trials are like watching paint dry, but he has a feeling that this case will be different.

The smooth and articulate lead defense attorney, John Alton, wears a dark top–of–the–line Burberry suit and is in the process of his final questioning of the young woman, Melita Colt, who sits in front of Stephen. Melita exudes a twenty–something passion for creativity. Her makeup is extensive but precise. Her dark lined eyes and hint of glitter on her cheeks enhance her youthful enthusiasm for the visual.

"Do you have any prior jury experience?" Alton asks in a voice that betrays just a hint of the Southern gentleman as he glides toward her.

"No, I don't. This is my first time."

Alton smiles and nods. "Do you watch the news, Ms. Colt?"

Melita tucks her chin as if slightly embarrassed. "No. It's not that I don't think it's important. It's just that I don't have a lot of free time."

"Of course. I understand." Alton looks right at Melita and smiles warmly as if this is the beginning of budding friendship. He then looks at his notes and continues, "I see that you work for Green Lawn Mortuary. What do you do?"

"I'm a funeral make–up artist, but I'm also a dancer," she answers proudly. "Thank you, Ms. Colt." Alton nods then sits back down.

Subsequently, the prosecutor, Elliot Mann, an athletic, middle aged black man with an appealing presence, except for the dark puffy circles under his eyes that give him the appearance of not having slept in days, approaches the jury box and directs his question to Stephen.

"Mr. Reeves, do you follow politics?"

"Not really in the last decade or so."

"Do you vote?"

"Yes."

"How do you choose your candidate?"

"Well, when the time comes, I look up information that I don't already know on the people on the ballot and what they stand for."

"You do your research."

"As much as I can."

"Do you have children?"

"Yes. My wife and I have two children."

"Thank you."

As soon as Mann sits down, Alton looks at Stephen and approaches, "Have you seen the press coverage surrounding Senator Claxton's arrest?"

"Some."

"How do you see the Senator as a result of what you've heard?"

"I try not to make a call based on what I hear in the press. I see more sensationalism than journalism, so I don't put much stock in it."

Stephen notices a few smirks from the Press. Alton has nothing more for Stephen and sits. The procedure continues with both sides asking questions of a few other potential jurors. A few minutes before noon, Judge Cohen recesses the court, allowing forty–five minutes for lunch.

After lunch, Stephen still has his seat in the jury box, but hasn't been asked much else. The hours flow by relatively quickly and near the end of the afternoon, with no movement in the jury box for the last hour, Alton stands and announces, "The defense accepts the jury as seated."

The prosecution follows suit and Stephen finds himself standing to be sworn in. He hasn't stopped to consider the ramifications of being selected for this trial until this very moment. This could be a very long trial. And a very public one.

Senator Claxton's presence at the defense table is captivating. His impeccable appearance and relaxed yet perfect posture give him an aura of bigger than life. He seems to take up more space than anyone else, even though he occupies generally the same amount of physical area. Claxton eyes the assorted people in the jury box who will determine his fate.

District Attorney Mann addresses the jury before they take the oath, "I'm sure you are aware that this trial will be all over the media and it is imperative that you take your oath seriously and not discuss anything you hear in this courtroom with anyone at any time until the trial has officially ended. We will resume here at 9 a.m. tomorrow morning. We sincerely appreciate your service and commitment to this process."

Judge Cohen instructs the jurors be sworn in. Stephen raises his right hand, along with the other jurors as the clerk recites, "Do you and each of you solemnly swear that you will well and truly try the cause now pending before this court, and a true deliverance make between the United States and George Claxton, the defendant at the bar, and a true verdict render according only to the evidence presented to you and to the instructions of the court, so help you God?"

The unanimous "I do" from the jurors in the box rings throughout the courtroom.

Stephen feels some anxiety at the prospect of what the firm will say to this development and even more anxiety in thinking about what Janet will say. This is clearly a longer leave than the five days of mandatory jury duty, but there's no way out now. This is a historic trial, and he can be part of something noteworthy. Something big.

* * *

So, these are the people the jury consultants, with all their expertise and fancy sociopolitical pattern–recognition programs, deem best for my chances of acquittal, George observes. The majority are women. He considers that good for him. There's a natural flirtation that frequently occurs between the Senator and most women. George Claxton is a tall, handsome, charming man and women tend to gravitate toward and respect his elevated position and his good looks. George wonders which of the jurors voted for him in the last Senate race and if that means anything under the circumstances.

The Senator won't have the opportunity to play to the jury during the trial. Alton, the best defense attorney in the country, forbids him to testify. Alton told the Senator that testifying is as much about the questions as the answers and Alton's concern is that he can't predict or count on the asked and answered objections and the defense attorney would have very little control over how George's testimony would come across. George has to count on the public's memory of their impression of him in the past, as well as how he appears in court now. Alton did say that he expects to allow George to let slip a few well–placed sound bites to the press as the trial goes along. The Senator has constituents that appreciate his stance on many issues, and many more simply like the tenor of his voice and personality, not having a clue about the issues. Most of these people will never wind up in a jury box, but impressions, opinions and information trickle down and across. George can't believe that Alton allowed Charlie Murphy onto the jury. The jury consultants flagged him, but he still wound up in the final mix. George can tell that Murphy doesn't like him. He knows in his gut that Murphy lied about liking people in power. Thinking about Murphy, George's expression shifts and begins to reveal his distaste for him.

Alton notices and leans in toward his client, "Careful George, we need them to like you. Imagine that you're in front of cameras at all times and we'll be fine."

George checks his expression as he runs the other jurors through his mind: *the older women seem okay; the middle–aged housewife is the kind I do best with, the receptionist will vote with the others; the young guy in the suit will be fine; that architect is a family man and won't cause trouble*…as he continues observing the jurors one by one, something strikes him. A recognition of sorts or what some might call an epiphany. He stares intently. His life rests in the hands of these people. He has the best counsel money can buy, but is it enough?

5

"Don't you find it strange that the guy fell on top of the Senator, then somehow the Senator is guilty?" Stephen asks Terry, taking a drink of his beer. They managed to snag a corner table at The Lawfully Wetted Bar, already bustling with the after–work crowd from Capitol Hill.

"It all comes down to what happened before that moment," Terry replies. "But if it was the Senator, why would he get into the elevator at all?"

"That's what a trial is for, man. The guy was the Senator's aide. The building was nearly empty. How did he get on top of that elevator? Who put him there or pushed him or whatever and why? Typical who dun nit stuff."

"The prosecution must have something no one knows about, otherwise they wouldn't be putting him on trial."

"Of course. Still, the DA's office is sweating this one."

"Why?"

"Are you kidding? They arrested a U.S. Senator. They have to present a rock–solid case to save face on this. The good news for them is that most convictions are won on a majority of circumstantial evidence. And juries are fickle, man. I've seen some weird shit go down with juries. No offense now that you're a juror."

Stephen fiddles with his jury badge – a clear plastic covering over a piece of paper with a bar code, court and case information and a number on it. He is juror 105827 and number 9 for this trial. "None taken. Thanks."

Terry raises his glass, "Here's hoping yours is a no brainer."

Stephen returns the salute and Terry adds, "They did tell you that this will likely take a while? I mean a while, like more than a month, maybe two, could even be three."

"What? I figured a few weeks tops." Stephen's face falls.

Terry shakes his head, "Oh come on, you know better than that. Remember OJ?

One hundred and thirty–four days."

"Holy fuck."

"I don't think they'll ever do it again quite like that; however, it's still big. Besides, I told you what to say to get out of jury duty, especially for a major haul like this. You could've done it."

"Well, I wasn't going to b.s. up there. Besides, I thought it could be interesting."

"Itching to get away from the firm, aren't you?"

"No," a defensive note escapes, and he thinks better of it. "Look, I thought I could contribute here. Ever thought of that?"

"Ookay."

Stephen sees the way Terry is looking right through him, so he confesses, "Okay, so yeah. I feel like I want to run sometimes. I'm getting stuck in sameness at work and I keep thinking I can change something there, but it doesn't happen. I really need to get out of there, go out on my own and I know it. I just keep waiting for the right time. I'm thinking now that maybe this will give me time away to get clear."

"Not a bad idea then." Terry motions to the waitress for another round.

"Not for me. I don't think I should," says Stephen.

"It's only two beers."

Stephen relents then gets the waitress's attention and adds, "Can I have some wings too please. If I'm going to drink, I need to eat something." He pulls out his phone and texts Janet.

"You didn't used to be such a lightweight."

"Some of us are adults with family responsibilities," Stephen regrets saying it the second he finishes. Terry sits back in his chair as the words hit hard. Stephen quickly adds, "Sorry. I guess I'm a little tense and maybe being referred to as a lightweight isn't exactly a warm and fuzzy. I guess I am a lightweight."

"You know I'm just joking. Everything all right, besides the work stuff?"

"Yeah. It's just that sometimes when I see you, I'm reminded that for you your time is your own and for the rest of us it'd be nice to have a day to just bust loose."

"Fear not Lancelot, now that you'll be in the neighborhood doing your civic duty, I can get you back to doing chasers. You'll want to wait for traffic to die down before heading home most days. And you're always welcome at the bachelor pad."

"That doesn't sound half bad, but I have a feeling I may be needing every spare second to catch up on work and kids' stuff and Janet. I'm starting to think I should've gotten out of this one."

"Nah, I'm sure it'll work out." Terry looks around the restaurant and waives to a couple of guys heading to another table, then turns back to Stephen, "There is one thing you may have a tough time with."

"What's that?"

"You're not going to be able to talk to anyone about anything going on in that courtroom. Not even to Janet. So, it'll be weird. I think there's a few things you should keep in mind going in."

"Like what?"

"First thing is, everybody lies on the stand."

"Oh, that's brilliant. You're not jaded. Come on, everybody?"

"Cops. Lawyers. Experts. Even jurors. Listen. That might seem preposterous but think about a few things: there are as many versions of reality as there are number of individuals in any given situation. Combine that with individual agendas and truth becomes an amorphous thing."

"Yes, 'Yoda', I can see that. But that's different than lying."

"In court, under pressure, let's say you have the certainty of conviction that your uncle, the defendant, is a greedy asshole. So, when you go up to relay what he said to you, you'll give it the spin from that conviction, even though that may not be at all accurate from an objective point of view."

The waitress sets down the wings and additional beers as Terry continues, "One place where you can see this, without any complex filters and in full swing and living color is divorce court. I did a couple of years there. Remember? Never again. There, truth is as formless as slime."

"Amen," the waitress chimes in.

Terry looks at her with a big grin. "You know what I'm talking about."

"The things my ex, that bastard, had the nerve to say about me; like that I was a voodoo witch. A real one that did spells and shit. Oh my god! And the judge took him seriously!" She scoots away shaking her head.

Terry turns back to Stephen and grabs a chicken wing, "I rest my case."

"That's a frightening perspective coming from a lawyer."

"Them's the facts jack. If you think about it, it explains some things in the law."

Terry takes a swig of his second beer. "Listen, everybody has a personal jury of sorts. The voices in your head for one. The people in your life are also your jury. Those you've loved, the ones you've hurt. These, my man, are your gods that declare your guilt or innocence, they are your judges on a daily basis. And every day your life is lived arguing your case before them. So, it's not a far stretch to recognize that those habits of arguing your own life have a way of twisting your perspective and coloring how you see certain facts, let alone how you relay that to other people, especially when you're under pressure."

Terry grabs another wing and chews.

"I thought you weren't hungry."

"What can I say, I'm a see–food eater."

"Don't let me be responsible for ruining your appetite. You are coming to dinner tonight. Right?"

"Wouldn't miss it." Terry wipes his face and takes another swig of his beer. The law excites Terry like nothing else. As pessimistic as his view of humanity can be, he loves his work and it's his life.

Stephen envies Terry's passion. He didn't used to envy it because he had that passion too, for creating angles and shapes and revolutionary ingenious buildings. But lately, he can't seem to tap into that excitement. Has he lost it forever? And if so, how can that be? He needs to find a way to get that old passion back. Feel inspired again.

"Let's get another order," Terry says and waives to the waitress.

Stephen shakes his head, "No. Dinner. Just get the check."

Terry always blazes his own trail – surrounded by some of the strangest elements of society in his public defender's world is in stark contrast to the most beautiful women who seem to gravitate his way. Stephen wonders if Terry is still not over Elise and that's why he won't commit to a relationship.

Terry's eyes light up as he talks about the law, "You'll notice that the one thing the law focuses on first, above all else, are certain facts that can't be circumvented or skewed by all those subjective realities. Those facts are considered real evidence.

"Because you have now been called upon as a steward of the public in criminal court, I'll use the examples of a violent case. So, facts will be a murder weapon, a dead body, blood, DNA, the crime scene, employment records, birth data, DMV data, etc., anything that can concretely or scientifically be proven. Other stuff is circumstantial, or hearsay or inadmissible but snuck in anyway. And believe me, a good attorney will always sneak something in. Better to apologize after the fact than ask permission beforehand and get denied. Even eye–witness testimony is fairly unreliable, although we tend to uphold it. Unless the person knows the perp they're identifying, it's definitely not even close to firmly reliable. Too many errors and overturned cases over the years to make eye–witnesses the cornerstone of any case. They are not that accurate. Sometimes a witness swears up and down that it's the guy, then we discover it's someone who simply looks like him and the wrong person ended up in jail."

"Isn't it your job to make sure people don't perjure themselves?"

"If I know someone is lying, I can't put them on the stand. If I don't know, but I'm afraid I might get surprised or something will come up that is proven to be a lie or even a half–truth, I also don't put them on the stand. Unlike divorce court, where it seems like all rules are ignored, in criminal court there are very specific rules in what you can and cannot ask or do as a lawyer respecting knowledge you have and how you use it. In other words, most of the time defendants aren't put on the stand, because if they're caught in one lie or something that even smells like a lie, then their entire credibility is shot. You would think that it's getting more difficult to prove cases without a lot of real evidence, because people on both sides are getting better at lying. However, it's quite the opposite. The side with the best spin tends to win, regardless of the truth."

"You've got to be kidding."

A mischievous smile spreads across Terry's face, "I don't know. Sure seems like it lately. It just makes my job more challenging. That's why I make the big bucks."

"Speaking of big bucks. Do you ever wish you took Griffith and Wheat up on their offer?" Stephen asks him.

"I have my days, but no. I guess I'm strange that way. There's something always surprising in the public arena. Can't get too comfortable. Besides, I'm the best and there are lot of innocent, poor people who deserve a good defense."

Maybe that's it. Stephen thinks maybe he's just too comfortable. Taking steps to start his own practice would disrupt that comfort and put him in the zone of uncertainty and risk.

***

"So, how'd it go today?" Janet asks Stephen, as soon as he walks into the kitchen with Terry.

Stephen gives her a squeeze from behind and nuzzles her neck as she puts the vegetables in a serving dish. "Good. But you had the big presentation. Did you get the Winston account?"

"I think it went well. I covered everything. Kathy was awesome and we had a good rapport with Mr. Winston. He asked questions and seemed pleased with the answers. A lot of nodding and smiling." Janet turns and wraps her arms around Stephen's waist and exhales, "I'm so glad it's over."

"You deserve it," says Terry. He points to the wine bottle and gestures to Stephen for a corkscrew.

"Hey you. Thanks. I hope that's a good bottle," Janet teases Terry.

"Of course. I do not skimp on my grapes."

Janet smiles then continues, "The Winston's are discussing the budget and said they'd get back to me in the next couple of days. I think it's really looking good." She looks at Stephen excitedly as she gets the hot pads. "Honey, I think they really liked my ideas. Keep your fingers crossed."

"Always." Stephen gives Janet kiss on the cheek and hands a corkscrew to Terry, who opens the wine.

Stephen looks for the salad bowl just as Janet's mother, Michelle, comes into the kitchen, coat and purse in hand, "Oh Stephen, the salad's done! I took care of it. It's in the fridge. You boys just relax," she says, then calls back into the other room, "Emily's coming to finish setting the table. Aren't you, dear?"

"Yes, grandma," Emily replies with the enthusiasm of a slug and comes into the kitchen to grab the silverware.

"Mom, why don't you stay for dinner," Janet suggests.

"Can't sweetie. Bridge night. You kids have fun. Tootles." Michelle slips out.

"Arlene invited us over for Thursday night. She's dying for me to meet the new boyfriend," Janet says to Stephen as she takes the roast out.

"I hope this one isn't a cheater," Stephen offers as he grabs the wine glasses.

"I know. She has the worst taste in men," Janet says.

Terry sniffs the cork just as his cell phone rings. Terry looks at the caller ID and mouths "Linda" to Stephen, as he hands him the wine bottle and turns away to take the call.

"I have a track meet on Thursday," Emily announces.

"Oh, that's right, the track meet. I'm not sure your father can make it in time. Can you?"

Stephen pours himself a glass of wine and watches Terry laughing and flirting on his call. Janet puts her arms around Stephen.

"Honey, what do you think?"

"What time does it start?"

"Probably at five."

"Well, that's tight. The courthouse shuts down at five on the dot, so depending on traffic, I can at least catch the end."

"Good. You need to see me in action this year," says Emily, "because I'm running the hundred–yard dash against the best runner at Eastwood and I think I can take her."

"Wow. I'm sure you can."

"No luck getting excused today, huh?" Janet asks, just as Terry hangs up the phone and Stephen seizes the opportunity to put the last of the food on the table.

"Let's eat," Stephen says, and everyone settles into their chair. "No, I didn't get excused. Actually, quite the opposite."

"You got on a trial." Janet's expression darkens as she helps Mark with his plate.

Terry sits back, avoiding Stephen's gaze.

"I think we would all agree that sometimes it's important for us to do something for our society that may seem like an inconvenience," Stephen speaks to the kids, deliberately avoiding Janet's gaze. "Jury duty is part of our obligation in a democracy. Your uncle Terry depends on good jurors. Right?" Terry puts a bite in his mouth and politely nods. Stephen continues, "I've never done jury duty before, so I thought it was time that I did my part."

"A courtroom like in the movies?" asks Mark.

"Yeah. Kind of like that."

"Cool."

Emily notices her mother's expression and asks, "Don't you want dad to be on a jury?"

Stephen seizes the opportunity and turns to Janet, "Yeah, honey. Why wouldn't you want me on a jury, upholding the people's rights under the Constitution?"

"Oh, that's priceless." Janet averts her gaze from her husband and turns to the kids and Terry, "It's not that I don't want us to participate. It's that sometimes a long jury duty can really interfere in a person's life and most of the trials are petty things and not that important and can drag on. Whereas your father is very important to his work and to us." She turns to Terry, "And because of that, he could have had himself excused. Right?"

Terry knows a time bomb when he sees it and replies, "I'm Switzerland."

"Oh great. Now you don't have an opinion," Janet says and turns her attention back to the kids, "Anyway, let's hope that whatever trial he's on won't last more than a few days."

"What if I got on a trial that was pretty important?"

Everyone's eyes turn to Stephen, expecting him to continue. He can tell that Janet is trying her Zen breathing technique to stay calm and positive.

"There's a United States Senator who has been arrested for murder and…"

"Wow!" Mark blurts out, "Murder!"

"That's definitely Law & Order stuff," Emily chimes in.

"The Claxton trial?" Janet asks.

"Yeah." Stephen looks at his wife, "Don't be upset, but I was there and it just sort of happened and I really think it could be interesting."

"There's no question that trial will go down as one of the biggest in this decade," Terry adds.

"No. Wow, that's a surprise. I get it. This is a big one, and important," Janet says, as she takes a drink of wine.

"Really?"

"They need good people on a jury of that magnitude." With a tinge of sarcasm, Janet adds, "People who have the time and resources to donate to the system. People whose personal and professional obligations are minimal enough that jury service is their offering to the world." Janet makes a poor attempt at hiding her upset.

Stephen retorts, "Well, as it happens, I'm in a good place for some time away from the office." He looks at the kids, "And just think of some of the good stories I might have after it's over."

"Cool," Mark adds, still thinking about the murder part.

* * * *

As night descends on the Reeves' household, Stephen, lying in bed in his boxers, flips through the channels on the bedroom television. He stops at the news. A reporter stands outside the Senate building addressing the camera, "The jury selection was completed today for The People versus Senator George Claxton, who is on trial for the grisly murder of his aide Joel Christiansen. The trial begins tomorrow. Despite public furor over the Senator's arrest, the prosecution claims they have ironclad evidence necessary to bring forth a conviction."

A shot of an older man in a crowd of people speaks to the reporter, "I think it's a setup. They just don't want him to lead the party." The reporter returns to the screen, "As you can see, the Senator has many supporters."

Stephen f lips the channel as Janet walks in from the bathroom, wearing her customary nightshirt, and slides in next to him. She gives him a quick kiss, then props herself up and grabs a book off the nightstand.

"Are you still upset with me?" Stephen asks.

Not averting her gaze from the book, she replies, "Mmhmm. I'm sure I'll get over it. Eventually. Maybe. I'll call the Hansons in the morning and tell them we won't be joining them this weekend."

Stephen winces. This three–day long weekend with their friends from Maryland had been planned months ago. Stephen knows how much Janet was looking forward to it. He was too. They haven't been away like that in a long time.

"We can still go."

"It's not like you can call in sick, Stephen."

"We'll just go separately and leave after traffic on Friday. We'll get there late and meet them, but I bet we really won't miss anything."

Janet puts down her book and looks at her husband. She needs to salvage something. "It'll be really short, but better than nothing. Okay, we'll still go."

"I love you. Always have." Stephen grins at her.

Janet cracks a smile and shakes her head, "Always will." She gives him a kiss. "Okay. Maybe I'm getting closer to not being mad anymore." She goes back to her book.

Satisfied, Stephen lies back and begins unconsciously playing with the remote – he channel surfs, then stops on a scene from the film 'Basic Instinct' between Michael Douglas, who plays Nick, and George Dzundza as the seasoned detective, Gus, discussing the Sharon Stone character, Catherine.

Nick says, "She's coming after me." Stephen turns up the volume.

"What is it between you?" Gus asks.

"I don't know."

"Something though."

"Yeah something."

Janet looks over at Stephen and clears her throat.

"Oh, sorry." Stephen turns the volume down and lays the remote on the bed next to him.

"Thanks. Try reading, honey, that usually works for you."

"Maybe later."

Staring at the television, Stephen watches the images, not really focusing on what he's seeing. The inability to sleep still plagues him. His mind turns to creating strange courtroom scenarios of famous people floating in and out, high drama between the press and the lawyers, and all eyes on the jury. Images come to him in bits and pieces. The faces he saw there today parade before his mind's eye. He invents stories about the people he knows nothing about: How that seemingly innocuous middle–aged guy sells cocaine on the side; how that old lady is really the gateway to an underground organization; how that receptionist at the mortuary hides national secrets in the lining of caskets when no one is looking. And maybe he is James Bond, ready to save the nation from doom. He snickers to himself. This must be what fiction writing is like. Despite the crazy thoughts and unsure of why, Stephen feels a sense of excitement. A sense that something is about to change.

6

A blustery wind makes its way through D.C. on the first day of Senator Claxton's murder trial. The front of the Pettyman building is a madhouse. Press vans clutter the courthouse parking lot and the curbs. Stephen has a difficult time finding parking. The place is swarming with people. Reporters and camera personnel line both entrances. A fight breaks out between a television reporter and someone going into the courthouse.

Stephen decides to park on the other side.

Stephen arrives on time and, once inside, checks in with the attendant. There is a separate entrance to the courtroom for the jurors, but some members of the press have found their way near some of the hallways and attempt to assess each passerby, hoping to glimpse a juror. Even though their names aren't on their badges, Stephen wonders if some of the reporters can run facial recognition software on them. That thought brings him back to images of James Bond and an imperceptible smile forms on his lips.

Everything is news in connection with the Senator and this trial. Reporters struggle to make stories out of speculating how this jury compares to others. The judge has ordered that the jury be anonymous to outsiders, but it hasn't stopped speculation of all kinds. Every news channel is resorting to reporting on rumors on some of the jurors' general backgrounds, such as believing that there is a diversity in the jury pool that might affect their bias in this case since the Senator leans to the right. The desperation of creating news for ratings rather than reporting actual news runs at an all–time high.

In the holding room, Stephen notices one of the jurors, he thinks his name is Ted, who looks like a politician. Ted is in his late thirties, wears a suit and paces the length of the room. Back and forth. Back and forth. His movements reflect a jittery personality. He probably feels naked without his cell phone. They had to turn in their cell phones upon check–in.

Fellow juror Mike Gresham approaches Stephen and extends his hand, "Stephen, right?" Mike wears a short–sleeved shirt and has a calmness about him that puts Stephen at ease.

Stephen shakes his hand, "Yes."

"I heard your name when you checked in. I was right behind you. Mike Gresham. This one's going to be a doozy. That's quite a swarm out there," he says, gesturing to the reporters on the other side of the door.

An older woman, absent–mindedly knitting, slides up next to Mike and motions at Stephen whispering loudly, "He has restless eyes."

Stephen hears her and is amazed that anyone would so blatantly say something like that, knowing they could easily be heard.

Mike, playing the diplomat, turns to Stephen as if in introduction, "This is Marge." Then to Marge, "Marge, this is Stephen."

Marge simply looks up from her knitting and nods at Stephen, then goes right back to ignoring him. Mike just makes a face like 'oh well.'

The bailiff enters, "You'll be going in in two."

Stephen now stands next to a blond woman he hadn't noticed before. She has long hair, a clean–scrubbed face with a pair of lightly tinted prescription glasses.

Something about her intrigues him. Feeling like he should meet all the people he'll be serving with, he extends his hand to her and smiles, "Stephen Reeves." She looks at him for what strikes him as slightly too long before smiling and reciprocating, "Eileen Harris."

Her delay makes him uncomfortable and self-conscious. Between that and Marge's reaction to him, he's grateful that he's not in a bar looking for a hot date. Thankfully, the bailiff opens the door and ushers them into the familiar, large courtroom.

Packed with reporters and spectators, the prosecution and defense teams make last minute preparations as the jurors take their seats. Once they are seated, all rise again as Judge Judith Cohen enters and takes the bench. Judge Cohen bangs her gavel for silence and addresses the jury, "First, I would like to say thank you all for your service. As you may or may not know, even during jury selection, I did not allow cameras to be used in this courtroom. I have also limited the number of people from media outlets. This is a publicity prone trial, and through my staff, I have been monitoring a good portion of the coverage. Unfortunately, that coverage is getting out of hand. It appears to be unceasing and filled with rumor and speculation and despite our efforts, the unfounded speculation seems to be proliferating and the potential for outrageousness increases once the trial begins. Therefore, prior to your entrance today, I granted a motion that due to the sensational nature and the continuous publicity surrounding this trial, you, the jury, will be sequestered for the duration of the trial and until a verdict is reached. We were hoping to avoid this, however it is necessary. You will be explained the procedure after we conclude today."

Stephen's eyes go wide. He hadn't even considered that possibility. The reporters are abuzz. A couple of the other jurors express their frustration by groaning and huffing. Marge seems delighted. This will be the highlight of her year. Stephen can't get a read from the people at either the prosecution or defense tables.

The judge bangs her gavel once again, "Order please. Mr. Mann, you may begin."

They say the burden is on the prosecution and District Attorney Elliott Mann looks burdened. His face maintains a sternness, and although he looks slightly more rested than the previous day, he nevertheless looks like a man under the strain of carrying an immense load. He stands up, gravely considers the jury and addresses them, "It is the prosecution's job to prove, beyond a reasonable doubt, that Senator George Claxton, with cold–blooded intent, brutally and willfully murdered his young aide Joel Christiansen." He walks over to the jury box, "Ladies and gentlemen of the jury, we have worked hard over the past many months and turned over every stone and in so doing we will prove just that.

"We will prove that Senator Claxton murdered this young man because the victim was a threat to the Senator. How so? The Senator's job depends not only on the favor of his constituents, the people who vote for him, but also on the favor of his party, a very conservative, right-wing party. What do you think would happen to the Senator's position if his very well–hidden homosexuality were exposed? Do you think his party would be okay with that? Would his voters? That is the threat the victim posed."

Most of the faces in the room register surprise and snap to attention. Stephen wasn't expecting this.

Mann gestures toward Claxton, "Due to the fact that George Claxton was up for the post of Majority Whip, he had to be assured of winning re–election this fall. He was a shoe–in. Or so he thought. However, exposure, or even rumor of any type of deviant sexual behavior, was sure to destroy his chances. And despite the wave of acceptance of homosexuality in much of this country, his district would not be tolerant of a homosexual representative. On the night of November tenth, when young Joel Christiansen threatened to expose the Senator's hidden predilection, they argued. They were alone.

"Much of the building was empty for the night. And during that argument, rage got the better of the Senator and it built up. And built up. And built up, until that rage took over and he acted to, literally, kill any possibility of a scandal that could ruin his chances of succeeding. This meant killing and getting rid of a man who trusted him, who was his aide and his lover.

"The prosecution will prove that the Senator was the last person to see the young man alive and that he delivered two lethal blows to his skull with his own personal award statuette that sits on the Senator's desk. He then carried the body and threw it down an elevator shaft, thinking that his victim's death would appear as a tragic accident. Unfortunately for the Senator, his plan took an unexpected turn when, unbeknownst to him, Joel, still barely alive, landed on top of the adjacent elevator, and pried his way into the elevator cab, where he landed on top of his killer, the esteemed Senator Claxton." Mann points to Senator Claxton, whose stoic expression shows no signs of fray. Mann goes on to enumerate the various elements of their case that they intend to lay out for the jury and just as it appears he may be going on too long, he concludes his statement, "The murder weapon was found in the Senator's office, wiped clean, but not clean enough.

"The Senator was the last person to see Joel alive and the Senator had motive to kill. I ask you to put aside status and fame and look at the facts in this case, and if you do as the law asks of you, I am certain that you will come to the right conclusion and find Senator George Claxton guilty of first–degree murder."

The room falls into a rapt attention. The jurors freely stare at the Senator and Stephen notices how the man keeps his eyes straight ahead, making every effort to avoid glancing at the box. He wonders if those were the instructions he was given by his attorneys or if they're of his own choosing. If he's honest with himself, Stephen has to admit to an inherent dislike of politicians. He equates them to a cross between members of the mob and used car salesmen. However, intellectually he tells himself that he can easily get past his bias and that he's determined to look upon the Senator as just a man with a powerful job.

A middle–aged woman with brown hair, haphazardly pulled back, sits in the first row behind the prosecution table. Her eyes are red and puffy. Her stare vacant. The dark circles around her eyes and the pallor of her skin suggest she hasn't slept in quite a while. This is Joel's mother, whose presence is obscured by the power of the proceedings and the attention on the defendant. She is rolling through the unspeakable in life. The loss of a child. No doubt that her body is going through the motions of what she feels obligated to do, but no one can know where her mind is at. Stephen cannot imagine that kind of pain. Next to her is a young woman bearing a striking resemblance, her daughter and Joel's sister. She's dressed in a business suit and every so often checks her phone between bouts of squeezing her mother's hand. She appears older than Joel and wears a wedding ring. There don't seem to be any other family members of the victim's present and Stephen wonders if the father is deceased. The family. Dominoes of the death. The other emotional casualties are the friends, who are gathered behind the family.

As the prosecutor returns to his seat, John Alton subtly shakes his head and slowly lifts himself from his chair behind the defense table. Standing tall, Alton clasps his impeccably manicured hands in front of him and looks seriously and full faced at the jury, then begins, "The prosecution would have you believe that this is a simple case with concrete evidence. Dear ladies and gentlemen, I assure you it is not." Alton's Southern accent is turned up a notch from the previous day. "Please take note of what is really considered evidence versus supposition or creative thinking, once you have heard all the facts." He releases his hands and gestures toward Mann. "Their story is absurd. Senator George Claxton had no motive to kill his aide. We will prove that what the prosecution is alleging is based solely on rumor and unfounded speculation, creating sexual innuendoes that are merely meant to shock you and bear no resemblance to the truth. There is no, and I stress, absolutely NO motive here.

"George Claxton is a well–respected civil servant who gave a young man a job, trained him and mentored him. He had great hopes for Mr. Christiansen and the Senator invested his time and effort into that young man. Their relationship was strictly one of mutual, professional respect. If the Senator's career grew, that young man would only benefit by that, and he knew it. In fact, he was looking forward to it. That is what every aide in Washington strives for. The prosecution's theory makes no sense whatsoever.

"The evidence to which the prosecution refers is purely circumstantial, with one exception – the weapon. We will show that anyone could have used that statuette, and returned it, simply to incriminate the Senator. We will also show that the Senator was in the Senate library during the time the victim was being attacked." Alton takes a long breath and stares at the jury as he makes his way toward his table, continuing, "Ladies and gentlemen, my client was set up in a cruel attempt to destroy him. In today's world, you all know that politics can be a difficult and an unforgiving arena." He picks up his glass and takes a drink of water. Then as if pondering the creation of the universe, he asks, "Who would want to set him up?" Alton smooths his sleeves and again drifts toward the jurors. "Perhaps an unhappy corporate lobbyist who realized George Claxton couldn't be bought off. Perhaps a political rival. Perhaps someone who merely saw an opportunity to throw suspicion his way. There are any number of possibilities. We live in a vicious, political climate and we cannot afford to be naïve about what people are capable of doing. In any case, we will show you that Senator Claxton is also a victim here because he is innocent. Not only does the Senator have an admirable and impeccable record as both a citizen and a public servant, but he also had absolutely no motive to kill Mr. Christiansen. Therefore, once you review all of the evidence, the real evidence, you will find plenty of reasonable doubt and with that, under the law, you must find Senator George Claxton innocent of all charges. Because, ladies and gentlemen, he *is* innocent."

A few exhibits are put into evidence and the judge calls for a lunch break, allowing fifteen extra minutes for the jurors to make their arrangements. Judge Cohen reminds Stephen of Janet's mother, Michelle. She has that classic face, a bit hard and stiff, but observing and intelligent. What she must see people doing to each other in case after case. No wonder she doesn't smile, he observes. The jurors are told that they can use their cell phones during this lunch break to prepare for their sequester. The Bailiff clarifies this, "These two individuals" pointing to his right, "...will take your sandwich orders, then you will have access to your phones in the jury room where you will remain to make your calls. Please understand that you are being monitored and as soon as you have completed your calls, you will again turn in your phones. If you experience a complication, please notify one of the monitors in the room and you will be instructed accordingly."

Stephen orders a pastrami sandwich and is handed a flyer on sequestration rules. He will be escorted to the bathroom during court sessions. He won't have access to his cell, the Internet, newspapers or television. They're going to give them movies through the hotel, but he's not really a movie watcher. The floor of the hotel, where they are staying, is guarded and permission is required to leave the floor at any time. If he were looking for time to work on his business plan, he sure found it.

The jury consists of seven women and five men with two alternates, one of each sex. Most of the jurors immediately focus on handling their own affairs in preparation for the sequester rather than fraternizing with each other.

Stephen calls Susan, his assistant, first to set in motion the necessary coverage for his schedule and to ensure that his work doesn't fall apart while he's away. He then speaks with Larry Simms, who is rendered speechless for the first time in a decade. And although Stephen can feel Larry's anger at the situation, he manages to resist the temptation to express it and Stephen suppresses his amusement. The K Tower partners aren't supposed to render a decision for several weeks and Stephen figures even if his firm does get the contract there's plenty of time for him to get back to the office. Stephen then calls Janet and tells her to bring him several books. He can sense Janet's disappointment about the turn of events and the now canceled plans for their weekend.

"Janet?"

"Yeah."

"You okay?

"Wow. I guess I forgot they did that anymore. That it was even a possibility," she says.

"I know. It didn't occur to me either. The judge didn't seem happy about it."

"I heard a blurb on the radio. It sounds like it could be intense."

"I don't think I'll be bored, during the trial anyway. Larry's not happy at all, but he says the firm will make adjustments. Fortunately, all the heavy lifting is already done on the Tower deal, by yours truly, and the bids are in so it's a waiting game anyway. I guess they can't exactly hold it against me since the entire country knows about this one."

"Do I get to see you tonight, when I bring your things?"

"Just for the drop off at the hotel, we won't get any alone time. From what I understand, we're monitored and chaperoned during this whole thing. We won't even know where we're going until the end of the day and I've given them your number, so you will receive a text with where to deliver my stuff. I guess some people are having it brought here, but because of work and kids, the rest of us get to have someone come to the hotel. We'll get to make phone calls from the room, but on a pre–determined schedule and they will also be monitored."

"Seriously?"

"I know. Nothing good about any of this."

This will be the longest time Stephen and Janet have spent apart since their wedding day. Maybe even since they began dating. A month before they got engaged, Stephen's mother died from a heart attack. Stephen went home to Denver to meet his brother Rob, put the house up for sale, have the service and take care of the estate. The entire ordeal took over two weeks. His father passed away from a struggle with bone cancer two years before and those eleven days were the longest stretch Stephen had spent with his brother since they were kids. During those two weeks, the first order of business was the funeral service and dealing with all their mother's friends and distant family members, some who were unconsciously scolding with, "It's good you're finally here. I know she missed you boys, what with not seeing you regularly," and "It's been years since we've seen you." And others who were helpful but tiresome to the two single men anxious to put it behind them. "Your mother was such a trooper after Harold passed away, I thought she'd outlive us all. I'm so sorry." In the days following the service, casseroles, lasagnas, and salads were delivered by fellow grievers to keep them fed while they dispensed with the furniture and personal items and finally put the house up for sale.

Stephen and Rob were never as close as he had hoped. Rob refused to go to college, got into extreme sports, married a stripper and divorced a year later. He eventually moved to New Zealand and started an extreme expeditions' business. The brothers' lack of common ground continued to exist throughout their life, but whenever they did get together it would be as if no time had gone by. They rarely spoke during the aftermath of their mother's death. For solace during that time, Stephen turned to Janet, calling her nearly every day to fill her in on his days and to let her know he was anxious to return. During this trial, that option won't be as available to him.

After lunch, the testifying begins. Most of the jurors start out taking notes. They are given pads of paper and pens and have been asked to leave them in the jury room when they aren't in court.

The prosecution establishes that a bronze statuette is the murder weapon. The statuette is some award the Senator won several years back for one of his innovative initiatives.

The prosecutor questions the forensics expert, "What else did you find in the Senator's office?"

A large bespectacled man, seated in the witness chair, answers, "The carpet had a few blood stains. It appears they had been cleaned and covered over with a chemical; however, we were able to ascertain that the carpet fibers contained blood matching the victim's."

"A DNA match?"

"Yes."

"In your professional opinion, where was Joel Christiansen beaten to death?"

Alton is on his feet, "Your honor, we do not know that the victim was beaten. We only know that he was struck and was still alive when the ambulance attendants retrieved him."

Mann jumps in, "I'll rephrase. Where did the victim receive his blow to the head, which through a series of events ultimately led to his death?"

"In Senator Claxton's office."

A murmur runs through the room. Stephen observes that Claxton continues to remain stoic.

On cross, Alton surmises, "So, with no fingerprints, anyone could have picked up the statuette, even days before, used it that night, wiped it clean, then returned it? Is that correct?"

"Yes, I suppose," the witness answers.

"As for the blood on the carpet, isn't it true that head wounds cause heavy bleeding?"

"Usually, yes, but…"

Alton cuts him off, "Is it possible that Mr. Christiansen had a cut many days or even weeks before? That those blood stains are not recent?"

"They had been cleaned within a twenty–four–hour period."

"Yes. But isn't it true that the cleaner masked your ability to determine how long the blood had actually been there?"

"That's correct."

"And, the victim did not die in the Senator's office, did he?"

"No, but…"

"No. We do not know with absolute certainty where the lethal blow was delivered, and we certainly do not know who delivered it."

Alton sits down, but Mann gets up to redirect. "Why do you believe there would be a relatively small amount of blood from this type of head wound, as opposed to other head wounds?"

"There was a very small point of puncture, and the victim would have fallen onto his left side. The puncture was on the right."

"Why do you believe that those stains occurred the night of the murder?"

"The small spatter pattern matches possible impact scenarios if someone of Mr. Christiansen's height were hit in the head in the manner he was hit while standing near the chair where the stains were found."

"In the Senator's office?"

"Yes."

"In your expert opinion and experience, is it likely that the blood could have come from a cut finger or from a bleeding nose, considering the evidence of the crime scene?"

"It's not likely."

For the first time, Stephen notices the Senator looking at the jury. The Senator's steel grey eyes continually observe yet reveal nothing. *How can he hear this testimony, look at the people who will determine his fate and remain so unaffected?* Stephen wonders. *Maybe he's been mildly sedated. Would probably be a good idea.*

Amazed at how long one person's testimony can take, Stephen feels weary by day's end. Approaching five o'clock, court is adjourned, and the jurors are taken through to their back room where suitcases are waiting for some of them. The group is gathered and directed outside toward a shuttle bus. Being one of the first to board, Stephen takes a seat near the back. He watches the others as they file in. Marge sits right up front and suggests that Mike sit next to her, but Mike spots Stephen and heads for the back, sitting next to him. "You're an architect, right?" Mike asks.

"Yes."

"Civil engineer myself. You have a family?"

"Yes. You?"

"Widowed."

"Sorry to hear that."

"It's been a few years. My kids live in Boston and my company has paid jury leave, so I'm okay. It's tougher when you have a family."

"You're probably right about that," Stephen replies, somewhat forlornly, thinking about what Janet is doing right now.

After a short ride, less than ten minutes from the courthouse, they arrive at their destination, a forty–year–old, two–to–three-star hotel besieged by beige and brown. Dull furnishings litter the surroundings. Stephen has never heard of this hotel and it's clear that this one is marked for occasions such as this with its institutional flavor and slightly stale odor. Not a place he'd pick for an overnight if he could help it. No fear of getting comfortable in this place. Stephen waits in the lobby with a few other jurors who also anticipate someone to bring them their clothes and personal items. A security area is set up where all the incoming items for the jurors will be x–rayed and inspected to ensure no communication devices are being passed on.

Juror number ten, Laura, thirty–something and wearing her hair back in some kind of strange bun, looks very serious in her business pant suit. No ring on her finger and she greets the young woman who enters with a hug. The young woman hands off a giant suitcase and a large tote bag to Laura, who then hands if off to one of the security officers and looks around the lobby with a mortified look. "Oh my God. How awful!" Stephen overhears her say. Next to them, the large, stubble bearded Charlie Murphy slaps a man of like size and appearance on the back and exclaims, "Thanks, brother. This'll be a hoot."

Before Stephen can think too much about his hotel mates for the next couple of weeks, Janet enters the lobby, rolling a suitcase and carrying a duffel bag.

"You're a sight for sore eyes," Stephen says. He gives her a kiss and a long hug and takes the bags. He has the items run through security, then leads her over to a couple of chairs.

"You okay?" she asks him.

"I'm not sure."

Janet takes in the place. "Maybe the rooms aren't too bad," she tries.

"Yeah. Maybe. Let's sit down for a minute. Don't leave me here yet."

"Oh honey, this place is…."

"Don't say it. I'm stuck now. Maybe this will turn out to be one of those stories we tell our grandchildren about what to watch out for."

"The kids really wanted to come, but I left them with Amy, figuring you'd call them before they went to bed. You can call tonight, can't you?"

Stephen pulls a piece of paper from his pants pocket and looks at it. "I can't call until tomorrow night. Then again on Friday. Sorry. I'm sure, in a weird way, Mark will think this is actually cool."

"I guess I was wrong about boring cases and all. But not so wrong about painful surroundings." Janet looks around the lobby and winces. "I also promised the kids I'd bring home Chinese, in honor of Wok night. That seemed to appease them."

"I love Wok night and Chinese take–out. Don't I get any?"

"I'm getting it on the way home. Oh no, I would've done it first and brought you some if I thought you were allowed."

"I don't know, I'm probably not. It's ridiculous how monitored we are. I have a feeling this will be a bigger pain than I imagined." He sees the restraint on Janet's face.

"You were right, and I should've listened."

"What?" Janet teases, "you want to repeat that?"

"No."

"Well, it's done. But we will miss you." She looks around, noticing the guards and a few other jurors. "This is kind of creepy. Knowing that we're being watched. I guess I should go."

"I'll really miss you guys," Stephen says. "Love you. Always have."

"Always will."

As Stephen hugs and kisses his wife, it registers that he's being placed in a restrictive and controlled environment. A strange concept, that the free people deciding on whether a citizen is innocent or guilty, whether he should or shouldn't lose his freedom, would be for the duration of the trial not free, while the accused is out on bail.

After a plate of pasta and salad in a cordoned off area of the small hotel restaurant, Stephen heads for his room. Only a few jurors stay to eat there, most take their food in the form of sandwiches up to their rooms. He opts not to sit with any of the others, figuring they'd see enough of each other in the coming weeks. He hopes not to be stuck having all his meals here, but it's doubtful.

He notices a sign for the gym. For most of his adult life his abs had been fairly cut, not Ryan Gosling kind of cut, but tight enough. In the last couple of years, he's gone up a waist size, and two since he's been married. Stephen decides to do sit ups every night while he's cooped up here. After Janet had Mark, she went through a period of despair over her figure. No amount of assurance helped ease her fears, so Stephen hired Charlie the trainer, who instructed her three times a week and Stephen mastered some lessons along the way. Charlie said that the only way to tighten abs was through various types of sit–up work and at least one hundred to two hundred repetitions every night until you achieved a certain core strength, then you could ease up, but constancy was imperative to keeping them. Charlie taught Janet a series of techniques – different ones for variety and to cover the muscle groups. Stephen did them with her on occasion to be supportive and they really worked for her. She still looks amazing. He remembers most of the sequences and now will have time to try them out – every night.

The modest room has a television, but only with restricted programing and movies. It's only eight o'clock. Stephen unpacks the suitcase. In the duffel bag he notices that Janet included a package of his favorite peanut M&M's, a small candle with matches, and she purchased a couple of new books for him. One's he's been wanting to read for a while. *The Devil In the White City* by Erik Lawson and *Leonardo's Brain: Understanding Da Vinci's Creative Genius* by Leonard Shlain. The note on top reads – *The candy will help get rid of any bad taste after a terrible meal, the candle smells good and might improve the lighting you're stuck with, and the books can keep you from watching too many movies and hopefully you'll be home before you have a chance to read both, xoxox*. He smiles to himself, pulls out the first book, leans back and opens the flap to …*White City*.

"…Beneath the gore and smoke and loam, this book is about the evanescence of life, and why some men choose to fill their brief allotments of time engaging the impossible, others in the manufacture of sorrow. In the end it is a story of the ineluctable conflict between good and evil, daylight and darkness, the White City and the Black."

7

George Claxton relaxes in his private study at home. Alton just left. He assured George that nothing had changed and that their defense remains solid. The first days of a trial are the worst for any defendant since the focus is solely on the prosecution's case and the arsenal put forth against them. Alton is a brilliant strategist – a shark among minnows. George reminds himself that this will all work out. He knows his way around a scrape and the scales are tipped on his side. He has confidence in Alton.

He pours himself a whiskey and looks out at the crisp night sky through the large window. He knows not to let his guard down. Regardless of the ways you cover yourself, there's always the possibility of an unexpected element. In this city, relying on predictability would prove unwise. You are either the hunter or the hunted. He is now the one being hunted, and his enemies are salivating.

Competence is a rare find in the halls of the self–obsessed, cat scratching, social climbing world of the Hill. Joel had competence and he had served George well, until now. Joel was a nice young man with potential, but this messy situation was not something George could've imagined.

He reclines in his chair and puts his head back. How did he get here? Before his arrest, he was in a position to make a real impact. Last year, he weathered the divorce from Cynthia, despite her Windsor family name. He wanted the divorce over as quickly as possible, so he conceded to some of her most ridiculous demands to avoid years of court costs and fees. He knows how to read people. Once he figured out how Cynthia operated in those negotiations, he worked it. Every time he made mention or proposed wanting an item, it would be that very item that she had to have. With that in mind, he put his finger on that hideous marble sculpture and the house in Sag Harbor and fought for weeks over it, finally feigning defeat and conceding those items to her, ultimately keeping what he really wanted.

No matter how hard Cynthia tried, she couldn't prove he was having an affair. Of course, she found nothing. He's not an idiot. Did she think that he would slip up after she filed the papers? That was the time to be hyper vigilant and it paid off. George is skilled at maneuvering through the truth. Some would call it lies, but he calls it life. It is in the average man's nature to believe that lies are necessary. That they somehow serve a purpose. The architects of society – the power holders – depend on lies. This he knows. In order to depend on them you must be skilled in using them.

To his surprise, his newfound freedom allowed him to score points with new constituents, men and women alike, in ways he couldn't have imagined. Also, despite his fears, money began pouring in and he moved into this exceptional brownstone near the Hill. His daughters, Bethany and Grace still haven't seen it. They said they wanted to come for the trial, but he won't allow it. George thinks it ridiculous to have them bear witness to the vile drivel that this spectacle will produce. The press is bad enough. Besides, the girls are in school. The last thing they need is to hear things that they can share with their mother, who would certainly use every shred of information to further poison them against him. He wonders if the girls will ever be free from Cynthia's venom to like him again. To embrace him fully as they once did.

He notices Sofia's sweater on the chair by the fireplace. He makes a mental note to make sure that when the girls do come to visit, to put away such things. Who he is or isn't involved with is something they don't need to know. Any parent can sympathize with that point of view, especially with an ex–wife still out to smear his character. That's one he just can't understand. Why would a woman want to turn her daughters against their own father? He's always been kind to the girls and even though he was gone a lot, especially these past ten years or so, they know they can always count on him, and have counted on him – successfully. He wants them to like his new place and to remember the times he did spend time with them – reading to them and taking them to the theater.

George drains the last of his whiskey and stares at the over–turned picture on his desk. He picks it up and smiles. It's been a while since he's had a picture of anyone other than Cynthia and the girls on his desk. Sofia put this here, but when Alton came to confer with him this evening, George turned it over, face down on the desk. The scrutiny he's under has substantially increased and every move he makes is noticed. He must be careful.

George sees Sofia as the type of woman a man in his position wants by his side. She doesn't have the prestige and the untainted family money that Cynthia brought to the table, but she's practical and ambitious. He believes her to be a woman who knows what it takes to get to the top and stay there and clears the way for her man. She isn't clingy or needy and understands the need to keep emotion at a distance when necessary. George sees emotion as the gateway to weakness. A truth that, in his view, few women understand. Sofia knows that sometimes people like him need to venture out and forge alliances by whatever means necessary, including sex. It's part of the game. George tells himself that when this is over, he'll take Sofia somewhere nice, as a gesture of his appreciation for all her efforts and for sticking by him. The woman is loyal, he'll give her that. He puts the photo in his drawer, face up, so he can look at it when he wants to, but won't have to worry about being questioned about it when people come over. He slicks back his hair, stands, and moves around the study.

Now he must deal with this. Murder. He can't believe it. Sleeping has been a challenge for him since this torment began. Maybe tonight he'll try not taking a pill. The trial is underway, and he's done everything he can possibly do to ensure his acquittal. He's wracked his brain for months to make certain that he's thought of every angle, potential minefield, or inconsistency. Now it's out of his hands and he needs to rest.

He's put the best people in place and it's their turn to deliver. They will do their job. They've committed to him. But something still nags at him. He has to be careful.

Perhaps a sleeping pill will be necessary after all.

8

On the fourth day of trial testimony, Stephen notices that his legal pad is three quarters of the way full of notes, making it inefficient. He decides to use bullet points and only for relevant insights. Up to this point the prosecution has focused on the nature of the murder, the forensics, and established the approximate time of Joel Christiansen being hit in the head prior to his being thrown down the elevator shaft to his death. The prosecution can't make the claim that Joel died at the time he was hit in the head since Joel's actual death didn't occur until after he landed on Senator Claxton in the elevator and within a few minutes after he was put in the ambulance. However, they can establish that it was the blow to the head with the Senator's statuette that inflicted the trauma and caused the series of events that led to Joel's death. The drop down the elevator shaft would have been instantly fatal if Joel hadn't veered and landed on top of an adjacent cab. That fall caused more gashes that resulted in the bloody mess once he fell on the Senator. With all the repetition of testimony, Stephen's mind drifts.

Currently they're in the process of establishing who was in the building during the time of Joel Christiansen's ordeal. Stephen notes that the security guard seemed quite certain about who came and went and the times of those events, but the man did take a bathroom break and the defense jumped on that point as if it were the discovery of the second gunman in the Kennedy assassination. Stephen ponders that unless someone had been casing the guard post for hours, the odds of someone sneaking in during the guard's bathroom break were slim. And if the killer were watching, then there was a likelihood that he would've been spotted, if not by the guard, then by someone on the street or on one of the street or building cameras. Janet and he watched enough crime shows to feel like he has some grasp of the process. The guard may not want to admit that he was in the bathroom long enough to create an opportunity for the killer. The guard had said that he would have welcomed talking to anyone coming or going. Boredom can skew a man's sense of time. What intrigues Stephen the most is the mention of the maintenance entrance. According to the guard, "It's locked up tight and only our maintenance guys have a key." But many things can happen to locks, they can be picked, and doors can be left open, and more importantly this means that there is another way into that building.

The trial breaks for lunch. Except for a few conversations with Mike and Marge, and with Ted, who's nervous energy can exasperate, and Joanna, who's only conversation revolves around her kids, Stephen has kept to himself during lunch and dinner breaks over the past few days, often grabbing a sandwich or burrito, sitting off to the side and burying himself in his book. The jurors eat in a separate and closed cafeteria style lunchroom. Stephen can tell he's not winning any points with his fellow jurors by remaining aloof. Today he puts the book down and engages in conversation with some of the others.

He grabs a tuna sandwich, chips and a coffee and looks around. He spots the sloppy Charlie Murphy cozying up to

Eileen. Stephen notices her hands. Long, slim fingers, but strong, not limp. Charlie bites into a greasy onion ring and chases it with a soda.

"This thing goes pretty slow, don't it?" Charlie says to Eileen. "Guess we'll be roomin' together for a while," he leans into her as he speaks, his oily complexion glistening, and Stephen notices her wince.

Eileen stiffly smiles and nods. "Okaaay. But I'm not sure I'd put it quite that way."

"Oh come now, down in Kileen we have a sayin' – the cow sleeps in the barn it's in. And well, we're kind of sharing the barn here." Charlie grins.

Eileen notices Stephen watching and turns and pulls her glasses down to reveal an eye roll in reference to Charlie's ongoing diatribe. Stephen briefly meets her eyes before the glasses go back up. The rims seem slightly too large for her face.

"I haven't been in this town long, but I suspect some things are the same everywhere," Charlie goes on between chews.

"Oh really? What things are those?" Eileen responds, taking a small bite of her egg salad sandwich.

Stephen feels compelled to rescue this poor woman. He approaches their table and stands next to Eileen's chair. "May I join you?" he asks.

Charlie momentarily appears confused, then glares at Stephen, "We're in the middle..." But before Charlie can finish, Eileen jumps in with, "Yes. Please do."

Charlie stands his ground, not budging and merely scowling at Stephen. Lunch with this guy is not Stephen's idea of a good time, so he takes it one step further, "Actually, now that I think about it, I've been having this breathing problem. Could be an offshoot of my claustrophobia and I think it'd be better if I were near a window."

"Great, buddy!" Charlie reacts and points across the room, "There's one."

"Oh, what a good idea. That looks much better anyway," Eileen says to Stephen, then adds perfunctorily to Charlie, "You don't mind, do you?" as she picks up her tray and starts across the room.

Stephen looks at the utterly shocked Charlie and says, "Thanks man," before following Eileen.

Charlie doesn't follow them. "Why, you son of a bitch," he mutters under his breath and makes a mental note to keep an eye on Stephen.

When Stephen sits down across from Eileen, she smiles at him, "Thank you."

Alone at the table with Eileen, unease sweeps over Stephen. "I noticed that you seemed put out by the guy, so I thought I'd be a buffer. My intention was not to stir up any trouble."

"Oh, don't be silly. I think Charlie will drum up new business in no time," Eileen says and nods back toward the middle of the room. Charlie has moved over and joined Melita and two other jurors and is in the middle of sharing his stories.

"He's not shy," Stephen observes.

"Surprisingly, neither are you," Eileen says.

Stephen unwillingly blushes and begins to feel nervous. *How ridiculous*, he thinks. He needs to get off this subject and discuss the trial or the weather or anything else.

"I don't think any of us expected to get on this trial or that we would be sequestered," he begins.

"You were following the news of all this before the trial?"

"More in passing, really. I knew the gist of it."

"What does that mean?"

"Well, it means that I've been trying to limit my news intake and be more selective about where I get my news and how much of it. I don't know about you, but I think most of what passes for news anymore is really a bunch of celebrity gossip, shameless promotion, and weather or financial hype than anything of substance."

Eileen slips her glasses off for a moment and massages the bridge of her nose.

Stephen notices that she keeps her eyes diverted, away from him.

"I know exactly what you mean," she responds and returns her glasses to their rightful place on her face before looking back at him, "I think it's crazy what the press gets away with. Sometimes I think they can say just about anything, and people will believe it, then if it turns out to be incorrect, the correction is so small or put somewhere where nobody sees it and nobody cares. It's difficult to turn an opinion around once it's been formed. What did you hear about the Senator?" Eileen seems genuinely interested.

"I knew the aide was murdered, landed on the Senator and that certain facts led them back to arrest Claxton. And now we get to see those facts firsthand."

Eileen nods and eats her egg salad sandwich. "Did you ever hear anything about what facts led to his arrest?"

"Only that he was the last person to see the guy alive. You?"

"No. I didn't hear anything."

First on the stand after lunch is a young, red–headed woman, Allison Gibson, professionally dressed in a dark suit. She exemplifies the eager young people clambering to excel and to be noticed on the Hill. Just out of college and still new to certain hard realities, her puffy eyes and sad expression betray her youth and fraying nerves. Anxious to be accurate, she takes her time answering each question.

Mann circles the witness chair. "Did you see Joel that Thursday night?"

Alison stares straight ahead, inhales and answers, "yes." Her lip begins to tremble, but she manages to carry on, "At around eight. He said he was waiting for the Senator to finish something so he could talk to him."

"Where did you see him?"

"He came into my office to get a chocolate. I always have them on my desk."

"What happened then?"

"I had to leave, so I packed up my things and he went back to his office."

"What time did you leave?"

"Sometime right after that." Allison tries not to look in Senator Claxton's direction.

"Was anyone else in the offices besides Senator Claxton and Joel when you left?"

"Not that I know of."

"Thank you." Mann faces the jury in a momentary pause before resuming his seat.

Alton rises and approaches Allison. "Not that you know of," he begins.

She swallows hard.

"So, you don't know if anyone else was in any of the other offices?"

"I don't think so."

"Did you check?"

"No. But no lights were on, and it seemed empty on the floor."

Alton nods, "Ah, so you don't really know. How good of friends were you and the victim?"

"We'd see each other at work. We'd sometimes have lunch."

"Lunch. Is that all?"

"What do you mean?"

"I mean did you have phone conversations or were you ever intimate?"

Allison's face registers shock, "No, of course not. I have a boyfriend." Allison stares ahead, trying to keep the tears from filling her eyes.

Alton presses on, "Okay. Do you have any way of knowing if anyone entered the victim's or the Senator's office after you left?"

"No."

Stephen feels sorry for the girl. Probably not what she imagined she'd have to do as part of her first job. But life is like that, Stephen reminds himself, surprises pop out of left field when you least expect them – like Janet's pregnancy that derailed their Africa trip – and you learn to roll with it.

The attorneys in this room are among the nation's finest. Their edge and intensity is apparent and they use it to intimidate when necessary. They also use gesture and tone to suggest a particular meaning or attempt to elicit a specific response. Performance, spin and jury consultants take up a greater role than justice. The two sides each try to use the system more cleverly to ensure a win. Certain facts and some evidence never see the light of day. They're suppressed because of technicalities, others are hidden under the guise of ignorance or relevance, and the jury will never get to see or hear about those.

Stephen wonders which of these attorneys is the more ruthless and which facts, if any are out there, the jury will never know about.

The first week of the Senator's trial comes to an end with the prosecution's last witness for the day that causes quite a stir. Joel's roommate, Scott, takes the stand. His red and puffy eyes quickly glance over at the Senator and, feeling immediately intimidated, Scott makes a deliberate effort not to look at him from then on.

He keeps his focus straight ahead. Young and handsome in an awkward, cherubic sort of way, Scott cannot stop his right leg from continuously vibrating. It appears to be an unconscious act, but it creates the impression that he is about to bolt out of his chair at any minute.

As the prosecution establishes that the two men were roommates, had known each other for several years and had numerous friends in common, Scott's face reveals hints of pain that recollections of Joel bring to the surface.

With attention to the night of the murder, Mann establishes that Scott had spoken with the victim minutes before the chain of events that led to his death. Scott speaks slowly. He attempts to stay composed and answer as succinctly as possible.

Mann asks, "And what did Joel say to you?"

"He said he needed to talk to the Senator right away and would be working late."

"Did he sound angry?"

Alton objects, "Calls for state of mind."

Mann switches gears, "No need to answer. You're sure you spoke after eight o'clock that night?"

"Yes. I had just started watching my show when he called."

"What was your relationship with the victim?"

Scott gulps and eyes the prosecutor. He exerts great effort to keep from crying. Scott doesn't want to betray Joel, but he can't lie either. "We were roommates and good friends."

"How good of friends? More than friends?"

"We were very close."

"Please explain to the court what you mean by very close, Mr. Birch."

Scott looks down and wipes a tear that squeezed its way out. After a moment he states quietly, "We were lovers." Joel had told Scott that he hadn't told anyone at work that he was gay. He was waiting until after the next election when he believed he would have greater job security and being open about it would no longer matter to a growing number of socially progressive constituents.

Stephen glances around the courtroom and notices a few people murmuring and shaking their heads.

"I thought he was cheating on me, and we got into an argument," Scott blurts.

"Who did you accuse Joel of cheating on you with?" Just as Mann gets the question out, Alton is on his feet objecting.

"Objection! Speculation."

"This goes toward possible motive, your honor," Mann offers smugly.

Once the judge overrules the objection, Scott continues, "I thought he might be having an affair with his boss, the Senator, because he always worked late."

Claxton appears calm listening to this testimony. Stephen wonders if he's not rattled on the inside.

Emotional, Scott adds, "…but I think I was wrong. I know I was..."

"That'll be all. Thank you," Mann instructs him.

The words "Because Joel loved me," escape from Scott before the judge silences him. This statement has the effect of a plea rather than a fact and Mann is betting that the jury can see the young man's desperation as he grasps at every possible confirmation of his lover's fidelity. Mann wears the expression of pity for the jury to see.

Alton approaches the witness, before Mann can sit down. "You have no way of knowing if your roommate actually saw the Senator after he spoke with you, do you?"

"Joel told me the Senator was still there, so…"

"Yes or no?"

Flustered and upset, Scott says, "No."

"And you have no way of knowing if Mr. Christiansen saw anyone else that night or even if he saw the Senator, do you?"

"No."

"Why did you think Mr. Christiansen was having an affair with the Senator?"

"Well…I don't know." Scott wipes his sweaty hands on his pants. "He always talked about how great the Senator was. And Joel worked late a lot. I mean a lot. And he liked it. It was like he wanted to work late."

"So, you're saying that Joel, like every other aide in this town, worked late and enjoyed working with Senator Claxton." Alton lets that sink in before continuing, "Did Joel ever tell you that he was in love with the Senator?"

A flash of scorn runs across Scott's face, "No, of course not."

"Did he ever tell you that the Senator had made a pass at him or that he flirted with him?" Alton asks with a bit of a smirk as if to imply the absurdity of such a thing.

"No."

"Thank you, Mr. Birch," Alton dismisses him.

Stephen unconsciously stares at Eileen who is seated in the row in front of his. He notices that her hair is brushed back away from one side of her neck. She is slender and her skin has an olive tone that isn't common with blondes. All week, she was reserved with the others, not talking much at all. She wasn't that way with Stephen at lunch. *Maybe she's one of those people who is better one on one than in groups,* Stephen conjectures. Next to her is the young, attractive guy wearing hip clothes, Ronald. He notices that Ronald hardly takes any notes. The jurors will be given a transcript of the trial. Stephen wonders how Ronald would remember nuances and unstated connections that he may observe without taking notes. They might be hearing testimony for weeks. That thought looms like an elusive bubble in his head. To most people being on this jury would seem like a frustrating and inconvenient obligation, but to Stephen it feels strangely like one of those things he wants to do, but probably shouldn't.

9

Janet, wearing only a bra and panties, walks out of the bathroom into the master bedroom. She doesn't turn on a light as she rubs lotion on her arms and walks to the window. The view looks out toward the back of the house. Around the edge of the building across the way a small glimpse of the city's vista is visible. One of her favorite things to do this time of year is to stroll through the cherry blossoms by the Potomac with Stephen and the kids during the National Cherry Blossom Festival. They'd make a day of it by picking a festival event, then coordinating the rest of their activities around it.

One year they did the boat tour, another year they did the parade and the fireworks, eating crabs from a huge pile on a table at one of the riverside restaurants. A festival event is a perfect way to revisit the monuments one by one, subtly teaching the kids about the nation's history and making it fun. Right before Stephen left, they talked about going to the kite festival. They started building a tradition around the cherry blossoms, but this year it's not going to happen unless she takes the kids by herself. Janet stares out into the night as she loosens her hair from its clip. The air is still, with scattered lights visible in the distance.

Stephen usually checks all the locks and makes sure the outside sensor lights are on every night. Janet forgot several times already and had to go back downstairs once she remembered. Even though the three of them are still here, without Stephen the house feels empty when the kids are asleep.

Noticing her reflection in the windowpane, her eyes instinctively travel to the little bulge extending beyond where she wants her thighs to end. She takes note of the softness in her belly. *Probably normal after bearing two children,* she thinks, but a far cry from the steel abs she used to sport. No matter how much she works out, she can't seem to get back to that same firmness she insists must still be in there somewhere. She's hitting that tipping point between a woman in the prime of her mature sexuality, where experience coupled with good looks and enough youth is considered sexy, and the onset of the signs that herald the beginnings of slight decay seen in older women brought on by middle age. She doesn't mind aging as much as she minds the constant reminders that it's somehow unacceptable. She turns from the window and away from her reflection without noticing the perfect roundness of her breasts, the long lines of her legs, elegant feet and hands or the way her eyes catch the small beam of light and brighten her face when she smiles. Maybe tonight she will sleep through the night. She completes her ritual in the bathroom and slides into bed, flicking on the side lamp.

Janet tries reading, but the vacant side of the bed bothers her more and more, as does the dormant remote control on Stephen's nightstand. She misses Stephen. He makes her feel great about herself and her sexuality. Before the kids came along, and even after Emily but before Mark, when she was feeling down or had a bad day, Stephen would take her out for a walk, a drink, a meal or a movie, or bring a bottle of Proseco home and pour her a glass, assuring her that all would soon be well again. Proseco is still her drink of choice.

Her cell phone buzzes, and Janet anxiously grabs for it. It's Stephen. "It's Friday night and this sucks," she says.

"I know. Can you believe I'm already halfway through the book? You'll turn me into a novel reader yet," Stephen says.

"That's a good thing."

"Yeah, but all that serial killer stuff in the book at the same time I'm listening to this trial is making me paranoid. Are you guys okay over there?"

"Of course. Other than we miss you. Your absence makes it painfully apparent how much you do around here."

"Well, I'd say that's a benefit."

"Yeah, for you. Terry's coming over tomorrow for Mark's practice."

"Good. Just don't let him get too comfortable."

"It's Terry."

"My point exactly."

Terry has a way of talking her off the ledge whenever she gets anxious about anything or worried about Stephen and now she particularly looks forward to seeing him.

"Ask him to go to the kite festival with you guys," Stephen suggests.

"I don't know…"

"You guys go and let me know if it's worth it, then you can take me next year."

"Maybe. Hey, speaking of the kids, couldn't you call any sooner tonight? They really wanted to talk to you."

"We were carted off to a restaurant, a bad one, as soon as court adjourned, for an early dinner, then they allowed those of us who wanted to, to change and be escorted to the gym to work out. I lost track of time, but it sure felt good to get some blood pumping."

"You're working out? Wow." Reflexively, Janet's hand goes to her belly.

"It's a start."

"Well good. I wish you could tell me more about what's going on there. You wouldn't believe the news…"

"Don't tell me anything. Remember the conversations here are recorded."

"Lovely. Good reminders every step of the way."

"On a positive note, I think the trial is moving along quicker than you might expect."

"I'm not sure what I expect."

After a long silence, Stephen adds, "Love you. Always have."

Janet responds, "Always will. Sleep well."

10

On the second Saturday morning of the sequester, as dawn breaks, Stephen notices that Washington D.C. is in for a gorgeous weekend and that he will miss out on being able to enjoy the traditional family outing. At least Terry will be there. There's a bus leaving at ten, taking the jurors who want to go outside by the river for a few hours, but Stephen plans on staying in his room and working on a business plan. He pulls out his laptop and positions himself at the small desk. They're allowing laptops because they've insured that they have no Internet access. Immediately a sense of oppression sets in. The longer he sits, the more the walls close in. The window won't open, and the air is stale. He tries to focus on his notes for an organizational chart, but his mind keeps drifting. He feels tight. Contained. This room is too dark and depressing. *How am I supposed to think?* Surely there's a room downstairs that's better. One that's he's allowed in and that the guards can recommend. He takes a last sip of his room's bitter coffee and decides he'll get some breakfast after all and investigate where they'll let him set up to work. The hotel has a small breakfast buffet for the jurors, but every time he'd looked at the scrambled eggs, he remembered what Janet said about them. That they're not real. What are fake eggs made of? Not important enough to taste and find out. He grabs his laptop and heads downstairs.

As he walks out of his room, he notices Eileen coming out of another room down the hall. Strange that he hadn't noticed where everyone's rooms are before today.

They're all on the same floor, but most rooms are to the right of the elevators and curve around, not to the left of the elevators like his, so he hasn't been paying attention. Most mornings, they all meet in front of the elevators and are escorted down, then at the end of each day they quickly retreat to their rooms from there. He never paid much attention; except he has noticed that Eileen was usually ahead of him in the morning and took the second elevator up later at night. The guards that bookend each of the halls are a dead giveaway that this is no ordinary floor.

"Good morning," Eileen greets him as they both reach the elevators together.

"Good morning."

"Are you going to breakfast? We only have another thirty minutes before they shut us out."

"Let's go."

Hard–boiled eggs, coffee and toast seems like a safe bet. You cannot fake an egg in a shell. Stephen selects his food and passes Marge on his way to the tables. "Hello, Marge," he says.

"Hello," she responds coolly as she brushes by him and makes her way to the coffee. No matter how hard he tries, this woman just won't warm up to him. Older women usually like him. Go figure.

Eileen sidles up next to Stephen with her tray and they sit down. "She doesn't like me," Stephen says, referring to Marge.

"Me neither."

"Oh great. You don't like me either."

Amused, Eileen says, "No. Marge doesn't like me. But I don't think she likes too many people."

"Apparently she loves Mike."

"Jealous?"

"Terribly."

Melita and Ronald are seated with four others, Laura the creative ad executive who apparently refuses to dress down for any occasion, Sam, one of the alternates, in his early sixties enjoying early retirement, Joanna, the middle–aged empty nester, and Ted.

The group, having finished their breakfast, chat over coffee, as Stephen and Eileen sit down at the long table. Melita waves at Marge to join them, but the older woman simply turns her back and heads to another table. Melita says, "I think Marge just feels vulnerable. She's the oldest one here, you know. I've noticed that old people can be really picky about everything. So, I've learned not to take it personally. With all this talk of murder and stuff, she could just be pissed off that she's the closest to dying of all of us."

"Theoretically that may be true, but none of us knows when we're going to die. Look at Joel. He was your age Melita. I'm only three years older than he was when he died. Fuck," Ronald adds.

"Oh wow," she returns as if that fact just reached her for the first time, "I guess that's true. Huh?"

"It usually happens when we least expect it. And nobody knows it's coming, unless you're a killer and you're planning it."

"Do you think this murder was planned?" Melita asks.

"Pretty sloppy planning if it were," Sam says.

"That's a good point," Stephen interjects. "That's why the charge is second degree murder. That alone says that the evidence points to the fact that it was an 'in the moment decision'."

"Like when a guy walks in on his girl in bed with another guy and loses it," Melita says.

"Something like that," Stephen replies.

"It's called heat of passion. Something set the killer off and because of that he reacted and killed the guy," Ted jumps in.

"I'm taking careful notes, because I think it's already starting to get pretty complicated," Joanna says.

"I think it's pretty simple. I believe the truth always comes out. By the time we hear everything, we'll know what we have to do," Laura declares as she pours herself a third cup of black coffee.

Ted leans back and looks at Laura, "No. We'd like to believe that, and we tell ourselves that to make us feel better, but Oscar Wilde said it best 'The truth is rarely pure and never simple.' You should know that. Aren't you in PR?"

Flustered, Laura counters, "Yes. But this is a court of law, not an article that someone is spinning a certain way."

"You sure about that?" Ted says. Laura just glares at him.

Reminded of what Terry had told him, Stephen offers, "Even in court, each side will try to spin the facts their way."

"The key being *try* and *facts*. We will have certain facts and if we stick to those without complicating things with the spin, then it will be simple," Laura asserts satisfactorily.

"Well, I guess we'll see how it unwinds," Sam says, then changes the subject to the day of leisure at hand. The majority of the jurors are going to go on the excursion. Only a few will stay at the hotel. Stephen thinks about his business plan, but Eileen says, "You should come. We'll be cooped up here enough, don't you think?"

Stephen realizes she's right. Maybe that's the smarter and healthier move. It doesn't take much convincing and he joins the field trip.

* * *

The day takes on a surreal quality. Ten jurors board the large van and proceed to the Jefferson Memorial located on the Tidal

Basin. The timing can't be more picturesque. A tapestry of fluffy pink and white blossoms cover the Basin's shore. The beautiful Japanese Cherry Trees are in full bloom cascading along the edge of the basin meeting their reflection in the water and creating a breathtaking sight. Stephen immediately thinks of Janet and the kids and how they should all be enjoying this together. But that's not possible and brooding isn't going to do him any good. They'll go to the festival tomorrow, probably with Terry, so why shouldn't he go today and enjoy being outside too? After all, he's the one stuck in a dull hotel room and court all day, he reminds himself.

Most of the jurors, while appreciating the weather, don't really take it all in. They walk around in groups and chat, some sit on the steps, talking or reading magazines, but Stephen senses that Eileen is different. That she appreciates this. Her face lights up as she languidly breathes in the fresh air and gazes across the water. When she closes her eyes, standing motionless, soaking up the sun and air, Stephen finds himself smiling. Although social and pleasant, Eileen has spent her time mostly listening this past week. That's a quality Stephen admires. Listening. He decides to follow Eileen's example and bask in the elements. Book in hand, he finds a spot against a tree and settles in to read.

Over the next few hours, he and Eileen share a few private exchanges, nothing about the facts of the trial, but some general concepts. Stephen also engages in small talk with Mike and Ronald while stretching his legs. A delivery of sandwiches and fresh salad arrives, and the group enjoys their first fresh and decent lunch in days before being brought back to their confines.

The weekend passes with little to show for it, except that Stephen spends plenty of time working out. Ted and Ronald give him a run for his money on the treadmill.

Those guys are in great shape. A shape Stephen used to resemble. They're younger, but Stephen's not old and he should be able to keep up. Surprisingly, the exercise isn't quelling a growing anxiousness that continues to plague him.

In Stephen's conversation with Janet on Sunday evening, she fills him in on every detail of their trip to the festival, trying to make him feel included. "We took tons of pictures and Mark brought a photo of you and would hold it up next to his face every time I took his picture. It started to get ridiculous, but he said it was to let you know you were with us in some way," Janet says with satisfaction, "What a gorgeous weekend. I'm sorry you didn't get to enjoy any of it, but we'll make up for it when you're done there."

He barely hesitates and then replies, "You bet we will. I'm glad you guys had such a great time." He thinks about saying something about his trip to the Memorial and that he was near the festival and thought about what a great time they would have, but he chooses not to mention it at all.

"I think I'll sleep well tonight," Janet says. "Speaking of which, we really miss you."

"I miss you guys too. I can't wait to see the pictures."

He doesn't know why he isn't telling her about his weekend and now he's starting to feel guilty. But now if he says something, she'll wonder why he didn't say anything sooner and made it sound like he's been cooped up, so she won't believe that there's no real reason for not saying anything. He can't explain it himself. It doesn't make sense that he doesn't want her to think he's enjoying himself at all while he's here. Janet would want him to get out and enjoy a moment or two away from this seclusion. Maybe there's some truth to the idea that he wants her to think this is hard on him.

Stephen hangs up and lays back on his bed wondering why he feels so disconnected. Almost as if a part of him is searching for something and whatever this part is searching for it's meant only for him, not for anyone else, until he figures it out.

11

Well into the second week of testimony for the prosecution, their case is on solid ground and Mann moves with more confidence and appears to have caught up on some sleep.

The expensively attired Cynthia Windsor sits in the witness chair. She's an attractive woman in that wealthy, we've all gone to the same plastic surgeon kind of way. Recent Botox injections prevent the upper half of her face and the lines around her mouth from moving. Even with the masked expression, her distain for her ex–husband comes through in her icy stare and body language. To keep herself calm, she resorts to constantly fiddling with her pearl and diamond bracelet.

Mann addresses her, "So, your divorce was finalized nearly a year ago?"

"Yes."

"Who filed for that divorce?"

"Objection. Relevance?" Alton is on his feet.

"Goes to establish motive," Mann responds.

"I'll allow it," the judge says.

Cynthia looks straight at her ex–husband, George Claxton, and says, "I did. I filed for divorce."

"On what grounds?"

With bitter and hurt intonation, Cynthia explains, "He lost all interest in me. And I don't mean just in the bedroom. In anything that was important to me. Anytime I expressed a desire for us to go somewhere as a family or even just the two of us to go out to a place I wanted to try, he'd brush me off. Make some excuse of why it was impossible for him to participate. Work became his automatic excuse, but I knew it wasn't always true. Certain things are understandable after so many years of marriage, but a complete disregard of your wife in anything other than her required attendance at a political function? Well, that became intolerable. And it had been years since he was interested in sex with me. Even when we first got married the sex wasn't overwhelming, but it was steady. I think our marriage was a career move for him. My girls were grown, and I got sick of it, so I filed."

At the defendant's table, Claxon shakes his head. *Always only 'her' girls when it's convenient.* He takes a deep breath and attempts to remain calm as he leans over and says something to Alton, who then stands up, "Move to strike, your honor. Relevance."

"Your honor, I need some leeway here," Mann pleads.

"I'll allow it. Get there quickly, Mr. Mann."

"Why do you think he wasn't interested in you sexually?"

"Oh, he was cheating on me," she says with certainty. "Probably from the very beginning, now that I think about it, but definitely in the last several years. I couldn't prove it, but I know it. For all I know he could've been sleeping with that boy."

Stephen notices the stirrings and hushed conversation in the courtroom at this statement. Joel's mother shakes her head and closes her eyes, as if to shut out this world around her. Alton, once again, objects and pleads with the judge, but before he finishes, Cynthia takes one last stab and adds, "He could be bi–sexual you know."

"Cynthia, for Christsakes!" Claxton can't contain himself any longer. Alton gracefully gestures for his client to still himself.

Cynthia doesn't look at him. She taps at her blonde hair to make sure it's in place and stares straight ahead in a self–righteous pose, twisting that bracelet, thrilled to get a rise out of her ex–husband. Her lower lip quivers just enough to make her point that she is also a victim here.

The judge instructs that Cynthia's last statements be stricken and, in an attempt, to return order to the proceedings, she calls for a fifteen–minute recess.

The jurors file into the jury room.

"Ooooooeee! That woman has an axe to grind," Charlie says as soon as they're all in the door.

"She's been wronged, and she's hurt. I can understand that," Laura contests.

"That may be so and the guy's probably gettin' some on the side, but she wants a piece of him to pay, somethin' bad."

"I know the judge told us to strike what she said, but I don't think I can just forget it," Melita adds.

Marge nods, "A woman knows her man, and something just isn't right with him."

"I think we should just stop and take a breath here. This is an angry ex–wife, and she made some good points, but we have a lot more testimony ahead, so jumping to conclusions right now isn't going to help us. Our job is to remain as objective as possible until we've seen all sides of this case," says Mike, the voice of reason.

"You're right," Ronald agrees.

"Yeah. Divorce is ugly, but we should stick to the facts." Right after Laura says this, she notices Charlie rolling his eyes and shaking his head. "What's that for?" Laura asks him.

"You want ugly, honey. Murder is ugly and when the emotions are all hopped up, it gets real ugly. A lot uglier. Sure, seems like he could've been gettin' some action from that kid. And from what I can see the facts are adding up to this guy goin' bye bye," Charlie replies smugly.

In the interest of peace and easing tensions, Mike changes the subject, and they all begin discussing the matter of security in the Senate office building. Stephen isn't sure of what to make of Claxton's ex–wife. Clearly born with a silver spoon in her mouth, to say she was spoiled is probably an understatement, but people don't usually give damning testimony like that if there isn't a kernel of truth in there somewhere. After all, a woman would consider the fact that this is the father of her children. *Wouldn't she?* He wonders what Eileen thinks of her. Eileen's expression doesn't reveal anything. He notices that she's watching the jurors carefully as they talk. Occasionally, she looks over at Stephen, but he tries to remain neutral, although his thoughts are all over the place. Getting into early banter in the middle of testimony isn't productive. They're being asked to decide a monumental fate and they need to stay rational and focused.

After their break, the prosecution rests and the defense now has the opportunity to shoot holes into the story the prosecution presented. Alton begins by placing the Senate building's janitor, Frank, who looks older than his fifty–six years and is modest and good natured, on the stand.

"How did the Senator seem?" Alton asks.

"Like usual, you know, busy. All dressed up for some fundraiser thing, but he always has time to say hello. Very friendly."

Alton establishes a few facts to his satisfaction and sits down.

"Redirect, your honor." Mann rises and approaches Frank, "After you spoke to the Senator, he got in the elevator and that was it?"

"Right."

"What did you do after the Senator left?"

"Well, I went on with my rounds."

"Did you clean the Senator's office?"

Frank eyes Mann suspiciously, unsure what he's getting at. "Like I always do."

"Right away after you saw the Senator?"

"I did two other suites first."

"What did you see in the Senator's office?"

"The same as always."

Stephen can see that Frank feels a loyalty to the Senator.

"Let me rephrase that. Did you notice the condition of the carpet by his desk?"

"It looked like some spilt coffee to me, that's all."

"Had you seen it the night before?"

"I don't remember."

"How about any night before that?"

"I don't think so."

"But you do remember the stain from that night?" Mann presses.

Hesitantly, Frank responds, "Yes, sir."

"Did you attempt to clean the stain?"

"No sir."

"Why not?"

"It looked like it was already cleaned up a bit and my carpet spray wasn't on my cart."

"Why not?"

Frank begins to show signs of sweat and swallows hard. "I don't know. It usually is. One of the other guys must've taken it. But I made a note and was going to clean it some more the next day."

"Thank you."

"Redirect." Alton stands, a bit frustrated. "Was your carpet spray on your cart earlier that day?"

"I'm not sure, because I didn't need it, so..."

"How about the day before?"

"Yes. I think I used it the day before."

"Where do you keep your cart when you're cleaning?"

"Outside the office I'm in usually."

"So, anyone could have walked by at any time that day and taken your spray."

"Sure. I suppose."

The Senator doesn't seem like the type that would steal spray and clean his own carpet, Stephen muses. But, then again, if he killed someone, he might scrub tiles with a toothbrush.

"Isn't it true that one of the elevators in the building was repaired just two days prior to the night in question?"

"Yes sir."

"Did you notice any special tools used for the repair of elevators?"

"I seen a bunch of elevators being repaired and they always have some fancy tools I don't recognize."

"Did they leave any of these tools in the building?"

"They were by the elevators for a while, then I don't know."

"But it's possible they stayed in the building?"

"Sure."

"Now, let's talk about how you get in and out of the building every day. You use the maintenance entrance, correct?"

"Yes."

"You have a key?"

"Yes."

"Do all janitors have a key?"

"No. Only the senior ones and supervisors."

"Have you ever lost your key, misplaced it or lent it to anyone?"

"No, sir."

"Do you know everyone who works in the maintenance department with you?"

"Most all. There are new folks on the other shift sometimes that I don't know so well."

"Could one of those new folks have entered the building that night?"

Frank appears confused.

"Could they?" Alton prods.

"I suppose. But we mostly see everyone there, on and off."

"Could someone else have come in through that entrance if they had a key or even broken in? Is the door ever left open or unlocked?"

Mann stands, "Objection. Your honor, this would call for pure speculation."

The next day, the defense continues their case. After numerous witnesses who don't do much to rip apart the prosecution's case, the last testimony comes from a small bespectacled man named John Wing. A researcher for one of the other Senators.

"Where were you on the night in question, Mr. Wing?" Alton begins his questioning.

"In the Senate library."

"Who did you see in the library that night?"

"Senator Claxton came in to return some books."

"What time was that?"

"Around eight fifteen I believe."

"What time did he leave?"

"He looked up some information and spent some time reading. I'd say about a half hour later."

"Which puts him in the library until eight forty–five." Alton smiles confidently.

On re–direct, Mann stands begins, "How do you know it was eight fifteen, Mr. Wing?"

"I looked at the clock."

"So, you say that the Senator walked into the library, and you immediately looked at the clock and saw that it was eight fifteen?"

"Yes."

"There is no clock on the wall in the third–floor library. Which clock would you be referring to?"

Taken off guard, Wing becomes flustered, then recovers, "I had a watch on. I didn't express myself well."

"Is that it, or is it that you really aren't sure?" Alton attempts an objection, but Mann's point is made.

* * *

Nearing one in the morning, Stephen lays in the lumpy bed staring at the ceiling. So far, his instincts tell him that the Senator could very well have done this at least from an evidentiary point of view, but the motive isn't yet clear and that thing about him being gay strikes him as iffy. Probably not true. But it's the only thing the prosecution can come up with. That doesn't mean there isn't a real and plausible motive. Just that no one has uncovered it yet. What he can't quite wrap his head around is the fact that this guy Joel was hurled down an elevator shaft. *How would you get the doors open? Probably one of those tools the janitor mentioned.* As an architect, Stephen knows a little about elevator shafts, but who else would know that? These days there's always the Internet and you can get a tutorial in just about anything. He makes a mental note to bring that up with the others and maybe try it on one of the hotel elevators.

Sleeping is still a challenge. Although he's discovered that after working out, he falls asleep much easier, but he doesn't stay asleep. He feels restless. He started reading the book on Leonardo DaVinci, but he doesn't feel like reading now. Or working.

Maybe he can try a movie. He spots the can of soda he brought up from dinner sitting on his nightstand – probably warm by now. He gets up, throws on a pair of pants, grabs the can and ice bucket and heads for the ice machine down the hall. The guard sees him, nods and goes back to thumbing through a magazine.

Stephen sees Eileen kicking the vending machine next to the ice machine. "Need some help?" he offers.

"It ate my money."

Stephen tries pushing a few buttons, strategically hitting the machine in a few places, but no luck. He turns to her and finally takes her in. She's not wearing her glasses. He notices how strikingly dark and intense her eyes are. He hasn't really noticed that before. Maybe her makeup is different. Her face looks much more beautiful without the heavy lenses. A silk robe, loosely tied, shows off Eileen's stunning figure. A figure that her daily clothes mask well. He wonders why this woman doesn't dress to accentuate her beauty. Perhaps she doesn't know how. After all, physicists aren't known for their fashion sense. Stephen holds up his soda. "You're in luck. I'm a sharer."

"Great. Thanks." She smiles at him and hands him her cup. He notices her unusual gold charm bracelet as he puts some ice into her cup and pours the soda. Eileen watches him, making him nervous.

"That's a beautiful bracelet," he manages.

"Thanks. It was a gift from," she hesitates just a moment then continues "a family member. I was told it's a one of a kind."

Stephen wonders which family member but doesn't dare ask. Instead, he just says, "A family member with good taste," and hands her the full cup.

"Thank you. Can't sleep?"

"No," he responds.

"Is that unusual?"

"Unfortunately, not for a while now."

"Me too."

"You have a family, right?"

In all the conversations he's had with her and the others, no one revealed much about anything personal, except Joanna about her kids and the little bit from Mike and maybe some basics from a few others, but mostly they focus on employment, what they're seeing in the trial and small talk. Her question shouldn't make him uncomfortable, yet it does, and he shifts.

"Yes. Wife and two kids. Very average, I suppose."

"I think it's nice. You always have someone there for you. Young kids?"

"My son's nine and my daughter's twelve going on thirty."

They share a laugh and Stephen begins to feel more comfortable, "You?" he asks.

"No. I travel too much."

"I love traveling. Don't do much of it, but one day maybe. It must be exciting."

"I guess it can be exciting or exhausting, depending. At first, I thought that was the source of my insomnia. Then I started Googling it and did you know that supposedly the cause of insomnia is usually because something is bothering you and you're not willing to face it or even accept that it may be a problem."

"So, what's your problem?"

Eileen looks at him with amusement and playfully responds, "I have no idea. I'm clearly not ready to face it, so no sleeping for me. And you?"

"I don't know. I could land this huge client and make partner, so that's great. I don't know, just feels like something's off. Like is this really my life?"

"I know exactly what you mean." After she says that there's an awkward silence and a tension between them.

Stephen breaks it. "Sometimes routine and responsibility gets in the way, but you never know, I am thinking of starting my own firm and doing more daring projects."

"That's great. You should. This trial is making me realize just how much shorter life is than we think. I mean, one day you think you have all the time in the world and this big future ahead of you, then the next – poof! – it's all gone." Eileen takes a sip of soda. "Sorry. I didn't mean to start getting maudlin."

"No. No, you're right. The kid was only twenty–six."

Another silence ensues and Stephen begins to feel awkward. Eileen remains comfortable just staring at him, sipping her soda and smiling slightly. She isn't wearing anything under that robe. He begins to feel warm. His mind grapples with where to go next. The subject of the trial provides simple relief. "The trial is getting pretty heated," he offers.

"Yes. It scares me to think that someone like the Senator...I mean that his fate is in our hands. I feel like some of the others are ready to hang him right away because I would be easy. But we can't afford to make a mistake. This is a man's life. One life was already taken, and I'd hate for us to get it wrong and take another one."

"Yeah, you're right. We need to be careful." *And you're beautiful*, he thinks. Her hair is brushed away from her neck and he looks at the long smooth nape. Then at her full lips and the way they glisten after she takes a drink of her soda. He can't stop staring at her and he knows he has to get out of there and back to his room. "It's late. We should really get some sleep."

Eileen gives him an amused smile as she retreats for her room. "Or try. See you tomorrow," she says.

Back behind closed doors, Stephen finishes his soda. His heart pounds as he brushes his teeth and crawls between the sheets. He needs to get some sleep. He hears Eileen's voice, "or try" and laughs. Eileen's dark eyes and her black silk robe flash through his mind. The night closes in and plunges Stephen Reeves into dreamland.

12

The motive remains the weak link in the Claxton case and the defense intends on discrediting the prosecution's allegations of any homosexuality. A tall, impeccably dressed, attractive woman in her mid–thirties, Lynette Saunders, answers the questions Alton poses to her, "How long did you have a relationship with the Senator?"

"Almost one year," she replies very matter of fact and without embarrassment.

"Was it an intimate, physical relationship?"

"Yes, it was." She brushes a strand of her long auburn hair off her shoulder to her back.

"In your opinion, is Senator Claxton a healthy, heterosexual male?"

"Absolutely. I have no doubts."

"Why do you have no doubts?"

"George loves women. I mean he really gets into the sex and relishes…"

"Your honor!" Mann is on his feet.

"Goes to discredit their claims, your honor," Alton jumps in.

"I'll allow it."

"Please continue," Alton instructs Lynette.

"Not many men love going down on a woman, but to George it was like breakfast. He would get so turned on by licking and…."

"Thank you, Ms. Saunders, I think we get the picture," Judge Cohen intervenes.

The jurors' impatience at the length of the trial starts to show. In the jury room, reactions are mixed about the motive. Charlie Murphy remains of the opinion that where there's smoke there's fire and bisexuality among actors, politicians and the eccentric rich is practically a given. Some of the others, including Sam and Marge, feel that the motive might not ever be certain, but it doesn't matter because the evidence is solid. Most of the jurors, including Stephen, Eileen, Mike and Ted, keep quiet about any of their opinions on the proceedings.

Stephen's mind wanders back to his dreams of the last couple of nights. Not only does his insomnia plague him, but now his dreams do as well. Images of rain streaking plump green leaves, creating mud on skin, on skin against skin, lips devouring each other, hands urgently pulling flesh closer…

Stephen remains true to his intent to not leave his room at night. He calls Janet and the kids, then settles onto the bed, wearing only boxers. He decides to watch a movie – something that will take his mind into other–worldly territory. He tunes into to a classic science fiction film, *Blade Runner*. Quickly immersed in the world of dark visuals and replicants, he thinks of how unexpectedly life can change in a single moment. Engrossed in both the film and his thoughts, Stephen jumps when he hears a knock on his door. He pauses the movie. "Hold on," he says, quickly putting on his pants and a t–shirt. Barefoot, he opens the door to find Eileen standing there in a pair of jeans, holding two cans of soda.

She smiles at him and looks over her shoulder. "I ditched the floor guard. I'm starting to feel like a caged animal, and I figured I owed you one," she says, entering his room. Stephen finds himself immobilized, as if in slow motion. A part of him wants to let her know that she can't be here. It's not allowed. But not one–word escapes.

Eileen sets the drinks on the small desk; her charm bracelet jingles with the movement. Stephen looks at her beautiful hands. Graceful. Elegant. No rings. He feels the thick gold band on his own finger. He says, "This isn't necessary, but thanks."

Eileen motions to the chair, "Do you mind?" she asks as she sits and pours the drinks.

"No." It would be rude to ask her to leave immediately.

She notices the scene on the television in pause mode. "What are you watching?"

"Blade Runner."

"Old movie?"

"Yeah."

"You can turn it back on. Or I can get out of your way."

"No. No, it's fine. I've seen it before." *Did I just say that?* He takes a sip of soda. "I think the trial is coming to a head. It should be over soon. The evidence against the Senator is pretty overwhelming."

"That's exactly what bothers me. It seems as if there's all this evidence, but it's all circumstantial."

"Not the forensics, just the conjecture. But that's how it is with most cases. Besides, the hard evidence is pretty compelling, and it just makes our job easier."

"Or more difficult. The people who know this man the best all say good things about him. About his character as a person."

"Except for the ex–wife," Stephen reminds her.

"Well, I don't know any divorced people who say nice things about each other. Do you?"

Stephen thinks of Terry and his breakup, and that wasn't even a divorce. "That's true."

"My intuition tells me something is wrong."

"In what way?"

"I don't know. It'll probably get cleared up."

"We'll have a chance to go over everything in detail when it's over. I'm sure that'll help."

"Strange to think we're so removed from the rest of the world right now," she says as she sits back in her chair and takes a sip. Her lips seem redder, and her white t– shirt clings around her full breasts and small waist. She usually wears bulky clothing. To have her here dressed like this is disturbing.

They catch each other's stare. Stephen gulps from his drink and tries to smile, uncomfortable in his own skin. Eileen moves to put her glass on the small table. Her bracelet catches the edge, and the glass topples over. Soda spills all over her.

"Whoa!" Stephen exclaims.

Eileen pulls her shirt out of her pants and away from her skin. "Shit! I'm sorry. What a klutz."

"Don't worry about it. Let me get a towel."

Eileen grabs some tissues and sops up some of the liquid off the table and floor. When Stephen returns with the towel, instead of handing it to her, he instinctively wipes the soda off her jeans. He realizes what he's doing and stops abruptly. He looks up at her. "Sorry," he offers. Their faces inches apart.

"It's okay," Eileen replies softly.

Neither one moves. Stephen hears his heartbeat pound in his ears and time takes on a slow, surreal quality. How can he be feeling this overwhelming desire for a woman he barely knows? And yet, the sensation lingers. Looming real and undeniable. He doesn't remove his hand that rests on her thigh. She slowly places her hand over his, leans into him and gives him a quick gentle kiss on the lips. She then backs away and says, "I shouldn't have done that." Her eyes remain fixed on his.

"No, you shouldn't have," Stephen agrees, as the world shrinks to only this moment in this drab little room filled with nothing but raw craving and a need to escape into pleasure. An urgency he hasn't felt in ages courses through his veins. A hunger rises in him, slow at first, a whisper from the inside. A small surge carries him into the vaster regions of his soul, silently consuming pockets of duty, patience and self–control, eroding the pillars of conscience he so fervently counts on. He looks deep into those onyx eyes and feels calm and consumed. She doesn't turn away. He stands up, holds her hand, and pulls her up toward him. Her arms slide easily around him. Their bodies conform to each other as they fall into a long, passionate kiss. The electricity between them flows and escalates in an uncontrollable wave until the kissing gives way to searching for the feel of skin on skin.

Eileen deftly undoes Stephen's pants and lets them fall to the floor. Feverishly, he pulls her shirt over her head and removes it, revealing full breasts in a see–through lacy bra. She pulls off her jeans and the two of them topple onto the bed. Her skill is undeniable and remarkable. Stephen can't believe that the outwardly reserved woman in the group is the same one he now holds in his arms. The agile strength of her body against his seems the most natural feeling in the world. He embraces her with an ardor he barely thought possible, demanding more and more. Erasing the memory of what he used to focus his life on, his only sight and desire lies in the unfulfilled hunger that ravages him harder and faster. He presses his mouth on hers, kissing her deeply, searching. She caresses him, building the intimacy. Their love–making cascades through urgency and gentleness, without apology.

After climaxing, Stephen pulls himself off Eileen and lays, out of breath, next to her. She turns her head and kisses his shoulder. Slowly, the surroundings of the colorless room come into focus. Remnants of the soda and the glass on the table; Eileen's rumpled shirt clinging to the chair; the towel on the floor next to the bed. The frozen image of Harrison Ford and Sean Young radiate from the television screen across the room. How everything can change in a single moment. Stephen feels Eileen's breath next to him.

She props herself up on her elbow and stares at him. He keeps his eyes riveted straight ahead, afraid to move. Afraid to think. Afraid to look at her. Afraid that all this is real. A slow dread begins in his belly. What has he done? How can he have done this? Who is he?

Eileen isn't that much younger than Janet, maybe seven or eight years. She isn't necessarily more attractive either. Although she'd borne no children and is clearly a workout machine – so well–toned and supple. Maybe it's just hardwired into the DNA. Maybe a heterosexual man's genetic predisposition when a young, attractive, female throws herself at his disposal is instinctive. An instinct to pounce on her without regard to any other factors. Terry probably knows this better than anyone. Much like Pavlov's dog. A conditioning that spans eons.

Eileen senses his growing tension. "It's okay," she whispers.

Did she really just say that? "How can you say that?" Nothing about this is okay. Not in his world. She has nothing to lose, but he...well, he has everything.

"I know you're married, and I have no intention of causing trouble. In any way. We're in a strange situation. A kind of time capsule, away from the real world, so let's not panic."

Stephen turns to her and brushes his hands over her breasts. "This isn't something you just forget. At least not for me. I'm not built that way. I made vows. I'm so sorry if I've led you on."

"Stop. Take a deep breath and just stop. I'm okay with this just being in the time capsule. Really." She strokes his face, then rises from the bed and begins putting her clothes back on. "I'm a big girl and I think it's crazy to be cooped up here like chickens and to not expect some relief. And..." She turns and looks at him gently, "I like you. Not in the I'm a crazy fatal attraction woman who's going to stalk you, but in the you're a nice guy and the one bright spot in this strange arrangement. Does that make sense?"

Stephen retrieves his boxers and puts them on. Relieved, he says, "Yeah. Actually, it does. I can't believe that it would, but it does." He grabs her hand and fingers the gold bracelet. "Thank you," he says.

She smiles at him. "Now let's see if I can sneak back to my room without getting caught."

Once she's gone, sleep is impossible. Stephen is charged up. His unease about what he's just done won't abate. Watching the end of the movie does nothing to ease his fire, so he resorts to pushups, sit ups and squats until he can do no more. Finally, nearing four in the morning, exhaustion takes over and he finds some solace in sleep.

13

When Stephen sees Eileen the next morning in the dining area, she's finishing her coffee and talking to Ted, who apparently must own an entire room of suits. Stephen's first impulse is to jump to Eileen's side. *Jealousy?* Can't be, he tells himself. He suspects that Ted is probably gay and nothing in his body language indicates that he's flirting with her. Stephen takes a deep breath and sees that she's relaxed and acting normal. He needs to do the same. She seems true to her word. He reassures himself that she will keep what happened between them in its own time space continuum, not behave like they have something going on or be clingy. Their actions will remain tucked away and non-intrusive. They are mature adults. Stephen tells himself that events with Eileen can indeed exist in a time capsule and that he will easily and gladly slip into his real life when all this is over. He grabs his coffee and sits next to Mike until it's time to leave.

In court, the day creaks along and the defense finally rests. But the prosecution isn't ready to end the trial and calls a young aide, Jill Jenks, as a rebuttal witness.

"Where did you see the Senator that night?" Mann asks her.

"In the hallway, outside the library." Visibly scared of what testifying here means to her future in a town that easily makes political pariahs out of newbies, Jill speaks softly and keeps her eyes down. "I stopped to get a drink of water on my way out, and I saw Senator Claxton go into the library carrying some books."

"What time was that?"

"Around seven forty–five."

"We had Mr. Wing here who testified that the Senator entered the library at eight fifteen. How can you be sure it was seven forty–five?"

The young woman gulps and begins softly, "I'm sure because I take the..."

Mann interrupts her, "Can you please speak up."

"Okay. I'm sure because I take the eight–p.m. bus home every night and I had a few minutes to go back to my desk and get my things and still make it to the bus stop."

Stephen looks over at the defense table and notices the grave faces of Alton and Claxton as they confer about what was just said. Apparently, they have nothing to offer and are unhappy that the trial is ending on this note. Closing arguments are scheduled for the next day.

That night, Stephen watches another movie. At least he tries watching. His mind constantly drifts to images of Eileen. He looks in the duffel bag. The M&Ms are still there. He'd forgotten about then. He opens the bag and begins eating nervously. Part of him hopes there will be a knock on the door, while another part, a more rational part, is relieved there isn't. What will he do if she comes by again? He will have to turn her away. That is for the best. Absolutely, yes. But she probably won't. Come by, that is. He lays back on the bed, holding the remote and playing with the volume. When he glances to his right, he realizes he's on the left side of the bed and there is no one next to him. He thinks of Janet and the churning in his stomach grows. He turns his attention back to the TV. The movie ends after midnight and he should be exhausted, considering he barely slept the night before. Yet sleep won't come. He relives the prior night's events in his mind and slowly, uncontrollably, he finds himself longing for a repeat.

* * *

In court the following morning, Stephen looks and feels haggard. He goes through three cups of coffee before he feels remotely ready to engage in the day.

The prosecutor confidently delivers his closing argument. "You've been witness to the facts in a very shocking case. When you leave to assemble as jurors for deliberation, we ask that you bring justice to a young man's senseless murder. Make sure you consider all the facts. The defense tells you that the Senator was set up but hasn't offered one shred of evidence to back up that claim. Who would set him up? Why?

Nothing except vague generalities has even been suggested, because that is not what happened. What we have here is a cold–blooded, brutal murder committed by Senator Claxton who couldn't bear the thought of losing an election. Winning the election and becoming Majority Whip was his dream, his very clear and what he believed practically assured goal. This goal became even more important in light of the fact that his wife recently divorced him, and the Windsor name no longer backed him." Mann paces effectively and addresses both the jury and the press seamlessly as he speaks. His face has the color and demeanor of a man whose confidence has continued to escalate since the trial first began. "Let's examine the facts. The state has proven that the murder was committed in the Senator's office; the murder weapon belongs to the Senator; the blood stains in the Senator's private office indicate that poor Joel Christiansen, a young man with his entire life ahead of him, was brutally assaulted in front of the Senator's desk with whatever object was at hand and the blood was cleaned up. I will grant you that this was not a planned murder, rather one that occurred in a moment of rage. That is why the charge is one of second–degree murder. But, ladies and gentlemen, that makes it no less vile and no less a murder. Second degree murder is a non–premeditated killing, resulting from an assault in which the death of the victim was a distinct probability. That is exactly what happened here."

Mann proceeds to mention each and every piece of evidence. Collectively the evidence appears substantial. The temperature of the spectators in the room cools toward the Senator and all eyes are on him to see if he will finally flinch. George Claxton has long ago steeled himself to the proceedings in the room and even Mann's weaving everything together doesn't appear to get to him. Claxton remains stoic.

"Why was Joel Christiansen killed? Because he loved this prominent, high–profile man and wanted the world to know it. He was young and young love is unreasonable. We all know that lovers' quarrels can be some of the most heated and irrational, but they are never an excuse to beat, let alone to kill, another human being. Young Joel, in the prime of his life, suffered not only horrible pain and death from the blows but also from the fact that he adored and completely trusted this man." Mann points to the Senator and pauses just long enough to make his point. "The man inflicting those blows. Imagine someone you love and trust suddenly attacks you. Sadly, it happens every day from jealous rage. And none of us are immune to jealousy, not even Senators. We have heard testimony that the Senator had been unfaithful to his wife in the past. That she felt betrayed by this same man. The ability to betray another is, regrettably, the nature of many men. Something the young must come to realize, sometimes in the costliest ways."

Stephen feels the sting of the prosecutor's words regarding faithfulness and betrayal, but pushes them away, certain that his very recent actions bear no resemblance to what is being said. How can they? He is a loving, honorable family man, scared of even cheating a little bit on his taxes.

"But there is no greater betrayal than what the Senator did to this boy. He inflicted rage induced blows and did not stop until he believed Joel was dead. Then he tried to cover it up. Sworn testimony has shown that George Claxton has no real alibi for the time of the murder. That is because he committed murder to prevent Joel from going public with the fact that the Senator was gay or perhaps bi–sexual. It doesn't matter which. This is information that would ruin him. We showed you how a man of the Senator's build could easily have carried an unconscious Joel to the elevator and throw him down the shaft. Which is what he did. In an ironic twist of fate, Joel did not die when George Claxton thought he did. And we showed you how it was possible to throw Joel on top of an adjacent elevator where his sheer will helped him pry open the vent in the roof of that elevator and land on his very killer. Senator George Claxton is, without a doubt, young Joel Christiansen's murderer." Mann's closing leaves a powerful impression. Stephen sees Joel's mother staring at the jury with her haunting eyes, pleading.

At a break between the attorney's closing statements, Eileen is contemplative.

She chats briefly with both Ronald and Ted, but otherwise keeps to herself and listens to the others, who seem anxious to get to deliberation. She can tell that the tenor of the room leans toward conviction just by some of the comments. She and Stephen avoid each other, but she watches him out of the corner of her eye. He too appears in a reflective mood.

That afternoon, Stephen watches as Alton stands and takes a stab at his side of the closing argument. His previous record shows him to be a master weaver of his client's side of the story. Today he has a great deal to overcome, but all he needs is one juror.

Something he never loses sight of. He begins there, with the jury box, addressing the jurors, trying to get them to view him as an affable proponent of the unjustly accused.

"Thank you, ladies and gentlemen, for doing your civic duty here and for recognizing the seriousness of the responsibility you bear. I know it must be difficult for all of you to be away from your families, your jobs and your lives all this time and I can only express my gratitude and understanding for your willingness to do so. A man's well–being is at stake. A good and honorable man. The life of a valuable civil servant to our nation. Make no mistake, the evidence in this case is all circumstantial and the motive is a complete fabrication. It's true that the well–spoken prosecutor tells a marvelous tale.

"But that is all it is. A tale of fiction. First and foremost, you must ask yourselves, why? Why would one of the most respected U.S. Senators in our time do such a mad act and ruin his life? Senator Claxton is not gay. That is absurd conjecture. We have shown that the Senator is not, nor has ever been homosexual. Never a hint anywhere in his past. So, those speculations by the esteemed prosecutor have no bearing here. Mr. Mann admits that Mr. Christiansen enjoyed working with the Senator and trusted him. Why would George Claxton do this to his most trusted protégé, in his own office? It doesn't make any sense. And right before going to a dressy fundraiser? The Senator was Joel's mentor. He had invested time and energy into Mr. Christiansen. He had absolutely no reason to kill this young man." Alton pauses and looks concernedly at the jurors.

"I submit to you that there were other people with strong motives who could have killed Mr. Christiansen and framed the Senator for their crime. Sad as it is, our country's leaders have enemies. Yes, we have tightened security since the tragic events of 9/11, but not in such a way as to prevent acts such as this. Let me submit to you, that the time of the beating cannot be pinpointed, therefore anyone could have been in that building and snuck out without being seen amidst all the chaos when the body was found. The building was not sealed off until over an hour later. And we know there was at least one other way in and out of that building – through maintenance. And right there, we have the existence of doubt."

Alton goes on in an attempt to explain away some of the evidence. Stephen feels that the man's arguments are well spoken but are still weak. The defense attorney makes some good points, but all in all Stephen leans toward the prosecution. If the others feel the same way, they could be out of here as early as tomorrow. That thought should excite him, but instead it stirs up a quiet panic.

By four in the afternoon, the judge officially concludes the evidentiary portion of the trial with her instructions to the jury. "You, as jurors, are the judges of the facts. But in determining what actually happened on the night of Joel Christiansen's death – that is, in reaching your decision as to the facts – it is your sworn duty to follow all of the rules of law as I explain them to you. You have no right to disregard or to give special attention to any one instruction that has been given throughout this trial or to question the wisdom or correctness of any rule I may have stated to you. You must not substitute or follow your own notion or opinion as to what the law is or ought to be. It is your duty to apply the law as it is explained to you, regardless of the consequences. However, you should not read into these instructions, or anything else the attorneys or I may have said or done, any suggestion as to what your verdict should be. That is entirely up to you. I realize your sequester has been difficult on you and your families, but that is no reason to rush to a verdict. It is your duty to base your verdict solely upon the evidence, without prejudice or sympathy. That was the promise you made and the oath you took when we began here."

After Judge Cohen concludes, the jurors are filed back into the jury room. Here a white board, pads of paper, pens and drinks wait for the twelve men and women in whose fate rests the freedom of a prominent United States Senator.

As their first order of business, the group quickly selects Mike as their foreman.

Mike has managed to be the least objectionable. Polite, non–threatening and uncontroversial. He begins methodically, "Should we start with some of the basics, or..."

Charlie cuts him off, "What's to discuss. I say we take a vote. Chances are we won't be needin' a discussion."

"Okay. We could certainly see what our first inclinations are. All those who think the Senator is guilty raise their hand."

"Wait," Joanna jumps in. "Can't we vote on little pieces of paper anonymously, like they do in the movies?"

Charlie rolls his eyes. "Come on, we all know he's guilty."

Marge nods in agreement.

"If that's more comfortable. Sure," Mike concedes and passes out small squares of paper to each person and instructs that they all fold it twice when finished and pass them back to him.

Everyone casts their vote and Mike goes through the papers, "Well, it looks like we have nine guilty, two undecided and one not guilty."

"Oh, come on," Charlie blares, staring right at Joanna. "That's why you wanted to be anonymous. Bein' that foolish I would too."

"Think what you want. But you're wrong. Exactly your attitude and assumption is why I wanted it to be anonymous. I don't think anyone should be bullied here. You should not take this lightly." Joanna's face grows crimson. Standing up to men like Charlie does not come easily to her.

"This is a great start. Let's go over what we all agree on first," Mike suggests.

Laura leads the way with, "Joel was beaten with the Senator's statuette in the Senator's office the same night that the Senator was still working."

As the jurors call out some of the key, undisputed facts, Mike writes them on the whiteboard, briefly discussing each point to ensure agreement of the facts. During the process dinner arrives to the deliberation room. Pizza and salad. The group continues with the process as they consume their food and discuss the case. The whiteboard begins to fill up:

- Joel – beaten with the statuette from Claxton's office and in his office the recording for the security cameras on that floor had some time periods, including the time around the murder, that appeared to be frozen on a still frame. The image corrected itself after 30 minute intervals. No way to be sure if they were tampered with. Cameras only monitored entrances and exits on each floor. Joel was beaten sometime after his conversation with Scott – probably just after 8pm
- Joel's body came off the top of and into one of the elevators between 9:00 and 9:15 pm
- The Senator was seen in the library sometime between 7:45 and 8:45 but was only there for 10–15 minutes.
- Someone tried to clean up the blood in Claxton's office
- Claxton had no blood on his clothes when anyone saw him, but he had a coat on when Frank saw him, so no way to know if there was any blood on his clothes underneath. If so, it would have been minor. He also has

his own bathroom in his office and extra clothes. The Senator was covered in the victim's blood when the body dropped on him

- Joel was still alive and waiting for the Senator just after 8pm
- There is no proof that the Senator was ever gay or whether that has any relevance

As Mike writes this last statement, Charlie blurts out, "There sure is some proof. Come on, even his ex–wife says he's got a problem bein' a man. You gotta take the word of someone who knows him in the bedroom."

Eileen can't resist retorting, "His ex–wife was clearly trying to hurt him. She would say anything to hurt this guy. There is nothing to prove that the Senator is or ever was gay. The one woman he slept with, Lynette, she proved that he likes women. A lot."

Ted looks at Charlie, "You're immediately assuming something criminal just because someone's gay?"

"Oh, look here. You gonna defend those sweet asses, or maybe you're one of 'em?" Charlie gears up for a row.

"Better than some ignorant hick."

Charlie jumps to his feet and lunges across Melita toward Ted.

Stephen puts out his arm to stop him, "Cool it!"

Charlie, visibly disgusted, looks straight at Stephen and sneers, "Aren't you tired of sticking your face where it don't belong?"

Stephen's anger surges at the comment, but he maintains his cool and refuses to take the bait, remaining silent.

"We've all had a long day. So, I think we've got a good start and maybe what we need is a good night's sleep before we come back to this. Why don't we just call it a night?" Mike suggests.

"It's after eight," Joanna says.

"I'm all for cutting bait," Ronald agrees. "We can pick up in the morning."

Mike adjourns the deliberations. The guards are notified, and everyone moves back to the hotel and to their rooms.

Stephen feels anxious. He loads into the hotel elevator with the six others who deliberately wait until Charlie goes up with the first load. Aside from a few, 'excuse me's' and assents to 'glad that's over,' no one talks. When the elevator stops on their floor, Stephen's eyes catch Eileen's, and he thinks they share a moment of understanding. As he walks back to his room, he relives the look in his mind. What understanding does he think they just shared? Maybe he's making the whole thing up and his mind is playing tricks on him. He's been cooped up here way too long. And yet, a sensation deep inside expects Eileen to come to him tonight.

Once he's in his room, he grabs a fresh pair of boxers from the newly delivered laundry pile on his bed and decides to shower. He looks at his door and quietly opens it just a fraction, just enough to prevent it from locking so she can enter if she comes by while he's in the shower. He strips off his clothes and remembers that it's his call night. He wraps a towel around himself and picks up the phone, asking the hotel to connect him to his home number.

Janet's voice answers, "Stephen?"

"I'm so sorry. We began deliberations and got back so late."

"So, no quick verdict."

"Not yet. Maybe tomorrow."

He talks to Janet with his back to the door and doesn't notice Eileen slip into the room. She sits on the bed and startles him. He gasps. She mouths 'sorry' and gets up and goes into the bathroom.

Janet detects a shift in Stephen's voice and asks "What happened? Are you okay?"

"Sorry. Yeah, I almost dropped something. I'm fried."

"I'll keep my fingers crossed that this will be over tomorrow."

Eileen comes out of the bathroom and notices the candle that Janet gave Stephen sitting on the desk with the matches next to it. She moves to the desk and lights it. She hears Stephen say softly, "Always will. Give my love to the kids."

He hangs up the phone and looks at Eileen, avoiding her eyes, "I'm sorry," he says. The apology comes automatically. He feels foolish. He tightens the towel around his waist. Self–conscious. He wouldn't have anything to be sorry about if he weren't doing anything so...wrong. The strange thing is that none of this with Eileen feels like his real life. He's sorry because he doesn't feel that much guilt because he can't connect any of this to his actual life. How can a man who made vows to a woman he loves more than anything not feel guilty in the moment he's cheating on her? Unless there's something wrong with him. Some weird brain defect. Maybe he has a brain tumor, and it hasn't been discovered yet. Unlikely. He feels guilty afterwards and when he thinks about it, but not at the time. He begins to feel guilty about not feeling guilty.

"Nothing to be sorry about. It's fine." She positions the candle and turns off the main light as Stephen approaches her, then he stares at the candle. Eileen looks at him and begins unbuttoning her shirt. She takes it off and tosses it on the chair, then slips off her pants. She stands in front of Stephen in a sheer bra and lace panties. Looking at her, a voice in Stephen's head begins to sound. Time capsule, time capsule, time capsule. He repeats the words as a mantra in his head to compel himself fully into the present moment.

Stephen reaches out his hand and runs his fingers along Eileen's belly. His towel drops to the floor. In a swift motion, Stephen swoops Eileen into an embrace, her legs wrap around him as they succumb to a hungry kiss. Their heat grows. They fall onto the bed, groping and devouring each other. The remainder of her lingerie is hurriedly removed. Eileen winds up on top and breaks her mouth away from Stephen, her eyes search his face. She pins his arms by his shoulders. They stare into each other's eyes.

She lowers her face and kisses him gently and deeply. Pulling her mouth away, she sweeps her hair over his face as she continues to kiss, first his neck, then his chest and slowly begins descending downward. Stephen reflexively reaches for her hair, but she deflects him and pins his hands to his side as she makes her way down. Lingering between Stephen's thighs until he is achingly hard, she then thrusts herself back in his face and violently, passionately kisses him again. Stephen rolls her onto her back. Eileen digs her nails into his back as they make urgent love.

Both spent, they lie in bed unmoving. He looks over at the naked woman by his side then back up to the ceiling. "This could be our last night in this place," he says.

Sitting up, she adds, "That's right. I meant what I said about what this is." She looks him in the eye. "Our own bubble?"

Stephen wistfully replies, "Yeah. Our own bubble."

"Yes. Okay." Eileen puts on her underwear, "Do you see the reasonable doubt in the case?" she asks.

"So, you are the 'not guilty' vote," Stephen states. "I'm one of the undecided."

"Okay. Well, what's holding you up?"

"I'm inclined to go with guilty. I just want to talk it out first. I don't think they have the right motive, so I want to make sure I'm solid on the concrete evidence; so, whatever the motive is, it doesn't matter if we know it or not."

"I think your right about no plausible motive." Eileen grabs a water and settles back down on the bed. "Have you ever heard of groupthink?"

"No. What is it?"

"It's a method of thinking that people get into when they're put in a specific kind of group. We're a great example – a jury talking through a specific thing with each other, and we keep circulating those thoughts among us until something is decided or we move on to something else. If I look at who said what tonight right after the trial, I would say that our goal to reach a unanimous verdict and to go home is greater than our desire to really look at everything as carefully as we should. The jury as a whole is not really inclined to realistically assess other possibilities. That becomes our groupthink and it's easier for those who have some doubts to just go along with the majority rather than fight it."

"Well, we could have just as easily all gone for not–guilty if that's the case."

"Except that Charlie started the groupthink long ago with his absolutes of guilt, and some of the others seem to agree, so I think subconsciously we all assumed that's where we'd go."

"Wow. Ms. Psychologist. I had no idea. That's a pretty good point, but I think we need the facts to back up the validity of that."

"Okay, well let's talk about some things. I can't help but wonder how it makes any sense that the man would go to a fund–raiser right after he dumps a body. And he dumped it where he works. Also, would you casually get into the same elevator you just threw a body onto? The Senator's behavior that night doesn't seem like a man who committed a brutal murder. Something just doesn't add up."

"I agree that not everything is tied up. But there is no other plausible scenario that I can see. He thought he dumped the body into the bottom of the elevator shaft. I think he was shocked when it came down into the other car. And remember he was going to be very late to that fundraiser, maybe to pad his alibi."

"According to the testimony, the Senator was in the library until eight forty–five, I know that's been disputed, but if it's true Joel could have been killed between eight fifteen and eight forty–five by someone else. You know a guy like the Senator has enemies and what better way to get rid of him than a trumped–up murder charge. Coming in through the maintenance entrance has never been ruled out." Eileen gets up and starts pacing. "The attorneys have glossed over one comment that I think is really important." She looks at Stephen's curious face. "The camera for that hallway strangely just happened to freeze on a still frame during that same time?"

Stephen is about to say something, but Eileen puts up her hand to silence him and continues, "I know that it has stuck before that week, but that also could have been pre– planned, staged or footage was erased. The camera would have covered the elevator bank. Anything is possible. We need to consider all possibilities, don't you think?"

"I do," he responds as he puts on his boxers and a shirt.

As they go over, piece by piece, the past weeks' testimony, Stephen wonders if perhaps she could be right. There are some holes in her theory, and you have to have quite an imagination to weave anything plausible, but it's worth considering.

14

In the morning in the deliberations' room, Stephen insists that they discuss how the Senator could have dumped the body. There were no drag marks in the hallway from the Senator's office to the elevator, so the Senator didn't drag the body to the elevator.

Ronald, Ted and Mike enact possible ways the Senator could have accomplished this. What emerges is a scenario where the Senator propped up the dying man with one arm over his shoulder and practically carried him to elevator. Joel had a slight built and weighed barely one hundred and sixty pounds, so a man the Senator's size, at least two hundred pounds, could easily have carried him in this manner.

"Okay." Stephen is convinced, then challenges, "Now open the elevator doors while the elevator is on a higher floor."

Ronald offers up, "Firefighters and repair men use an elevator key. The elevator repair guys were there that day and the janitor said they could've left tools. The whole thing wouldn't be a reach at all if two people did this. A guy the Senator's size could've done it alone, but it'd be trickier."

"Maybe he did have an accomplice," Laura chimes in. "Maybe he's the one with the partner. Maybe that's exactly the explanation we need to tie all this together."

"After they tossed the body, his partner could have gone down the stairs and either hid on another floor or left through the maintenance entrance when he saw an opportunity, before the body was found," Ted suggests.

Melita jumps in, "Either way, with or without a partner, it looks to me like the Senator is guilty. You don't just sneak into the guy's office, beat his worker to death, clean up and dump the body, without the Senator having a clue – no way."

"Yeah! I agree," Charlie chimes in. "No matter how you slice it, he's guilty somehow."

"Here's a fact," Marge blurts out, "that Senator has shifty eyes." Laura rolls her eyes. "You don't have to believe me, young lady, but it's true," Marge insists. Laura mumbles something under her breath and goes back to doodling.

"The body fell on the man. It's too big of a coincidence," Eileen says. "Nothing about his actions that night shows any indication that he could have been a person who did something like this."

Stephen has to admit that it's seeming less and less rational to think that one man accomplished this type of killing, then dressed for a fundraiser and the guy he killed fell on top of him. His instincts tell him the man is guilty, but he doesn't want Eileen to take the brunt of the argument alone. He decides it's worth exploring.

"People like that have an ability to cover up their emotions. They are harder than the rest of us," Joanna offers.

"What if someone else did kill him, like his jealous lover, and the Senator was set up?" Stephen offers.

"If it was a set–up, why would the killer try so hard to clean up the carpet?" Ronald argues.

"If it was that obvious, it wouldn't be a plausible set up," Stephen responds.

"We don't have anything to indicate any theory like that. No evidence for that kind of thinking. No evidence points to an outsider," Mike says calmly.

"That's right. They said the evidence in the way he was killed didn't indicate a pre–meditated act. Having someone sneak into the building and pull off a set up would definitely take planning," Joanna adds.

Ted injects, "But if the Senator killed him, he could've called someone to come help him clean up. And they could've used maintenance."

"It still could've been a setup because the killer could have deliberately staged events to look like a rage murder," Eileen immediately rebuts.

"You are just muddyin' the waters. What if this, what if that. You could do that with anything 'till the cows come home." Charlie scoots back in his chair and puts his feet on the table, shaking his head.

Laura increases her fidgeting, "I'm having trouble with wasting so much time. It all comes down to this. Is there any indication that it could've been anyone else?" She glares at Stephen. "Most of us here can rationally see that the answer is no. We know the kid was killed between eight and eight forty or so and no one else was on that floor then, except the Senator and that janitor, who arrived at later at eight forty–five. If there were another possibility, there would be some indicators. And even if someone did sneak in, the Senator was there."

"We have no way of knowing that," says Eileen.

"Look, I can see what you're trying to get at here. I was one of the undecideds. But what convinced me is that Scott, his roommate, said Joel was waiting to talk to the Senator. Whatever he wanted to talk about could be the reason the Senator killed him. Even if the sexual angle doesn't exist, we don't know what other possibilities could exist for that talk. Maybe something even more devastating and problematic for the Senator," Ted declares.

Although they haven't taken another vote, Stephen can tell that Eileen is the only holdout. He understands her desire not to want to make a mistake with a man's future. For her sake, he feels increasingly more interested in exploring this line of thought. "Right now, I think it's possible we have reasonable doubt," Stephen says.

"Only an idiot would go to not guilty from all this. Even tinkerbell finally voted guilty," Charlie says, referring to Ted, who winces in disgust and snaps back.

"I came to my vote despite the musings of the ignorant hick there." Ted gestures toward Charlie.

"Name calling is not productive Mr. Murphy," Mike tries.

"Too late," injects Laura.

"I'm just saying that I think we would all feel better in the long run if we thought through all the scenarios, so that when we submit our verdict we are as sure as we can be," Stephen persists.

"We're already there," Ronald responds.

"Well, I'm not," Stephen asserts.

"How long you want to…" Charlie does air quotes, "explore."

"Look, we can go through one by one only those things that lend themselves to some disagreement," Mike puts forth.

"As long as it takes," says Stephen, envisioning another night with Eileen.

Groans and sighs emanate around the room and Charlie offers his final sentiment for the day, "Aw shiiiiittt!"

15

Certain that Stephen will be home tonight, Janet shops for all the ingredients needed to prepare his favorite dinner, roasted chicken, mac and cheese and a tomato and onion salad. She plans to season the chicken with garlic and rosemary, drench it in butter, then turn it every fifteen minutes during roasting. She buys special salt rubbed bacon to add to the recipe. Stephen loves bacon. Dinner will take a couple of hours to make because of the homemade chocolate tart she's adding to the menu. The kids will go nuts. It's been strange for all of them without Stephen for this long.

Michelle offers to assist her when Janet arrives with the groceries.

"No thanks, mom. I really appreciate your help with the kids. Now you get a break, and you should stay for dinner," Janet talks as she empties the bags.

Michelle can see that her daughter wants her family to herself tonight, so she replies with "Oh no honey, I need to…" Janet's cell rings and Janet motions for her to hold on as she answers. It's Stephen, but from the hotel number.

"Hey there. Are you about to leave?"

"Unfortunately, we're still deliberating, so it's going to be another night. I can only talk for a minute; we have a break to make our calls and get back."

"Oh." Janet feels overwhelmingly deflated. She shouldn't have planned this dinner for tonight. It was silly of her to assume that Stephen would be home. Michelle sees the expression on her daughter's face and jumps in to help put away groceries. Janet moves to the window and completes the call. Agreeing on a verdict can take a long time. Even Terry told her that juries are a fickle and alien beast. And yet, something in addition to the long absence, something inexplicable, is making her anxious to see her husband again, and soon. This trial is testing her every nerve. Stephen's absence emphasizes all the ways she relies and counts on him. All the ways he is an inextricable, firmly woven thread in her life – their lives. Not only has his absence put more on her daily plate, it's also made her long for their connection. She misses the daily downloads of their workdays and the way they tag team dealing with the kids.

For the first time since she can remember, she's had a hard time sleeping. The lack of sleep adds to her anxiousness. With each passing day of his absence, her tension grows. Increasingly, she's spent more of each night on alert. Much like sleeping with one eye open. This past week has been especially difficult with all the dreams. She can't recall the specifics of those dreams, only the panic and morose feeling after waking up. A feeling that sticks to her like a hot mist and takes all day to shake, if she can shake it at all. She's been short and testy with the kids and Emily is being particularly difficult as a result. Stephen will be home soon, she tells herself. Then why does something still feel off.

Stephen hasn't been sounding like himself since last Saturday. This worries her, but she can't pinpoint why. This must be stressful for him too, after all, he's the one cooped up for weeks on end in that hideous hotel. That's probably all it is. Everywhere she turns, information on the Claxton trial comes at her. From the news. From people she knows. The kids. Even in the street. She can't wait for things to get back to normal.

Hopefully, tomorrow it will all be over. She goes back to the counter and puts the food away with violent fervor.

"Are you alright?" Michelle's voice comes through.

"Yeah mom. I'll make this dinner another day. He's still stuck."

"No decision yet?"

"No. But I still want you to go home. I'm sure you can use some time to yourself."

"Honey, I don't mind at..."

"Mom. Please. Just go."

Janet heads into the family room where Mark and Emily are doing their homework. "Looks like your dad has to stay another night."

"Great. Fantastic. He can just miss all my events." Emily seizes every opportunity to exercise her newfound teenage sarcasm.

"Aww, man!" Mark exclaims.

Michelle is on Janet's heels, "You two lay off your mom tonight. I'll see you tomorrow." She kisses her grandchildren, then says to Janet, "Take a bath tonight. Relax. It's almost over. He'll be here before you know it."

"I wanted to hear about all the gory stuff. John said there was a bloody body and everything," Mark says.

"It's not like dad got to see the body, stupid," Emily snaps.

"You don't know that."

Janet shakes her head, "Cool it. Don't call your brother stupid. I'm going to make dinner."

She returns to the kitchen and opens the refrigerator. She stands there staring into its contents hoping something will jump out and figure itself out for dinner.

16

The rest of the evening's deliberations fail to yield an agreement. As they go over the evidence and Stephen listens to the other jurors, he feels fairly certain that Eileen will not yield to the guilty vote and the others most definitely won't let the Senator off.

That night Eileen visits Stephen's room again. Stephen assures himself that this is and absolutely will be the last time. They fall into their lovemaking easily and this time slowly. They're developing a natural and dangerous rhythm that comes comfortably to both. They've been together only a few times and Stephen is amazed that their rapport feels as if they've known each other and have been together for years. The only time Eileen deflects his hands is when he tries to touch her hair. Probably smart not to look obviously rumpled if caught. But Eileen has become a master at eluding the guards and it never occurs to Stephen that they could get caught.

"I'm worried that I'm the only one creating a problem for everyone on this. I really appreciate that you tried to get the others to at least look at my point of view, but they're just upset now. I know that everyone wants me to just shut up and go along so we can all get out of here, but..."

"You can't vote guilty, can you?" Stephen asks.

Tears fill Eileen's eyes and this tears at his heart. He rubs her back. "I understand where you're coming from. It's okay. It's a man's future at stake and we all have to be sure. If you don't think you can get to 'sure' then you can't."

"I'm sorry. I don't know what else to do. I know everyone..."

"Look, I don't feel the same way, but if you have that much doubt then for you there's reasonable doubt. You're smart, Eileen, and there's a reason there is a twelve–person jury that all have to vote the same way. You make some great points."

"They all hate me and they're not going to stop badgering."

"No, they're not." Looking at her, Stephen realizes that this will be their last time together. He offers, "If it'll make you feel better, I don't think it's going to matter if it's one or two of us that hangs the jury. The result is the same and you won't have to be the only hated one."

Eileen's face lights up, "Are you saying..."

"Yeah. Why not? I'll vote with you."

Eileen jumps on Stephen and squeezes him so tightly he knows he just did the right thing. If they can't get any of the others to agree to reasonable doubt, it still won't make a difference in the outcome of the trial. The jury is hung, and the Senator will have to be tried again. But Stephen's actions will make a huge difference to this vulnerable woman with whom he feels a strange and binding connection.

"Thank you," she says.

Stephen rises from the bed and puts on some clothes. "Of course. No reason delaying the inevitable."

She dresses, then slowly opens the door and peeks out. She turns back to him and strokes his face. "Time capsule," she says as she looks back out the door. When it's clear, she gives Stephen one last kiss and slips out quickly and quietly. Stephen doesn't move, unsure of what to feel. A heaviness descends on him. A sense of loss? Or perhaps the weight of something having shifted within. Surely, he'll begin to feel like himself as soon as his life returns to normal. This feeling is the remains of the tail end of living in a time capsule. The past weeks have left him unmoored. He must start right now, tonight, to gather his wits and focus on his family and his future.

* * *

In the morning, tempers flare inside the jury room. Charlie stomps his fist on the table, "This is bullshit!" he declares. "There is nothin' in what you've said that makes me think that he might not be guilty. You're just chatterin' on about doubt here and doubt there, and what if this, then that, and what if that then this. Jesus! There can always be doubt, but it has to be *reasonable...*" as he draws out the word, a drop of spittle scoots out of the corner of his mouth, "...doubt and you are not being reasonable."

"Okay. I think we need to assess where we are right now and where we can possibly go," Mike announces and calls for another vote. The vote reveals only ten guilty votes. The outstanding two are Stephen and Eileen and they firmly declare their unified not guilty stance. Mike sits back and looks at the group. He turns to Stephen and Eileen and asks, "We've been over the evidence numerous times, is there anything that you're confused about that we can clear up so that you would vote with us?"

Stephen regards Mike. Ever the logical, calculating and practical engineer. He glances at Eileen and notices the slight shake of her head. Stephen answers, "Look Mike, I appreciate that you think we might be confused here. But I think it's quite the opposite. This isn't a slam dunk and I think you all know it. We may not have something else that's concrete to offer up that proves he's not guilty, but I can't send a man to prison for life if I think there's a chance he didn't do it."

"There will always be a chance that a person who's on trial didn't do it. But that's not how the law is set up. Einstein said, 'Whoever undertakes to set himself up as a judge of Truth and Knowledge is shipwrecked by the laughter of the gods.' I really hate to say it, and you know I do, but Charlie's right. I may have some doubt, but I don't think it's reasonable," Ted says, exasperated.

"That's right, young man. You've spun in the wrong direction," Marge says to Stephen. "That man has a dirty guilty secret in his eyes."

"What is it with you and the eyes?" Ronald mutters.

"You can roll your eyes all you want, young man, but mark my words, the truth is in the eyes every time – if you know how to look."

Eileen says calmly, "Nice quote, Ted, but I have another one for you, 'There's a world of difference between truth and facts. Facts can obscure the truth.'"

"Geez," Ronald mumbles under his breath. Several jurors sigh and shake their heads.

Everyone digs in their heels and Mike suggests that they report a deadlock. All agree. He notifies the guard.

The crowded courtroom bustles in anticipation of the verdict. George Claxton swallows hard and remains calm until the jurors are brought into the room. Claxton observes a trickle of sweat as it meanders down his back. He feels a dampness in his palms. After seating the jury, the judge enters, sits, reads the piece of paper handed her, then addresses the jury, "Has the jury tried every means possible to reach a verdict?"

This question causes a stir and Claxton feels his heart race. Mike stands and answers the judge, "We have, your honor."

"And is it as a result of your best efforts that you have been unable to reach a verdict?"

"It is."

Judge Cohen attempts to hide her disapproval and leans toward the jurors, "You all are aware that if you need additional information or additional time, it can be provided?"

"Yes, your honor."

"In your opinion, Mr. Foreman, is there anything further that can be done that might lead you to a unanimous verdict?"

Mike remains resolute and responds, "We have asked ourselves that question and unfortunately, no, your honor."

Murmurs run through the courtroom and all eyes are on the jury or the defense table. George feels an urge to smile but suppresses it. Instead, he stares hard at the jury in curiosity.

Judge Cohen shares a concerned look with the prosecution and announces, "The jury is officially deadlocked." Turning to the jury she adds, "Thank you for your service. You are dismissed."

Mann stands up and loudly asks, "I request the jury be polled, your honor."

The courtroom grows louder, nearing pandemonium, and judge Cohen bangs her gavel to restore order.

"Very well." She gestures to the jurors to sit back down. "Beginning with the back row and to your left, please stand and state your vote," she instructs.

Eileen turns pale and several of the others are also uncomfortable with this request. Marge begins the process with announcement of her guilty vote, then Charlie, then Ronald and so on until it's Stephen's turn. He glances at Eileen for courage, but her stare remains straight ahead. Stephen slowly stands and says, "Not guilty."

As soon as he says it, the reporters begin their frenzy of writing and texting furiously. He glances at Claxton, but the man remains impossible to read. After several more "guilty" announcements, Eileen stands and Stephen feels relief and camaraderie, then she says, "Guilty."

Stephen snaps his head in her direction. *What?* Did he not hear her? *She didn't just say that.* As the rest of the votes conclude, he is left as the sole standout. He whispers to Ted, next to him, "Did she say guilty?"

Ted shrugs and replies, "Probably scared. Doesn't want reporters on her ass. And since you were first, she didn't have to."

The room begins to spin. Stephen's head suddenly feels enormous, and he tries desperately to will Eileen into turning around, even slightly, to give him some acknowledgment of what just happened. Instead, Eileen's countenance remains stiff and aloof. *This can't be happening.* His face flushes and suddenly he becomes aware that all eyes are on him. He swallows hard and tells himself to breathe. He must breathe, stop fidgeting and calm down. This will all straighten itself out. *Just avoid reporters. Do not look at Mann. She probably panicked because of all the press and the pressure.* He can understand that and if she needs him to be the rock, then he can do that. Certain that Eileen will explain this to him in short order enables him to relax more.

"Ladies and gentlemen of the jury, you are excused. Thank you for your service." The judge dismisses the jury.

As soon as the judge vacates her seat, pandemonium breaks out. The next several minutes blur together in a kaleidoscope of color and motion. Stephen hears voices, the scraping of furniture, doors, yelling, yet no sound reverberates louder than that of his own breathing, his pounding heart, and the roar of agony in his mind. His main goal remains to get to Eileen, yet at every turn and opportunity, she eludes him. The guard ushers the jurors out through the jury room. Eileen is among the first in there. By the time Stephen arrives, she's already heading for the door to the hallway. He rushes toward her, the urgency in his voice unmistakable, "Eileen." She won't turn around, instead she grabs the door and opens it. He reaches for her arm, and she pulls away, refusing to even look at him. Eileen rushes out, vanishing down the hallway. Members of the press already circle their way. Shock and confusion set in. Mike says something about making sure everyone grabs their phones. Stephen gets his phone and runs out into the hallway looking to catch a glimpse of her.

He thinks he spots Eileen get into an elevator. When he tries to follow her, reporters trap him. He is the juror of interest. It's his picture, his interview and his statement that everyone wants. She doesn't even look back. Never once does she look at him. *How can that be?* Maybe she's trying to protect him and their affair. Maybe she's just simply too freaked out and embarrassed. Maybe... He invents a dozen scenarios, but none of them matter. As he makes his way out of the annex, he is hemmed in. The press hurls questions at him. They call upon him to answer for his position. Unwilling and unable to deal with the cameras and the reporters, Stephen steels himself and repeatedly says "No comment," as he pushes through. One reporter reflexively grabs for Stephen's arm and Stephen recoils with "Don't touch me!" With each step, his face grows more flush and his heart races faster. Trying to focus on the predicament at hand – getting to his car – he tries to remember where it's parked. Weeks have passed since he first parked it here. Does he have his keys, or did he leave them in his hotel room? Reaching in his pants pocket he feels the familiar jingle. *Okay, just keep walking.*

17

After the verdict, or lack thereof, George Claxton mulls over the jury. The architect. And only the architect. *That's a surprise, and yet perhaps not. How did this marvelous turn of events come to pass?* He's curious, but he doesn't want to waste too much time surmising. He doesn't have to. A more preferred scenario, besides a not guilty verdict, would've been a few more holdouts on the guilty vote. But he's free for now and the likelihood of going through this again is slim. It's costly and people have no patience for repeats. He knows the prosecution threw everything they had at him on this one and they have nothing more to throw.

Regardless of the outcome, the trial cost him. George wonders if there's a way to come back from this black mark of suspicion. In time such things are possible. Look at the historic tally: Ronald Reagan and how he shook off the taint of Iran–Contra; the Downing Street Memo was buried, and the public looked the other way; the sex scandals of Kennedy, Clinton, and dozens more were ultimately pushed aside in favor of other attributes. He chose this road of public scrutiny. With it comes a range of jealousy, of obstacles and obstructionists. He knew this going in. He'd prepared well for it. Well, for most of it. Admittedly, there are some things, and a certain breed of person, he hadn't anticipated over the years. People who made certain claims to get him on their side, then put him in precarious positions when those claims turned out to be quite different than originally presented. He dealt with it in the only way he could in order to keep his position. Now he has to deal with the fallout of this travesty.

Alton moves him away from the table and toward the bench. He advises Claxton to keep calm and quiet when they leave the courthouse. Alton wants to handle the press. A recent poll uncovered that a slim majority suspect the Senator to be guilty of something and are just waiting for a reason to sling more mud his way.

Alton is a lawyer, and the game of politics is a different beast from lawyering. Handling the press is familiar territory for George. Perhaps now the Senator needs to begin reconnecting with his constituents and show his faith in this great nation.

As Claxton and his attorney exit the courthouse, the press swarm around them like vultures to a slaughter. Questions come at George from all directions:

"Senator, how do you feel about coming so close to being sentenced to prison?"; "Senator! Will you be officially resigning?"; "Are you surprised by the outcome?"

Alton leads the way with his "No comment" mantra. Only one time does he stop and say, "Senator Claxton is an innocent man, and we are grateful that our system of justice still works."

Without warning, Claxton stops and takes one of the microphones. Alton, displeased, braces himself.

"I love this great nation," Claxton begins. "And I have and have always had faith in our system of justice. Today is no different. The system works. I am an innocent man and I recognize that not all people can see that, but it takes only one person to further the cause of justice and for that I am grateful. I will continue to serve my country in any way that I can. I will not simply walk away from all that I believe in. I will still do everything I can to continue to make ours the greatest country on earth. Thank you." He starts walking again.

"Do you believe you were set up?" asks a young reporter.

Alton intercedes, "This is still an ongoing case, so please no more questions. Thank you."

Claxton and Alton make their way to the waiting black town car and speed away.

"I wish you wouldn't do that George," Alton admonishes.

Claxton replies, "It was necessary. I know the game and I'm not about to say anything to weaken my position." He pulls off his jacket. "The question is, now what? What's next?" he asks his attorney.

"We'll meet with the prosecution in a few days and see where they are in pursuing a new trial. You need to stick around your home for the next couple of weeks until we can get a read on things."

"I intend to resume a normal life. You're saying I should do it slowly, discreetly."

"Exactly. Look George, while it's true the public has a short memory, you need to stay out of their sight for a while. We dodged a bullet in there."

George wonders when he'll be able to see Sofia again. She can come to him. To his brownstone. Perhaps in a couple of days.

18

After he grabs his bags from his hotel room, Stephen check's Eileen's room but it appears that she's already gone. He waits in the hotel lobby on the chance of spotting her. The front desk won't give him any information. He manages to dodge the few reporters who have found the hotel and gets in his car and heads for home. Stephen tries to shake the sinking feeling in the pit of his stomach as the dread continues to grow. Both Terry and Janet keep calling his cell. He can't talk to them. Not yet. What the hell is he supposed to say? *Yeah, so it was all me. No problem and I'm proud of it. Damn it!* He texts Janet that he's on his way home, but that's the most he can bring himself to do. He needs time to think. To sort out what's happened from what everyone surely assumes has happened. He's not the one who thought there was enough reasonable doubt, but now he's taking the sole blame for the deadlock. All he wanted to do was help. The other jurors know it wasn't just him, but that doesn't really matter, and they don't care. Either way it's a done deal. A new trial may happen, or the state will have to drop it. Maybe he should have voted guilty regardless of the fact that it wouldn't have changed the outcome. It would have changed it for him. Then she would have had to tell the truth. Stephen tries to understand how she could just leave him like that. Did she think she was doing him a favor because of their affair? Maybe in a way that makes some sense. Maybe in her own strange way she's merely trying to protect him. There might be something to that. Then why does he feel so disturbed?

Traffic continues to engulf him, and he feels grateful for the extended solitude.

How will he explain this to Janet? To Terry? Looking at the time, he should be home in less than an hour. He can tell Janet the truth about there being some reasonable doubt even if it was Eileen's reasonable doubt and not his. Janet will support him in his stance. He tries to convince himself that he doesn't need to say anything else. His decision stemmed from the fact that he knew there was a question of reasonable doubt somewhere. The fact that that doubt resided with another juror is irrelevant. It existed and that's all that matters, he tells himself. Whatever happened or didn't happen with Eileen no longer matters. Those events remain in the vault of the time capsule and have no bearing on his real life. Eileen made some valid points and the more he thinks about it, the more plausible the Senator's innocence seems. Maybe he was right in voting not guilty regardless of Eileen. The possibility of the Senator's innocence calms him. Thinking that perhaps he just saved the direction of a man's life acts as a salve on his frayed nerves. That's nothing to be ashamed of. Stephen's breathing begins to relax as he focuses on the positive in all this. He refuses to see himself as a cliche. The middle–aged married man who strays because he's un–evolved. So, he's had a blip in his life and instead of working through it, he did what every other self–pitying bastard does – had an affair. It's over. It'll never happen again.

Pulling onto his street, he notices a news van parked near his house. He has to make it into the garage fast. As he pushes the remote button for the garage door and it begins its ascent, a woman jumps out of the van. Stephen makes a quick turn into his driveway before she reaches him. He's in the garage and quickly closes the door as the reporter calls to him.

"Dad!" Mark exclaims and runs toward Stephen as he walks into the house.

Stephen picks up his son and squeezes him tightly. "Hey. I missed you, big guy."

Mark squirms out of his grasp and excitedly says, "Some reporters called here looking for you! Is it true that you're famous now?" as Janet and Emily come running to join in the greeting.

"What?" He can't believe they found him so quickly. He can't allow this to invade his family. Not anything that happened during that trial, not the reporters. None of it. "No one talks to any reporters," he commands.

After the initial enthusiasm of seeing each other, Stephen searches Janet's face for a sign that everything will be all right.

"We did get some calls, but I told them that if you wanted to talk to them, you would contact them. Is that okay?" Janet says.

"Yes. Thank you." Stephen sighs in relief, "I could use a drink."

"From what we saw on the news, I'm sure you can."

Stephen's eyes plead for a respite from the trial, and he says to the kids, "First things first. I want to talk to you guys about you and everything I missed. Okay? We can talk about the other stuff later. Your dad needs a break from all that right now. And, no, I'm not famous."

While Mark and Emily both fill their father in on the latest events in their lives, Janet pours herself and Stephen each a glass of wine. The family convenes in the kitchen and Janet happily completes preparation of her husband's welcome dinner. Mark returns to the topic of the trial, "Dad, Bobby says you let a killer go free. That's not true, right? Bobby never knows what he's talking about."

"The man on trial, a Senator, isn't a killer unless he's found guilty, and Bobby doesn't know the facts. That's what a jury is for and every person on the jury has to vote the way they think is right. That's why a person is innocent until proven guilty. And all the people on the jury have to agree. If they don't, then there is not enough proof to find him guilty." He looks at Janet for a sign of approval.

She smiles at him. "Your dad is not someone who would make a decision like this lightly. He's the most honest and responsible person I know and if he isn't sure that the Senator is guilty then there's a really good reason for it."

Stephen swallows hard at Janet's words. "Why I did what I did, I can't explain to you right now. I thought I was doing the right thing. And sometimes all we can do is our best."

Mark accepts that answer and Stephen manages to avoid discussing any more of the trial by promising Mark they can talk about some of the gory stuff another time. As the wine courses through his veins, Stephen reminds himself that it's done. Over. He relaxes and feels more normal than he has since before the summons. *This will all blow over.*

He takes a shower and changes his clothes, deftly avoiding intimacy with Janet, saying, "I need some time to decompress. You understand." He's never been this manipulative in his life, but he assures himself that it's for her sake.

Janet completes her intended meal and announces dinner. As Stephen happily devours his food, he looks at the loving faces of his family. An overwhelming sense of gratitude engulfs him, then for a split second his mind wanders back to his hotel room and a gold charm bracelet, and a flash of darkness crosses over his features along with a slight welling of tears.

Janet notices Stephen's shift. "Are you alright?" she asks.

He stares at his wife and shakes it off, "Yeah. Just so glad to be home. This dinner is great, honey. Thank you."

"I helped," Mark chimes in.

"You did not," Emily snorts.

"Did too." And so, they go on and Stephen smiles at his kids.

After the kids are in bed, Janet sees Stephen staring out the family room window into the darkness. He looks great. She can tell he's been working out. She comes up and hugs him from behind, running her hands around his middle and his pecs. "You really have been working out."

Stephen stiffens, "Not much else to do after sitting in a chair all day."

"You want to talk about it now?"

How can he tell her that he never wants to talk about it? Ever. That he wishes that the entire thing would vanish from their life. That none of the ordeal, not the trial, the other jurors, the result, his absence, none of it belongs anywhere near them, even in conversation. Instead, he shrugs and says, "Not much to say. It's really what I said to the kids. Honestly, I want to get some distance from it right now. Do you mind?"

She turns him to face her and looks in his eyes. He doesn't hold her gaze. He seems distant. "I understand. You do seem exhausted. Besides, it's late. Why don't we get some sleep and maybe we can talk tomorrow, catch up on us."

"Okay. I guess I am pretty tired."

Once in the bedroom, a restlessness returns to Stephen. He notices Janet watching him, but he can't think about that now. He turns on the television to anything but current events hoping it will help his mind relax. Animal shows always seem like a safe bet.

Janet comes in from the bathroom wearing a tight camisole. He hasn't seen that one in a while. Stephen wonders if she expects him to want to make love tonight. That would be the normal thing to do. But the last thing he feels right now is normal. She did point out that he needs rest, and he intends to cling to that. As she approaches, his anxiousness increases.

"Stephen, are you sure you don't want to talk about it at all? I'm sure it's stressful. It might help. They were talking about you all over the news today and you don't seem like yourself."

"What do you mean?" His defenses kick in. "Myself, like a normal guy with a normal life? Or myself, like a guy who's been cooped up for weeks in a dump, listening to hours and hours of 'he said, she said', and a shit ton of detailed evidence, eating crappy food? I don't think it's unreasonable to think that guy number two can't just jump in like nothing happened."

"Wow. Feel better now that you got that out?" Janet sits on the bed. "Look, I'm sure this got to you. How could it not? But you're home now, we've missed you and it's over. You've been distracted and jumpy every time we talked on the phone these past couple of weeks. I'm worried about you and what went on over there."

"Nothing went on," Stephen bristles. "It was a murder trial. A big one and people got tired, and everyone just wanted to go home." He sits up, then slides off the bed and begins pacing.

"Are you saying that that's why they voted guilty, because they wanted to go home, and you didn't?" Janet watches him carefully.

"That's not what I said. It's just too hard to explain and it's not even worth talking about. It's over and I just need it to be over." His heart starts racing. The room suddenly feels warm. Very warm. And stifling. "I'm going to get a glass of water. You need anything?" he asks.

"No. I'm fine," Janet says deflated. She thinks about how not fine her husband seems.

In the kitchen Stephen pours himself a glass of water and chugs it. His mouth is parched. Whatever normalcy he felt earlier has vanished. Something feels wrong. Very wrong. But there's no one he can tell. Maybe Terry. Terry left several messages. He'll call him tomorrow. Terry will chalk it up to the weirdness of people on juries and especially under a sequester where quirks run amuck. He can't reveal the truth about Eileen and him. That never happened. Not in this life of his. No way and not a soul can ever know. He too will have to find a way to forget it. Cancel it from his mind. But he can't forget being publicly betrayed like that. Not that the public has any clue that he was betrayed. But they think they know that he is the only one that hung that jury. Everyone at the office surely knows – his clients, people at the kids' school, their friends. He must find a way to get comfortable with this or else it can cause problems. Unfortunately, at this time there's only one person who can give him the answers and assurance he needs so he can return to some sense of order.

Stephen routinely charges his cell phone in the outlet near the small desk in the kitchen. With the push of a button, it powers on and stares back at him. Now what? He doesn't have her number. Luckily, the Internet offers a wealth of resources and search options. Stephen pours through the Eileen Harrises in several databases, then remembers the area where she lives. She mentioned a lake near her house a couple of times in the jury room. After several minutes that feel like hours of searching, Stephen finds her number. He knows she's single, but does she live with anyone? No matter, this is more important, he tells himself. Grabbing a sweatshirt off a chair, he slips out of the kitchen into the backyard and dials.

Voicemail answers. Stephen speaks softly, yet his upset comes through, "It's me. Look, I don't know what the hell happened in there today, but we need to talk. Call me at the office tomorrow." He leaves her a number and mumbles something about how this is the last thing he would have expected from her and hangs up.

From the kitchen window, Janet stares out into the darkness at her husband.

Nearly midnight. Who can he possibly be calling at this hour? She takes a deep breath and decides not to let him see her here. He's clearly upset. Surely, he'll come around and talk to her about what's bothering him. Tomorrow he will allay the suspicions surfacing in the back of her mind. Until then, she will give him some space.

Unable to sleep at all during the night, Stephen slides out of bed at four a.m. He scrambles up some breakfast and writes Janet a note telling her that he can't sleep and wants to get a jump on all the work he's missed. She'll understand. She has to. He just needs some time to settle back into his life. To get into a rhythm with work and his schedule before he can get back to normal with her. He puts the note on the kitchen counter and makes it out the door while the rest of the household still slumbers.

The offices of Graeber, Fike and Simms are modern and highly polished.

Stephen has one of the large offices with a view and floor–to–ceiling glass on two sides. Not a partner's office, but close. He's their top designer. Stephen busies himself going through stacks of memos and drawings left for him on his desk. It looks like his big deal with K Tower may happen after all. The meeting is scheduled for this afternoon, they pushed it a week for him, hoping he'd be back.

Stephen spends a few hours catching up before the rest of the firm funnels in.

Some of his colleagues politely pretend that he isn't the guy who hung the jury. Others look at him with clear disappointment. Only a few dare inquire:

"So, what aren't they saying on the news, Reeves? Was some of the evidence suspicious?"; "I'm sure there's a lot none of us know, so don't worry about it."; "Wow, I'm sure this is weird for you. To be the guy who didn't convict. I'm sure you had a good reason though."

Stephen drinks copious amounts of coffee throughout the morning to keep up the stamina to deal with people. He fields a few calls from clients, but his disappointment multiplies every time Eileen isn't the one on the other end of the line. Terry calls him again, fortunately on his cell, so he can easily ignore him. But Terry's messages become increasingly more difficult to brush off, the latest being "Hey, what the hell is going on with you? You need to call me. Now!" Instead, Stephen texts him that he'll call after work.

By noon, every time his desk phone rings, and Eileen isn't on the other end, his anxiety builds. He knows that if he could just talk to her and understand what happened, he can put it in a place in his head that makes some sense and be able to let it go and move on with his life. Last night, the contact information on Eileen included her address. Maybe if he sees where she lives and runs into her, maybe he can resolve this and finally get some peace. A part of him considers this as being a very rational idea. The other part of him, screaming silently though a recessed portal from the back of his consciousness, suspects something closer to stupidity or sticking your hand into the face of a sleeping lion. A growing impatience takes over and Stephen tells his assistant that he needs to leave to go look at a building.

"The Tower meeting is at 3:30," she reminds him.

"Don't worry. I'll be back in time."

Eileen's neighborhood, lined with modest middle–class homes, takes only forty minutes by car from Stephen's office. Stephen's mind remains focused. The second a thought about anything other than clearing this with Eileen enters his mind, he brushes it off. Talking to her will clear up everything. He slows the car as he nears the correct address. There. The house on the right. It has a closed white garage door and no car in the driveway or out front. She's probably at work. He should've thought of that. He doesn't know which firm she works for, or he could go there. Maybe he should leave her a note. The peeling paint strikes Stephen as incongruous with Eileen's personality and demeanor. She's so elegant. Maybe you really can't know a person in such a short time. Some of her traits that he's come to know aren't common to any scientist types he knew. He doesn't personally know any physicists at all. But he'd met a few other kinds of scientists and they were socially awkward by comparison. She wasn't, except maybe a little bit in the larger group, but only because she was reserved until the end. He pulls into the driveway and walks up to the front door. The railings are frail and in disrepair and the frames around the windows seem loose. Maybe she's having some financial trouble. Stephen rings the doorbell. No answer. He knocks. Nothing. *Yeah, probably at work. What was I thinking coming out here now? Does she really live like this?*

Curiosity prevails and he tries to look in the front window, but the drapes are too concealing. Then he hears a tea kettle whistling inside the house. Could she be home and deliberately not wanting to see him? Her car must be in the garage. He pounds on the door. "Eileen?!" The kettle stops whistling. Stephen tries opening the door, but it's locked. He can't believe this. He looks across the street and sees a guy, walking his dog, looking at him. He takes a breath. If she doesn't want to see him, so be it. He's a grown man. He's just going to have to deal with it. He did what he thought was right and a Senator is not in jail. Maybe he is innocent. There's nothing wrong with that. It's not like he sentenced an innocent man and ruined a life.

Stephen gets back into his car and drives away. He uses the drive back to the office to call Terry. Stephen dials and Terry answers right away, "Finally!" he exclaims.

"Hey, I'm sorry. It's been a shit storm."

"I can imagine, but I expected an update. The prosecution is a mess over this thing and seeing your mug on TV freaked me out. I confess, I was worried about you."

"Certainly not what I had in mind."

"What happened in there?"

"We can talk about it later. I've got the Tower guys coming in this afternoon. It looks like they may be going with us."

"That's huge. Your first big skyscraper, guy. You must be excited."

"It's not official yet, so we'll see today. Hey, you around this afternoon?"

"I have a pile of paperwork, so probably be here until six."

"I'll stop by after the meeting. Is that okay?"

Terry's surprised by this, "Oh, okay. Yeah, man. Great."

"See you then." Stephen feels both relief and concern that instead of going home early, he's going to see Terry.

19

Terry sits comfortably behind his cluttered desk. He's on the phone with feet up and motions Stephen into his office. Stephen plunks down in the dilapidated chair in front of Terry's old desk and begins to crack his knuckles. Stephen observes his friend. Terry's life is so uncomplicated. He has only himself to worry about. And his work. In his personal life, he can do whatever he wants when he wants without panicking that his life will blow up. He doesn't have major obligations like kids, a wife or even a steady relationship. He can work late or not. He can eat whatever he wants, when he wants.

Stephen's leg begins a nervous twitch. Terry's life is clean and transparent. Relationships are messy. Families, social agendas, politics, love–all messy. Terry finishes his conversation, hangs up and turns to his friend, "You look like shit."

"Thanks. Good to see you too."

"So? K Tower?"

"Yeah. We got it." Stephen attempts to muster some enthusiasm.

"Congratulations! We should celebrate."

"They popped open some champagne at the office already. Everyone's cutting out early."

Terry observes Stephen's twitching.

"What?" Stephen asks defensively.

Terry stands and closes the door. "For a man who just landed the biggest account of his career, you sure aren't acting like it. Something's up with you. I can smell it? What gives?" he asks.

"Well, aside from a minor detail that I look like the guy who let a killer go free, I couldn't be better."

Terry stares at Stephen, concerned, "You think you made the wrong call?"

"No. It's just that" Stephen stands and begins pacing. "Well, it freaked me out when it looked like it was all on me."

Terry studies Stephen carefully. "It wasn't?"

"No. This other woman also voted not guilty but said guilty in the polling. What am I supposed to do about that?"

"Ah, the old *volte face* in the heat of public pressure. It happens. Either they panic or if they were on the fence then something triggers them to switch. I told you juries get crazy. People are strange, man."

Terry knows Stephen better than to believe that he would be this insecure about a vote that he took ample time to arrive at just because someone else changed their mind. He presses, "Why does it matter?"

Stephen sighs and leans against the desk for a moment. "I guess it doesn't." Then his chest begins increasingly constricting and he resumes his pacing, while taking deep breaths. Why can't he let it go? Juries *are* crazy. And he is one of them – the crazy ones. Something he couldn't have imagined.

"Crazy is right," he adds. But then so is Eileen. Maybe that's really all there is to it – the jury crazies.

Terry studies his friend, noticing something dark, heavy and unsettled about his countenance. "How crazy are we talking?" he asks.

Stephen stands still and stares at the floor, a growing hysteria begins to show.

Terry takes the cue, "Come on. Let's go. I'm buying you a drink. Or four."

The two settle at a corner table at the sparsely populated Lawfully Unwetted Bar. Still too early for its regulars. Neither man spoke a word on the way here. Consumed by a cacophony of thoughts, Stephen requires all his energy just to remain upright and to go through all the motions. What's he going to tell Terry? Can he tell him what he's done?

He isn't cut out for keeping secrets like this. He has to find a way to get back to his life with Janet without blowing it up first. Terry sits patiently, staring at Stephen.

"I slept with her," Stephen blurts, never much good under guilt–gnawing pressure.

Terry's eyes go wide, and a flicker of shock runs across his face. Before responding, he presses his lips together and inhales, then slowly nods, wondering who 'her' is.

Stephen looks at him and says, "Well, aren't you going to say anything?"

"Who is she?"

"The woman who originally voted not guilty."

"Ah." A barrage of scenarios crowd through Terry's mind, but he still refuses to speak. Processing.

"What do you mean, 'ah'?"

"This isn't exactly what I expected, so give me a minute. I'll go get our drinks."

Terry stands up and goes to the bar for their drinks. Stephen watches him, filled with angst. Maybe he shouldn't have told him. Maybe he should've made something else up. The problem is that Terry can always tell when he's lying.

Returning with a pitcher of beer, Terry pours glasses for each of them and then asks, "How the hell did this happen?"

"I don't know. I've been wracking my brain for a smart answer to that one. It just seemed...I don't know. We were cooped up. It was…as if my real life wasn't a part of it."

Terry stares at Stephen, unconvinced.

Stephen snaps back, "And who are you to pass judgment on me anyway? You can't sustain a relationship for more than two months."

Despite Terry's status as a player and his philandering ways, honesty is the one thing he doesn't compromise. Not one of his women are misled into believing he is faithful to them, and he lets them know up front that he is not interested in a long–term relationship.

"Hey, this isn't about me. And you don't have to get ugly. What you did is...well, you cheated on Janet. Just tell me what happened."

'Cheated on Janet,' the words ring in his ears. He is not that person. And yet...he is. "It was like I was living a different life there. Like it wasn't even me. I know that must sound insane. Maybe it is a little insane. I don't know."

Stephen finishes one glass of beer quickly, then pours another. He explains to Terry how after a few weeks of being cooped up, away from everyone and everything, he and Eileen developed a natural rapport, an ease and a heat he hasn't felt in a long time.

And that's true. She isn't pretentious, or insecure. She's a lot like Janet. He sees Terry's disapproval when he talks about the sex, but his disapproval is no worse than his own. Terry cares for Janet and Stephen doesn't expect any approval here. What he needs is to find a way to move beyond this.

"Did she instigate this?" Terry asks.

"No. It just happened. Almost by accident."

"Yeah. I'm familiar with those kinds of accidents," Terry states and notices Stephen's angry glare. "Sorry. Alright, was this event love–making, screwing or just taking the pigskin bus to tuna–town one time?"

"I don't know."

"Oh boy. So, it was more than once and…" Terry stops, recognizing that Stephen isn't really capable of a one night bang–da–bang and that's why he's still torn in some way.

"We both agreed that it was a time capsule thing. That it was just in the moment – there – in that time. She knows I'm happily married."

"Look, I'm not judging you. Maybe fifteen years ago I would have, but now that I've got a little life on me, I see that events are gray. Life is gray. And people are gray. Everyone can go to an edge, maybe even one they didn't know they were capable of. Shit happens."

Stephen finds Terry's words soothing. He opens up and talks about how smart and secure Eileen seemed and that's why changing her vote during the poll is so upsetting.

"Did she think the guy was innocent from the get–go?"

"Not innocent per se, just not guilty."

"So, she didn't coerce you in any way?"

"Holy shit! I can't believe you'd think that!" The raw nerve of truth hits hard. Stephen is aghast that a guy who's known him nearly all his adult life would actually think that he could be influenced like that. The reality that that is what happened lives in an alien vortex. He could never even have believed it about himself, but to think Terry can believe it.

"Hey, I'm just saying that in the heat of passion, a lot can happen."

"Well, Mr. Attorney, it didn't happen in the heat of passion. Yes, we discussed it, but rationally and we raised all sorts of questions with each other and in deliberations. So, that's not what happened."

"Okay. It'salways good to be sure."

"Why would it matter anyway?"

"I don't know. Probably wouldn't."

Stephen drains another glass of beer. Terry watches him, knowing that the guilt must be choking him. He knows something like this is an enormous departure from Stephen's code of conduct and how he sees himself. "Hey. I know how much you love Janet and that this can't be easy to handle. Being sequestered and the jury crazies, well now it's over and you'll find a way to forget it." He leans in toward Stephen. "You have to."

"I do. I do love Janet. More than anything and I can't even believe this happened." Stephen's distraught face borders on frenzy. "I will find a way to make it up to her, I swear. I just need to find out why Eileen switched her vote. Get some closure."

Terry stiffens. "Whoa! You aren't even thinking about seeing this woman again, are you? You can't possibly be thinking that."

"I just want to talk to her and find out why she lied about her vote. She won't take or return my calls and it's eating at me."

Terry shakes his head, amazed that Stephen of all people can be suggesting this. "Not a good idea on any level. Trust me on this one. There is nothing to be gained from ever again going near that well, my friend. I understand that when you were away from civilization you could get away with it, but Janet is in your world. The world you are in now. And I'm telling you, don't take any chances. I know of what I speak."

"I'm not going to sleep with her again," Stephen insists. "I just need to know."

"Why can't you just let it go? The trial's over. It's done."

"I know that seems like the rational thing..."

"Because it is. It's the sane thing. It's the only thing."

"...but there's something wrong about what she did. I can't explain it. I need to feel some peace so I can go back to my life and feel normal." Stephen looks at Terry and can tell that Terry doesn't believe him. "I have no intention of sleeping with her," he says emphatically. "I really just want to know."

Terry takes a big swig of his beer. "I believe that you think that's the problem here. What you don't want to admit is that no matter what she tells you you won't feel normal. The real problem is that you can't be normal around Janet, because you're no longer the same guy you were before Ms. Sexpot. Take some advice, cheap though it may be – talk to Janet."

Stephen's face registers genuine panic and he leans away from the table.

"I'm not saying you should tell her you slept with this babe." Terry quickly adds, "Hell no. No way. Definitely not that. But you've got to say something. You've got to tell her what happened with the verdict and why you're bugged. She's got to know something's going on. Women always know when something's up."

"Yeah. You're probably right. She definitely thinks something's wrong. I stink at faking it."

"I know. And from now on, don't do anything that stupid."

"Thanks a lot."

"Anytime."

Stephen knows that Terry is right and yet full acceptance of that fact eludes him.

The right, sane, and logical thing to do takes a back seat to the absurd impulse. The office is on his way home, and he should probably stop in and see if he needs to take anything home with him. He knows full well that he rarely takes work home and the last thing he's going to be doing now, especially after the Tower news, is working at home tonight, but he makes his way into his office anyway. A few stray cups and a champagne bottle are strewn about from the earlier celebration. Seemingly harmless lies, even, and perhaps especially those to himself, seem to be proliferating. He knows he shouldn't call Eileen from his cell phone. Janet isn't the type to ever snoop through his things and their relationship certainly never gave her cause for such action, but he wants to make sure that he keeps things as clean and unencumbered as possible. If that too were true, he wouldn't be calling Eileen at all. But he calls from the office line. Again, no answer. *Why won't she take his calls?*! A rational person might think that maybe she isn't home. But he knows that's not the case. He can feel it in his gut. He knows she's deliberately avoiding him and it's making him angry. He gets her voice mail. After the beep, Stephen says, "Eileen, I have to put this thing to rest. You can't do this to me. I need some answers. Leave a message on my office line. I'll keep checking my voice mail. If I don't hear from you by ten tonight, I'm coming over. And I'm not going away until we talk." He hangs up the phone in frustration.

He'll talk to Janet. He will. Stephen tells himself. Tonight, after dinner and once the kids are in bed, he will reconnect with the woman he's built a wonderful life with.

He'll tell her how he felt publicly vulnerable because this woman changed her vote during the poll and he was left holding the bag. He'll mention his frustration in trying to do the right thing, but then wondering if he missed something crucial. Something a man with his wits about him shouldn't have missed. No. No reason to think he didn't have his wits about him. Janet would point out that he is known for having his wits about him. That he graduated top of his class and never drops the ball when people are counting on him. Until now. He dropped the ball – big time. But he has to pick it up again and make sure no one gets hurt, so he'll find a way to talk to Janet that will bring them back to a normal communication pattern. Back to where they were before this mess began.

At home, Stephen falls into the routine of the family dinner and the evening progresses without incident. After the kids are in bed, Stephen pours himself a bourbon and checks his watch. After nine he calls his office voice mail. Nothing. Janet enters the family room, "Well, now we can finally have some time to ourselves." She sits on the couch and pats the spot next to her, "Come here and let's relax. I'm so proud of you landing that deal. I should know about the Winstons next week. Wouldn't it be amazing if we both got the big accounts right now?"

"Yes. Absolutely it would."

"Stephen, aren't you happy about all this? Is there something that happened at the trial? What's going on with you?"

"Of course, I'm happy." Stephen moves toward her and sits, "I know, I'm not being overly enthusiastic. It's just that I'm still reeling from that trial, and it seems like reporters keep cropping up everywhere. They're still outside our house. I can't stand that."

"I know. Just the one is left. It's a pain for all of us, but we've got a system now and I'm sure they'll give up soon. I think we should talk about what happened during the trial."

Stephen gulps his drink. "I want to talk to you, Janet. I need to talk to you, and I will. But..." He notices Janet's face shift and her body stiffen. All he needs is a little more time, then he'll be fine. The last thing he needs is for Janet to sense this craziness inside of him and she will. She knows him. She really knows him, and he can't take that chance. "I need you to bear with me just a little longer," he says.

"What does that mean? I'm worried about you."

"Everything's fine. I'm just sorting some things out in my head. You go upstairs. I've got to go run an errand, but when I come back, I'll explain everything. It has to do with the trial, and I need to check on one thing, then I can make sense of it and lay it out for you. I promise, okay? We'll talk it all out."

Stephen sets his drink down and stands.

Janet looks up at her husband and a slow panic starts to build. "No, it's not okay."

Stephen grabs his keys and heads for the garage.

"Stephen?" Janet grabs him, "Where are you going?"

He shrugs her off. "Don't worry. Please. I just need to do this one thing. Just trust me on this, okay? I will explain everything as soon as I get back," Stephen pleads.

"Something's not right here. I'm your wife and I have a right to know what's going on with you. What are you doing?"

Stephen sees Janet's confused and stricken face, yet he knows he'll be back to fix it. She just needs to be patient with him. Just a little longer. "You have every right. You are absolutely right. And I will explain. I'm sorry I can't do that right now, but I just need one last piece, then I can. I won't be long, and I'll explain everything when I get back. Love you. Always have." Stephen practically flies into the garage and into his car.

"Always will," she responds, unconsciously but weakly, to the empty space in front of her. Janet's first impulse is to follow him, but she can't leave the kids alone. Her instincts are on fire with warning sirens. Unfortunately, she can't imagine what can be going on with Stephen. Did he have an affair? Can a man having an affair be so blatantly obvious about it? Sadly, this is Stephen, not just some man and that is not something she thinks he is capable of. He looks so good since coming home. The working out while on the jury. But his weirdness on the phone, he was so distant last night, so not normal... As inconceivable as it seems, the answer might be yes, he might actually be seeing someone else. A deep sorrow sweeps through her as a piece of her heart cracks from the mere thought of the love of her life even thinking of finding someone else.

20

Driving down the street, he wonders if he's officially lost his mind. That the insanity is permanent. *What the hell is wrong with me?* He feels like a man possessed – his body and actions being controlled by someone or something else. A someone or something he can't seem to stop, no matter his mind's otherwise rational directive. This compulsion is maddening. Why can't he get her out of his head? He received a couple of calls from reporters at the office and it's been easy enough to let them know, in no uncertain terms, that he would not now or ever comment on the trial or his verdict. His assistant, Susan, has fielded the rest of the calls with those same instructions. Privacy is his right and asserting it with conviction seems to ward them off. And Janet's right, they will soon get tired of it and move on. So what's his problem? He feels like a fool, that's what. He doesn't want to think it even remotely possible that he has somehow been manipulated by Eileen to do what he did. Surely the circumstances of their coming together and deciding to vote for acquittal have no bearing on their personal attraction for each other. Eileen determined to not let a man go to prison because she had doubt. Lots of it. He helped ease her difficulty with that decision and that is all. He has to believe that. But if he really believed it, would he be leaving his wife in a state of anger and driving to Eileen's house tonight? Stephen can't find even the slightest clarity in the jumble of thoughts attacking his brain from all sides. It's as if he's been bitten by a disease–ridden mosquito and the symptoms are taking hold. Driven to keep going, he hears Terry's words in his head "Don't do anything else that stupid." Well, he has no intention of sleeping with her ever again. That is certain. Maybe going to see her doesn't qualify as the epitome of intelligent behavior, but he needs peace of mind. Surely that's worth something.

The streets appear peculiarly quiet, and colors have faded to shades of grey. The stirrings of life in the darkness move to a different rhythm. Stephen turns on the radio, but the sound, any sound or song, bothers him, so he turns it off. He prefers the silence. He remains focused on getting an answer to the gnawing questions in his head. Staring at the lights in the houses and watching cars pass by going the other way give Stephen a sense of calm. As if he's moving through the world cocooned in his own bubble. An observer of humanity, rather than a participant. The roads become narrower the closer he comes to Eileen's neighborhood. This doesn't seem to be much of a family neighborhood. He wonders if Eileen ever wanted a family. She said something nice to him about it once, but that doesn't mean she ever wanted or wants one. Or maybe she had one once and something went wrong. You never know about people and their secrets. She told him she didn't have anyone, but maybe she really lives with a guy and that's why she's avoiding him. That would be awkward, but not insurmountable. He could be prepared for that. He'll just explain the jury verdict situation and, maybe if there's another guy there, she'll be more willing to talk about it. Yes. All they need to do is have a simple conversation and then they can each go their separate ways.

Arriving at her house, he sees no car in the driveway or out front, but the porch light is on. No visitors so she's probably alone inside. That would be best. He pulls into the driveway and turns off the engine. No interior lights are visible from the front.

Maybe she watches TV in her bedroom or another room at the back of the house. Maybe he's crazy and will scare the living daylights out of her when she sees him here. The love–making juror turned lunatic stalker. But he did leave her a message. Maybe he should turn back. If he does he knows the angst will persist, maybe even grow. No, he has to see this through.

Stephen approaches the front door and rings the doorbell. No answer. He knocks. Still no answer. He has a feeling that she's home. Maybe if he checks around back, he'll know if she's home and avoiding him again. A small gate at the side of the house provides easy access to the backyard. Stephen enters through the gate and walks around to the back of the house. The neighbor's dog barks at him, causing him to jump. He stops and goes still, waiting for the dog to stop barking, then he slowly heads deeper into the backyard. Grass, a few trees and a small flowerbed make up the entirety of the yard.

Fairly simple, but not well maintained. That continues to surprise him. Eileen strikes him as the type of woman that insists on a high level of care, yet everything about her house speaks to the contrary. No lights shine from the rear of the house, except for a dim glow somewhere deep inside. Stephen spots a broken window. That's not very safe. He peeks through the opening and sees a woman's shoe on its side in a hallway, illuminated by a light from an interior room. Could she bc home? And in trouble? That would explain a lot. He opens the unsecured window and crawls through into the house. He calls out, "Eileen?"

His eyes adjust to the interior darkness. He stands in what appears to be a family room. A flower–patterned couch. A matching chair. A TV. A small coffee table and a basic bookcase filled with books. A small desk filled with papers. Not too cluttered and decorated for use rather than for looks. Nothing looks out of place. As he approaches the hallway, he notices that one of the paintings on the wall hangs askew. A sliver of light shines from a room at the end of the hall, illuminating the shoe – a beige low–heeled heavy pump. Stephen moves it out of the way.

He heads toward the light, "Eileen?" No response. His stomach clenches and a chill runs up his spine. He just broke into a woman's house and is snooping around. Not a good start. He peers into a bedroom – dark and empty with the curtains still open as if she hasn't been in here since darkness fell. The only light comes from the end of the hall. He continues toward it to a partially ajar door.

"Eileen?" He pushes against the door to reveal more light. This is a bathroom, but he can't open the door because it hits against something. "Eileen?" He pushes with more force and slides into the bathroom to see what's blocking his passage. "Oh God!" The yell escapes involuntarily as Stephen looks down.

His eyes meet with a body of a woman on the floor. Her clothes are disheveled, and her blond hair is matted in blood with a part of her face missing. Her slightly tinted glasses are bent and partially off what's left of her face. The body is strangely askew. Unnatural. She wears a full, pale blue skirt that appears to go just below her knees. She is on her side and the beige blouse looks like something that was in style decades ago.

His shoe is millimeters from the blood. Blood is spattered on the tub, the walls, the shower curtain, the towels, everywhere. Instinctively he begins to reach for her, then abruptly stops himself. No. She's dead. He can't be here. *Don't touch anything. How can this be happening? No. This can't be real. Fuck, fuck, fuck. I am not here*. He knows he must get out. The room begins to spin. Breathing is tight. Stephen stumbles out of the bathroom. His car. He must get to his car and get out. *Get far far away and never look back.*

Staggering down the hall, he spots the front door, grabs for it and runs out of the house. How can this have happened to Eileen? His Eileen. He takes a few breaths to stop his hands from shaking and gets in his car. He tries to inhale and get control of his hands. He turns the car on then grips the steering wheel to control the shakes. He peels out of the driveway much too fast, driving like a mad man on a quiet street. Slow down, he tells himself. He definitely doesn't want to attract any attention. His mind doesn't know where to go. Something like this exists so far out of his realm of possibility that he feels paralyzed. She's dead and he's been in her house. Nothing about this is okay.

Stephen slams on the brakes, just in time to prevent him from running a red light. He drives around aimlessly, turning randomly and not paying any attention to where he's going. Shadows loom toward him as he chooses deserted streets. His tires nearly miss a cat crossing the road. He wanders into a part of town foreign to him, where some tough characters wander the streets and even the buildings appear menacing. Everything is encroaching on him. His only goal is to get as much distance from Eileen's house as possible.

Did someone break into her house and shoot her when she happened upon them?

That window was broken. But the house wasn't ransacked, and nothing seemed out of place. He remembers the plasma TV on the wall in the living room. Robbers surely would have taken that. Was she someone's target? That seems so unlikely given what he knows about her. What could she have been involved in to get herself killed? What does he really know about her? Just what the court knows. And only that. When he googled her, he only found her contact information and her name in connection with her company. Nothing else. Everything else could bc a lie. Maybe she's one of those people who can't help themselves and they lie about everything. Having different lives in different circumstances. Images of her twisted leg and her matted hair and all that blood creeps in among the jumbled images in his head. He should tell someone that she's in her house dead. Someone killed her and he can't just pretend that he didn't see her. What if someone saw him there?

Stephen slows the car and takes a long, deep breath. He looks around at his surroundings – a rundown neighborhood near a commercial street. He has to do something. As his adrenaline tapers down to a more normal level and his mind begins to clear, his insides began to heave. He pulls into a gas station and goes around the side to the bathroom. His stomach convulses. The broken lock allows for easy access into the filthy accommodations. Flies buzz around the stench filled toilet. The corroding sink is only slightly more inviting. His insides constrict harder. As Stephen steps inside, he can't hold it together any longer and vomits into the small basin. After wiping his face with a few squares of harsh toilet paper, he turns on the faucet and splashes cold water on his face. The mirror has been long broken and corroding, thankfully not allowing him a good look at his frenetic appearance.

His head throbs with panic and confusion. He can think of only one option – to tell Terry. Terry will know what to do. He will sort through this, but Stephen will have to be prepared for being blasted and reminded of what an idiotic maneuver this was. Well, he already knows that; but what can he do about it now?

Stephen notices that Janet has called his cell three times already. He's created an even bigger wreck to clean up with her. He doesn't have the capacity to think about that now. He puts

Terry's address into his GPS and hits go. Janet will understand after he sorts through this latest development. Development would be an understatement. A woman lying shot to death on the floor, and he discovered her after breaking into her house. Nothing strange there. Maybe he has become just a little unhinged through all this. He's used to a life of routine and order and rational behavior. A normal life without much drama. The drama of their lives comes from the kids and the angst of growing up. Petty issues at the office or with friends. Nothing like this. He hears the pounding in his temples and feels his heart tearing at his chest. He can sense his blood pressure.

Probably a record high. It's as if he can feel and hear the force of it. He begins driving, summoning all his strength to keep the car on his side of the road at a normal speed.

He needs to get away from everything for a while, even the city. Maybe he and Janet can take a three–day weekend and go somewhere and regain some sanity. That sounds like a good plan. His mind races in all directions – concocting travel itineraries, images of Eileen, both during the trial and dead on the floor, Janet looking right through him, and thoughts of the once normal life he'd created and how to return to it. Every now and then, he remembers to breathe and focus on the road and that eventually leads him to Terry's apartment.

Terry sits on the couch as he reviews some briefs with the television on and enjoys a bourbon. Not a typical bachelor pad. Terry's affinity for art is evident in the unusual sculptures and paintings well placed around the large main room. Stacks of books fill the built-in bookcases and the room opens to a modern kitchen at one end. His apartment is both cozy and tasteful. Comfortably welcoming. A pounding on the door interrupts his peace. Terry opens the door to a disheveled, frantic looking Stephen who smells bad and immediately pushes his way in.

"Hey, man, what's…" Terry begins.

"She's dead," Stephen blurts.

"Who?"

Stephen tears off his jacket and begins wildly pacing and gesturing as he talks. "I went to her place tonight." Stephen stops and shoots Terry a murderous look, "Don't say a word. I know it was stupid. I just wanted to talk to her. You know, like I said before, to be able to finally put this thing behind me. I wanted to do it before I spoke to Janet and, you know Janet, she wanted to talk right away. Anyway, I called her – Eileen that is – but she wasn't there – wasn't picking up anyway. I told Janet I was just going to do this one thing. I didn't tell her what it was, of course. That would've been even more idiotic. But, anyway, then when I was done, I planned on telling her everything, except the sleeping with her part. So, I thought, okay, this could work out okay. So, then I went over, and she was dead. There was blood and her hair was all matted and blood and her legs were so...I…"

Terry's jaw drops and he turns pale. Stephen's eyes are wide and unnatural and the veins in his neck are bulging and throbbing. Terry grabs Stephen by the arms and makes him stop moving. "Stop. Just stop talking for a minute and sit down." Terry leads Stephen to the couch and makes him sit. "Take a deep breath," he instructs.

"Who would've thought she…" Stephen begins.

"Shhh. Give it a rest for a minute. I'm going to pour you a drink, then we're going to go through this slowly, okay?"

Stephen acquiesces, accepts the drink and gives Terry a play by play of the evening's events. This time Terry does the pacing as he listens, deeply concerned about his best friend. "You parked in the driveway and walked up to the front door, then around to the back?" Terry clarifies.

"Yeah."

"Why did you go in the back? What in the name of God made you trespass? I just can't..." Terry stops himself, knowing this would not be fruitful. What's done is done. "Never mind. That doesn't matter now. What matters is that a neighbor may have seen you. You have to report this."

"Can't we just make an anonymous call?"

"No. Chances are they will find out that you were there tonight anyway. Your car could have been spotted, someone saw you getting out or in, or any number of scenarios. This way, you go in person and report the crime, showing you have nothing to hide, and it puts this thing to rest, insofar as your connection to it."

"Janet's going to kill me."

"Yeah well..." Terry prevents himself from finishing that sentence and instead asks, "Did you speak to Eileen at all in any way since the trial?"

"No. I told you, she wouldn't take my calls." Stephen's palms begin to sweat again. "I need to call Janet."

"Call her on our way. First, you need a reason to have gone to her house tonight."

"Well, her house needs serious work, so maybe I offered to help her with a contractor or something."

"Or you could tell the truth about wanting to talk to her about the verdict."

"No. I can't do that. That would open that whole can of worms during the trial and suspicions of all kinds. And the last thing I need is Janet suspecting something."

"You're not being rational. I don't like it. Any of it," Terry remarks and moves to grab a jacket.

There's no convincing Stephen to bring the verdict or the trial into his report to the police. He refuses to tell the truth. Terry has no choice but to let him step forward as an innocent person who stumbled upon the body and freaked.

21

Janet can't believe Stephen just walked out without an explanation. This is way out of character for him. Something happened during that trial, and she wants to get to the bottom of it. Even if it was an affair, she has to know. Nearly midnight and he won't even take her call. What can be going on with him? For a man like Stephen to stray, there had to be a reason, maybe even a long buildup of reasons. She knows he's been restless this past year, what with wanting to do more with his work, but not knowing how to approach going out on his own. And drinking more than usual. The fact that he so easily accepted jury duty also struck her as a symptom of this unease. Maybe she's missing something. He hasn't been able to look at her, really look at her, since his return. That's a sure sign of guilt of some sort. Janet's mind spins out of control. She frantically searches for a clue as to what's going on with her husband. Stephen is one of the most rational, kind and considerate men she's ever known. He was the sensible one, the one who always thought ahead and planned. She likes to wait to see how the mood strikes her before making certain choices. She likes to do things in the spur of the moment.

Live more impulsively. He is methodical and structured. A planner. Was he planning something now?

Janet completes three loads of laundry and folds and re–folds clothes on the couch. Anything to keep herself occupied. She tries to remain calm and not project too much on worst–case scenarios. She always trusted him and now should be no different. He asked her to trust him, so she will. It's just that the way he said it gave her an eerie feeling. No, she has no basis for that. Paranoia never brought anybody to a good place. She pushes the clothes aside and looks down at the coffee table and realizes she's polished off two thirds of a bottle of wine. She can't remember the last time she'd drunk so much. It's not helping.

Her cell phone rings, and Janet grabs it. "Stephen?

"Hi, honey. Listen, I'm with Terry and we're on our way to the police station."

"What? Are you okay?" Her reaction is a mix infused with worry, relief, and a wine buzz.

"I'm fine. I found something that I have to report..." Stephen sees Terry glaring at him and decides it's probably better to tell Janet over the phone and give her time to digest the information before he gets home. This way he won't be under scrutiny with her watching him say every word.

"What do you mean?" she asks.

"I found a body…" Stephen begins.

"What? What do you mean? Where are you?"

"It was one of the jurors. I had to meet with her tonight and when I got there, she was dead."

"My god, Stephen." Janet can't quite wrap her head around what he's saying. "Where were you meeting?"

"At her house. I'm so sorry. I should've told you and just stayed home and talked this through."

Janet stands up and begins walking around the room. Her head is spinning. "Why did you go to this woman's house? Who is she? Was she old?"

"Just one of the jurors on the trial. Look, I've got to go. I'll be home right after."

"Don't hang up on me. We are not done here." Janet becomes intense. Stephen gets quiet and looks out the window away from Terry.

"Where did you find her? How did she die?" Janet asks.

"She was shot at her house."

"Jesus, Stephen, what the hell…?"

"I know. It's crazy."

"Are you okay?"

"Yeah. I'm fine. It was quiet when I got there so…"

"Was anyone else with you?"

"No."

"I don't understand. Why would you go to one of the juror's homes at that hour, and for what purpose?" Janet contends.

Stephen sighs, deflated, then, "I know it must seem strange, but I went because of the trial. It's all about the trial. This thing has been gnawing at me and I just wanted to get to the bottom of it. Get some answers. In the beginning, she was one of the only people doubting the Senator's guilt, then she became certain and was the one voting not guilty and she had a great argument."

"Clearly she convinced you," Janet replies. The words fly out of Janet's mouth before she can catch herself. She isn't sure where it came from. She abhors jealousy and suspicion and yet here she is. The entire conversation feels surreal to her.

"No. It wasn't like that." Stephen tries to sort through the confusion in his mind.

Listening to Stephen, Terry realizes that this isn't exactly the story Stephen delivered to him earlier and wonders if Stephen's guilt stems not only from the affair, but also from feeling like he's made a mistake.

Stephen focuses on being clear with his wife. "I started to examine all the facts and I realized I couldn't put a man away if I had this much doubt. So, we had two not guilty votes at the end. But when we were polled, she completely changed her vote, which made it look like I was the only one who hung the jury – and I just don't know why."

"Why does it matter?" Janet asks.

That is the question of the day. The answer that causes Stephen endless struggle. "I thought if I got a rational answer, I would feel like I hadn't misread anything...I don't know. I thought it would make a difference. But now...she was killed. And I don't know what to think." Stephen slumps in his seat. He concludes the conversation letting Janet know that as far as he knows, Eileen is as ordinary as people get and he can't imagine a thing like this happening to her. Maybe she was robbed or something. He'll be home as soon as he's finished at the station.

Stephen hangs up and can feel Terry's eyes on him. Instead of looking at his friend, Stephen silently turns his attention back out the passenger side window toward the city lights. Terry clears his throat and at first Stephen ignores him. After a minute, Stephen finally turns to Terry, "She was probably robbed or something, right?"

Terry shrugs, this time keeping his eyes on the road. "It happens. She came upon a perp, and he panicked and boom."

Stephen winces. As they pass by some restaurants and bars, he sees couples and groups of friends drinking and laughing through the windows and people walking to and fro. He sees a blonde woman and as she turns toward him, he sees Eileen's face, then suddenly half of it is missing and he gasps.

"What? You okay?" Terry asks.

"Yeah. It's nothing."

"Listen, when we get to the station, don't volunteer any extra information. None," Terry instructs him.

"Yeah, got it."

"I'm serious. Not even an extra word."

At the police station, the officer taking Stephen's statement pauses and eyes him carefully when he asks, "You're telling me that you saw a dead body and fled the scene to get your lawyer, before reporting it?"

Flustered from the beginning, Stephen's demeanor doesn't change much when he answers, "I was totally spooked and this isn't my lawyer, this is my friend, who just happens to be a lawyer..."

Terry jumps in and addresses the officer, "Look, Mike. You know this kind of thing happens all the time. People get freaked and panic and don't know what to do. It's not like there's a handbook on what you're supposed to do when you come across a dead body. I helped him calm down and we came right over."

The cops are familiar with Terry and his type of defendant and Mike seems to be able to tell that this one's different and he eases up.

By the time Stephen completes reporting what he saw, and they let him go, nearly two hours pass. Terry heads back to his apartment and Stephen goes home, battered and catatonic. When he arrives home, Janet lays scrunched up on the sofa sound asleep. She tried waiting up for him and this makes him feel even worse about his behavior. He grabs a blanket and covers her, then makes his way upstairs, feeling thrashed and confused. Maybe this is a bad dream and he'll wake up in the morning to his normal life. If only.

22

At dawn, Janet crawls into bed next to Stephen and he puts his arms around her. Neither one speaks. They just lie there in a moment of togetherness. An aura of fear and dread hangs over them. Sleep eludes them. Last night was not a dream. Finally, Janet kisses him quickly and gets out of bed. "What did the police say?" she asks him.

"Nothing to say, they went out there to look at it I guess." He sits up.

Janet sees the horror of what he witnessed flash across Stephen's face. This entire scenario defies her reality, and she can't imagine what he must be feeling. "I'm sorry you had to see that. It must have been awful."

"Yeah."

An awkward silence threatens to take root, but Janet pushes on, "What did they say about you?"

"Nothing. I told them what happened and that was it."

As she tries to put the pieces together in her mind, she sits on the bed and looks at him. "Where was the body? Was there blood?"

"Yeah, there was blood. She was shot in the face."

"That's so…ugh…unbelievable. Were you scared?"

"I don't know. Shocked more than anything, and then I knew I had to get out of there, so I called Terry to figure out the best thing to do. I figured he would know."

"What do you think happened?"

"I don't know. I can't imagine." Stephen squirms, needing the questions to stop.

"I still don't understand why you went to her house last night?" Janet can't hide her disbelief.

"I know how this looks and that it's hard to believe, but I really did go there to get answers."

"Do you think her death had anything to do with the trial?"

"I don't know. Probably a robbery."

Janet sits back, her mind racing. "Something doesn't feel right about any of this. I think there's more you're not telling me."

Stephen reaches for his wife. "Come here," he says, thinking how marriage is the riskiest proposition of them all – a love that hovers permanently on the precipice of collapse. He sees now that every day he risks a fall that can shatter it irreparably into splinters and blow it all to hell. He guides her to sit on the bed next to him. "I know this is crazy. I know I must seem strange to you right now. But I'm through the worst of it. I've been tortured by this thing. You're right. Something about her changing her vote doesn't feel right. I can't really explain it. It's the way we talked about the case and the way decisions were made in the jury room. Hard to explain. Just that a part of me wonders if I made my decision based on something I didn't see the right way and…. I just don't know what to do with that. I thought if I talked it through with her, she could put the thing to rest for me."

"What about talking it through with me? Ever thought of that?"

"Clearly it would've been the better idea." He looks at his wife as she examines his face. Her look probing. He still can't hold her gaze for long, so he hugs her instead. She needs more time to absorb what he's told her. They move apart and into their morning routines.

Stephen takes another shower. The one he took before bed, only a few hours ago, doesn't feel like enough. The events of the last few months are over. Finished. With Eileen gone, nothing remains for him to resolve. He reminds himself to be grateful for the privileged life he leads and swears to be a better husband, a better person, because the line between here and there is very thin.

The television is on in the kitchen and Janet intently turns her attention to the news. Emily bounces in, "Mom, can I go to Suzy's house afterschool?"

"Shhhh." Janet puts up her hand and Emily rolls her eyes.

Stephen enters and immediately focuses on the screen where a reporter stands in front of Eileen's house, "Last night, a Virginia lakeside community was beset by tragedy. A young woman's body was found in her lakeside home. She has been identified as thirty–two–year–old Eileen Harris. A solar energy physicist with..."

"She's young," Janet says out loud.

"Mom? Can I?" Emily persists.

"Fine."

Mark jumps in with, "Dad, how come she always gets to go and I don't?"

Stephen needs to hear what's being said so he snaps, "Mark, not now."

Mark plunges back into his cereal after sticking his tongue out at his sister, who responds with a sassy smile.

The reporter informs the public that the victim had been shot in the head. A photograph of a smiling Eileen pops up on the screen. Janet checks Stephen's reaction as he watches this, and she sees confusion playing out on his face. Stephen stares at the photo of Eileen. Something about it is strange. It looks like a standard headshot, but that doesn't look like the Eileen he knows. Not completely. The glasses are the same, but the way they rest on her face look odd. Different. And thirty–two? The woman he knew seemed older. That's not to say she didn't look great, she did, amazing in fact, but her demeanor and mannerisms suggested more maturity and…there's something about the face in the photo that isn't quite right. The image switches to another picture of Eileen, this one without her glasses. She looks similar and yet he knew her face and that wasn't it. Something looks wrong. But the report is clear that she was one of the jurors. After watching the news coverage, silence ensues between Stephen and Janet – a sickening that defies words and rises out of such a violent act entering their personal space.

"They said they're investigating a possible connection to the trial," Janet points out.

Distracted, Stephen says, "I can't imagine that will lead anywhere."

Janet rests her hand on Stephen's arm, "Stephen, can we talk more tonight?" she asks.

"Of course."

She needs her husband back.

After Janet and the kids leave, Stephen goes online to better examine the media's photos of Eileen. The first photo pops up and Stephen blanches. He scrolls through a couple of others. His hands begin to shake. Not many images of her are available.

Dread overwhelms him. This can't be right.

On his way to work Stephen calls Terry and informs him that the pictures of Eileen on the news and on all the news sites online are not of the same woman he had been with. Not the Eileen that he was on that jury with.

"You can't be serious?" Terry begins to wonder about Stephen's mental stability.

"Yes. I'm serious."

"It could just be the pictures, man. I certainly don't look like the same guy you knew twenty years ago."

"No. There were a few pictures and I looked at all of them. It's not the pictures."

"Women have work done on their faces all the time now. It's not like in the old days my friend. It's not unusual."

Stephen is insistent. He can't be assuaged. Terry wants to beg him to give this thing a rest and not stir up any more dirt, but he senses that this is another one of those times that Stephen is determined and won't budge. To appease him, Terry offers, "Let me make some calls and check into it. See if there's any way something is messed up."

"Please do. I would really appreciate it."

Stephen knows he must seem irrational and maybe he is, but he can't remember a time he felt so unsettled. And it's not just about the affair and her death. He feels certain of that. There's something else at play.

A young reporter catches up to Stephen as he parks his car at his office building. "Mr. Reeves, right?" Says the casually dressed man, holding a phone.

"No. I'm not going to talk to you. Not now, not ever. Leave."

"You found and reported the body of Eileen Harris. How…"

Stephen lunges at the guy and spews "Get out! Get away from me!" The guy backs off, leaving Stephen shaking in the parking lot. *They know that I found the body. How is that possible? The fucking information age. This is hell!*

23

The night is crisp and clear. Janet insisted that Terry join them for dinner again tonight. Somehow, having him around helps both her and Stephen feel that their lives are normal or getting back to it. He's a testament to them that recent events are nothing to worry about. Conversation around the dinner table focuses on sports and the kids and both Stephen and Janet do their best to block out their underlying anxiety. After dinner, Stephen and Terry leave the kids with Janet while the two of them sit outside by the workshop, each nurses a glass of bourbon.

"I checked into it. It was the same woman who was on the jury with you," Terry says to Stephen. Stephen hasn't mentioned his doubts about Eileen's identity to Janet and Terry has advised him not to. That there is no reason to keep wading in those waters and risk more hurt feelings.

"I'm telling you; I don't think so. I saw other photos in the paper and online this afternoon and the woman who was killed is not her," Stephen insists.

"Maybe she doesn't photograph well. As I said before, but you probably weren't listening, maybe the babe had a nose, chin and cheek job since the pictures were taken. Who knows? But it was her. I'm telling you. The cops found her jury docs at the house. And everything on her application identifies her as *that*

Eileen Harris. The one you were on the jury with. She even filled out the proper forms to get excused from work for jury duty. So now, just put it out of your mind. Look man, you've got other problems." Implying Janet. "And you've now got the big project, so put your neuroses behind you."

Stephen shakes his head. He knew her face. The nuances of her contours as she slept, as she laughed, as she sat deep in thought. He'd studied her face as a way to try to reach some understanding of why she'd captivated him. Why he felt compelled to keep moving toward her as a moth to a flame. He tried to read into the angles and curves as if they were a crystal ball, soon to reveal the source of his behavior. Without a doubt, he knew her face.

Terry sees Janet through the window, and she waves to them. He waves back. Stephen looks up and smiles at her. She turns away and follows the kids out of view. Terry leans toward Stephen and looks him straight in the eye, "You're delusional. Maybe your guilt is making you remember differently. Maybe something went on that makes you think you know something about her. Maybe you projected a certain image onto her and that's what you're clinging to, for whatever reason. It happens. Whatever. I don't know what happened to you, but if you don't want to fuck it all up, you have got to get a grip on yourself and let this thing go. Don't think about her and especially don't talk about her. Ever."

Stephen takes in the words. Being delusional means having a belief that is contradicted by what's generally accepted as reality. Also, delusion is a precursor to mental illness. Do his actions come across as mentally unstable? Looking at Terry, he can see he's perilously close to the edge. It's true he hasn't been making the best choices. Maybe it's time to take his cue from someone else. He decides to acquiesce. Terry's probably right. A strange thought, considering their relationship histories.

"You need to get some sleep," Terry tells Stephen. "Every time I close my eyes, I see her lying there…"

"I can't imagine, but you have to find a way. Take something. Get a prescription. Anything."

Later that night, after Terry has gone and the kids are well on their way to dreamland, Stephen looks at Janet as she brushes her hair in their bathroom. He smiles at her from the doorway, holding out two glasses of dark liquid. Janet looks at him questioningly.

"B&B," Stephen says.

"It's been forever since I've had one of those."

"I saw the nearly full bottle and I thought, why not?"

She smiles at him, leaves the brush and grabs the glass. The two of them find their way to the chairs by the window. Stephen takes the first mouthful of his liquid and makes every effort to calmly and rationally talk to Janet. She deserves as much information as he can give her without damaging their marriage and hurting her. He expresses his feelings of wanting to start his own business while at the same time having insecurity around his ability to succeed and how the time at the trial gave him a chance to examine his options and to really see that if he wanted to make that change, he needs to make it sooner rather than later. He also tells her about the other jurors and how they instantly jumped at the guilty verdict and that he too succumbed to the same conclusion without really working through other possibilities and how this made him feel like a bit of a failure. As she sips her drink, Janet asks questions about Eileen, and he manages to answer them without giving anything away.

"I guess she seemed like the only one who was really thinking, so I realized that asking questions and really analyzing each piece several times over was a smart approach. Her questions made me see that I was doing what everyone else was doing just to get out of there. I think for the first time in my life I felt like part of the herd and just a bit stupid, so I really took time to go through all the evidence, even though the others were not happy with me." Hearing himself say this out loud makes him realize that this is the story he's selling to himself as well. A new version of revisionist history that he can live with.

"But *she* was happy with you," Janet says, looking for something, but unsure of what. Stephen feels the impact of her comment, but wisely allows it to slide off.

"I don't think that made a difference to her really, but then when she changed her vote at the end, I wondered if it did. But Terry said that she probably just got scared and didn't want the press after her. He's probably right. Especially since I had already said the Senator was not guilty." Stephen empties his glass.

"So why go to her house at night? And why tell the police you went for repair work?" Janet persists.

"It was stupid. I did tell her I'd look at a couple of things for her, but I went at night because I really wanted an answer on why she changed her vote. It was a time I figured she'd be home and couldn't avoid me. Her doing the about–face just didn't make any sense, considering her position in the jury room. It kept haunting me and I felt the sooner I knew, the better I'd sleep. I didn't tell that part to the cops because I was afraid that they'd think I had a reason to be mad at her. It was stupid and I'm sorry."

Janet recognizes Stephen's sincerity and reaches out to her husband. That night, they make love, and both find a way to believe that they are moving closer back to normal.

24

After a few days, Stephen begins to feel better. His face still shows signs of lack of sleep, but the generic sleeping pills give him at least a few hours without tremors. A light rain fills the morning as he sits in his office. Grateful that Janet is the woman he loves and has built a life with, he thinks about doing something romantic. He used to do that sort of thing all the time – before the kids. Too much time has passed since they'd had any extended alone time together. They need a weekend away. Stephen's mind searches for ideas on where they can go, when his phone intercom buzzes. "Yeah."

"There's a Detective Phillips here to see you," Susan announces, "He's in reception. Do you want me to send him back here?"

His good mood vanishes. "No. I'll be right out." *Stay calm.* This must have something to do with Eileen's death. This can't be a good sign. Maybe this is just a follow up to his statement. Maybe he just has a simple question. Probably no big deal. No need to jump to conclusions. Stephen steadies his hands and walks into the reception area to find a tall, average looking man with a receding hairline scrutinizing the place. As soon as he spots Stephen, he steps forward and smiles, "Mr. Reeves?"

"Yes," Stephen says extending his hand. "How can I help you?"

"Detective Phillips. Can we go someplace to talk? We have to talk to everyone who served on the jury with Ms. Harris."

"I already gave a statement."

"Yes, and we need to go over that and perhaps gather some more details from you," Phillips says casually.

"Sure. No problem." Stephen leads the detective to the small conference room.

Phillips' shoes squeak as he follows. After plying the detective with a cup of coffee, Stephen sits across from him and tries to relax, "What else can I tell you?"

"Why did you go to her house that night?"

"I already explained that. Do you not have that?"

"In your report it says that you went to speak with her about some repairs to her home. Is that correct?"

"Yes."

"After ten o'clock at night?"

"I know it probably seems strange," he begins, trying to stay cool, "but, with our schedules, we hadn't been able to find another time. Frankly, I wanted to get it over with and not drag things on. I didn't really have time to help her out, but I made the offer, so..."

Phillips nods, seeming to accept the answer. Consulting his small writing pad, he continues, "Did Ms. Harris' behavior strike you at all odd at any time during the trial?"

"No. Well, except that she lied about her vote. So, not during the trial, but I guess right at the end there."

"Some of the other jurors thought she panicked in the end and didn't want the publicity. How about afterward, in your conversations with her?"

"No. We just spoke on the phone – once." The lie echoes in his head.

"Did you know her prior to the trial?"

"No."

"So, you got friendly with Ms. Harris during the sequester?"

"What does that mean?" Stephen bristles.

"Didn't you agree to contact each other after the trial?"

"Oh, yes, well that. It was business. I'm an architect," he adds, a redundancy not needed.

Phillips gives an amused nod. "Did she say anything to you about being afraid or nervous about something?"

"No."

"Did you ever sleep with Ms. Harris?" Detective Phillips slides the question in as smoothly as if he were inquiring about the weather.

Taken aback, Stephen's heart skips a beat. The guy didn't just ask him that. How the hell? "What?" Stephen's dislike for the detective and suspicion grows instantly.

"Did you?" Phillips persists.

"No. Why would..." Stephen begins.

"It seems that one of the other jurors thinks they saw her enter your room on one occasion."

"Oh that." Stephen tries to remain unfazed and feigns relief. "She just stopped in to see if I had an aspirin. She had a headache. And I did. Have an aspirin, that is." The lies just flow. From where he has no idea. He can't believe deception suddenly comes so easily to him. This worries him to no end. This absolutely has to be the last one, because what if he has to remember what he said when? He wonders if Phillips can tell that he's lying or sweating.

Phillips' expression remains neutral, but Stephen suspects he isn't buying it. The way he smiles and nods his head. Quite possibly mocking him. The other jurors, especially Charlie, that blowhard, aren't models of articulate calm, so maybe he'll be fine. Noticing that Phillips finishes writing and closes his pad,

Stephen can't resist asking, "Are you sure the dead woman is the same Eileen Harris that was on the jury?"

"Positive. Why would you ask that?" The detective's eyebrows goes up.

"It's just hard to believe, that's all."

Phillips shoots Stephen a look of suspicion. "Mmmmhmm. Is there anything else we should know, Mr. Reeves?"

Assessing that he should quit before getting himself deeper into trouble, Stephen stands leading the way out for the detective. "Not that I can think of Detective. I hope you guys get whoever is responsible for that poor woman's death." Stephen opens the door.

After detective Phillips is out of sight, Stephen looks at his hands and notices they are unmistakably shaking. He notices Susan trying to be nonchalant, but she was watching him with Phillips. He immediately shuts himself in his office and calls Terry. "The cops were here. A Detective Phillips," Stephen announces.

"Okay, hold on. Let me get off the other line."

While on hold, Stephen doodles on a pad and breaks two pencils. Maybe he's just being too paranoid. The cops ask all kinds of questions to get people flustered. Had he seemed flustered? Who wouldn't get flustered if accused of sleeping with someone who'd just been murdered? *Wow. She really was murdered.* The entire incident still feels like a bad dream that he can't fully import into his reality – except for the images that continuously seep into his nights.

"Alright, what'd Phillips want?" Terry returns to the line.

"Well, he said it was just routine. That they were questioning everyone on the jury."

"And that would be standard procedure in a case like this, so that's nothing to worry about." Terry seems relieved.

"Thc guy also wanted to go over that night again. The night I found her."

"What'd you tell him?"

"I stuck to my story."

"Good. Then there's no problem that I can see."

Stephen looks down at his doodles. Sharp jagged angles. Black.

"Stephen, you there?"

"Yeah. Listen. If this thing gets out of hand, could you help me out? I mean legally. You're the only one I'd trust."

"Christ. What the hell are you talking about? You are wound way too tight. Give it a few days…"

"I mean it. Could you help me if I needed it?"

"You won't need me, but if you did, you know you can count on me. My first suggestion is just fuckin' relax. You don't panic just because a cop asked you some questions."

"He asked me if I slept with her."

Terry's silence speaks volumes. Stephen has a feeling that the game has changed.

He slept with a woman whom he found murdered. Terry makes Stephen repeat every word he told Phillips. Stephen fears that there were likely going to be more questions.

"There may not be more questions," Terry says, "They may pick up a lead on what really happened. We have no way of knowing this woman's life and they will dig and dig. If there's any kind of follow up, you cannot tell any more lies. They have her phone records; they will know you didn't talk to her. Chances are this won't matter, but from now on, keep your mouth shut as much as possible. Most likely they will find something that explains why she was killed, and you'll be fine."

Terry's words are fairly reassuring, and Stephen decides to focus on the positive and trust that the truth will come out around what happened to Eileen and who actually killed her.

25

Janet looks at the beautiful bunch of orange tulips Stephen brought her. Spring is her favorite time of year and Stephen surprised her yesterday announcing his intention to whisk her away to the wine country for the weekend. Michelle agreed to watch the kids.

Feeling inspired and excited to feel the sparks fly again, Janet decides to take off early from work and go shopping for something new and fun for their weekend away.

Boutique lingerie stores are a luxury and only for special occasions. The last time Janet patronized one was nearly ten years ago, after she finally lost some of the pregnancy weight from Emily and in preparation for their anniversary. Entering one again after all that time feels invigorating. The clean smell of refined sachets and scented candles waft through the exquisitely displayed merchandise. Nightgowns, teddys, bras, panties, satin and cashmere robes and silk slippers surround her in a high brow palette of colors. She feels special just being a customer here. Then she looks at the prices. Can she be this out of touch? A sexy lacy bra and panty set for three–hundred and fifty dollars! One bra for *only* a hundred–and–twenty. *What normal person can afford this stuff?* She needs to change her thinking. She's a successful, nearly middle–aged woman who can afford this, not on a regular basis but on a rare occasion and this is definitely one of those, so she brushes the sticker shock aside and smiles at the overly serious older saleswoman looking at her.

Blue is Stephen's favorite color, and it looks great on Janet, enhancing her eyes. Janet finds a blue/gray sexy silk camisole and panty set that fits her superbly. She opts for the camisole to hide the stretch marks that still persist on her stomach. Bikini days are over by her standards, but she still looks good. Once the saleswoman realizes that Janet is a serious customer who intends to buy, she suddenly becomes all smiles and overly helpful. Janet adds two marvelous smelling candles to her purchase and happily heads home.

That afternoon, both Stephen and Janet leave the kids to their homework while they adjourn upstairs to enjoy the anticipation of their getaway. Stephen sits in a chair, enjoying a bourbon, as he watches Janet pack enthusiastically. She coordinates shoes, jewelry and bags for every outfit and make sure she doesn't forget essential items, like her hair gel and spray, without which the humidity would have a field day.

"I'm so glad we're doing this," Janet says.

Stephen grins from ear to ear, enjoying her excitement. "Me too. It's long overdue." The truth of that strikes him and he adds, "I'm sorry if I haven't been very romantic lately, it's just…"

"Don't go there. I already did a head–trip on myself. I'm sorry too. You know, I started thinking that you being away for that trial might have been a good thing for us."

"Oh?"

"Yes, it's made us see that we *really* need some time for us without the kids. I'm so glad we're not letting it go any longer." Janet goes over to her husband and kisses him. "Thank you for arranging this."

"We'll make it a regular thing." Stephen shifts in his chair and changes the subject. "The weather's supposed to be sunny, so the winery tours will be great."

Janet smiles at him and says, "You said we're going fancy on Saturday night, right?"

The doorbell rings.

"Yup." Stephen takes a sip of his drink and stands. "I'll get it."

When Stephen leaves the room, Janet pulls out her new purchases and adds them to the contents of her suitcase. She wants to surprise him.

26

Mark beats Stephen to the door and opens it. Michelle stands there holding a grocery bag and before she can get a word out, Mark pulls her inside. "Grandma! Come to my room, I'm making a space shuttle."

"You go. I'll be right there, Markie. I just have to put a few things away."

Stephen turns to Michelle as Mark runs back upstairs. "Let me help you with that." He grabs the bag, and they head into the kitchen. The doorbell rings again.

Stephen comes from the kitchen and opens the front door. Standing there are two men. Stephen recognizes one as Detective Phillips. Three other officers come up from behind them. Stephen's face betrays the crushing feeling in his chest. Phillips nods to the other man, then steps inside. The other man follows. Stephen freezes. Phillips looks at Stephen and says, "Hello, Mr. Reeves. Detective Phillips." He flashes his badge.

"I remember," Stephen mumbles.

"This is Sergeant Sloan, and these are officers Harlin, Mathews and Case." Phillips hands Stephen a folded piece of paper. "This is a search warrant for the premises."

"A search warrant?"

Phillips nods to the three officers who enter the house and fan out to begin searching. "And we have the authority to arrest you. Please put your hands behind your back," he says to Stephen.

Sloan pulls out handcuffs as Stephen's jaw drops open. His mouth feels dry and as much as he wants to scream and protest, not a sound comes out. The room begins to spin, and time slows. Sloan snaps the cuffs on Stephen's wrists. They feel cold and sharp.

Stephen feels each metal clasp of the cuff as it clicks into place. Each click sounds so loud and clear in his ears.

Michelle comes back around from the kitchen, "Stephen, I…" and stops dead in her tracks at the sight of the scene in front of her.

"Stephen Reeves, you are under arrest for the murder of Eileen Harris," Phillips states formally and gestures to Sloan who recites, "You have the right to remain silent. Anything you say can and will be used against you in…"

Constriction engulfs Stephen and the feeling of being trapped descends like a boulder. He sees Michelle's face and it jolts him. "What the hell?" he finally manages to Phillips.

"...the court of law. You have the right to an attorney. If you cannot afford one, one will be appointed for you."

Michelle yells for her daughter, "Janet!!"

"I don't understand this," Stephen says in protest. He looks up and sees Janet coming down the stairs. Her face contorts in a strange combination of shock, suspicion, and panic. Stephen looks pleadingly at his wife.

"Mom!" The call comes from Emily in the family room. Janet's reaction is instantaneous as she runs down the stairs and yells, "I'll be right there. Hold on!" Then she looks at Michelle, who immediately goes to Emily.

Janet turns to her husband, "What's going on? Why are..." she stops, noticing the officers looking through her house, then her eyes land on the cuffs around Stephen's hands. Frozen, Janet just stares at the cuffs, panic overtakes her.

Phillips looks at Janet and says, "I'm sorry, ma'am. We have a search warrant for your home and cars and your husband is under arrest." Turning back to Stephen and Sloan he adds, "Let's go."

Janet grabs Stephen's arm as she asks him, "What's this about? Please tell me it's not about…" Stephen's eyes tell her everything she fears.

All he can manage is, "It's some sort of hideous mistake. I swear. Call Terry."

Phillips and Sloan push him out the front door.

"Where are you taking him?" asks Janet.

"To the station on Easton. He'll be booked, then you can petition for bail. If..."

Emily trudges out of the family room with Michelle on her heels, "Mom, grandma says..." and stops short, gawking at the bizarre scene before the open front door. Phillips turns and continues out the door.

"Go back into the family room, honey," Janet says, but Emily won't budge. "Now!" Janet insists and Emily instantly vanishes.

Janet walks out with the men arresting her husband and finds herself staring at a police car as Stephen is pushed into the back seat, behind the metal screen. He looks at her and mouths 'Call Terry.' She manages a nod, turns toward the house and sees Michelle and the kids in the doorway. Stephen sees them too. They're visibly scared.

Janet rushes up to them.

"What are they doing to dad and why are they in our house?" Emily asks, pointing to the other officers going through the house.

"Where's he going?" Mark asks, half fascinated by being so close to a real police car and half afraid for his dad.

"It's just a big mistake. I have to call Uncle Terry and get this thing straightened out. Come on. Inside."

The front door closes as the police car pulls away. Stephen knows he's innocent. Surely, this is some sort of joke or tactic to try to get information from him that they think he has. This can't be a real arrest for a real murder, Stephen tells himself. The two men are engaged in small talk in the front and not paying any attention to him.

"Hey, Detective Phillips," Stephen begins, "why are you guys doing this instead of looking for the real killer?"

"You'll get your day in court, Mr. Reeves."

"This is ridiculous. I..." Stephen has a lot to say, but Terry's voice inserts itself into his head to not offer any extra information, so he stops. "Never mind."

Once at the station, they place Stephen in an interrogation room. Stephen lets them know that he is waiting for Terry. The District Attorney, Bill Devoe, enters and immediately takes a gruff stance, "What is it you really wanted to speak to the victim about, Mr. Reeves?"

"I already told you that. I'm not saying anything more until my attorney gets here."

"That's fine. You don't have to say a word Mr. Reeves. Just listen." Devoe puts a tablet on the table and opens a file, then hits play. The sound of Stephen's voice booms from the small device. Devoe turns up the volume.

"...you can't just do this to me. I need some answers. If I don't hear from you by ten tonight, I'm coming over, and I'm not going away..." Devoe taps it off.

Stephen feels like a man stripped and splayed open. He always believed that he's in control of his destiny. That he's willing and prepared for the consequences of every action. This is the credo of men with integrity. Stephen has always considered himself to be an honest man, who prides himself on a sense of personal responsibility and honor.

One that has nothing to fear when it comes to revealing the truth. In the past this was true and it should still be true because he has not committed murder. Except that there is a piece of dishonesty that has lodged itself in his life and begun to grow. He assumed that an affair conducted behind the veil of sequestered circumstances could remain in a box, apart from his real life, and never acknowledged thereafter. He assumed that no consequences would come from something done in secret and out of the way. In his assumption, he made a mess. A mess of outstanding proportions.

"It's not what it sounds like," Stephen declares as if there exists the possibility of their believing that. Fortunately, he's spared the additional humiliation of these men treating him like a killer when the door opens and Terry bursts in.

"Stephen, don't say anything." Terry angrily turns to Devoe "Where the hell do you get off interrogating my client without me being present?"

"I was simply being generous and disclosing some facts."

"You've got nothing to hold him on."

"Wrong, counselor." Devoe holds up the tablet.

Terry looks at Stephen and sits down. Devoe plays the recording again and Stephen can tell that Terry is pissed. Really pissed. He doesn't blame him. He did tell him everything. The main things anyway. But he left out the messages he left for her, because why seem more like a crazy person to your best friend than necessary?

"I need some time with my client. Alone," Terry asserts.

The men clear the room, leaving Terry and Stephen sitting in strained silence.

Finally, Terry leans in and, knowing they're being watched, says in a controlled voice and gesture, "They're watching, so stay cool. Now, what the hell's the matter with you? First, why in god's name would you ever leave a message like that, and second, why didn't you tell me this? Now you're coming out looking like a liar straight out of the shoot."

"I wasn't thinking. And..."

"Obviously not with your brain." Seeing the genuine fear on Stephen's face, Terry immediately wishes he hadn't said that. "Look, this isn't good, but you didn't kill anybody, so it'll get cleared up."

"I don't know what's going on, but I can tell you it's not this – me. This has nothing to do with me. I don't even know how this can be happening. This is crazy, so insanely crazy..." Stephen's breathing becomes erratic.

Terry stands up. "I'll get you some water and I've got to talk to the DA and see if I can get some insight into what they've got on you, then I'll make some calls and see if we get an arraignment hearing today and get bail posted. I'll get someone to cover for me at PDS while we get you squared away and find you a top attorney. In the…."

"I don't want another attorney. I'll pay you. I'll do whatever I have to, but you've got to handle this."

"I'm a PD and…"

"But you can find a way to do this, right? You have to." The look on Stephen's face is full of fear and pleading and Terry could never walk away from that.

"You sure you want that? There are guys with a lot more clout than me and a lot more resources."

"Are you kidding? You're the only one who really knows what happened and you know me, and you know I didn't do it. You've got to help me."

Terry nods. "Okay. I'll work it out. First, is there anything else you haven't told me? "

"No."

"Any other messages you left?"

"Well. One, but I was just asking her to call me back."

"Great. How many times did you call her?"

Stephen looks up at Terry. He feels like a child being reprimanded. "I don't know. A few. Maybe six."

Terry sighs and takes it in. "Anyone see you with this woman in the hotel in an inappropriate way?"

"No. We were careful. She always snuck into my room."

"So, you wouldn't know if someone saw her or not?"

Upon hearing that question, Stephen realizes that Janet will find out about his affair. One way or another, she will know, and he won't be able to hide it. Life as he knows it is officially over.

"Hang in there," Terry says and leaves the room.

Stephen's mind stops. A numbness invades his body and soul, and he takes on a sensation of being suspended in time and space. The room takes on an amorphous quality and he wonders if this is what an out of body experience feels like. Right now, he prefers the feeling of suspension to the one of facing what comes next. He suddenly feels very old.

27

The officers leave the Reeves' home after a few hours of searching. They left things in disarray, and they found nothing. Janet clings to the idea that she must remain composed for the kids. That she can't allow her nerves to unravel. She helps Mark and Emily pack a bag. Her mother is taking them to her house for the weekend. She's never seen her mother so frozen and incapable of functioning. Understandable. How can anyone be normal right now? Janet does her best to reassure Mark and Emily that someone made a big mistake and that she and their father will take care of it. Not to worry. Their life will be back on track on Sunday, and they'll all have dinner together and laugh about it. Right. It's late and they're all exhausted and Michelle has never seemed so ready to take the kids and leave.

Terry finally calls. He managed to pull some strings and got a bail hearing right away. Stephen was granted bail, but the amount is steeper than Terry hoped. Terry won't give her any answers over the phone, and he evades her questions, saying "We can go over everything once we get him out of here." Then he adds, "It'll be okay." But Janet doesn't believe him. She knows that Stephen must be keeping something from her regarding the trial and that night and that woman. She knows why. No man goes to a single woman's house that late at night for house repairs or to get an explanation he can easily get over the phone. Something had transpired between them. Something that threatens everything she knows about the man she married and their relationship. Terry won't say it, but she knows this must be a factor. The sick feeling in her gut tears at her with each thought of the possibility of his betrayal, yet the tears don't follow. Trying to get in touch with the possibility of Stephen doing something like being intimate with another woman fails her. She can't make herself get there, at least not now. Not yet.

Good people sometimes do stupid and bad things. In her heart, Janet knows Stephen is a good person. A truly good man, who neither would nor could ever murder anyone. That much she knows. That's not to say he probably hasn't been stupid, but stupidity and murder are quite different things. Right now, her focus has to be on getting her husband out on bail.

Putting together enough collateral for Stephen's bail takes some time, but she manages it. She calls her mom and Michelle willingly puts up the majority of the needed cash. She's always been a big believer in liquidity. Thank God for that and for online banking andstocks.

Janet's hands shake as she drives to the station. Shestill manages to remain composed on the outside. A woman with her wits about her. Except for the hands. On the inside, a mass of mounting monumental hysteria and outrage builds. They were supposed to be in the car together, heading to dinner on their way to the wine country right now. That's not going to happen. Janet immediately puts a lid on any more thoughts aboutthe romantic weekend that will never be. Her husband has been arrested formurder.

When she arrives at the station, Terry is waiting for her. "Where is he? How bad is it?" she asks him pleadingly.

"Look, we know he didn't kill anyone, so it will get straightened out." Terry takes her hand, "Just…well, it may get a little rough for a few days, so try to keep in mind the Stephen we know and love. Okay?"

Janet knows what he's asking of her, but she just stares at Terry, as a barrage of conflicting emotion flows through her. Terry directs her down the hall, "Come on."

They go through the necessary procedures and Janet produces the bond and turns it over. Stephen is brought out and looks like hell. The terror and dread from within has twisted his expression. She can't look at him. Terry tries to be overly accommodating to the two of them and continually fidgets and talks about some upcoming procedural steps as they make their way out of the station. Janet can see that he is uncomfortable around her and Stephen. Always the good and loyal friend. With Terry's history with women, he would be the more likely candidate in this scenario, not Stephen. Janet remembers a woman Terry dated years ago, Goldie something, who never let him pick her up for a date. She always insisted on meeting him at work or the place they were going that night. Janet only met her once at a dinner and was immediately struck by the way Goldie avoided eye contact and kept looking around the restaurant. Goldie claimed she worked on most weekends and conveniently excused herself from most Saturday night dates. After nearly two months, Terry insisted that the relationship seemed perfectly normal to him. Until the day Goldie's husband, an ex–football player, followed her to one of their dinners, waited until Terry showed up and began beating him until other patrons managed to pull the man off of a bleeding and battered Terry. Terry walked away with bruises and a broken nose and immediately shredded Goldie's number. That was just a year after Elise left him. Terry always said that the only reason he has a shred of belief in any kind of marriage is because of Janet and Stephen. That thought makes Janet nauseous. The only thing that would make her feel better would be knowing that this is all some sick joke or a nightmare that must come to an end. She wonders what's going through Stephen's mind right now and how he thinks she should respond to this predicament.

Terry walks with them to the parking lot and hesitantly says his goodbyes. Janet and Stephen continue their silence as they walk to her car. She can feel his eyes on her. She slides into the driver's side and as soon as he's in, she backs out of the parking space. She drives slowly at first then begins speeding as they move away from the police station. The tension in the air grows thicker with each passing second. As does the speed of the car. Stephen clears his throat and Janet instinctively looks over at him with such ire in her eyes that he barely manages to swallow any sound he's thinking of making. She tries to find a way to keep her anger from escalating. She envisions a calm, rational conversation with Stephen, where he explains in detail all the events and nuances that have led up to this clearly unforeseen and erroneous outcome. A conversation where his explanation and the fact that he's kept things from her somehow make sense and they come to a mutual understanding and vision of how to get through this. Despite her desire for this vision, her body screams a different tale, as does Stephen's presence. The look on his face. The fear in his eyes.

Finally, Stephen speaks cautiously and softly, "Thanks for handling the bail. I know..."

Suddenly and without warning, Janet violently slams on the brakes, bringing the car to a dead stop in the middle of the road on a quiet residential street.

"What are you doing?!" Stephen exclaims.

"What am I doing?! You want to know what I'm doing? Because that is clearly the question of the day, isn't it?" Her eyes flare, thick with sarcasm, "Oh yeah, it's all about what *I'm* doing, what *I've* been doing. Whereas you. Well, you, you just get to be you. No questions asked. Let's just explain this all away as some fluke of bizarre coincidental events. Or better yet, a case of mistaken identity."

"Janet, I..."

"What do you think? You think I'm an idiot? That I believe you were arrested for the murder of a woman you say you were a passing acquaintance with?" She stares at him, but he can't hold her gaze. "Normally I would believe that. I would believe it if I didn't know that you were hiding something from me even while you were away on that trial. You started acting strange over the phone. I could feel something was wrong."

Stephen doesn't speak and this infuriates her even more. She puts the car in park, gets out and slams the door.

"Janet!" Stephen fumbles his way out of his seat belt and goes after her. "Janet, wait!"

With each angry step Janet takes, tears fill her eyes. "You fucked her! Just admit it! You brought this down on yourself and on us."

Stephen catches up with her and grabs her arm. She yanks it free with a fury and turns to face him.

"I'm sorry. I'm so sorry," he offers.

"You owe me the truth. Take responsibility for yourself. You fucked her, didn't you? Then you lied to me. Say it!" She looks at his completely distraught and pain– filled face. This is the moment she needs in order to be sure. Now she knows. He slept with someone else and there is no going back. Her tears begin to flow.

"I know I screwed up…"

"Say it!!"

"Okay yes. I fucked her. But I didn't kill anybody!" Stephen grasps at whatever straws he can to find his way back to some sense of normalcy.

A neighborhood patrol pulls up behind their car. They both see it, but Janet ignores the security guy and walks away from Stephen toward a small wall on the perimeter of someone's property. Stephen returns to move the car and park it properly.

Janet's goal is to get a handle on her hyperventilating and the flood of tears that have now found a life and abundance she didn't know possible. Her husband cheated on her. Her Stephen. A responsible, loving man devoted to his family. Or so it seemed. We can't really know the inner regions of another – the deepest thoughts of even those closest to us. Sometimes we don't even know our own deepest thoughts until something triggers them to surface. She doesn't know Stephen's fantasies. That was the one thing they never talked about. She figured he would tell her if he needed something else, something different in their sex life. Maybe that was naïve. She should have asked more often.

Could she have been so blind to think their relationship was solid? It felt solid. She wracks her brain for any red flags or moments that she brushed over, but nothing comes to mind. Some things are not meant to be understood. How can you possibly understand another person whose inner reality must be so different from your own, even with all the same external factors? They share the same life – the same house, the same kids, the same days, vacations, all of it – or so she thought. Then one day it all shatters. Caused by the one person she would have bet her life on could never willingly shatter it. But he did. What does he think of their life? How does he see her? Had she changed and become dull? If he were so unhappy, why didn't he tell her? No, damn it! He wasn't unhappy and she knows it. They had a good life, a great family, and their relationship was solid, he's just....

Stephen walks up to Janet and sits next to her. She simultaneously wants to kill him and to never let him go. What a strange feeling – that fine line that stretches between love and hate. She desperately wants all this pain to go away. Instead, Stephen begins talking, "At first, I just helped her get rid of this guy who was hassling her. Then we started talking..." Janet feels transported to a place where pain knows no bounds. She hears his voice. At first the sound hits her like a strange reverberation heading toward her. Slowly she begins to recognize the words leaving his lips and feels every carefully crafted word as it rips at her, piece by piece, until she wonders if anything will remain.

"I felt like I was a different person. Almost as if I was more curious than anything. Curious to see if I could do this. Then once it happened and I woke up and realized what I had done, I couldn't fit it into my life, our life. It's as if it happened somewhere else to someone else. I know it sounds crazy, but we were trapped, and it didn't feel like my life. None of it." Stephen looks at Janet's ashen face as she stares at the pavement. "Janet. Please look at me. It didn't mean anything on any level. I swear. Please. Look at me."

She can't look at him. Instead, she manages "So, you slept with her just once?"

Silence. The fury behind her eyes begins to burn again. This time she looks at him. Straight in the eyes. But he looks away. "Wow," she says, "That's some kind of story if you were not yourself and not in your life and curious more than once and over and over again. I guess when you say you woke up and realized what you had done, you mean woke up after weeks of being asleep and in a stupor of fucking this woman over and over again, right?!" She begins to shake and more tears flow. How can there be any more liquid in there? Janet huddles into a ball and screams into her hands.

"No. I don't know how it happened and I don't really understand why. I just…" Stephen reaches out to Janet. She slaps his hand away.

"Don't touch me! Don't you dare touch me." She stands up and storms back toward the car. He quickly follows.

Getting into the car, Stephen tries again, "Janet, please, we've..."

"Shut up! Stephen don't say another word. Not now. I beg of you. I can't take another word. Just shut up."

They drive home in silence. Her nerves are shot. Janet needs a break from the pain. She resolves to take that edible gummy that her girlfriend, Carol, left in the guest room medicine cabinet when she came for a visit. Carol wanted Janet to try it, but Janet explained that she didn't need it. Carol left it there, in case Janet ever wanted to see what it was like. Now she wants whatever might help calm her. Maybe it will help her sleep. She has to sleep. A long, long sleep, away from all this. Away from Stephen.

* * *

The house is dark when they arrive. She pulls the car into the garage and quickly gets out and retreats inside. She grabs the gummy from the guest room and pops it in her mouth. Taking action, focusing on one step at a time, no matter how small, soothes her. She makes her way upstairs to the bedroom. Stephen is already there.

Janet takes one look at him and says, "Get out."

He freezes. "Okay. I'll sleep in the guestroom," he manages. Then he slowly approaches her. "I will do anything to make things right between us again. I can't bear the thought of losing you."

She can't believe it. He's like a dog with a bone, wanting her to buy into his bullshit. She needs some space. "You were just arrested for murder. I found out you cheated on me, and you think for one minute that you can just wave a magic wand and things will be right between us. That ship has sailed Stephen. You made sure of it." She grabs her head as it starts to throb. She sees the suitcase she packed for their trip still partially open on the chair. She walks over to it and flips the top all the way open. The beautiful grey and blue silk camisole stares up at her. Tears burst forth, but she doesn't make a sound. She picks up the camisole, fingering the satiny fine fabric. Slowly she says, "You went to her house that night because you wanted to be with her again, didn't you?"

"No."

"You left me and your family late at night to go fuck her, didn't you?!" As the words come out of her mouth, she begins ripping the camisole.

"NO!!" His voice booms, surprising both of them in its volume. "I swear that's not why I went. I told you the truth about that. I was pissed. I felt like I'd been used, and I just wanted answers."

Janet shakes her head as she violently rips the satin and lace in half. Stephen grabs her arms, but she fights him. "Let go of me!" she spits at him and flings free of his grasp. Her face is wet with tears and wild with frenzy as the venomous words escape, "I don't believe you."

The torn garment hangs from her hands. He looks at it and his expression reflects a man standing in quicksand. "I have no reason to lie now," Stephen says emphatically. He looks Janet squarely in the face. "I did not go there to sleep with her. You've got to believe that. If you believe anything, that is the thing to believe. I swear that's not why I went. That's the truth."

"God, Stephen. You just couldn't let it go." She throws the fabric into the room and topples the rest of the suitcase to the floor. Her head throbs more fiercely.

"The woman is dead. Something strange is going on." Stephen's adrenaline won't let up and he's frantic. "Having an affair while we were cooped up for weeks is one thing. A horrible thing that I'm sick about and if it's the last thing I do, I will find a way to make us right again, but this is murder. I don't know how I got to this. If you know anything, you know I'm not a killer," he implores.

He is not a killer. That is a statement she believes. She stands still, closes her eyes and tries to get the throbbing to stop. She remains quiet.

He continues, "All I keep thinking is that I've been set up. The woman whose body they found is not the same woman who was on the jury." Janet opens her eyes and looks suspiciously at her husband. Stephen sees the nearly imperceptible shake of her head and explains, "I know it sounds crazy, but hear me out. The woman on the jury had the same hair and looked similar, but it wasn't her. I told Terry. He said he checked into it and he seems to think I'm wrong, but he's going to poke around some more because I'm getting more and more sure that it wasn't her. I've seen all the photos and that's not her. I know it's not."

"And of course, you would know better than anyone." The bitter words hit him hard. Janet moves past him toward the bathroom. The drug will kick in soon.

Stephen feels marooned, yet he keeps paddling. "I know I've hurt you, and I know I can't erase it. I'm not sure I still have the right to ask, but I need you, Janet. I always have."

She shuts the door between them, walks to the sink and looks in the mirror. A stranger stares back at her. Black smudges streak her wet face. Her hair sticks out in random directions and her eyes are puffy, creating slits where her eyes should be. Very desirable, she thinks sarcastically. Very sexy. *Oh yes, here's the little wife looking like the Tazmanian devil while the glorified mistress is immortalized in youthful death.* She begins to laugh, wondering if this is the way to insanity.

* * *

Stephen lies in the dark on the bed in the guest room. He's never spent much time in this room. They had few guests over the years, but Terry stays in this room on an occasional weekend when they stay up late, and he's had too much to drink. Stephen has never not slept in the same bed with Janet if they were in the same city and especially under the same roof. Her face tonight… In her eyes he saw hurt beyond his wildest imagination. And he was the cause. A reality he refuses to allow in tonight, because if he did, he would cease to function. The way she looked at him and the agony and rage on her face play in his mind over and over again. From here, he can feel her anguish wafting from the master bedroom, their room, down the hall and through the walls and into every fiber of his being. It's palpable through the air and ingrains itself into his cells. He is no longer welcome in his own bed. Denial proves useless. The choices he made, and his actions brought this pain into their lives. His self–hatred grows. How could he alone destroy the peace and happiness of those he loves the most? Be that kind of person? And for what?

The horror of Eileen's death still feels unreal. Images from that night flow through his thoughts – the shoe, the blood, the rooms. Images of her lying on the bathroom floor repeatedly flash in his memory. Something about her... Stephen hadn't wanted to relive that night, but now he needs to. Thinking back on that image – the way her hips were twisted and her skirt... wait. Her hips. They were larger. Too large. Even more proof that the woman he found isn't Eileen, not his Eileen anyway. In his gut he knows it. Not that he can make sense of it or prove it, but he knows that the woman in the photos and the body in that bathroom is not the same woman he was with. He's certain.

In the past, when he found himself in difficult situations, he procured comfort in the fact that he had Janet by his side and on his side. She had the ability to help him understand himself in ways he can't always arrive at alone and they had a habit of brainstorming together and coming up with solutions. Turning to her now is not an option. Acting on an impulse that he thought would remain buried for the rest of his life has instead ripped his world to shreds – in an unimaginable way. Stephen finds himself in territory so foreign and invasive and succumbs to a terror he has never known. He and Janet won't be leaving for the vineyards. They won't be having romantic evenings and planning his break from the firm. Shame fills him as he considers what she must think of him. How will he ever be able to repair this damage? He will spend his life trying. Of this he has no doubt. First, he needs to find a way out of this predicament and to keep his family from being touched by it as much as possible. The thought of Mark and Emily finding out about his arrest hits him between the eyes and is too much to add to his already tortured thoughts. That will come tomorrow.

Their lives are now consumed with straightening out a false accusation of murder and keeping him from going to prison. Prison. Prison is something they only see or hear of on television and in the news. Prison and the people who go to prison exist apart from the world he knows or has ever known. The closest he's ever gotten to a criminal was through Terry and his work and that was only through stories told. Now the idea of prison enters his life and thinking about the possibility paralyzes him. Could he really be prosecuted for this? Stephen stares at the ceiling as the terror increases. The panic takes over his body. He has to find a way to escape, yet no hope of escape exists. Stephen gets up and begins writing down notes. It's going to be a long night.

28

Saturday evening. Janet sits in the rocker on the back porch, a glass of wine in hand, looking out at the changing light. Stephen left this morning, and she spent the day avoiding phone calls, thinking and putting ice packs on her face in between crying bouts. She texted Michelle not to worry and to please keep the kids until Monday after school. She would talk to her then. Her mother didn't press her. That's the one good thing about having a parent who wants to avoid discomfort and confrontation at all costs.

She hears Stephen return. She feels calm. That's a lie. A wrong word or the slightest disturbance can blow the lid off that calm in a second. Staring out at the trees, the flowers, the grass and at an occasional fly, caters to her precarious state of numbness, which to the untrained eye masquerades as composure. Torn from the inside out until nothing but a quiet, sharp, yet constant despair fills the spaces that have been blown apart. How do you still the rage? The pain of being so personally violated? Betrayal, like a sharp blade, pierces the body, slowly, inexplicably and without warning or compassion. The high helped throughout the night, then it wore off and she was fully awake. She spent most of the day in bed. Thinking. Crying. Thinking some more. That's the worst part. The thinking. The imagining of his hands all over that woman. His lips devouring her in the way reserved only for her. No longer. She doesn't have the luxury of wallowing in self–pity or storming off to Bermuda for reflection and recovery because Emily and Mark deserve better than a basket case for a mother. Not that she doesn't feel like one. She's only required not to show it or to come unglued.

She hears his footsteps echo through the front room, then upstairs, checking to see if she fled or if she remained. He doesn't call out for her. He probably thinks she's left. Good. Let him think that for a while. She's glad her father is not around to see this. He's been dead almost ten years now.

From the time she graduated high school on, Janet believed she could have a family, a loving husband, and a fulfilling career, all in one life. And she has. Stephen always encouraged her. She never doubted that he's the right man for her. She respected and admired his willingness to evaluate himself under even the most ego shattering circumstances. Would he have eventually told her about the affair if he hadn't been caught? Even amidst the grandest notion of always being honest with each other, she doubts his honesty would extend this far. In a situation like this, a far more primal element kicks in – self– preservation. He probably told himself that it would only hurt her. And that is true. And really, if honesty is the standard she insists upon, she would rather not know. She would have been okay with it going away into the dark depths we don't know about each other and that stay on the outskirts of a life together. She wonders if that makes her a hypocrite.

Stephen steps out onto the back porch holding a drink. "Oh, hi. I didn't know if you were here."

"I'm here."

He looks at Janet, not knowing what to do. The awkwardness of the moment strikes her as absurd after more than two decades of familiarity. Stephen tentatively sits down in the chair to the side of the rocker and looks down. "I know I may not deserve the time of day from you right now, but I just want you to know how truly sorry I am." Something catches in his throat, and he swallows hard. "I don't know what to say to you except that I'm so sorry and I'll do whatever you want me to do."

Janet hears him but continues to look out into the yard. A long silence ensues. Finally, she says, "All this came at me at once. First, your finding a dead body, then I didn't even get to catch a breath between finding out you cheated on me and were arrested for murder. So, I get to be furious and disgusted with you and..."

"I know. I'm so sorr..."

"Stop. Just don't say anything." Janet shifts in her seat and pushes the rocker into a gentle motion. "The murder thing, well...I know you didn't kill anyone. I've thought about this, and I will help you in getting this charge cleared."

Stephen immediately reaches for her, "Janet, th…"

She slaps him away. "Don't, Stephen. Don't touch me. I mean it. We have Emily and Mark to think about and they come first right now. I could say look what you've done to me or what you've done to the children. But nothing's been done to them until and unless we do it and we can choose many ways to go with this. I will not be the hysterical woman here and make things worse. I choose to have control over myself and make the best choices for our kids. That is our responsibility." Her eyes pierce him as she says this. She continues, "Yes you cheated on me, betrayed me, kicked me in the gut, cut out my heart. All of the above. And that I will deal with in my own way, in my own time. I take responsibility for my life and my choices and I'm a big girl so I will deal with this. I will not use our children to do the guilt manipulating thing. That would be the easy way to go and the most harmful…to them."

Stephen opens his mouth to speak, but Janet stops him. "Don't say anything. I don't want to hear anything from you right now. One of the things we've always had between us is honesty and that is something, no matter how hard the situation, we assured each other in the very beginning we would not abandon. Remember? Even if we wanted to go our separate ways, even if we came by some fetish we had to explore, we would first tell the other person so that no one would ever get blindsided, because we had respect and love for each other. I want to ask you something, but I don't want you to answer. I just want you to think about it. These past couple of months and now, who are you? This…" she gestures indicating him "...is not the man I know. A man who lies to those he professes to love. A man who betrays his vows and secretly plans things. Did you wake up one day and say, hey I think this could be good 'cause I'm bored? The only thing that really matters now is, is this who you want to be? That's really the only question here. For all of us. What matters now Stephen is what you do from here on out."

Janet stops the rocker and stands up. "I'm going upstairs. Maybe in the morning we can talk about Mark and Emily. Mom will keep them until Monday afternoon." She turns to leave, then looks back at Stephen and says, "You made me a promise." With that she leaves Stephen alone on the deck.

He looks out into the darkness. Janet will stick by him through this ugly mess. God, he loves her. She is the most courageous person he knows. Mark and Emily are the luckiest kids alive to have her as their mother. She is right and he can't let them down. This is about him. His choices and ultimately their effects on others. Who does he want to be? As a man, as a role model for his children. She's right about the promise they made to each other that no matter how painful, they would share their truth if it impacted the other person and the relationship.

They even made a pact that when they reached forty that if either one wanted to stray, they would each be given one hall pass and during that time they would have a mini separation, believing that afterward they would come together stronger. He had forgotten about that, or maybe he just wanted to forget so he wouldn't have to face it – face himself. They were young, but as a result of that openness their relationship grew stronger over the years, until recently. He knows who he is and who he wants his children to know him to be. He has to reclaim himself. He cannot fail them.

29

"The woman's family and friends all confirm that she was on jury duty. All the records indicate the same thing. It's virtually impossible for it not to have been her," Terry says in exasperation, running his fingers through his hair.

Terry and Stephen sit in a diner having an early breakfast at Stephen's insistence. "It wasn't her!" Stephen states emphatically. "I don't know how else to say it." He's been going over every detail from his first encounter with Eileen up to the night at her house. "You're the only person I can tell this to, but her body was not the same as that woman in the bathroom. Come on, man, you know when you know. She had these lean, small hips. But the dead woman, her hips were too big. And the skin. In the pictures, it looks like Eileen had pale skin, but I slept with a woman with the most remarkably silky olive skin."

Only a few patrons inhabit the diner at this hour on a Monday morning and the waitress keeps looking over at them.

"Okay. Let's say you're right and it wasn't her. Who the fuck would it be?" Terry asks.

"I went over everything last night, and during the trial she wanted the Senator to get off. She made sense and some good arguments. So good that I thought she was right. At least right enough for her to cling to her not guilty position. She kept saying how there wasn't enough proof for a conviction. How the evidence against him could have been planted. Her argument was solid. She based it not on the idea that he was innocent, but because there was enough doubt surrounding his guilt. Not once did she even come close to changing her mind. I thought she had a point. But now I wonder if I missed something." He sighs, "if I were played."

"Sounds like quite the deliberations. A bit like Twelve Angry Men. You were going to vote guilty, weren't you?" Terry finishes the last of his coffee and motions for a refill. Stephen just stares at him.

"Wow," Terry says. "*Were* you played?"

Stephen recoils as if being struck. "Look, I still believe that if I hadn't voted not guilty, she would have stuck to her vote. So, no. The result would have been the same."

"If that's true, then even more reason why this different woman notion doesn't hold much water."

"I'm missing something." Stephen puts some money on the table, preparing to leave, "Can you get me a copy of the trial transcript?"

Terry promises him the transcript by the afternoon.

"I'll pick it up after work," Stephen tells him. Work. The work he should be doing on the Tower deal they all just celebrated. The deal that he worked his ass off to make happen and would lead him into the partnership. *Would* have led him there. It all seems like a distant memory. He knows that at least one of the partners has seen or read the news over the weekend and they're bound to know he'd been arrested. John Graeber left a message on his cell, requesting to meet this morning, but not until ten. He dreads going in there. By the end of the day, everyone will know. How will they handle him? Fire him? Would that be legal, since a person is innocent until proven guilty? Chances are he'll keep his job in some way or another. Unless John thinks he's capable of murder. If not murder, then in any case of something stupid that landed him in this predicament, which is the case. No denying that. Regardless of what happens, he has a responsibility to the Tower project to at least make sure he does everything he can to ensure it gets off to a good start. That's why he's coming in early. To get as much done and organized as possible before his meeting with John.

Stephen only has an hour to himself before the first of his co–workers arrive. As uncomfortable the thought of facing his colleagues is, it's nothing compared to his family. Usually, people wave or smile at him through the glass panes of his office as they go by, but this time, nearly everyone passes with averted eyes, head down or staring at their coffee. Anything else but him. Susan usually pops her head in with a "Good morning. Can I get you anything?" but today, she promptly goes to her desk and sits. How would he behave if one of his colleagues fell into to his situation? Maybe he, too, wouldn't know how to behave and would choose to distance himself.

The question makes him realize that he isn't that close to anyone at the firm. No social ties formed over the years, other than functions somehow linked to business – a building unveiling, a client reception, a holiday networking cocktail party. Janet only knows two of the partners and a handful of the others and only superficially. Even after all these years there are no close bonds. Early on he had visions of working in a company with people he could call friends with real camaraderie that extended from their work into their personal lives. Graeber, Fike and Simms do have a high turnover rate, but maybe he is also partly to blame. Some of the others seem to have much closer ties. Larry and Neal play racquetball every Friday. And he knows that Elliot's wife is in the same book club with the partners' wives.

Nearly ten o'clock. He leaves his office and heads down the hall. John motions for Stephen to enter. "Stephen, how are you holding up?"

"Fine. Just fine." And the lies keep rolling out.

"Listen, we heard about the arrest. I had breakfast with Alan and Larry this morning and we just can't even imagine what you must be going through, and we'd like to help."

"Oh? Listen, John, it's a crazy mistake. I can't even believe I have to deal with it. I…"

"Of course, of course. No need to say anything more. We know you have a wife and kids, and you need to take care of your situation. How is Janet doing?"

"She's fine."

"Well, good. I'm sure it'll all work out. In the meantime, we think you shouldn't have to worry about work here."

"You're firing me." Stephen states it as an expected fact.

"No, no. Not at all. We're giving you a sabbatical of sorts, so you can focus on yourself and your family."

Sabbaticals are voluntary and usually for something positive and life enhancing, not for digging your ass out of a tar pit. Stephen replies, "John, I don't need a sabbatical. I'm the lead on the K Tower and they requested that I guide the project. I assure you I will not drop the ball."

"We've already spoken to Craig and Bernie, and they understand and think it's best if we all support you in taking care of your situation."

They sure didn't waste any time getting him out of the way. His instincts were right. It's in the worst of times you find out who your real friends and supporters are. At least he can turn over his plans, notes, budgets and schedules all in order. Stephen and John exchange a few more pleasantries, pretending that Stephen's world isn't on the edge of an abyss.

Everything around him begins to blur. It's as if he's watching and moving among his surroundings through a hazy film that has been slowed down just enough to not seem natural. Stephen packs a couple of boxes from his office and has them brought down to his car. No one says anything to him about what's happened. Just tense smiles and nods hello and ridiculous small talk. He calls Susan into his office and begins to tell her what's happened and that he'll be taking some time off, but in talking to her he can see that she already knows. John probably called her ahead of time. They're efficient if not compassionate. Before he leaves Graeber, Fike and Simms, he looks around the office. Instinctively he knows his days here are over. Even if all this goes away tomorrow, the stain and the rift can't be erased. Rather than feel sorry by the loss, he feels slightly lighter. The decision has been made for him.

He calls Janet. No answer. He leaves her a voicemail, "Hi, it's me. I got called into a meeting with John. They're giving me a sabbatical. I'll be home by the time you and the kids get there. We can all talk then. If you want to go over what I should say to the kids, give me a call, otherwise…well I know this is on me and I don't want you to have to feel...well, I just want to do whatever I can. I will tell them. Okay. Lo…Bye."

* * *

The door from the garage opens and Mark is the first one in the house. At first sight of his father, Mark runs to Stephen, hugging him hard. Emily follows with more caution. Janet stands behind Emily.

"Did you go to jail?" Mark asks.

"No, pal. I didn't. Come on, let's sit down and I'll explain what's going on." He gives Emily a hug, but she stiffens. Janet nudges Emily toward the family room. They all sit down and promptly stare at Stephen.

"David said his dad said that you killed somebody. Did you, dad?" Mark begins.

"No. I absolutely did not. I did find the body though."

"What?" Emily grimaces. "Mom, did you know?"

"Yes, honey, I did. And your dad is right. He did notkill anyone. Those are just vicious rumors and those kids…" She stops herself. "You can't listen to rumors."

After a half hour of explanation and question and answer, Stephen feels like he did well. Both Mark and Emily are now included in what's going on and hopeful that this mistake will get straightened out soon. Janet doesn't let on that she's upset about anything other than worry over Stephen's arrest and the task that lies ahead. Stephen decides to tell her about the firm after the kids are in bed.

PART 2

"The man who moves a mountain begins by carrying away small stones."

Confucius

30

"Come on, grandma, I can't be late!" Mark yells.

"I'll be right there," Michelle answers as she looks over at Emily putting on her shoes. "Are you ready, dear?"

"I'm coming. Go ahead." Emily's frustration is unrestrained these days. Her adolescence has ramped up since Stephen's arrest and her dour mood hasn't let up for weeks.

Janet looks over at her daughter, "Do you have the permission form?"

"I got it. Bye." And she's up and out the door.

Janet pours herself another cup of coffee and sits down at the kitchen table. She sees Stephen in his workshop. There's a blustery wind outside. A few clouds. The backyard is mostly well tended and has some leaves flying about, but it's starting to brown with winter coming. Since the DA is pursuing the case against Stephen, Stephen moved into his workshop. He sleeps on the couch, then spends his days frantically researching and doing everything he can to assist with his own defense. They decided to have Michelle move into the guest room so she can always be on hand for the kids and act as a buffer, helping to diffuse the tension between Stephen and Janet.

Janet has known this man eighteen years, but can we ever really know someone?

How many stories do you hear of the man who had an entire other family and his first wife and kids didn't suspect a thing? Is it possible? To not suspect a thing, if a thing is happening? Is it possible to be so blind? So completely wrong? They say love is blind. Young love and new love, sure. But eighteen years blind? 'Only if you let it, dear.' 'Only if you choose to be blind.' Michelle used to say that the married people who were blind sided had a reason to not want to look or to see. Did Janet have a reason to not want to see? Was the idea of preserving her family and this life reason enough? The idea of Stephen being unfaithful to her is a shock. But it's not the kind of shock that rips out the core of everything you believe about mankind and people. Fundamentally, she believes that any marriage is susceptible to an affair under the right circumstances.

Granted, she didn't think theirs had reached the right circumstances and she was wrong. But murder? Is it possible? Could he have done it? Is she deluding herself? Maybe accidentally? Maybe he did see Eileen that night and they talked. Maybe she threatened to tell Janet about the affair, and he panicked. Maybe…but it was a gun. She has never heard Stephen talk about ever shooting a gun. He abhors guns. He certainly doesn't own one – *does he?*

Nothing about the man she married hints at his being capable of such a violent act. Quite the opposite. She always believed in her ability to intuitively know. To sit with herself. To meditate and allow those instincts to come forward, no matter how unpleasant. She followed that knowing all her life and it served her well. She had avoided some minefields. Like the time in high school when her friend Betts tried to convince Janet to come along to this guy Robbie's house after school for a "mellow" party and some beer. She had a bad feeling about Robbie and refused to go. That afternoon, an ambulance was called to that address and one of their mutual girlfriends, Olivia, was taken away after a bad reaction to drugs that were slipped into her drink. An early version of a rufi. Her intuition had not let her down.

Right after Stephen's arrest, Janet landed the Winston job for the museum event – the largest account of her career. What should have been an incredible celebration never happened due to the circumstances. She felt compelled to do something to mark the occasion, if only for Kathy, whom she counted on more than ever now. To make it special, she took Kathy to an extravagant lunch, but she could barely remain present, and Kathy kept looking at her with large, puppy dog eyes. Janet tried to focus on the Winston job and bounce around ideas, but she sounded stilted, even to herself.

During the ritual of perusing the menu Kathy graciously said all she felt like was a salad, so they cut it short and went back to the office where Janet buried herself in work. All Kathy has ever said about Stephen's arrest is, "I can't imagine what you're going through. But I want you to know that if you ever want to talk about it, I'm here. I'm also here one hundred percent on the job." Janet has chosen not to discuss anything about Stephen's predicament and Kathy has remained respectful of that. The Winston account has kept Janet preoccupied and is helping keep her mind off what lies ahead. As much as anything can. Kathy and she have managed to plan and coordinate all the elements for a three–hundred–person gala. Now they must flawlessly execute it. The Museum event is tomorrow night, so until then Janet will be immersed into making sure it goes off without a hitch. She can't think about what comes after that.

31

Stephen and Terry have been meeting for breakfast three times a week at the same diner. They now have "their" booth, and the waitress has warmed to them.

"There's one thing that bothered me then and I've re–read that part of the transcript and it still bothers me. It was the stains in the Senator's office. The maintenance guy saw the stains the night the body was found. But, when the Senator's office was searched, the stains had been cleaned. The janitor said they looked like they had been sopped up, but I don't think he would have noticed them if they were cleaned like the forensics described later."

"Okay."

"Well, who cleaned them? It wasn't the cleaning guy, and it wasn't the Senator, he wasn't there between finding the body and the police searching his office. So, who cleaned them? I thought it might be the real killer. But now, I'm thinking the Senator had an accomplice."

"The woman?"

"Why not? If I were played, it's possible."

"The only way you could've been played is if she were connected to the Senator in some way. And as you know, we've come up empty on that end. Eileen Harris had no connection to the Senator."

"You've got to believe me that it was a different woman. I'm telling you, I'm sure of this. If you don't go talk to the other jurors. I will." Stephen hasn't had a decent night's sleep since all this began. His already tenuous sleeping habits have now become merely a series of catnaps throughout the night.

Terry sees the determined look on Stephen's face and treads lightly. "Do you have any idea how difficult it would be to switch out a juror or impersonate a juror or set up something like that?"

"But not impossible." Stephen has fire in his eyes as he continues talking, "Our jury was picked on a Friday. We all went home for the weekend after that and that's when the switch could have happened. What if another woman made herself look close enough to the Eileen who was assigned to the jury and then took Eileen's place by the time we all returned on Monday?"

Terry considers this and is skeptical but wants to throw Stephen a bone. "The DA is alleging that your motive in killing Eileen was to cover up your affair. If we can't prove that you had an affair with a different woman, whose name you don't even know, we're sunk. So to put your mind at ease, I'm willing to talk to the other jurors and see if anyone can back you up. You will not get involved or speak to anyone. Got it?" Stephen nods and Terry continues, "If anyone can corroborate that it was a different woman in that jury room then we may have something. But, if not, I've got to spend most of my time building a solid defense. One that makes sense. Right now, this isn't it. If we come up empty, we have to go with another defense. Okay? I mean it. And I need you to get that and let me do my job."

"I'll keep looking into Claxton's background. You'll see it wasn't her."

"Stephen, this isn't something you can keep going with if we come up empty." Terry leans forward and stares intensely at his friend. "The slightest misstep can blow up in our face. This is serious, man. This is murder. No more missteps."

Stephen forcefully sweeps his fork and the sugar off the table. "You don't think I know it's serious!" What he really wants to do is to rip the table from its bolts and throw it through the glass window, but he manages some semblance of self–restraint. The waitress looks over, alarmed, but stays back. "I just blew up my fucking life. I may have lost the only woman I ever loved. I can't even think about how to deal with the kids. They know I'm living in the workshop and we're making up some shit about oh, it's because I can't sleep and need to be able to get up and work and not wake their mother.... blah, blah blah. But they know something's seriously wrong. I'm being accused of murder, and you don't think I know it's serious!"

"I'm sorry. Hey, take it easy. I can't even imagine what you're going through with Janet."

"No, you can't." Stephen takes a few breaths and calms down. He's managed to keep himself focused on making sure he knows every fact on everyone he's come in contact with, on everything he's overheard from when he started on that jury and on every detail of Claxton's trial. This focus helps him maintain some sense of functionality. If he turns his attention to the stakes involved, he will become completely unhinged.

Stephen grips his coffee mug and takes a deep breath.

"Look, I know she must be wanting to take your head off, but she loves you. You two have the real thing and I can't imagine..." Terry stops and just shakes his head.

"You didn't see her face that night we left the station, that first night, after we left you. I crushed her. That look is still there. I thought with time...but it's not going away. I don't know how you come back from that."

* * *

Wanting to do everything and anything he can to help Stephen, as well as put his mind at ease, Terry places calls to the other jurors and sets up meetings with a few to get a read on them and see if any have the slightest inkling of the same suspicion concerning Eileen's identity as Stephen. Charlie Murphy's need to hear himself talk immediately affords Terry his first face–to–face.

Murphy's front room reflects the sloppy manner of the man. The worn, sagging couch looks like its last good day harkens back to the sixties. Beer cans and paper plates strewn haphazardly around the room in front of the giant screen television testify to the man's preoccupation with the tube and the smell of dog makes breathing difficult upon first entrance. Charlie motions for Terry to have a seat, "I just let Elmo out the back."

"I'll just be a minute," Terry informs him.

"Suit yourself. But I'm gettin' me a beer. Want one?"

"No, thank you." Terry remains near the front door, keeping it partially open to let air in.

Charlie lumbers to his kitchen and calls back to Terry, "I don't know what I can tell ya 'bout that woman. Who'd you say you were representin'?" He returns, beer can in hand, and takes a gulp.

"I'm representing Stephen Reeves."

Charlie's demeanor turns cold. "Uh huh."

Terry notices Charlie bristle at the mention of Stephen's name. "Is there a problem?"

"I don't see one. You wanna ask me somethin'?"

"Do you have something against my client?"

"Well. Seein' as the man killed someone."

"That's not a statement of fact, Mr. Murphy. He's under suspicion, yes, but he didn't kill anyone and we're going to prove that." Charlie slurps his beer and stares suspiciously back at Terry. "Is there some other reason why you would think my client capable of something like this?"

"The two of them were all chummy and held us up at the end. They were all 'he could be innocent because of this n' that' but who knows what was really going on?"

"Did you see or overhear anything that..."

Charlie's patience comes to an end. "Look. I know yer just doin' your job, but I got nothin' to say to you. I don't know what they were up to, but I got nothin' to say."

Terry pulls out several photos of Eileen Harris and shows them to Charlie. "Just one more thing Mr. Murphy, please. Is this the woman, Eileen Harris, you were on the jury with?"

"You know it is. Her face was all over the news. Why would you be askin' that stupid question for?"

"Can you please take a really close look at the photos. I know some of these are the pictures the press put up, but here are a couple more. Did she look different when you saw her during the trial?"

Charlie takes one of the photos. "This ain't a very good picture of her. That's all. She was a pretty woman. Prettier than this here picture. But some folks just don't take good pictures."

"In what way prettier?"

"For one. This here picture, she's got no make–up and her eyes are plain. I only ever saw her with her glasses on and I think she had makeup on too, so that'll make a gal prettier." Charlie hands the picture back to Terry and shakes his head. "The cops said it was her, didn't they? So why wouldn't it be her? Yeah, it's her." Charlie opens the front door all the way, clearly indicating that he is done talking. Terry thanks him and leaves.

"The guy really doesn't like you. Any reason I should know about?" Terry relays his recent visit to Stephen over the phone as he drives to meet Melita Colt. Stephen tells him about the incident with Eileen at lunch and how it must have shattered the guy's ego. Terry doesn't like the idea of any of the jurors having a less than favorable impression of Stephen, but this seems harmless enough.

Melita's studio apartment brims with bright colors both in paint and various fabrics that are draped over chairs and tables. She motions for Terry to have a seat on the floral love seat at the foot of her bed while she studies the photo of Eileen Harris he handed her. "I thought it was already for sure that this was her," Melita notes.

"We think it may not have been."

Melita cocks her head suspiciously at Terry. "Would you like some herbal berry tea?" she offers.

"No thanks, but you go ahead."

"No. I'm good." Melita positions herself cross legged on the floor opposite Terry. "You think Stephen is innocent?"

"Yes, I do."

She looks at the photo again. "Hey, I don't know. I didn't spend my time gawking at her, you know. And she sat at the other end of the table most times. Maybe she looked different, but so what? I try and change my looks sometimes. You can really do a lot with makeup and accessories."

"So, she did look different than the woman in these photos?"

"Sure. But I can't tell that she didn't just have a makeover. Women can change their looks a lot. It's probably her."

Exasperated, Terry stands. "Thanks for your time."

While Terry hunts down jurors, Stephen situates himself in a corner of the library with his laptop, near the newspaper archives. He isn't sure how far back he needs to look to get a hit on anything on Claxton or a woman who may have been the Eileen he knew, so in addition to the Internet he checks out old newspaper articles that may not have been digitized. In the media, George Claxton cuts a majestic figure. Prior to joining the Senate, Claxton spent eight years in the House of Representatives, making friends and influencing people. He has an MBA from Wharton and before his political life he held a position with a private equity investment firm, Windsor Jones Capital, where he met and married his boss' daughter, Cynthia Windsor. On society pages they appeared the perfect couple – giving to highly publicized charitable causes, rubbing elbows with high profile titans of industry and politics alike, always caught smiling together and inserting a daughter or two to give a complete family portrait. Contrary to the legacy left in the media, Stephen saw first–hand the effects of that 'perfection' when Cynthia had testified. On the surface, the road to the Senator's seat appears paved with gold, graciousness, and good intentions. But Stephen feels certain that something stinks beneath that veneer. He digs further back into some of the articles regarding Windsor Jones and makes some copies of client lists. His eyes begin to burn. No sleep and no food aren't a good combination.

He asks a clerk to keep an eye on his things as he goes to get some coffee and a sandwich. His thoughts stay focused on Claxton. The Senator's background, his associates, his movements. Stephen searches his brain for a clue, any clue to give him some direction. For the past three years, Claxton served on the Senate Appropriations Committee. This is one of the most powerful committees in the Senate, which decides how the money from the Treasury will be spent. For the past two years, Claxton served as the subcommittee chair. This means that Stephen can find and go through the various spending bills that Claxton championed, but how can he find the man's ties to a random woman whose name he doesn't know?

"Here you go sir." The woman behind the counter hands Stephen his cup and a ham and cheese sandwich.

"Thanks."

Walking away, he notices a poster with a photo of a group of young people that reads "are you on board with us?" *That's it!* Photos. He's got to get his hands on as many photos of the Senator with otherpeople.

* * *

Terry manages to get only three other jurors to meet with him, but none of them will commit to saying that Eileen's identity is possibly in question.

"Sorry man," Terry tells Stephen. "I'll talk to a few more next week, but it's not looking good. So far, the other jurors aren't willing to say that it wasn't her. Although I suspect that there could be some doubt there."

"I told you. They just don't want to get involved. People are cowards. Let's put some pressure on them. There's got to be one who will step up. I think Mike or Ted might."

"I've been mulling this over and over and even if one of them would say they think it wasn't her, it wouldn't be enough for us to build a case on. I'll keep digging and I'll ask for a continuance before we have to commit to our defense. Maybe we can find something else. Did you come up with anything?"

"Nothing yet. I've started going through photos and I've found some areas where I need to keep digging. I'll keep at it. I have a feeling that there's some mold in the Senator's closet, I just don't know where it's coming from yet."

32

The Library of Congress has become a refuge for Stephen. He tries to stay away from the house as much as he can during the day. Michelle is often there and even with time the awkwardness isn't getting any better. In the neighborhood and at Mark and Emily's school, Stephen suspects that not only the teachers, but the parents and students wonder about him now. Did he do it? Is he one of those guys whom you'd never suspect of anything more malevolent than jay walking, then one day... boom! Surprise! He turns out to be the maniacal, serial slasher. That's why he won't pick up the kids from school anymore. He just let's Michelle or Janet handle all of it. It's embarrassing. Not just for him, but for them too.

At home, when everyone is there, their day–to–day life and group conversations revolve around the kids. After Janet pulled off the Winston event, and has no new impending business, due to a lull in the season, she chooses to maintain her schedule of going to work early and returning early every evening. Although she hasn't been able to publicly bask in the success of pulling off the museum gala, the money has given her business some breathing room and her office has become a refuge from the tension at home. She and Stephen attempt to interact casually and to discuss things with the kids about schoolwork and activities and occasionally about where they are respecting Stephen's trial. They still eat dinners together. Michelle does much of the cooking and her presence keeps everyone on their best behavior.

The excruciating part of all this surfaces every time Stephen looks at Janet. With each passing day the chasm between them grows. Their exchanges are matter of fact, efficient and seemingly professional; however, any thread of intimacy has disappeared. That weighted tension from the first couple of weeks catalyzed into a low–grade undercurrent, and if left undisturbed will remain dormant and dominated by the demeanor of two roommates living together and working on solving a mutually unpleasant problem. Michelle runs interference through the tension, but Mark and Emily still feel the undercurrent and have become exceptionally and strangely obedient children at the dinner table. Emily is no less moody, but she retreats to her room as much as she can.

Stephen speculates if his children ever look at him and wonder if he is really a bad man somewhere under the good dad they thought they knew. Both Janet and Michelle keep telling the kids that yes, people are saying mean things, but they aren't true, and they just need some time to prove his innocence.

At his post at the library, Stephen sifts through more articles and selects an array of photos for copying and several for printing from his computer later. He needs to have several blown up in order to really see the people clearly, especially the few where Claxton is with a larger group. Feeling discouraged and with persistent dryness in his eyes, he decides to call it a day and goes to see Terry.

"No, not even Mike or Ted will say that they don't think it was the same Eileen. I'm sorry. I don't know what else to do. We have to go with our first line of defense," Terry explains to Stephen.

"I can't believe this. We have to have more time. I think I may have found something, so I don't think we need them. This could be the break we need. I'm having some photos digitized and blown up. They're too blurry on my printer. We just need a little more time." Stephen paces in front of Terry's desk. He found an old photo in one of the newspaper articles on a small mining company in Claxton's state that was being touted for job creation. There's a group of people in the photo with Claxton and the woman next to him looks familiar, but the picture is black and white, grainy, and too small to be sure.

"We're out of time. The judge won't grant another continuance," Terry tells him. "I tried, but without any concrete reason, she won't give it to us. The prosecution has been pressuring to proceed quickly. I've done what I can. We've got to proceed. Our defense here is your character, your history, the lack of evidence of an affair, no weapon. No motive. We've got nothing else that's got any backing. I'm ready for this. We'll be fine." Terry says the last sentence almost reluctantly. The case the prosecution has been building against Stephen is not a slam–dunk by any stretch, but it has legs and some punch, and this has Terry worried, especially in light of the fact that they now have to rely on a jury.

33

The jury has been picked and on the first day of Stephen's trial, Stephen and Terry meet an hour early in Terry's office.

"Janet's coming?" Asks Terry.

"Yeah. She said she'd meet us in the courtroom after she gets the kids off to school. She wanted to go today instead of Michelle."

"Good. Try to relax," Terry instructs.

Yeah, that'll happen, thinks Stephen.

Relaxing lives in the past. Stephen hasn't had a day of feeling relaxed since the first days of the Claxton trial, when innocence was a concept he embraced. Is any adult ever fully innocent? In an across the board, including the niggling of their subconscious sort of way? He was guilty as hell, just not of murder. Would the jury sense that in him and crucify him? Stephen fidgets and moves his pacing to the other side of Terry's office.

"You're going to have to sit still in court and stop emitting that frantic vibe or else the jury will think you're a nut case and we're not going for an insanity defense. Can you do that?"

Stephen stops. "Fine. Yeah, I know. Can I get some coffee?"

"You can have decaf."

The People v Stephen Reeves trial is in a smaller courtroom than the one for the Claxton trial, but the similarities give

Stephen the creeps. Sitting at the defense table as the accused, knowing your life is about to be dissected publicly, is terrifying. Stephen suddenly feels a camaraderie with drug addicts – he would love something to anesthetize him right now. All he has is the water in front of him. Terry tells him to focus on the area immediately in front of him. That helps. As the jury files in, Stephen's attention is on Terry as he goes over a few initial notes. Then he looks over at the jury box. At first glance at the final, fully seated jury a slight nausea comes over him, but he manages to push it aside and stare at one point, slowly slipping into a comatose state. He remembers Claxton and how his features remained impervious to too much scrutiny from others. He takes his cue from the Senator. Devoe and his second chair sit at the prosecution table conspiratorially mumbling to each other.

All rise as Judge Emily Ramen sits on the bench and Stephen's fear grows. He feels as if he's been squeezed into a funnel and as he looks out into the room, everything appears distant and blurry. He hears Devoe's opening argument as the prosecutor talks about the "mountain" of evidence. Then the hairs on his neck and arms prickle as a sense of *deja vu* engulfs him. Where has he heard this before? He feels overwhelmingly warm. His emotions are a mess. He takes a drink of water. Maybe the Senator was innocent after all. Good for him and his holdout, but that jury was ready to hang him. Can he possibly get out of this?

Terry pats Stephen's arm. "Breathe," he instructs him, then he takes the floor.

Stephen feels completely disconnected from his body as he hears Terry's voice speaking to the room, "…I'd like to take a moment and talk about what's it like to be accused of something you didn't do." *That's right. This I did not do*, Stephen thinks. "Maybe as a child your mom accused you of spilling a soda on the carpet, but it was really your sister, and it was up to you to prove it because she wasn't going to admit it. Or your teacher thought you cheated when in reality you studied like a hawk to get a good grade. Or a friend accused you of telling, when you know you didn't. Whatever it is, it's hard because it's up to you to refute their accusation. Is that fair? Is that how it should work?" *No!*

Stephen feels his heart beating faster. He can almost hear it. The beat louder than the sound of Terry's voice.

34

The prosecution presents their witnesses during the week. Janet instructs Kathy not to take on any new clients unless their events are at least three months out, so that she can be present in the courtroom during Stephen's trial and not have to worry about work. Terry has been adamant about the importance of her visible support of her husband. Having the jury see Janet in the room day after day will have an impact.

Doug and Jennifer Harris, Eileen's parents, an average looking couple in their sixties, wear a trail from the DA's office to the courtroom, determined to get justice for their daughter. Their grief pours into anger and demand. Midweek, as Janet makes her way down the hall to the courtroom, a weary Jennifer Harris exits, head down, to make her way to the restroom. Mrs. Harris glances up and stops as Janet approaches, she looks her right in the eye and shakes her head as she speaks to Janet, "She was my little girl." The words come out strangled through tears.

Startled by the encounter, Janet is overcome with a paralysis – she wants to speak, to comfort, to say anything that might be appropriate, but nothing comes forth. They are each driven by love into this agonizing situation. There is nothing Janet can say to the woman to ease her pain and she knows it, so she chokes down her emotion, gives a nod, and continues.

Throughout the week, Stephen's demeanor is stoic. He can't find an appropriate expression in a situation like this. Part of him feels indignant and righteous due to the injustice of being falsely accused. Another part descends into the distress of being so close to a woman so brutally slain and the depths of a terror so foreign that it creates a physical paralysis of sorts. A third part insists that he find a way to connect and appeal to the people who hold his fate in their hands. But when he thinks about the jurors, he knows the volatility and lack of any real empathy that exists among them, because he's been there. This thought brings forth anger. An anger that must remain hidden, at all costs.

He and Janet rarely carpool to and from court, attempting to minimize their alone time together. However, they strive to keep a sense of family togetherness by having dinner together nearly every night. Friday night is Michelle's bridge night, so take–out is on the menu. Janet insists that her mother not cook at least a few nights a week. Janet wants to make sure that Michelle does not abandon the few things that are important in her own life. She also wants to put on the most normal mommy face for the kids, no matter how much she doesn't feel like deciding about and preparing meals. Listening to people take the stand and talk about her husband and murder has been accumulating an anger inside Janet that she's managed to contain but is finding more and more difficult to keep up.

Stephen arrives with the Thai food and dinner procedures begin. The kids discuss what matters most to them – their friends, sports, and injustices at school. Janet barely touches her food and mechanically responds to Emily's and Mark's questions and comments. Stephen finishes his plate without tasting a thing.

Janet sends the kids upstairs to finish their homework and get ready for bed, then stands and begins clearing the table. Stephen grabs some cartons and follows her. He begins loading the dishwasher. Janet watches him put the utensils in. He never separates the spoons, allowing them to stick together. They don't get clean if they're left stuck together. She's told him over and over again through the years, but he still does it. Janet grabs the spoons out of the dishwasher and holds them up. "Why can't you do this right? You can't put them in like this." She separates them and puts them around the other utensils so they can't 'spoon'. "Like this. You're supposed to do it like this," she says this without looking directly at Stephen as the tears begin to flow. She storms out of the kitchen.

Stephen immediately follows her into the dining room. "I know these past few months have been hell." He grabs Janet's arm to turn her toward him. "As soon as this thing is over, I'll do anything...."

She extracts herself from his grasp. "Don't you get it? I don't think you killed anyone, but when this is over, I don't know where I'll be. Where we'll be. Just leave it at that and let's get through this without adding more crap on top." Janet returns to the kitchen.

"I just..."

"Stephen." Janet grabs a small plate off the counter and throws it on the floor where it shatters at their feet. Stephen jumps but remains silent. She speaks. "Over the last fourteen years, we've been poor, we've moved, we've had problems with our families. Through all that the one thing I have counted on has been your love and your honesty. That's been the constant." More tears spring forth. "That's what has made sense for me in my life with you. No matter what, I was always able to crawl into bed next to you and find sanctuary. You've taken that away from me." She turns away from him and begins putting other items away, leaving the broken plate pieces on the floor. "I don't know how to get that back."

Stephen stands there as a crushing weight descends upon him. He feels helpless in the wake of Janet's tears, so he does the only thing he can think of and crouches down and begins picking up the plate fragments.

35

Terry sits alone at the defense table in a full courtroom tapping his pencil and staring at the clock on the wall. He spoke to Stephen ten minutes ago, who assured him that he was on his way. Terry informs the clerk that his client merely hit a traffic glitch – and prays that this is true. The prosecutor glances over at Terry and raises his eyebrows as he gestures to the defendant's empty chair. Terry's unease mounts.

"All rise," the bailiff begins. Terry stands and stares at the door.

Just as the judge enters, so does Stephen and rushes to his chair. "Sorry," he mutters to Terry as he takes his seat and the trial resumes.

Much to Stephen and Terry's dismay, Charlie Murphy testifies for the prosecution and has nothing favorable to say about Stephen. Throwing out tidbits like, "I knew right off that he was interested in her," and "I hear them carryin' on together in his room."

Despite Terry's objections, damage is done. It had never occurred to Stephen that he and Eileen could've been heard. Their rooms were to the left of the elevators, and everyone else's were to the right. Then he saw the layout of the hotel floor. The wall from Charlie's room abutted the wall to his room, even though they entered from two different directions going around the building. But they were so careful and quiet and…. Stephen can feel the jurors' eyes on him. Is this what Claxton felt like every time they stared at him? Claxton. Somehow all roads lead back to Claxton, he knows it. He wouldn't be here if it weren't for the esteemed Senator.

When court breaks for lunch, Janet leans over to Terry and Stephen, "I'll pick up some sandwiches and bring them to your office."

"Thank you. I…" Stephen begins, but Janet just nods and is off.

Terry gathers his papers and he and Stephen make their way out of the courtroom. "Did you hit massive traffic this morning?" Terry asks.

"Sorry about that. I forgot I had those old pictures blown up. The trial started and…anyway, I swung by to pick them up. Took longer than I thought." Stephen stops and pulls out the envelope from his briefcase. Terry grabs his arm.

"Are you serious? You cannot. I repeat – CANNOT – ever be late again. Unless you are dead or bleeding by the side of the road, you are to be in my office a half hour before court to ensure that this never happens again." Terry is furious and Stephen can see it, so he simply nods in assent to give Terry time to simmer down. Stephen returns the envelope to his briefcase and continues walking with Terry.

Once in his office, Terry seems calmer. He turns to Stephen and offers, "Okay. Let's see the photos."

Stephen pulls out the envelope and sifts through the images, forwarding them one by one to Terry after first taking a cursory look. One black and white photo startles Stephen, "Oh my god."

"What?" Terry asks.

Stephen slams the picture onto Terry's desk, "It's her!"

Terry grabs the image. The image is quite grainy after that much blow up, but the woman among the group of men is recognizable. She has sharp features and short dark hair. Her hand holds her scarf close to her chest and on her wrist dangles an unmistakably unique charm bracelet. A bracelet Stephen is intimately familiar with.

"This is her?" Terry's tone indicates doubt.

"Yes! Don't treat me like I'm one of your slobs who's grasping at bullshit to get a lesser sentence. This is her. She had blond hair and didn't wear much make–up at the trial. She also wore those damn glasses in public, but I've seen her face without them and know it well. And the clincher is that." Stephen points to the bracelet. "Same one she wore and it's not some designer brand you can pick up anywhere. She told me it was custom made especially for her." Stephen's excitement mounts.

He pulls out more papers, including the article with the original photograph and hands it to Terry. "Look. Her name is Sofia Arden. She's not mentioned in the article, only below the photo. This a groundbreaking ceremony for Benjamin Mining in West Virgina. There's Claxton, next to her. This photo establishes her connection to Claxton, doesn't it? Can't we go to the judge with this?"

Terry sits back in his chair and continues reading the article.

"Well?" Stephen presses.

"Unfortunately, this photo only establishes that a Sofia Arden was at a groundbreaking ceremony with the Senator. Does it mention Claxton's role?"

"He backed their bid to mine in his state, even though it was new turf for them."

"It doesn't help us much. First, it still doesn't prove she somehow replaced the real Eileen Harris on that jury or why. What's her connection to the Senator that she would take the risk and do something like that? Right now, all we've got is your word that this is the woman..."

"It is."

"...and that she had met the Senator. You're still the only one who's sure it wasn't Eileen Harris in that jury box. Look, I believe you, but we're dealing with evidence and probability and proof. And we've still got nothing."

"Bullshit! Now, we've got the identity of the woman."

"Okay. But what are we going to do with that? Tons of women know the Senator. So what?"

Stephen's head swims with notions of tracking down Eileen, or rather Sofia, confronting her, dragging her into court and blowing this thing wide open. Before he can say anything, Janet enters with the food. "Hi."

Terry holds up the photo of Sofia, "Your husband just found the woman he claims posed as Eileen Harris on the jury."

Janet puts the sandwiches down and takes the photo from Terry. She stares at the image. Stephen can't bear to watch her face as she studies it, so he begins to distribute the food. Sofia exudes a smoky sexuality even from a grainy blowup and this makes Janet uncomfortable. She puts the photo down. "What does this mean?"

"Nothing yet," Terry says.

"There's a reason she replaced the woman and it's connected to the Senator. We need to talk to the Senator," Stephen says.

"There's an idea. Sure. Let's chat up the Senator and say, hey we know that you're guilty of murder, so you and this woman who we now know you've met in the past, rigged the jury so you'd get off. I can understand why the Senator might go through jury rigging, but why would this woman risk it?" Terry asks.

"Maybe she loves him," Janet offers.

"Who? The senator?" Terry asks. "That's a lot of love. A woman who could manipulate a situation like this doesn't strike me as someone who would take a risk like that merely for love. Maybe there's something bigger involved."

"Like what?" Stephen asked.

"I don't know. Right now, we're just writing fiction. We need to do some serious digging to see if there's anything here."

"We need to find Sofia Arden," Stephen says as he bites into a sandwich.

* * *

After court adjourns for the day, Janet watches an exhausted Stephen walk to the men's room, leaving her with Terry in the hallway. "Terry, be honest. What are his chances in there?"

"I can't answer that, Janet. With a jury, you never know."

"What do your instincts tell you?"

Terry looks down at the floor, then slowly raises his eyes to hers. A worried look spreads over his face, but he attempts a smile. "Today didn't go so well. But we have a long way to go, so let's not get stuck in doom and gloom. We'll find a way. The truth is on our side."

Janet appreciates his attempt at optimism, but she feels disheartened and for the first time since Stephen's arrest a sense of actual terror raps at her psyche. Stephen going to jail is inconceivable in the world she knows or in any world that she can imagine.

Terry looks at Janet. Regardless of the outcome, he wonders if Janet and Stephen's marriage will come out of this intact. He can't imagine a different outcome. "Hey, you know you are the love of his life, don't you?"

Janet shakes her head, "Please Terry, don't go there. He obviously didn't feel that way when he jumped into bed with her."

"I know this may be impossible for you to understand, but I am a thousand percent certain that he didn't..."

"Stop. I've been thinking about this endlessly from a lot of different angles and no matter what – our actions have consequences. Yours do. Mine do. And his do. Some more serious than others and this was as serious as it gets in a marriage. To say 'oh, it was a mistake, a lapse, an aberration, so no problem, you can still stay in the game.' That's not okay, because you can't stay in the game at the same place you were when you squirreled it. You of all people should know this." Janet sees Terry's face darken at this last statement. Terry doesn't know that both she and Stephen know the reason Elise had backed out of marrying Terry. It was because Elise had found someone else. Janet doesn't want to bring that up, but she wants to press her point. "You can't just stay in the game as if nothing happened. Why not, you ask? Because the game as it was being played is over. The game has changed. One of the players changed the game. Do you get it? He changed our game. Now the only thing we can hope for is that we can find a way to somehow create a new game."

Terry's discomfort shows on his face as his mind grasps at all the implications.

He can't pretend not to understand how deep this cuts. Finally, he asks her, "Do you think you can? Create a new game, that is."

"I don't know. But there won't be any game at all if he goes to prison."

* * *

That night, after the kids are in bed, Janet shuts herself up in the bedroom and tries to distract herself with television. The photo of Sofia keeps popping up in her mind. She's beautiful. Much more so than Eileen. This eats at Janet more than she cares to admit. They do look alike, but Sofia exudes something that attracts. Even in a grainy picture. She's sexy. Men are visual creatures and left to their primal instincts they're dogs. If it's sexy and looks good and there's nothing to stop them, they're all over it.

Good relationships and common sense usually stop the smart ones from blindly jumping in. Did he consciously pursue her? Is she that much sexier and more attractive and interesting than Janet? Janet looks at her hands and the skin on her forearms. Small spots of discoloration are beginning to appear. Sofia is younger than she is. Not much, but enough, so she probably doesn't have any spots. Considering this, she realizes that Stephen may be a lot of things, but he isn't that shallow. Then why? Why did he do it? She can understand that being desired by someone new can heighten the senses. Does Sofia do or have something that Janet doesn't? What Sofia doesn't have is the years of experience together. Of memories. Of kids. Of building a good life together filled with so much happiness. She and Stephen managed to keep unfolding freshness in their relationship through the years. Those years peeled away old layers and revealed new ones that grew with time. They grew into something more solid. Until about a year ago. His schedule became intense, their time together lessened, and he started questioning his career and maybe everything. They just had a lapse, and he used that lapse to screw the whole thing up.

Regardless of where she tries to focus her mind, a clenching pain seizes her and tears suddenly gush forth without warning. As her tears flow, Janet grabs a pillow, buries her face in it and screams, over and over again, muffling her voice into the thick down.

36

Tracking down Sofia Arden proves to be a task much like tracking a polar bear in a snowstorm. Her footprint is barely visible on the Internet. Stephen turns his workshop into a war room for his defense. He's turned his nightmares of seeing death into an obsession of finding the truth – the entire and larger truth of what happened and how it happened to him. Now he's not merely trying to prove his innocence in a murder but proving that the Senator's trial was a trap for him and that he's not crazy and can come back from this. Maybe then the nightmares will stop. A large grease board covers one wall, with photos and markings and arrows. Another corkboard tacked with articles, photocopies and documents hangs above the cluttered desk. Laptops, files and papers cover the other surfaces in the room. All this produces some interesting ties between the woman he chose to bed and the illustrious Senator on trial for murder.

Sofia Arden is the stepdaughter of Robert Benjamin, whose father is the founder of Benjamin Mining. Historically they looked and smelled like a family company providing jobs in their states of Alabama, Tennessee and Kentucky. Through their lobbying efforts and Senator Claxton's championing of their cause they acquired a struggling mining outfit in his state. The

Senator pushed a bill through the Appropriations Committee to assist Benjamin Mining's enterprise with various financial appropriations for the sake of community job creation and to prevent additional job loss, which enabled them to create a huge mining enterprise in West Virginia. Claxton ran his campaign on being the guy that would increase jobs in his state and Benjamin Mining seemed a natural fit. Since coal is the primary source of fuel for generating electricity in the United States and has been around since 1890, no one thought it unusual to focus on it for the benefits of retaining and creating more jobs. The Senator gained popularity, using the community job increases as a beacon for his good works. The grumbling about the devastating effects on the environment from mining was still in its early stages of public awareness and those involved in coal mining were doing everything in their power to discredit and debunk the findings.

A light knock at the edge of the open door turns Stephen's attention. Janet stands in the doorway. "Having any luck?" she asks.

The circles around Stephen's eyes appear darker, his weight has dropped over the past few weeks, and she can tell that he's in trouble. He shakes his head. "Not really."

Janet needs to feel useful in helping Stephen and Terry win this. It's Saturday and the kids are both at play dates. *Mark and Emily cannot, will not, grow up with a father in prison for a crime he didn't commit,* she tells herself. Janet realizes that she has to do everything she can on her end, or she won't be able to face her children or live with herself if this goes from bad to worse.

"I made some lunch, if you want to take a break," she says.

During lunch, Stephen fills her in on some of the pieces he's uncovered and takes Janet through the players, however loosely aligned with the Senator, hoping a new insight will surface.

When nothing new comes to mind, Janet notices his somber mood set in.

"Maybe you need a fresh pair of eyes. Let's go over what you've got," Janet offers and leads the way back to the workshop. "Sometimes a piece of information surfaces when you least expect it."

Stephen watches his wife sink into the quagmire of information and his heart goes out to her. He can't imagine a better partner for himself in life. For most people, an affair signals one of two things: one, that there's a problem in the marriage or two, that they've either outgrown their partner or aren't with the right one. Janet and he may have been a bit disconnected because of their workloads last year, but if he really looks at it, it was hardly a problem. Some people he knew were hitched to a spouse that made their lives miserable or held them down in some way or simply provided a life of malaise and a slow death. And for them, an affair was a signal that it was time for them to cut their losses, get out and grab some sliver of happiness before life came to an abrupt halt. Stephen's straying stemmed from something entirely different within himself.

Something he could have, and should have, handled in another fashion. In his case his straying signaled a dissatisfaction with himself that should've been dealt with differently. How he could have completely discarded and forgotten everything he believes in remains a mystery to the saner part within him. In Janet he always felt he had a partner. Someone he could talk to about anything. Someone who always had his back and kept him honest about himself even when it wasn't what he wanted to hear. Someone who made him a better man. He struck the jackpot with Janet and in a nanosecond threw it all away. His father always used to say that a reputation takes years to build, but only a minute to destroy. The bilious feeling surfacing in his stomach every time he thinks about it doesn't help him improve his situation any more than it assists him in knowing what he can possibly say or do when it comes to Janet to ease her pain. He needs to ensure that he will be around to have the chance.

"Okay, so how good a company is Benjamin Mining?" Janet asks, after reading through numerous documents.

"When Claxton went to bat for them, they were no worse than others. Probably a lesser evil, because they were still doing underground mining." Stephen explains that underground mining still does damage, such as bringing waste from deep under the earth to the surface, which often becomes toxic when it comes into contact with air and water. It lowers the water table, changing the flow of groundwater and streams, which causes enormous water waste. When the mines collapse, the land above them starts to sink, causing serious damage to buildings. And, all coal mining produces mine methane, twenty times as powerful as a greenhouse gas that is released during the coal mining process. While this methane is often captured and used as town fuel, industrial fuel, chemical feedstock and vehicle fuel, it's very rare that it all gets used, the rest is released as a dangerous pollutant.

"But then they began strip mining," Janet says, following along.

"Yes. But that's after the Senator's involvement and there's still nothing illegal about it."

"It should be illegal. Every time I look at one of those mountains, or what used to be a mountain, I feel sick."

"I know. But back when this deal went down, almost ten years ago, people weren't seeing the problem."

"Or they didn't want to see," Janet states. She recalls her reading on the subject and how strip mining's impact is even more harsh. "You know how freaked out I got when we took the kids to the National Forest, then drove through the mountains down the parkway and saw what was happening. Even then, people knew that strip mining was destructive. My god, they lopped off entire mountain tops, and all that coal dust and debris pollutes our water, causes flooding and erosion and all kinds of horrible things."

"I'm finding out that the land and water remain contaminated and that it continues to pollute long after the mine shuts down," Stephen adds.

"Look at this." Janet points to an article, "after only five years, their impact on the environment raised alarm bells when Benjamin's strip mining caused soil erosion so big that it took out several homes in a small community. And contrary to the Senator's job creation assertions, everyone knows a large portion of the miners lost their jobs because of strip mining, because it requires a lot less manpower. But there's only this one article on it."

"Probably not big news because it only affected a few families," Stephen says, grimacing.

* * *

Sunday evening Terry arrives at the Reeves' house with pizzas and a bottle of wine. "You are a godsend," Janet greets him at the door and ushers him in. Michelle is out for the evening at her book club.

"How's he doing?" Terry asks.

"He's out back with the kids, getting away from it I think."

"Rob texted and he should be on the plane any minute now," Terry says. To Terry's delight, Stephen's brother insisted on being a character witness and on being on hand to help.

"I think Stephen's embarrassed. Not the way he wants his big brother to see him," Janet suggests.

"It's good for the jury to see him here."

"I know."

As Terry and Janet set out the food in the kitchen, Stephen, Mark and Emily burst through the back door.

"Pizza!!" Mark yells out in delight.

"Aren't *you* the favored one around here," Stephen says to Terry.

"Not that pizza is any substitute for Janet's culinary expertise, but hey, I don't do cooking. I did, however, get a decent bottle of wine."

"Can I eat in the family room?" Emily asks.

"If you take your brother with you so we can talk, okay?" Janet replies.

"Ugh! Fine," Emily consents.

Once the kids are settled and the adults are into the pizza and wine, Stephen asks Terry, "Anything come up on your end?"

"A lawsuit was filed by Clean Earth N Air against Benjamin Mining last year alleging contamination of the water table and toxic poisoning of local citizens from that water."

"What's happening with it?" Stephen asks. "It looks like it's been settled and sealed."

"Is Benjamin still active there?" Janet asks.

"It would seem so."

"Does Sofia work for the company?" Janet continues.

"According to the company records, her mother was Anne Arden. She married Robert Benjamin when Sofia was only five years old. Anne died three years into the marriage and left Sofia her shares of Benjamin Mining."

"So, she's an owner."

"Yes, but it looks like she went away after college. Her stepfather remarried within a year and had two sons of his own. And, of course, now they run the company," Terry tells them.

"What did she do?"

"Sofia graduated from Clark University and worked in Germany for five years before coming back to West Virginia and taking a position with the company. So, it would seem that she did indeed work for Benjamin Mining when the Senator pushed their appropriations through. From little bits here and there, it looks like she tried putting together a lobby for the company, which was failing until she met Claxton. There must have been a bribe or something to lure him. What's weird, is that after they got the green light and the appropriations money, she went dark. She left the company. No records of her – no address, no employment, not even credit card bills."

"She could be using a pseudonym," Janet says.

"But why? Where's the dirt?" Stephen pours himself another glass of wine.

"If there were a bribe and she was the insider, maybe Claxton couldn't afford for anyone to put them together."

"Who cares. They already got their money, and there's no reason to suspect a bribe or anything else." Stephen's frustration is again visible.

"Maybe there is a reason. Right after the appropriations bill, Benjamin Mining started racking up violations of all kinds of health ordinances and someone's been covering it up."

"Claxton," Janet states.

"It would derail him politically if he supported a company that proved to be corrupt, and he kept covering up for them."

"Could be, but this is just speculation," Terry informs them. "We've got no proof and we've got nothing illegal to point to yet. But we did uncover that Sofia did the original deal with Claxton nine years ago. That could tie her to him, but that too is no guarantee, because Claxton can claim he had no direct involvement."

"I hate to stop this train, but after going over and over all the information that we've been gathering, isn't our primary objective with all of it to prove that Eileen Harris didn't serve on that jury?" Janet questions.

"What are you getting at?" Terry inquires.

"Where was the real Eileen Harris, if she wasn't at that trial?" Janet responds.

37

Monday morning, Terry has no choice but to begin presenting his case based on his original defense strategy. His goal is to show and solidify that Stephen is a man of irreproachable character, that he did not have an affair with the victim and therefore had no motive to kill Eileen Harris and that he had no gun or history of ever owning or possessing a gun to do it with. He can honestly maintain that Stephen did not have an affair with Eileen, because he had the affair with Sofia, so there is no perjury.

The only rub is that the existence of Sofia cannot be brought up, but that is a complicated morass, and legally he has no grounds upon which he can go there. His witness call sheet in favor of Stephen's character includes people from Stephen's past and current clients, his employers as well as friends and family, including Rob.

Janet is not in the courtroom at the beginning of the session. She is waiting in her car outside of baggage claim at the Dulles airport for Rob to alight. Neither Stephen nor she have seen Rob in person in years. Skyping him on holidays has made it seem like much less time has gone by, but she's nervous none the less. Despite the distance between the brothers, both literally and figuratively, Janet is surprised but delighted that Rob insisted on being here for the second part of the trial. This is not the best circumstance under which to enjoy a reunion and yet the brothers seem to come together during times of crisis. Rob doesn't know about the affair. No one does except for Terry and herself and, of course, Stephen, and she intends to keep it that way. Terry offered to have Rob stay with him. This will help avoid personal questions about the marriage.

In order to prove that Sofia was really on that jury and Eileen Harris was not, Janet finally broke down and confided in Kathy this morning about the other woman theory because they need as many hands–on deck trying to track down Eileen Harris' movements prior to, during and after the trial. Kathy will spend the day with one of Terry's paralegals looking into airline flights and car rentals.

The passenger door opens, "Hey sis!" a booming voice startles her. Rob's robust, bearded face smiles at her as he tosses a backpack and jacket into the car.

"I didn't see you come out." Janet gets out of the car and gives Rob a hug, then opens the trunk for his large suitcase. "Thank you so much for coming."

"Hey, no question. This is surreal. I'm not sure I understand how this can be happening."

Janet sighs as they get in the car and begin driving. "Me neither," she says, then proceeds to fill him in on the general facts and Stephen's claim about another woman and his being set up and that they can't mention any of this during the trial unless they can get some proof and approach the judge and prosecutor with it on the side.

Terry is pleased with the morning's witnesses and their portrayal of Stephen's character and history. Jason Willis, one of Stephen's fellow architects, isn't effusive, but his accounting of Stephen's dedication, responsibility and good humor can't be ripped apart. Devoe is unable to tarnish any of the morning's testimonies, but not for lack of trying. At eleven forty, the judge calls for recess until one o'clock.

Stephen and Terry head out to meet Janet and Rob for lunch and to prep Rob for his testimony. He is scheduled to be first up in the afternoon.

"Great to see you, Stee!" Rob gets up and hugs his little brother.

"Hey. Thanks for coming, but it really wasn't necessary," Stephen responds. "You look good."

"Wish it were under better circumstances. You look a bit buggered yourself. No surprise, I guess. It's incredible what's going on," Rob observes.

"Yeah," Stephen responds as he looks his brother over. "You're becoming more of a New Zealander every day."

"Not a full–fledged Kiwi yet. But it's tremendous down there. You must come visit. The whole family. You'll love it."

Stephen would love nothing more than to think of that as something he can plan to do, but the prospect of jail looms large. The mood immediately deflates as reality descends on them.

"I've been filling Rob in on the Eileen–Sofia theory," Janet says. Stephen shoots her a look, and she adds, "about Eileen being replaced and setting you up that night." Her look assures Stephen that no mention of the affair was made.

Terry emphasizes to Rob to keep his answers short and to not reveal anything new to what is being asked. The prosecutor will probably want to know about their current relationship and will dig for a clue to any secrets or scandals. Terry has an advantage over another possible attorney in his shoes because he knows his client better than anyone. Terry and Stephen have been privy to each other's secrets more than most.

Devoe will also likely ask about their childhood and any proclivity to get into trouble. "Ha! If only I could ever entice little brother to join in some of our riskier adventures. Nothing to worry about there, mate," Rob points out.

The Lawfully Wetted Bar is not known for its gourmet cuisine. It's a down and dirty place to grab a quick lunch and a staple for afternoon and evening drinks for those in need of getting through the legal system with some of their sanity intact. Janet checks in with Kathy several times during lunch.

"Nothing yet," she informs Terry and Stephen halfway through lunch. "I'm also having them look into bus and rail options." Janet exasperatedly bites into a nacho. "I can't believe I'm eating this crap." The group continues to brainstorm on other possible avenues to pursue in their hunt for Sofia.

* * *

Rob's testimony proceeds without a hiccup. Rob is likable and the jury appears to respond well to his open and good nature after statements like "Stevie was the studier, got good grades and all that. Very responsible. I was a bit more the mischief maker." Rob's sincerity comes through as he says, "I couldn't ask for a better brother." That statement makes Stephen realize that despite the Reeves' family's historic lack of intimate conversation, Rob is someone he can fully trust. He realizes that it's time to break the pattern and reveal himself to his brother. He needs to fill him in on everything. No point in keeping any secrets.

After the last witness of the day, Janet leans over to Rob, "I'll meet you in the hallway. I have to make a call." She heads out and calls Kathy to get a report on any progress they may have made regarding a lead on Eileen. Her face registers a growing disappointment as the others file out of the courtroom. She hangs up and looks at Stephen and Terry, "Nothing on airlines. And they came up empty on car rentals too," she announces in frustration. "She probably used an alias, and we have no way of knowing what that could've been. Damnit!" Janet slams her hand on the wall.

38

"Uncle Rob, wanna see my new plane?" Mark pulls on Rob, after the perfunctory greetings.

"Whoa mate. You have an airplane? You bet."

Emily rolls her eyes as Rob trails upstairs after Mark. "I made it!" Mark exclaims.

Both Stephen and Janet know that it's an important family dinner, because the kids haven't seen their uncle since Mark was three, but both are itching to get back to work to get some answers surrounding Eileen. They assist Michelle in the kitchen while Terry talks on the phone in Stephen's workshop and uses the time to continue going over his case.

Throughout the dinner, despite best efforts at small talk and focusing on Rob and his adventures and the kids' updates, Terry appears frayed and stressed and more worried than either of the Reeves wish to admit. Rob is acutely aware of his brother's mounting anxiety. Michelle remains focused on making sure everyone has enough food and drink and uses her best efforts to not think about anything else but the tasks at hand.

"How about I take my niece and nephew out for dessert and, Michelle, you come along," Rob offers.

"Oh no, dear. I'll just take care of the dishes and head to my room. You go ahead."

"I wanna go to the cupcake place!" Mark shouts.

"Fine, brat," Emily concedes.

"Em, please," Stephen scolds, as a momentary semblance of normalcy returns to the household.

"Stee, I'll take your wheels, okay?"

Stephen gets the keys for Rob as Janet and Michelle clear the plates. In the kitchen, Michelle pats Janet's arm. "Let me do this. You go do what you have to do." Janet opens her mouth to begin to say something, but Michelle shakes her head to silence her and says, "Go."

In the workshop, over glasses of bourbon, Stephen, Janet and Terry go over the next day's court strategy.

"Eileen had to have been hiding somewhere," Stephen says. "If she were just staying at home, her best friend would have known. The neighbors would have known."

"Maybe she just stayed locally," Janet says. "Okay, so…" She begins typing, "I'm sending Kathy a text to start calling local hotels. She can start with the A's going down and I'll start with Z's going up."

"That information is confidential. We need an order to get them to cooperate. I already pulled my favor on the transportation lines," announces Terry.

"Can't we just use the same order? How many of these clerks will really check? Besides, we can probably get most of these places to talk other ways," Janet says eagerly.

"We can try. Let's print up a list of all hotels and divvy it up," suggests Terry. "I'll get Janice to help."

The workshop looks like combat headquarters as the three of them make calls, write things down, and pace around. After a couple of hours and nearly half a bottle of bourbon, the mood is grim.

"I've been thinking about it." Stephen sits back on the couch and polishes off his third glass. "You've got to put me on the stand," he suggests.

"No way," Terry responds, "It's suicide."

Janet nods in agreement.

"Not tomorrow, but maybe on the last day. I need to tell that jury what really happened."

"We've got nothing to back you up on your story. It's quicksand. You'll get sucked in by your version of the truth. And that will prove their case for them. You will look like a liar. A crazy and delusional liar. Right now, we stand a chance with reasonable doubt. If you get on that stand, you have to tell the truth about your affair and our defense goes down the toilet."

"The Senator didn't testify and even though we were told that we couldn't consider that, I know it had an effect. We couldn't discuss it, but I wondered about it, and I know others did. You can't not wonder. I could stick to everything the way we've got it now and just explain how confused I was by her changing her vote and I wanted to know why. I think the jurors would understand my position. I think they need to hear from me. They'll be able to see I didn't kill her."

"And Devoe will eat you like a light snack."

"Not only that," Janet interjects, "I don't think you could avoid saying that it wasn't Eileen Harris. You won't be able to keep it in, Stephen."

"And with nothing to back you up, you'll look desperate and pathetic."

"Oh great. That's something to add to my already growing reputation, desperate and pathetic, along with suspicious and adulterous."

"Save the pity party right now," Terry continues, "aside from proving that Eileen Harris wasn't at jury duty, we would have to prove that Claxton killed his aide and was involved with Sofia in some way, giving him a motive to rig the jury. Then we'd need another juror to confirm that Arden could have posed as Harris and then, if we don't sound completely and utterly crazy, we'd have enough reasonable doubt to get you off." Terry tops off his glass and puts the bottle away. "We have to focus on what we've got."

"You do that. But we can't just give up. Let's try to think of other possibilities we haven't thought of," Janet offers.

The three of them look at each other wanting to continue, but the deflated expressions and exhaustion on their faces lead them to call it a night and to leave that option for tomorrow.

Rob fell asleep on the family room couch waiting for Terry to take him back to his place. Stephen needs some time with his brother, so he tells Terry, "You go on home. Let him stay here tonight and we'll move him over tomorrow."

After Terry leaves and Janet goes upstairs, Stephen wakes Rob, "Hey, bro."

Rob rolls his head. "Hey, sorry. Must've dozed. I'm up."

"I need to talk to you." The look on Stephen's face informs Rob that this is going to be a long night.

Stephen takes Rob into his workshop and, over another round of drinks, tells him the truth about Eileen, really Sofia, and his affair. "I don't know how I got to the place where I would ever consider it, let alone do it."

"Yeah, well, you decided to give your ferret a run in the wrong field. That sucks, but it happens."

"Jesus, you make it sound so trivial."

"No, but it wasn't love, it was just a fuck, right?"

"Right."

"So, look…everyone gets their wires crossed for one thing or another at some time in their life. It just so happens that you were in the wrong place at the wrong time when yours got crossed."

"Yeah, but I had all the control in the world, and I let myself be at the mercy of a stupid situation. I even knew it at the time. I'm an idiot."

"You're human. You've got to forgive yourself. It doesn't help you to keep beating yourself up over it."

"How can I forgive myself when my wife and my kids can't forgive me?"

"It starts with you. They can't forgive you until you do it first."

"I just want to make it right."

"Look, what you did was a bonehead maneuver. Now all you can do is prove your love to your family again." Rob finishes his drink, rubs his face and leans back on the couch. "Remember when mom and dad had fights – which you know they had a lot of?"

"Oh, yeah," Stephen agrees.

"Well, they always made up in the same way. They went back to the place where dad proposed. You remember that little park on Maple? Mom said it was the shittiest and most romantic park in the world. They went back to the place that reminded them of why they decided to be together in the first place. It kept reminding them of their love."

"Who told you that?"

"Mom. After dad died."

"Wow. You are such a romantic, big brother. You know that? How are you not married?"

"I haven't found my Janet."

39

Around three a.m., Stephen situates Rob back into the family room and returns to his workshop to get some sleep. He tosses about with visions of Sofia and the Senator. Laughing together. Plotting. Secretly knowing their plan with him as their patsy.

Mocking him. And now, letting him lose everything so they can go on as if nothing strange or illicit happened. So, they can be together. Both free to wreak havoc on other people as they see fit. As if their lives are more important than anyone else's. Sleep proves impossible so Stephen quietly slips out of the house before dawn. The question 'Where was Eileen Harris if not at the trial?' is not the only question he can't get out of his head. The other question 'Where is Sofia Arden now?' grips him just as much. He knows that the answer of Sofia's whereabouts lies with the Senator. Stephen suggested to Terry early on that he go check out the Senator's house. Terry's reaction, "Absolutely not! Under no circumstances can you be seen anywhere even remotely suspicious, besides, right now anything there is a dead end. We don't have anything to start with." That was then. Now, we do have something to start with. Sofia and some background.

Maybe they're together.

Stephen knows that the Senator has security, but he's not going to try and see the man. He only wants to look at where he lives. Check out the area. See if anyone comes and goes. Merely a drive by. Nothing more.

The streets surrounding the Senator's home are empty. The substantial three–story brownstones are encircled by large trees and manicured landscapes. Stephen slows the car as he approaches the address. Quiet. A dark SUV sits in front of the Senator's side entrance – probably the security detail. Stephen pulls onto the front street and parks a half a block away across the street. He has a large coffee and a scone to keep him occupied as he waits. As the sun rises, he takes out his binoculars and looks at all the windows and doors. The curtains are still drawn and there are no traces of movement.

He has plenty of time before he has to leave for court. He finishes his coffee and begins glancing through the paper. An hour passes before he wonders if he might be wasting his time. Terry mentioned that it would not be in the Senator's best interest to be seen with Sofia at all, especially now, until a final decision is made on whether he will have to succumb to another trial. He's probably right. Stephen turns on the engine and prepares to leave. As he shifts into gear, the Senator's garage door opens, and a car drives out. Stephen doesn't need his binoculars to recognize that a dark–haired woman is driving. She passes him going the other way. It's Sofia. He's certain. He pulls a U–turn and follows her. As she keeps increasing her speed and pulling some evasive maneuvers, Stephen thinks she's spotted him. He can't let her get away. He speeds up trying to catch her. They're approaching the main boulevard and traffic will be getting thick. He has to try and catch up to her here. He guns it, runs a stop sign and finally draws close enough to get side by side. She quickly glances his way, then immediately turns away and tries to evade him. Her face appears even more beautiful than he remembers, surrounded by short black hair and sporting a deep red lipstick. The contrast enhances her stunning features. The same features she managed to downplay and to nearly obliterate from notice during the trial. He opens his window and yells at her, "Pull over!" Sofia ignores him, but he persists, "Sofia! Pull over!"

She ignores him as he struggles to keep up with her. She maneuvers away from him, finds a clearing, accelerates onto the boulevard and is gone, leaving a jumble of traffic in her wake.

"Damn it! Damn it! Damn it!" Stephen slams his hand against the steering wheel.

She was here, she knows what's happening to him and she isn't going to do anything about it. How can the woman he knew, if only for a moment, do something like this? Not just to him but to anyone. Now there's no doubt of her connection to the Senator. They're lovers. What else? He has proof. But Terry will let him know that he doesn't have any proof at all. Only the word of a man desperate to get off on a murder charge. It would be the word of a distraught man against the word of a prominent Senator. He is so fucked. Terry probably shouldn't know about this. Janet shouldn't know.

He'll have to keep this excursion to himself. Any more signs of instability could cost him with the relationships he has left.

* * *

Stephen brings bagels, coffee and fruit into Terry's office.

"What did you do? What do I need to be worried about?" Terry asks, eyeing the offering.

Stephen skips a beat for a minute, then realizes Terry's just being Terry. "Funny. I just don't want to risk my defender busting a gut worrying about my being late, so I thought I'd try early."

"Still not sleeping?"

"Not really. Had a chat with Rob last night. I told him everything. I figured he has a right to know what's really going on."

Terry digs into the bagels, "Good. I'm glad you did that. That way I don't have to worry about slipping up."

"Oh yeah. I forgot, it's all about you."

"Always, man." Terry smiles teasingly and adds another sugar to his coffee. "I've got John Graeber first up this morning."

"Do you think that's a good idea? The man did basically remove me from the firm. That can't be a sign of confidence."

"He did not remove you. Remember that. Do not ever say that. Do not let anyone ever hear you say that. His position is that he wants you to focus on your defense and that the firm is behind you one hundred percent. He comes across as confident in you as a person and we need someone higher up from the firm. I think this will be good for us." Stephen acquiesces despite his misgivings on the matter.

Stephen watches as Terry finishes his breakfast and gathers some final papers. "Listen, I think you should know that I saw Sofia this morning," he blurts out. Terry freezes and stares at Stephen as he continues, "It was in the street. She was driving."

Terry pauses, thinking for a moment, then checks his watch, "We need to get going. Look, I know you're anxious to prove this woman exists, but maybe it was someone who looks like her. We can talk more about this after court."

Stephen opens his mouth to start to protest, then thinks better of it and decides to wait.

Both Rob and Janet are in the courtroom as the proceedings begin. Rob looks rumpled and tired as he gives Stephen a confident smile of support.

John Graeber cuts a respectable and believable figure on the witness stand and Terry feels that the jury likes the man. Regardless of the confidence Stephen should be feeling as he watches witness after witness impart nothing but positive and honorable character traits, his mind keeps wandering to the image of Eileen, or rather Sofia, in her car. He still can't believe she's really this other woman. This seductress and con. Her face surrounded by that rich dark hair...the red lips... as another witness takes the stand.

Terry nudges Stephen and whispers, "Give her a smile. You can't tune out on these people."

After the day's testimony, as Terry packs his briefcase, he notices Stephen drifting away in reverie again and asks, "Is there something else I should know?"

"What?"

"You tell me. You've not been with us today Mr. checked out, even though today was our best day so far. You're probably thinking about what you think you saw, but either way it's not relevant right now."

"I *did* see her this morning."

Terry sets down his briefcase and slowly turns to Stephen, "There's more isn't there?"

Stephen continues, "I checked out Claxton's house. Don't freak out. I parked way across the street and just watched. I was about to leave, then his garage opened, and she drove out. I followed her, but she lost me."

"Look, it still could've been someone else. I know you want to see her, so maybe your mind just…."

"No. It was her. I pulled up next to her and she saw me. It was her."

"Jesus." Terry grabs his briefcase and motions for them to get out of there. "Let's go," he commands as he leads them out of the courtroom.

Once at the bar, Terry's logical side takes over. "Okay. Let's assume it was her. But now that she's seen you, you can bet she'll stay away from the Senator."

"I'm not so sure. She knows I'm in court all day."

"There is no way you can go back there. I'm not kidding. It's suicide if you get caught."

"I'll get Rob to…"

"No way. No one linked to you. Look, I've got a guy I can get to watch the place, in case she goes back. I'll get him to take photos in case we can put something together. But right now, even if she does go back, she does us no good."

"But she's the…."

"What do you think is going to happen? You think she's going to say, oh yeah, I impersonated someone and then I had her killed?" Terry takes a pull off his beer. "I know it's hard to hear, but the system isn't always in favor of the innocent. It should be, but it just isn't. Unfortunately, we are too far along in the game to be able to stop. There are a lot of innocent people in prison because they had no way to fight the machine. We do. I've been at it for a long time. But we can't be stupid about it. We're building your case right now and it's going well. I think we can get reasonable doubt. I think the jury, at least a few of them, will go our way."

Stephen looks down at the table. Everything begins to blur. He's not a big believer in God or prayer, but right now, inside, he's praying. He's praying for a miracle. For a change in the wind. A shift in his favor. Something, anything that will help end this nightmare.

40

Her mother was always looking to move up. Social climbing became her art and she excelled at it. As a little girl, Sofia loved her mother and longed for her approval and to feel close to her. She waited for hugs and kisses that never came. It's not to say that Anne Arden Benjamin didn't love her daughter, it's just that she was not into sappy displays of affection. She would give her daughter the obligatory good night kiss on the forehead and an occasional squeeze around the shoulders in a situation where it was expected, but overall, she believed that talking to Sofia and teaching her about what life was really like was a far more valuable parenting gift.

Sofia's biological father, Frank, was Italian on his mother's side. She was named after her paternal grandmother. One day before her mother officially left her father, Sofia overheard a conversation between them where Anne told Frank that he would never amount to anything. That she couldn't properly live and raise a child because he wanted to switch careers. That he promised her the family estate in the Hampton's and now it was going to his brother. Proper survival and the right circles were paramount to Anne. She told Sofia not to worry. They would have a wonderful life soon. Within a year of leaving Frank, Anne married Robert Benjamin. A step up financially and in social circles. Sofia believes that her mother was having an affair with Robert long before she left Frank. Thinking back on that time, Sofia remembers hushed telephone conversations and spa and beauty appointments that likely never happened.

Robert Benjamin was a fine stepfather, but she missed her real father, who moved back to Italy after the divorce. When Anne got sick with chronic bronchitis that eventually turned into severe pneumonia that led to her death, she said to her daughter, "Sofia, always remember, you have money. I have made sure that you will never be poor, but all the money in the world can't give you class. Always check yourself, Sofia. You have class. I have taught you and don't let anything else show. Regardless, you still need a man. A respectable, classy man, so your children will be respectable."

Her mother underestimated herself as an individual without a man, because she underestimated all women in that way. Upon her death, Anne's share of Benjamin Mining went to Sofia, but Sofia didn't really know what that meant until she was in college. Europe was a great training ground. Intellect was valued regardless of sex, and she pursued her studies with a vengeance. She even visited her dad in Italy during break one year, but she was disappointed by his obvious displays of fawning over his new family and not taking any interest in her This caused her to never want to see him again.

Once back in the States with a business degree, she vowed to make her mark on the company she had a stake in. Even though Sofia's two stepbrothers ran the company, it was Sofia that expanded their enterprise and turned it into one of the largest mining outfits in the country. Without her, they would plod along as they had always plodded, with no new insight, growth or vision for the future. They never recognized or admitted how powerful her role in the company had become. They were mesmerized by the money. Always the money, regardless of how it came to them. American men are so naïve about women. Even George. Sofia could see in it in his eyes. George Claxton underestimated her. You would think a man of his experience and stature would know better, but women still seemed to stump him. Yes, she had fallen in love with him and would do virtually anything to get him out of trouble. Virtually.

Sofia puts her laptop on her lap and pulls up a video of George Claxton when he was a bright–eyed, young and confident Senatorial candidate. In the video, Claxton stands in front of a medium sized crowd and speaks passionately to his voters, "I'm tired of hearing about all this greatness but not achieving it. Aren't you?" He begins,

"We should be achieving it. It's time to stop talking and start doing. We need to be the greatest country in the world on every front, not just say we are. Every policy we make, everything we set up and claim that we stand for, must be reflected in everything we do and in every action we take. I don't mean most actions; I mean *every* action. We need to back up our words with actions. *Back It Up*!" He exclaims each word emphatically and the crowd applauds. Whistles come from the voters holding various signs that feature *Claxton* and his slogan, *Back It Up*. Claxton gestures for them to stop, then continues, "Whenever you ask your representatives 'why did you cut that corner?' or you ask your neighbor 'why did you throw your trash onto our street or your neighbor's lawn?' you get a whole song–and–dance and they say, 'you don't understand, it's more complicated than that.' Well, I don't think it is more complicated. You cut that one little corner that one little time and it will build and build and build into the maelstrom we're in now. I'm here to get us out of it." The crowd cheers and claps and goes wild as he concludes with, "How you do anything is how you do everything! Back It Up! Thank you!"

Sofia stops the video, then closes her laptop and sets it back onto the passenger seat of her car. Love. That is the man she did indeed fall in love with. But she's too well trained and experienced to fall into a completely blind love, and at her expense. Most powerful men don't have emotional loyalties. Initially she felt George could be different, but she stayed observant. She knows what drives men like George. But that his rage would go to such lengths did take her by surprise; however, with great power comes great risk, so she moved ahead with him, keeping her eye on their future. Sofia was getting to the point where she didn't have many childbearing years left. When George called her the night he hit Joel, he sounded like a little boy. She talked him through it, then snuck in through maintenance to clean up his office. He had to show his face at the fundraiser.

His arrest stunned them both, but she again leapt into action. George appeared frail in the early days of his arrest and during jury selection and she felt strong and capable of helping.

What she hadn't expected was to encounter a man like Stephen within her web. At first, he seemed the perfect patsy. Average, middle–aged, good looking and open to some adventure. But upon closer involvement, looking into Stephen's eyes, brought her recognition of a sincerity and an honesty that pained her. Seeing him this morning rattled her. The plea in his face. She had hoped to never see that. Average this guy is not. In her circles, she never encountered men like Stephen. Men like that can't survive in her world. She wonders if women like Janet know how lucky they are. Or if they dream of some bigger than life manipulator like George. Grass being greener and all that.

George. Handsome, powerful, wealthy and... well, she knows if the ship were sinking and her weight meant the difference between his death or survival, he'd be the first to throw her overboard. Much like her mother did Frank. Consequences were for other people in his book, not for him. He is privileged and if he makes mistakes, it's other people that pay for them. He's above that. Or so he thinks. Is anyone above some consequence from their actions? That makes her sad. She never had to be involved in harming innocent people in the past. Not really. The pollution from the mining operations could be thought of, in a way, like that, but not directly. Besides, aren't the laws supposed to be enforced to deal with that? The players in her world, at the top of the corporate food chain, aren't innocent. They all know the game and the stakes. With skin so thick and hearts of steel, it's easy to remain disconnected. She allowed herself to feel something with George, but only after years of watching him and after what she thought would be the last of the bigger risks. She allowed his charm and political prowess to seduce her. And maybe her mother's voice in the back of her mind chanting, "You need a man. A powerful man," contributed to letting her guard down.

George's handsome face, great poise, powerful position, and disarming smile were too much when combined with a moment of vulnerability that only she saw when they were left alone on the rooftop in Paris after that second meeting. Her stepbrothers and their associates aren't capable of showing even a glimmer of vulnerability. She doubts they have any souls left. In George, she witnessed what she thought could be a brighter path for herself and she liked it. But in that moment, she forgot that he is one of them and will always choose the easier, emotional road of denial and manipulation to avoid having to deal with any pain or discomfort. Winning means everything and now she knows that no price is too great for men like George. Joel was so young, and his only crime was his great skill at putting together what they were up to. When Joel confronted George with the document he found; George claimed that he had a moment of blind rage. He was shocked and he lashed out reflexively, not thinking about what he was doing, and Sofia believed him. Initially.

Unfamiliar feelings of sorrow and sickness well up in her when she thinks of the mess with the jury and the wreckage of Stephen's life in the process. She should have told George less about Stephen. She sits in her car watching Stephen's house from across the street on the corner, with part of a tree blocking the front end of her vehicle. She wears a red wig, a baseball hat and a plaid shirt. What she hopes to accomplish remains a mystery, yet she feels a need to see Stephen's family. To see Stephen's life. Sofia hopes to find a way to live with what she set in motion when she singled out and chose Stephen to be the fall guy.

She watches Janet arrive home with someone else. A bearded man. Both look unhappy. Only a few days left before deliberations. Surely Stephen won't be convicted. But today, his desperation makes her wonder if he indeed could be found guilty. She had been careful and knows the prosecution can't prove the affair. Still, something gnaws at the back of her mind. George seems too confident that Stephen will be convicted and that he, himself, will not have to go through another trial. What does he know that she doesn't?

41

Two more days yield nothing new on the Eileen–Sofia front, other than Stephen knowing that Sofia is real and nearby. Janet, Rob and Kathy have come up empty and Stephen feels his panic rising. He trusts Terry, but even a spectacular alchemist can't make a diamond out of nothing but shit. He's been set up. He knows it. He just can't prove it. Closing arguments will likely begin and end sometime next week. They don't have many more witnesses to go, despite Terry's efforts at stalling and drawing it out as long as possible.

Stephen told Janet and Rob that he saw Sofia in her car, but he could tell that even they are unsure of whether his eyes aren't playing tricks on him. Stephen needs to get some sleep. To rest so that maybe some other thought will break through, and he'll know what to do. Where to turn next. Hoping that the weekend ahead will allow his mind to stop churning long enough to sleep proves too lofty a goal. Friday night brings continuous tossing and turning. Finally at the first sight of dawn, Stephen's body succumbs to the forces of exhaustion and drops off into a couple of hours of essential sleep.

Just after eight a.m., Stephen opens one eye. The boards and papers in his view quickly remind him of his current life. He quickly shuts it. He needs to think about something else.

Hawaii. He loves Hawaii. Several years ago, he and Janet went to Maui without the kids. First time they took a vacation by themselves since either of the kids were born. They stayed in a small rental in a remote bay, mere steps from the ocean, surrounded by sounds of nature and tropical breezes. Their days were spent swimming, reading, eating, making love, and sleeping. Pure bliss. That remarkable feeling of carefree days and nights, with no obligations in those moments, remains a touchstone for him. He wonders if some people feel like that all the time. What he would give to be in that place, in that state of mind right now.

The door to the workshop opens, but no sound follows. Stephen senses a presence and opens his eyes to find Mark standing over and staring down at him.

"You're awake," Mark says, delighted.

"Hi, champ. Good morning." Stephen props himself up and motions for Mark to sit next to him.

"Yeah. It's Saturday," he mutters as he sits. "No school today."

"You doin' okay, Gremlin?"

"Yeah. Yesterday, we caught a snake during recess."

"What'd you do with it?"

"Well...Jamie put it in a brown bag and brought it into class. But, when it was time to go home, we couldn't find it."

Stephen can imagine some teacher making that discovery after hours and furrows his brow as if contemplating the problem. "I see. Maybe you should make sure the snakes stay outside from now on. Most teachers aren't big fans of snakes you know."

"Yeah. I think you're right. I know Mrs. Brown isn't a fan."

"Oh, how do you know that?"

"She kind of started breathing funny when we mentioned that the snake had escaped."

"I see." Stephen stifles a smile.

Mark looks at his father intently. "Are you going to jail?"

The question takes Stephen's breath away. The prospect of jail looms over all of them. "I hope not," he manages, "I didn't do anything wrong, and I have to trust that the system will work, and that the truth will win. Do you understand?" He asks the question realizing he himself barely understands any of it.

"What if it doesn't?"

"We can't think that way right now, okay?"

Stephen desperately wants his son to understand that his arrest, this trial, and all the accusations can't possibly be true. He wants to find a way to guarantee that his son will be certain of his innocence. But he knows he has no way to assure that and no way to guarantee that the system will be of any help. His confidence in the justice system, even in people, has perilously eroded. His trust must lie in the relationship he's nurtured with his son thus far. He looks at Mark and can't imagine him growing up with a jailed father who is a convicted murderer. That thought must not enter his reality. Not yet.

Mark nods and asks, "Do you have to work all day today too?"

The question illuminates that in Stephen's obsession to clear his name, he's lapsed in the thing most important to him – time with his kids. "I think I can take a break today. No work, just hanging out with you and Em."

"Yeah!" Mark's face lights up and he jumps off the bed, grabbing Stephen's arm and pulling him along.

To an outside observer, the morning at the Reeves' household appears to be that of a loving family enjoying the beginning of another fun weekend. Rob shows up in time for breakfast and brings pastries.

"I hope you're hungry," says Rob as he plunks down a giant box of baked goods. Mark immediately opens it and yells in delight, "Bear claws! My favorite!"

As everyone gathers around the table and enjoys the food, the only giveaway that betrays the perfect family façade comes in the form of occasional worried looks and an unseen tension between Stephen and Janet, along with measured words and limited topics of conversation among them all.

"I need to get the rest of my art supplies today," Emily announces, then turns to Janet and adds, "and you promised to get me some new track shirts for practice."

"I know, you both need some stuff for school. I'll take you this afternoon," says Janet.

Mark makes a face akin to torture, fearing that he's expected to endure that adventure and tests the waters with, "I don't have to go, do I?"

Stephen assuages his fears, "Why don't we let the girls do their thing and the guys'll go get some ice cream and check out the model shop."

"And maybe the Air and Space Museum," adds Rob.

"Oh man! Yeah!" Mark's relief washes over him and both Stephen and Janet laugh – something they haven't done in a very long time.

In the afternoon, Rob, Stephen and Mark decide to walk to the ice cream shop.

As they make their way down the neighborhood's main street, Stephen notices unpleasant looks aimed his way. He's amazed that people recognize him from the media coverage, then decide to pass judgment without knowing a damn thing. He never notices anyone who's recognizable from the news or television on the street, not even celebrities. He lives his own life and isn't looking at who's who and judging them and wondering what and how they're conducting their lives. This time, he lets the anger the attention stirs up pass right through him. He didn't think it was a good idea in the beginning, but now he's happy that Rob is here. As unpleasant as his life is right now, having his brother with him feels good.

Mark orders a large scoop of double fudge in a cone, Rob goes with two scoops, rum raisin and peach, and Stephen sticks with vanilla bean. "Boring," Mark says.

While their orders are being prepared, Rob excuses himself for the bathroom.

Mark's cone is ready first and Stephen hands it to him. Mark moves and motions to the small, empty table by the door. Stephen nods as Mark heads over and grabs a seat.

"You had one scoop of double fudge, a scoop of rum…" The kid behind the register addresses Stephen.

As Mark enjoys his ice cream among a scattering of patrons, a woman steps into the shop and immediately approaches Mark. "Hi," Sofia says, "Mark, right?" He nods. She thrusts a large manila envelope toward him and sets it on the table. "Can you please give this to your dad when he's done?"

Before Mark can get his, "Okay" out, she's gone.

Stephen turns away from the register and his eye catches sight of Sofia's dark stiletto heel and perfectly shaped calf as she steps out the door. His gaze follows her leg up to an expensive silk skirt and tightly fitted top, and the glint of light from the bracelet as she rushes down the steps onto the street. He drops his change and runs after her.

Another patron enters at the same time and blocks the entrance just long enough for him to lose sight of her. He pushes past and looks up and down the street, but there's no sign of Sofia. Stephen attempts to breathe, but the air catches in the tightness of his chest and he freezes for a moment before he returns to the shop and over to Mark, who is now joined by Rob.

"What's going on?" Rob asks.

Stephen ignores him and sees the envelope on the table. "Are you okay?" he asks Mark.

Mark nods and points to the envelope, "That's for you."

"Did that lady give it to you?"

"Yeah. She knew my name."

Rob looks at Stephen, "Hey, what lady?"

"I think it was Sofia," Stephen tells him.

"Who's Sofia?" Mark questions.

"Just someone your dad knows from work," Rob answers, wanting to spare his brother more lies.

Stephen takes the envelope, opens it, and looks inside.

"Dad, you promised no work today."

"I know Grem. This isn't work."

"What is it?"

"Hopefully proof that your dad's not crazy." Stephen looks inside and sees papers and brochures. He closes the envelope and feels a fierce pounding in his chest. This must contain something that can help him. Sofia isn't some cold heartless killer. He's sure of that. She can't be. He knows she set him up, yet even now he wants to excuse her. What kind of pathology is this? Does he have some hidden, damaged need for self–sabotage? He grips the envelope and looks at Rob. Unfortunately, until he carefully examines the contents of the envelope, he can't focus on hanging out with his son or do anything else.

42

Terry, Janet, and Stephen sit around the kitchen table with the contents of the envelope strewn about. Janet talks on the phone as Terry and Stephen stare at her in anticipation.

"Thanks, Kathy, I owe you one, or by now about a hundred," Janet says as she hangs up then turns to the guys. "Bingo! One Eileen Mathis was on the manifest for the mining company's private jet on March sixteenth from Washington to the Cayman Islands."

Stephen sighs in relief.

"Great!" Terry exclaims, then sarcastically adds, "Now all we have to prove is that Eileen Mathis is the same woman as Eileen Harris."

Stephen shoots him a look, "It's here. We just have to put it together."

Terry acquiesces, "Sorry, you're right. I just don't want to jump the gun and get hopes up in a direction we may not be able to go."

Stephen reaches for one of the papers and begins reading, "That Monday, the same day as the trial started, $750,000 was deposited in an account for Eileen Mathis at the World Net Bank on Grand Cayman. I've got the account number here. Virtually all incoming funds to the bank are from an outfit in Kentucky and several outgoing transactions are to Alabama. I bet both of these are associated with the Senator in some way."

"What about the deposit for Eileen Mathis?" asks Janet.

"That deposit was wired from within the bank."

Terry stands up and begins walking around, his mental wheels churning. "This could be good. Really good. What's the account name that the money came from?"

"From one of the corporations on the bank's charter."

"Let me see." Terry grabs the document out of Stephen's hand and begins examining it. "FF Alliance Ltd. We can do cross checks and find out who represents that corporation. If Claxton is connected in any way in any of the threads attached to his corporation, we may have some grounds with the judge. I'll get my office on it first thing in the morning."

Both Stephen and Janet smile and hope pours out of them for the first time since testimony in his trial began.

"I'm sure there's a connection," Stephen says.

"I have to admit, I couldn't have imagined this." Terry looks at Stephen and shakes his head, then adds, "She just handed you this?"

"She approached Mark," Janet says as her smile instantly fades and she instinctively gets up from the table. Terry's simple question returns her thoughts to territory deliberately suppressed. "That scares me. She even knows our family."

"I admit, that's a risky move for a woman who doesn't want to exist in any of this. I don't get it, man. Why?"

Janet shoots Terry a look that warns him not to press for an answer to that. She then excuses herself and leaves the workshop. She needs some time to breathe.

Admittedly, she feels relieved that information has finally surfaced that could lead to Stephen's release, but the fact that the woman who set him up and seduced him now tracked him down and is giving him aid, tears at her psyche in a way she can't seem to control. Betrayal never simply vanishes. The nature of this type of wound is that even under the guise of healing, its tendency for ongoing reactivation exists and can be triggered with the most obscure or minute provocation. Janet's mind fills with thoughts of intimate and tender moments between the man she trusted with her soul and a sophisticated, attractive viper woman who obviously feels something for him despite her ulterior motives, otherwise she wouldn't have provided this information. If she can see that Sofia cares about him, Stephen certainly can. What else does Stephen know about this woman? And does he still feel anything for her despite what she did to him? Hard to imagine. These events create a freshness to Janet's still raw wound, and she wonders if she will ever find peace again. Tonight, she will take one of Stephen's sleeping pills. As much as she abhors taking medications of any kind unless absolutely necessary, the number of times she has deemed absolutely necessary since Stephen's arrest would be alarming if she thought about it. She opts not to think about it.

* * *

Terry agrees to meet Stephen at six a.m. at his office along with a couple members of his staff. This is one of the few cases Terry's assistants all offered to pitch in on the side with whatever he needs. They know how much Terry needs a win here. This morning they are all working full tilt on their computers. Even with four people searching through numerous databases, Terry is still surprised by how quickly they get a hit.

"Got it!" Ellen, Terry's right hand assistant, exclaims, as the others gather around her desk. "FF Alliance Ltd. has only four members – all of them entities, which we expected, so digging into each of those entities, a BMM, LLC, has a G. Claxton listed as Managing Member."

Stephen looks hopefully over at Terry.

"How do we know that Claxton is our beloved Senator?" Terry asks.

"The address for the G. Claxton of BMM is the same as the address for one George Claxton, our Senator, for his car lease – the very same P.O. Box. Coincidence? Me thinks not," Ellen responds.

Terry grins from ear to ear, "All right!" The smoking gun – Claxton is a signer on the account of the corporation that wired the money to Eileen Harris. They are certain that Eileen Mathis was an alias for Eileen Harris and a little time will bring that fact to light, so all Terry has to do now is convince the judge to give them that time. If the goal of the justice system is indeed to bring out the truth, then surely, he will be granted this opportunity in light of the new facts.

He calls for a special emergency hearing with the judge and presents all the new evidence, despite the raucous objections from the prosecution along the way. "This is an absurdity, your honor," Prosecutor Devoe injects, "We are nearing closing arguments and suddenly the victim isn't the woman the defendant met? Really? If they had known this all along and that were true, then why wasn't that the defense strategy? Why wait until now to bring this theory into it?"

"We knew we needed some proof," Terry retorts and wants to add 'you bastard' but restrains himself. "Your honor, if you can just give us a few days, we can find someone to identify Eileen Harris as the woman who used the name Eileen Mathis as an alias during..."

"I'll tell you why, because the defense is desperate and grasping and..."

Judge Ramen shoots a look at the prosecutor and interrupts him, "Enough Mr. Devoe," then turns to Terry, "Mr. Pollard, while I applaud your attempt at constructing an intricate conspiracy theory here, we don't have time for this level of reach, especially this late in the game. You already stated your theory for the defense and there is absolutely nothing that suggests a different woman sat on that jury with your client. That is an insult to the court system, not to mention that your conspiracy theory involves a high–ranking member of the Senate, which in and of itself requires a lot more than a little time. Don't you think?"

After reviewing the contents of the envelope, Terry's concentration has been so fixated on finding Claxton's connection to the money, certain that it would be enough to buy them time, that he sobers up quickly when the judge shakes her head insisting that conjecture and speculation won't win the day. "But your ho..." Terry attempts, but the judge raises her hand to silence him. "Court will reconvene in one hour."

Terry's cheeks burn at the futility of the system he's spent his life defending and being party to. He notices Devoe's face, feigning concern for justice but revealing the hint of a smirk, concerned only with tasting another win for his side.

As Terry storms out of the judge's chambers, Janet, Stephen and Rob approach to meet him.

"What happened?" Janet asks.

Terry waits until Devoe is down the hall, then shakes his head in frustration. "Why not?" Janet's voice betrays her growing panic. Stephen begins to turn pale.

"We know we need hard evidence to show that Eileen Mathis is Eileen Harris, but the judge thinks we're just stalling, and no amount of time can prove something she doesn't believe is possible. She doesn't believe it could've been someone else on the jury and the fact that Claxton is listed on the charter is just a business dealing for him and a coincidence for us and has nothing to do with anything here as far as she's concerned. She won't even give us a day. We're out of time. I have to wrap, then Devoe will give his closing."

"We can subpoena Sofia to testify," Stephen suggests.

Terry feels for the desperation lodged in the eyes of his best friend. "You know that's not going to work on so many levels. Nowhere in our defense to date did we or could we even hint at this theory and without all the pieces, it doesn't hold water. We all know it."

Stephen walks to a bench against the wall and the others follow. "I'm going to jail," he says as he sits down and stares at the floor.

Rob sits next to him. "Don't go there, bro. We've gotten out of scrapes before, and we'll do it again. From what I've seen in there, they can't find you guilty." Rob tries to restore some hope.

"That's right," Terry adds, "Just because we're not presenting what we know to be true here, we have to stop thinking that it's a certain death sentence. That's not what's happening here. We're forgetting that the jury may not convict. Let's not forget that there's no weapon, no motive that the prosecution has been able to prove, only conjecture, nothing to smear your character and I think we've done okay. Also, I get the last say. I think there's a real chance you will be acquitted."

"Bullshit," Stephen says without looking at him.

Janet regards the face of the man she's spent most of her adult life with and sees a pain she can't have imagined for him. Terry also wears a stricken look she can't bear to witness. "We can't just give up," Janet insists. Stephen offers no reaction.

Terry adds, "There's no reason to give up. We're the ones with the most important truth on our side – you didn't kill anyone."

Stephen shakes his head at that comment and Janet feels her anger rise. “Well, I can’t just stand here. There must be something else to make sure...”

Stephen feels Janet’s disappointment in him. He wants to reach out to her and say he has an answer for this problem, but he feels nothing but hopelessness.

Janet looks around the courthouse, then back at the three men. She’s not one to support a pity party. “I’ll see you later,” she announces and storms off.

“Janet!” Stephen stands and calls out, but she waives him off as she rushes out of the courthouse.

“She’s right you know. We don’t have the luxury of feeling sorry for ourselves because we can’t do it our way. We can and have presented a solid case. Now we stick by what we know to be true – you are innocent. Let’s go in there and do it. Get them on our side. Okay?” Terry offers, motioning for them to get going.

“That’s right. Let’s put on our winning faces. No time to whinge. It’s not over,” Rob encourages as he stands and the three head toward the courtroom.

Stephen looks at his brother and his best friend and it hits him that they’re here for him. That he led them all into this mess and to this place and it sucks. “I don’t know how to remotely make any sense of what I’m putting everybody through…especially Janet.” He stops, “hold up a minute.” He turns to Terry. “I am grateful for everything you’ve done in there. But I need you to make me a promise.” Stephen fixes his gaze on Terry, “if I go down, I need you to make sure Janet and the kids make it. I’ll go over all my accounts with you and there’s that property in Vermont I’ll want you to sell for them. I need to know that she’ll get through this and doesn’t have to worry about anything.”

"Jesus, man. This is not how you need to be thinking right now. Come on, get up and go to the bathroom, splash some water on your face and get back in the race in top form," Terry says.

"Yeah, man..." Rob starts, but Stephen stops him, "And I need *you* to help my family in any way and visit more often." Rob stands there stunned and simply nods. He's never seen his brother this way and is unsure of where to step next.

Stephen grabs Terry's arm and looks him in the eye, "I need you to promise me."

Terry sees the seriousness and despair in Stephen's plea. "Of course. You know I will take care of them. You don't have to ask. But you've got to focus on a different vision here. I need you to focus and channel your innocence through every pore of your body right now. We have to go into that courtroom and fight for the truth and I need you to be the pillar of that truth. I need your face and your eyes to help me convince that jury that you did not kill anyone. You cannot go in there defeated. Do you understand me?"

Stephen nods and adds, "Do you think Janet will be back?"

"Yes. You know she's fighting for you. Don't let her down. Don't let Mark and Emily down. Project your innocence to those jurors in there. You hear me?"

Stephen nods, then ducks into the bathroom to get his game face on.

The first order of business when court reconvenes and after Terry rests the case for the defense is the prosecution's closing argument.

Stephen looks at the jurors. He knows they can't possibly understand the enormity of their task. In theory, he had understood that Claxton's freedom was on the line, but he hadn't really understood the depth and severity of what that meant on the scale of an entire life and all those affected by it. Until now.

As Devoe prances around the courtroom, addressing the jury and shooting admonishing glances at Stephen, Stephen feels the emptiness of where Janet should be seated. He's suddenly aware of his need to soak up every moment of her presence.

Taking Terry's advice to heart, he tries to keep his posture straight and his face up. Stephen allows most of what Devoe recounts to pass right through him without registering or reacting to it. He finally allows himself to hear the very end.

"The State has proven that Stephen Reeves was frantic to see the victim, but she didn't want to see him. He was so enraged that he left angry, threatening messages on her answering machine. He broke into her house that night, determined to have it out with her. He would have you believe that she was already dead when he got there, but he didn't report her death until hours after he fled the scene and had time to be advised by his attorney. Those are not the actions of an innocent man. Those are the actions of a man who committed murder, needed time to dispose of the weapon, and knowing he left glaring evidence behind, to find a way to try to explain it away. Ladies and gentlemen, you know that we have provided you with more than enough evidence and testimony to conclude that this man had an affair with the victim, then killed her to cover it up. Let the law help you to do the right thing and find him guilty."

Terry feels relieved that he has another night to work on his close. He needs it.

Even with Stephen's attempts to put on a positive face, Terry knows that his friend won't hold up much longer.

43

Janet spends the rest of the day chasing any lead she can find. Her anger fuels her. Not only anger at Stephen for having brought this to their doorstep, but also anger at the pity party he's spinning into before it's even over. Already projecting a bad outcome. What the hell happened to the man she married? She can't imagine that this is how their life plays out.

The key lies in finding witnesses who can identify the real Eileen Harris when she was posing as Eileen Mathis. The first place Janet thinks of looking leads her to begin snooping around the private airport where Eileen purportedly boarded the company's private jet. The lobby or waiting area boasts sleek top of the line high–end furniture surrounded by two story green glass walls. This part of the airport appears empty, but Janet knows some staff must be nearby to cater to the heavy hitters if and when they show up. She can see men stationed outside one of the hangars off to the right. Probably security. This building appears to have cameras mounted in corners throughout. The thought occurs to her that Eileen would have likely been caught on camera if she'd come through here. The problem lies in who has access to that footage and if they would release it or simply erase it if instructed to do so by those pulling the reigns. Two hallways flank the waiting area. One leads to the restrooms and the other to what looks like a small office off to one side. It's locked, but a large window to its interior shows that no one is manning the single desk inside. Janet leans against the door and waits until a very tall, muscular man approaches and eyes her suspiciously.

"Excuse me. Are you Mr. Dole?" Janet inquires.

"Yeah. And who are you?"

"I'm Janet Reeves. I was told that you run this hangar and the bookings for jets including Benjamin Mining."

"I don't have any record of an appointment with you, Ms...?"

"Reeves. I don't have an appointment, but..."

Dole gives her cold stare and proceeds to open the door. "No appointment, no dice."

"Please. I just need a minute of your time. It's a matter of life and death," she continues. She takes a photo of Eileen Harris out of her purse and holds it out to him. "I just need to know if this woman boarded the company's plane at the end of last May?"

Despite the desperate and imploring look on her face, Dole continues his cold stare and announces, "I can't help you," as he turns and enters his office.

"Please. Wait. I just need..." The door closes on her. She looks at him through the window and continues her pleading until he finally shuts the shade.

Janet walks out to the hangar area, where two men are smoking and arguing. The large one notices her first and gestures to his rival and they both fall silent.

"Hello," Janet greets them. The large one smirks, but neither man speaks to her.

Janet approaches them, "Hi, I was wondering if you could help me. My sister..."

The door behind Janet rams open and Dole comes out, fuming. "Lady! You are not allowed out here. You need to leave."

"I just wanted to show"

"Now!" Dole inserts himself between her and the two crewmen. "I don't see..."

Dole raises his hand to silence her, and Janet quickly realizes that to push any further could result in disaster. She turns away in defeat, but something in Dole's vehemence to get her out of there encourages her to keep looking for a witness. One is out there somewhere. The plane landed in the Cayman's, where Eileen would have used her alias during her entire stay. The next step is to find out where Eileen stayed, where she ate, where she spent her time. Janet looks at her watch – barely enough time to get to school and pick up the kids. Her mom has a doctor's appointment.

As she drives, Janet leaves Ellen a message to call her when she has a minute. Ellen vacillates between the trial and Terry's office as needed. Terry hired Ellen three years ago and Janet knows her from an occasional crossing of paths throughout those years and has always liked her. Ellen is over a decade younger and smart and mature. These past months, Janet got to know her, not only out of necessity, but also out of fondness. The two women clicked and found themselves confiding in each other during down times in the case. Janet's phone buzzes. Ellen.

"What are you doing after work today?" Janet asks.

"I'm not sure work will end today," Ellen replies. "Devoe is just finishing, and it looks like Terry won't do his closing until tomorrow."

"I want us to contact hotels, vacation rentals, restaurants, and anything else we can think of in Grand Cayman to see where Eileen could have been seen and maybe find a witness. Do you think Terry would be okay with that?"

"Great idea. I'll get my intern to start right now, and I'll get on it when I get back to the office. You coming here?"

"After I get the kids settled, I'll meet you at your office." Her next call is to Kathy.

Janet convinces Stephen to spend the evening with the kids. She can tell he's frantic and impatient and wants to be useful, but this is exactly why he needs to chill. She reminds him of his priority to spend as much time with his children while he can. This is not an argument he can deny, and he and Rob decide to have game night with Mark and Emily after the kids finish their homework.

After hours at Terry's office, Janet, Joe the intern, Ellen and Kathy spread out in a small conference room, while Terry closets himself off to prepare his closing. The team methodically breaks down a list of hotels and rentals on Grand Cayman, looking for a clue. Ellen juts between Terry, when he needs her to look up something, and Janet and the team. As the hours pass, the list seems to grow and Janet's confidence in getting a result wanes. Not even one lead materializes. Would she be registered under yet another name? If so, then why wouldn't Sofia have given them that? Or under Sofia's? Janet suggests that they should check under both names with each call, just in case.

After ten, Terry surfaces and perceives Janet's weariness as she hangs up from another fruitless call. "Hey," he says.

"Hey yourself."

"I think I have a good closing," Terry pronounces. "I also think you need to get out of here. All of you. Go get some rest. You guys can pick it up tomorrow while I'm in court. Okay?"

Feeling tired, Janet acquiesces, knowing that she's losing steam and needs to recharge. On the drive home, she feels a strange chill and becomes increasingly alert. For a moment, she thinks she's being followed. She feels certain that the same set of headlights keep up with her same turns for several miles. She slows down to see if she can get a look at the car. With nothing but lights shining in her face, she can't even make out the model of the car, just that it's a dark sedan. Once in her neighborhood, the car seems to vanish. Probably just self–imposed paranoia. No surprise under the circumstances. Janet brushes it off and pulls into the garage, anxious to lay her head down for the night.

44

In the morning, Stephen and Janet take the kids to school together on their way to the courthouse. Last night, Stephen was just a dad. They played games, ate popcorn and for a few hours life existed as carefree and loving as he remembered it. It felt so good to feel like a regular person again. The few hours stood encapsulated apart from arrests, courtrooms and conspiracies. Rob was a natural fit to the family and Stephen now wishes that he had visited more or that they had gone to see him. Stephen slept for four consecutive hours last night. With dawn, reality once again sets in and Stephen's need to spend every possible minute with Mark and Emily magnifies as his hope diminishes. He misses not being able to sleep in his own bed with his own wife. He knows that once he was the creator of a safe and caring place for them all. Would that ever be the case again?

Today Terry will deliver his closing argument and that will be it. Fate will be delivered, and a life changed forever. What if he is acquitted? Will he and Janet repair their relationship? Can she ever forgive him and love him the same way? The extreme stress and ripping apart of some of the fundamental strands of their relationship created deep scars. A thread of their life, their bond, has been lost. He knows this. But the question is, can something else, a new something that also works, take its place? Can they rebuild and grow even stronger? He wants to believe that it's possible and he clings to this fantasy.

As they pull into the courthouse parking lot, Stephen parks the car, then puts his hand on Janet's arm and turns to her. He struggles to strengthen his resolve and says, "Janet, if for some reason things don't turn out well...I want you to know I..."

"Stephen, stop. Don't say anything. Not now. We have to focus everything we have on your innocence and coming out of this whole."

Stephen closes his eyes and silently nods. This woman, his life partner, deserves a good outcome. He opens his eyes and looks at his wife. Time seems to slow down enough for him to study the smooth strong lines of her face, the fire and determination in her eyes. If only he can preserve this moment forever. If only she can return to him.

"And Stephen," Janet adds as she gets out of the car, "I know." She says this to him with the sincerity and compassion of someone who knows you to your core. A certainty still exists between them. A knowingness of their deepest selves. The soul without the story.

Terry, with Rob in tow, meets them in his office a few minutes before they are due in court. Janet and Stephen notice that Terry wears a new suit and tie. He looks more polished than they've seen him in a long time. He must have already consumed several cups of coffee, apparent in his energetic gestures as he reads through some last–minute notes. Reminded of Terry's unwavering commitment to him, Stephen remains grateful for this rare kind of friendship.

"You two ready?" Terry asks them as they enter.

"I'm not going," Janet blurts out.

All three men are taken aback and Stephen's face falls in complete and utter despair. "What?"

"The jury needs to see you there," Terry reminds her.

"I've been thinking about this all night, and I thought I could just go along, but I can't. I have to see if I can come up with something. Anything. I might be bullshitting myself here, but I have to fucking do something," Janet apprises them. "I will go completely crazy if I just sit and watch this thing continue without at least trying everything I can think of. I cannot sit still. Do you understand? If I sit still, I start to think and if I listen to you in there I will start to think and I will start to get angry and when I start to get angry it shows on my face and I start to envision all kinds of things and I will want to kill someone. And the jury will see this."

Stephen winces at that last statement, knowing who that someone is.

"I cannot sit in that room anymore and see what's happening. You can tell the jury that I went to spend the day in church praying to make sure that justice is done. I don't give a shit what you tell them, but I just can't be there and behave. Rob is here. I asked mom to come. She'll met you there too." Janet crumples into a chair after she finishes and pulls out her cell phone. "Go. Call me or I'll call you or something." She waives them off.

Terry recognizes Janet's resolve and steels himself. He pats Stephen's shoulder reassuringly, "Let's go. We'll be fine and we'll get 'em on our side."

"Wait." Janet stands and walks over to Stephen, grabbing his arm and turning him toward her. She takes a moment to look at him, "I know you're innocent and somehow we will prove that. Terry will convince them. You need to know that going in there." She pulls him toward her and hugs him. Tears well up in his eyes as he feels her warmth on him. He holds on tightly and reluctantly releases her as she lets go and turns back into the office.

As Rob, Terry and Stephen walk toward court, Terry says, "She loves you, you know."

"I know."

"You okay?" Rob asks.

Stephen remains conflicted about not testifying. The senator didn't testify, and he knows that hurt him in the deliberations. On the other hand, his position remains quite different, and he knows that Terry and Janet are right and that he would invariably slip up and say something preposterous to make himself look either even guiltier or simply crazy. "Yeah. And I'm ready," he responds.

Terry prepared himself throughout the night, but standing in this nearly full courtroom, with the lives of his two best friends on the line, he chooses to simply speak first from the heart and go from there. He puts his notes down on the table in front of him and stands. "Ladies and gentlemen of the jury, I have been a lawyer all my adult life and I can honestly say I've never felt more strongly about a case." Terry puts his hand on Stephen's shoulder. "Stephen Reeves, who is on trial here, has led his entire life as a loyal family man, a professional, a father…" For Stephen the room takes on a strange immediacy. He can smell the wood that makes up the paneling, the desks and the

benches surrounding him. The ever–looming presence of Eileen's parents bearing down on him. The sounds, while clear, feel distant as if radiating through a vacuous space. He invokes the posture Terry suggested and tries simply repeating, *I am innocent* in his mind, but his overriding guilt around the affair makes that statement impossible to completely embody, so he revises the words to reflect a statement he can feel confident about, *I did not kill anyone*.

* * *

While Terry fights for Stephen in court, Ellen gives Janet her half of the remaining list of possible places Eileen Harris could have been in Grand Cayman. Ellen and some of Terry's other office staff will do what they can today to come up with anything that might help. A race against the clock. This is their last gasp. Janet calls Kathy and tells her to drop everything connected with their clients and help on this again. She asks Kathy to meet her at Janet's home so they can work together on combing through hotels and restaurants, in tandem with Terry's office, doubling their chances of finding something...anything to ensure Stephen will be safe. She's grateful for Kathy and her positive spirit, loyalty, and the way she honors and respects everyone's privacy and pain. At least Janet hasn't had to worry about her business going down the toilet during all this. She knows she owes Kathy. Hopefully someday she'll be able to pay that debt.

She settles Kathy in the workshop, and they begin going over the list. After a few frustrating calls, Janet gets up. "I'll go make us some tea." As she heads inside the house, she notices Mark's baseball glove by the back door. Stephen must have played catch with him last night. Maybe before they moved inside for the games. He is great with the kids. Calm, certain and always there for them. The sight of the glove immobilizes her. After standing and just staring at it for a while, she thinks she hears Kathy say her name, but brushes it off. Instead, she bends down and picks up the firm, well–worn leather. Feeling its texture and looking out at the back yard ignites an avalanche of emotion and without warning, one loud sob follows another and another. Tears flood forth until Janet drops to the floor, clutching her stomach, howling.

Startled, Kathy jumps out of her chair and goes to Janet. "Are you alright?" The question escapes her lips. An utterance so incredibly inadequate and absurd, yet the only thing she can think of. Janet nods, a likewise farcical response, yet the one individuals of western society are conditioned to give as a matter of protocol under overwhelming circumstances.

Janet releases the mounting fear and grief that's been building up inside of her over Stephen's predicament and its effect on everyone she loves. "I'm sorry," she finally says to Kathy as she stands up and wipes her face with the back of her hand.

"Don't be ridiculous. I can't even imagine."

"I still can't believe any of it. You'd think in this last year I'd get it through my head that this is really happening, but a part of me keeps hoping I'll wake up and it will all miraculously vanish."

"We all need a pill like that, don't you think?"

"Yeah." Janet manages a version of a smile. "Kathy, I don't know if I've properly thanked you for keeping me afloat through all this. Taking care of the business and helping me. I..."

"No need. Seriously. It's been my pleasure. You sit down and I'll get the tea."

There isn't enough time to indulge in her woes. Janet gets up, pulls herself together and goes into the kitchen to wash her hands and face. "Can you think of any other way she could have registered?" Janet asks.

Kathy hesitates a moment as she turns on the stove. "I hate to say it, but if she was put up in someone's private home, we wouldn't be able to track her."

"Oh my god. You're right." The room begins to close in.

"But we don't know that and, besides, there must be something she did, rented a boat, or booked herself on an excursion. I looked into a few common tourist attractions, and I'd like to get cracking on those, if you think it's a good idea."

The futility of that is glaringly apparent, but Janet doesn't have a better idea. "Yes, I think that's good. You start there and I'll call some of the private rental agencies."

45

George hasn't returned home. Good. She's counting on him being absent. It gives her time to double check the account numbers and make sure they haven't been changed. Sofia pulls out the token and activates it. Her fingers fly over the keyboard. They still work. The money is still there. Maybe George is being honest with her about everything. But no, there's more... She's seen him lie. He's convincing. And the voice inside tells her something different. He's up to something he's not telling her. She leaves the screen up and picks up a pad of paper. This obsession around Stephen, instead of easing up, grips her more fiercely with each passing day. Surely, she can exorcise it. She picks up the pen and begins writing. The sentences come slowly, and she scratches through some and revises others.

Sofia takes a deep breath and puts the pen down. Nearly lunch time. She hears the garage door. George must be back. Over the past two weeks, she sensed his confidence growing and the lust for more power re–surfacing within him. She doesn't want to believe that now that she has given him what he's wanted and needed most, his freedom, that his desire for her has waned. Yet their lovemaking feels hurried since the trial and his mind perpetually wanders. She wants him to step up and tell her how wrong she is, that he really does love her, and all this was truly for them. Sofia tears the page off the pad, folds it and puts it in her purse. She returns her attention to the computer.

George begins to feel better about his future. The debacle of being accused of murder has caused a setback, but the public's memory is short and already an outrage over the new scandal his opponent is generating over potential tax fraud is leveling the playing field. The press can always be counted on to go after a politician or celebrity if it means tearing them down. They can also be counted on for their short attention spans when it comes to the next new, sensationalized story. The last meeting with a few of his key supporters and his press secretary went well and he has been assured by his attorney that no second trial will be forthcoming.

He's looking forward to a drink and a relaxing lunch. Pulling into the garage, he notices Sofia's car. She handled her part well; he has to give her that. He loosens his tie and enters the study. A breeze wafts in through an open window as Sofia sits behind his desk, working on her laptop.

"I didn't expect you here before me," George says as he tosses his tie and jacket on a chair and moves toward the bar.

"Since we were having lunch, I thought I'd take the opportunity to work here this morning, so I grabbed some things and came back."

"Good news," George announces as if not hearing her, "Alton assures me there will be no second trial. Apparently, some evidence has been misplaced." He feigns surprise as he pours himself a scotch. "And that fool is going to prison any day now. I just got a call. The jury is going into deliberations this afternoon, and my source tells me he's as good as convicted."

"George, I can't help but wonder if it was really necessary to kill that woman," Sofia says, carefully studying his face.

"Now you bring this up. You're the one who said he could cause trouble if he talked to her."

"I said that to make sure we kept our guard up, not to..."

"Now it's my fault? If you weren't so good at what you do, made such a lasting impression, he wouldn't have been so determined to find you, now would he? We couldn't risk him talking to her." Claxton swigs his drink. "It's done Sofia. Relax. Lest you forget – we had tens of millions of dollars at stake. If that son of a bitch, Joel, had minded his own business and not read that original report in the first place, none of this would have happened. I usually do the shredding after everyone is gone." Claxton plunks himself down on the sofa.

"Yes, of course."

"We need to pursue future business, but not right away. Let some time pass until things become a fuzzy distant memory in the public mind. God knows, that shouldn't take too long," he says.

"Business. Yes." Sofia watches him for a moment. She notices how he seems to be concerned only with his comfort and the prospect of acquiring whatever whim he's seeking next. He didn't really see her when he entered. Oh sure, he saw her as one sees a chair, a table, a pet in the room. A physical presence that registers in the mind. But he didn't see her in the way one sees and ingests another's face, another's eyes, body language, real presence. Noticing another's mood or posture. He hasn't even kissed her. Now that she thinks about it, those kinds of greetings had gone by the wayside some time ago. Testing her theory she asks, "What about our plans? You and me? This was all supposed to be for us."

Their plans had included taking a month away to travel and to spend uninterrupted time with each other. Claxton had also hinted about getting married and she knows that would be a process of first attending numerous functions with him and being introduced into the community as his significant other.

Those plans began getting shelved even before he was arrested for murder. His excuse at that time had been his divorce and then after that the excuse was how it would look so soon after the divorce. She suspected those plans would continue to be shelved until he either finds a need for her or finds an alternative and a way out.

Claxton becomes uncomfortable and in need of a refill. He rises and returns to the bar, answering without looking at her, "Our plans." He begins as he pours himself a double, "Well, of course, eventually. Those too. But not now. You know that Sofia. I need to lie low and let this mess blow over for good."

"It's been months. We can go to Bali or the Seychelles. If only for a week or two. To get back to us. We've been so distant. It's normal for you to want to rest after all this."

"In my position right now it's not a good idea. I can't be seen with anyone suspicious in any way. You understand, don't you?" Glass in hand, he turns to Sofia and gives her his best charmingly concerned, duplicitous face.

"I do," she replies and genuinely means that her understanding has indeed reached a clarity long needed. That he would refer to her as suspicious is a new one.

"Almost forgot. I need to call Jack," George says. He pulls his cell phone out of his pocket and gestures to Sofia that he will be in the other room. Jack is his press secretary. She watches George's tall, handsome figure stroll out of the room. So confident. So charming.

A sadness descends over Sofia. Much like a veil falling slowly, enveloping every contour along the way. Just like that, he folded her up and put her away like yesterday's paper. No dialogue. No specialness. No accident. A silent, purposeful, ordinary decision. Perhaps there are too many things to feel, and he doesn't have the heart to feel them. Perhaps his heart is locked up in a safe place and to unlock it requires a strength that would shake his world – tear it to pieces and lay parts of himself bare so he would have to look at them, and his body couldn't survive all those tears. Perhaps he put her away because she resembles parts of himself he can't afford to have exposed and that would threaten his power. Whatever the reason, it no longer matters because its effect on her is something she's no longer willing to accept.

She turns her attention to the computer in front of her. The screen still reflects the correct URL for George's bank account at the World Net Cayman Bank. She refreshes the page and types in the password and logs back in. The total on deposit registers as $36,346,893. Right after George's trial, he was still flustered and in major damage control mode, so he was more relaxed with her access to his space when he was gone. He was grateful to her, and she knew that. She fed on that. It gave her hope for their future together. He allowed her in and out only under cover of darkness, but that seemed understandable. One night, she arrived before him and came across his passwords in his desk and something inside told her to copy them. The next time she looked in the place he had stashed them, they were gone. George had moved them. Initially, she thought of asking him for the passwords and asking him if he trusted her. She didn't ask. She wasn't ready to see his reaction then, in case it wasn't what she wanted. Over $36 million in just that one account and he still cries poverty. She could take it all and he wouldn't be able to do a thing about it. But, despite her anger, that's not who she wants to be anymore. She will only take what she needs to begin anew. She has an old Swiss account in the alias of Ann Hoffman that she's kept to herself and that she can now use as her way out. Sofia types in instructions for a wire transfer to Ann Hoffman in the amount of $13 million U.S. and pushes "send," just as George walks back into the room. "Chad should have our food here any minute from Café Milano," he announces.

She logs out and looks at him, "I completely forgot, I have to get some documents over to Jason before he gets up in the morning, so I have to go back to my hotel and get that file. Why don't we meet for dinner?" They had only been out in public a few times since the end of his trial and that was to out–of–the–way mom and pop establishments where she would meet him after he secured the premises. Her question is contentious, and she knows it, but it no longer matters.

"You can go to the hotel later. You have to eat lunch. I'll call him and see how close he is."

"No, really. I'll have it later. Dinner?'

"I pushed my lunch meeting to dinner, so now I have to stick to that. I can't move it again. You understand," George says, now irritated.

"I do. Listen, missing lunch is my fault. I wasn't thinking. Why don't you come with me? We can eat in my room," she continues baiting him, knowing he would never take the risk of being seen with her in a hotel in the city. Instinctively she knows she should abandon this urge to bait him and to find a way to leave.

"Don't be ridiculous. I can't be seen going to a hotel in the city right now. You know this."

"Yes, of course."

Something about Sofia's demeanor troubles Claxton. "What difference does it make if we eat here or there?" he asks, suddenly becoming flustered. "What is going on with you?"

Resisting the urge to deck him, Sofia dons a smile instead and replies, "Nothing. Enjoy your lunch. I'll see you later."

Claxton watches Sofia leave the room, carrying her purse and laptop. She cuts a fine figure, and he really does care for her. Perhaps the stress of what she's been through is making her increasingly irrational lately. Pity things have to be this way.

Private business just isn't private when in public office. He has a new image to create, and she may not work out to be a part of it. The Benjamin Mining violations are mounting, and he needs distance from that. Perhaps that will change. Perhaps not. Claxton turns on the stereo and drink number three makes its way into his glass.

46

He has always considered himself an optimistic man, yet fear, guilt and shame now take over so that summoning any shred of positivity prove to be too much for Stephen. He just can't feel it. Over the last several days, as the trial came to an end and they were no closer to finding any evidence to prove the real account of the Eileen and Sofia identities and of his innocence, he felt himself spiral down into a black hole of resolve for more punishment. Intellectually, he knows he's already been punished far beyond the weight of the crime of having an affair, yet in his heart somewhere he won't let himself off the hook. The jury doesn't begin deliberations until tomorrow morning. Terry assured him that he felt the trial went well for him. Stephen knows he may be blowing smoke, but he chooses to believe him anyway.

Stephen spends the evening with Mark and Emily. He lets them stay up late so he can get as much time in... just in case. Janet pops in every now and then, but her task remains sending emails, making calls and lining up more searches for the next morning. Janet desperately seeks identification of Eileen anywhere. Stephen decides this is her way of coping and, although he doesn't think it will go anywhere, he appreciates her efforts. Once the kids are in bed, Stephen pours himself a glass of wine. A habit he's taken up to help him relax in hopes of getting some sleep.

"Can you pour me one?" Janet says, walking up behind him.

"Gladly." He hands her his glass and pours himself another. Janet's face looks drawn and tired. "You need to get some rest," he suggests.

"Look who's talking." Janet can read feel Stephen's despondency. "You can never predict a jury," she offers.

Stephen just shakes his head and drinks his wine.

"Do you want Mark and Emily in court when the verdict comes in?" she asks.

"No. No kid needs to be put through that. Don't you agree?"

"Stephen..."

"Don't say anything. I played with fire...and... I lost my head...and I... I'm so sorry." Stephen looks longingly at his wife. He reaches out and touches her face.

She grabs his hand and holds it for a moment, then releases it and says, "Let's try to get some sleep."

Stephen finds himself running through long hallways and empty rooms. He senses he's being chased but isn't sure why or by whom. The hallways keep multiplying. Then in an instant, he stands in the center of an empty room. One wall of the room is comprised of large windows that look out onto a vivid, architecturally pleasing skyline with gardens scattered throughout like patchwork. He moves toward the view, looking for something and abandoning any anxiety. As he leans toward the window, he hears a distinct sound right next to his ear. A cocking sound. He turns slowly and his eyes meet the barrel of gun. The sudden sensation of that kind of terror jerks Stephen out of his sleep. The sheets are wet from his sweat and dawn's light already intrudes into the room. No more sleep.

Terry clarifies several times that there is no need for Stephen to return to court until the verdict comes in. However, they all agree that the best use of their time until such a call comes in is to continue digging and Terry's office has the most resources and proximity to court if and when they get the call. They can use the conference room. Rob will stay with Michelle, and they will come when they're needed.

The morning passes without word from the court and Janet decides to pick up a decent lunch for them and bring it back rather than ordering from the same places they've grown tired of. Besides, she needs a break. On her way out of Terry's office, something catches her eye. A quick flash of light, the way the sun hits a mirrored surface or metal. She turns to look and spots a woman rounding the corner away from the courthouse. She wears a charm bracelet that dangles and catches the sunlight. That bracelet! Janet runs toward the woman and grabs her arm from behind. She turns and both women stand facing each other. "Sofia Arden?" Janet's hands shake as her eyes exhibit traces of anger as well as a plea.

Sofia hesitates then says, "No, excuse me."

Janet holds on to her, "You're not going anywhere. Don't you dare do this to my family."

Sofia knew that coming back to the courthouse was a risk, but she told herself this would be a good way to end things, to complete this reckless cycle of her life – make one last stop and get some good news that perhaps Stephen has been acquitted after all. That way she can leave with peace of mind. She thought a verdict would have been in by now, but she can't wait any longer and almost made it out until Janet caught her. The upset she feels being face to face with Janet surprises her. Not wanting to get caught is certainly cause for discomfort, but this feeling rears up from a different place. A foreign place for Sofia. One that stirs up a jealousy and self–directed anger at her own choices in life.

Janet appears worn and harried. A woman simply trying to hold it together. Sofia knows her own identity is no longer of any consequence and to deny it would be pointless.

"I didn't set out to harm your husband. And certainly not to get anyone killed. Please. I had hoped a not–guilty verdict had been returned by now. I'm sure it will be. I have to go."

"No. That's not good enough. You screwed my husband," Janet spits.

"And I can't take it back. I'm not sure that I'd want to."

Janet releases Sofia's arm, then slaps her hard across the face. Two men passing by notice, hesitate for just a moment, then continue on their way. Sofia winces and calmly takes the blow. "You're luckier than you know," she says.

"Lucky? Hell no. There's a good chance that he's going to prison, but you probably know that. The trial didn't go well, and we don't have any way of proving Eileen Harris was Eileen Mathis. The information you provided isn't enough. We need more. You and the Senator must be thrilled to have your fall guy. I know you think you helped Stephen with that information, and I can only guess why." Emotion catches in Janet's throat, and she crams it down. "But we don't have what we need." Janet's resolve begins to crack and tears well up in her eyes. "We can't prove he never even met the real woman who was killed."

Sofia's flight is in a few hours, and she knows that George will find out soon what she's done, and there will be some satisfaction in that. She's surprised that she miscalculated that the information she'd given Stephen would be enough to lead them to the truth. This is her chance to begin to make things right – to begin to sleep at night.

She has no plans to ever return to the United States. Her stepbrothers will be thrilled. There is nothing here for her anymore. "Call Elias Jamison, Grand Cayman on Boreo Drive. It's a private estate that rents out. That should be enough. There's no more I can do for you."

Janet jots down the information into her cell phone, then reaches to grab Sofia as she heads out the door to the parking lot, but Sofia retreats and begins walking faster.

Janet follows. "I need to be sure. Can you tell the judge? Now. Please. Just say it, then you can disappear," Janet pleads.

Sofia slows for a moment, turning to Janet, "No. I am leaving. You have what you need," then proceeds to her car.

Watching the woman walk away, Janet is struck with a sudden need to capture her in another way. She raises her cell phone and calls out to Sofia. As Sofia turns around, Janet snaps the photo. The picture isn't great, but it does the trick. A host of emotions swim through Janet. With no time to indulge them, Janet shakes them off and runs back into the courthouse.

"That was fast," Terry says as Janet bursts back into the conference room. She relays her exchange with Sofia and immediately gets behind her laptop and uploads the photo of Sofia and puts it on a fob.

Stephen's temptation to run after Sofia grips him, but he knows it's irrational and fruitless. Besides, it's too far from Terry's office to the front of the courthouse for him to be able to catch her. Terry mentally tries to string it all together and see if he has any options left. He instructs Joe to search for information on Elias.

"I hope this one gets us something," Terry says.

Stephen stuffs his emotions and listens silently, not daring to hope.

Janet pulls the flash drive out and hands it to Ellen. "Can you get someone here to print this up, then photoshop it up to make her hair blonde, put glasses on her and mimic whatever else she did to make herself up for the trial. I think if we show Sofia as herself and then as Eileen, we have a better chance."

Ellen grabs the drive and dashes out. Terry kisses Janet on the face out of exuberance. "Brilliant!"

Stephen stares at his wife, amazed. "You are incredible," he says. "What can I do?"

"We're not there yet," she replies. "Go get me some coffee and a sandwich please, so I don't pass out."

"Done." Stephen leaves the office, grateful to be of some use.

Janet goes over to Joe to see if she can help him. A while later it looks like they have some numbers. Terry watches Janet as she gets on her laptop and pulls up anything she can on the Boreo Cayman estate, then cross references those numbers.

"Here it is. That estate is on one of estate rental sites and I had been going through, we just hadn't gotten to it. But this is the public reservation number, so this one might be the private one." She writes down the phone number, picks up her phone and hesitates. "I don't want to risk that these people were paid off to keep silent."

"What do you mean? We have to pursue it," Terry insists.

"Of course. I know. It's in how we do this. This is everything. We only get one shot here and I don't want to scare them off." Janet's mind races. "I have an idea."

Terry looks at her expectantly, but she waives him off, holding up her hand asking him to be patient. She leans back in her chair, deep in thought.

Stephen returns with coffee and sandwiches, "I brought extras." Terry points to Janet and instructs him to be silent. Stephen whispers to Terry, "What's going on?"

"We have a contact and now she's thinking."

Stephen is tempted to ask what there is to think about but stays silent.

Janet takes a sip of coffee and bites into a turkey sandwich as her mind churns.

She figures that Sofia secured the rental for Eileen and if any information would be imparted, it would likely be to Sofia over a stranger. Janet finishes her bite, takes a sip of coffee and closes her eyes. She sits there for a moment taking a few deep breaths before she opens her eyes, picks up the phone and dials the number. "Hello. I'd like to speak to Elias Jamison..." Terry, Joe and Stephen are all at rapt attention. "Is there any way you can get a message to him immediately. This is rather an emergency... yes my name is Sofia Arden."

Stephen and Terry exchange looks and smile. Janet leaves her message, supplying Terry's unlisted back line as the call back number, and they all take a deep breath. The waiting game begins.

Over an hour later, Ellen returns with the photos of Sofia, showing a sequence of how she transformed herself into Eileen's lookalike. She hands them to Terry. "I think these are really good – it's amazing that she did this. I still can't believe this could've happened," Ellen says.

"That's the problem, the judge can't believe it either. These are perfect to back up our argument. Any word on a verdict?" Terry inquires.

"No. Nothing, just that the jurors are finishing their lunch and will be back in the deliberations room by one–thirty," Ellen relays. "What about the estate?"

"The guy's calling back," Janet states with absolute certainty.

Ellen nods, "That's great." The tension in the room refuses to let up.

"I need to get a bead on Judge Ramen and see when we might get an audience, praying this guy calls and gives us what we need. Can you check on that?" Terry requests of Ellen.

"On it."

"The rest of us need to try and relax," Terry imparts, unconvincingly.

Every time Terry's back line rings, the trio hold their breath and let Janet answer.

The last call left them flustered. A clerk called regarding another case, and they immediately panicked that the verdict had come in. Two hours later, the energy in the room grows unbearable. "I'm calling again," Janet announces.

"Do you think that might seem suspicious?" Stephen asks.

"No. I think that when Sofia Arden wants an answer, she gets it." Just as Janet walks over to Terry's desk, his phone rings and they all hold their breath.

"Hello?" Janet answers. Her face lights up and she gives the thumbs up. "Yes, Mr. Jamison. We have a problem with our accounting department here and our client is furious. Sometimes good help is so difficult to find, and as we accommodate numerous clients, I need a confirmation on one of our people who stayed with you last May. We've had some extra charges for people who we didn't actually accommodate." Janet explains that she needs written confirmation that the woman she made the reservation for was indeed the one who had stayed at the estate and would he be so kind to look at a photograph to confirm this. She completes this task via fax and Mr. Jamison, aptly charmed, identifies the real Eileen Harris photo and happily complies with Janet's requests including signing an affidavit identifying the woman in the photograph as the one housed on the estate during that period, the same time period during which Eileen was supposed to be a juror on the Claxton trial.

The emergency meeting scheduled with the judge is just before four o'clock.

When Devoe gets wind of it, he hits the roof, and despite being in a deposition, he has to be there, either by going himself or by sending an Assistant District Attorney from his office. Devoe decides he needs to be there in person. The meeting takes place in the judge's chambers.

"What's this all about, Mr. Pollard? Please tell me we are not going down the same rabbit hole," Judge Ramen asks as she enters the room and begins removing her robe.

"Your honor, the jury is due back with a verdict at any time now," Devoe states the obvious. Terry realizes the man simply likes the sound of his own voice.

The judge gives the prosecutor a look of annoyance, which silences him. "I believe we are all aware of that, Mr. Devoe," she states.

Terry pulls out the signed affidavit, along with the photo of Eileen Harris, and hands it to the judge and a copy to Devoe. "These documents prove that Eileen Harris, the same Eileen Harris listed on the jury docket for the murder trial of Senator George Claxton, was in reality on the Cayman Islands during the Senator's trial. She went under the alias of Eileen Mathis and stayed at the address you see there. We have eyewitnesses prepared to identify her. This means that my client has not actually met the woman who was murdered."

"Your honor," Devoe begins to blow, "This outrageous theory again. This could merely be a woman who looked like her."

"I was hoping you'd say that," Terry says and pulls out the photo of Sofia at the courthouse today and hands it to the judge and a copy to Devoe. "This is Sofia Arden. The woman we believe was in the jury box masquerading as Eileen Harris. She was at the courthouse today and gave us the information on the estate. We also did a workup on this photo to show the court how she was made up to look like Eileen Harris." Terry pulls out the photoshop version and passes it out. He hands out a few more papers and continues. "Also, there is my summation of the facts and the contract you have there is proof that Senator George Claxton along with Sofia Arden, the woman who took Ms. Harris' place is involved in numerous violations' coverups regarding Benjamin Mining, the company in which Ms. Arden is a large shareholder. That is a separate matter, but it speaks to motive for the identity switch to ensure the Senator's freedom."

"Is this Ms. Arden prepared to testify?"

"No, your honor. We believe she's likely leaving the country, if not already gone. Giving us this information is certainly not in her interest, but according to our information, she has dual citizenship with Italy and maybe even Switzerland. We believe it's likely that she is not intending to return to the United States. We also believe she will likely be using an alias. Also, the Senator is a powerful man, and this information is of course not in his interest and therefore poses a danger to Ms. Arden. But I believe we have more than enough evidence to prove our case that my client never knew or even met the real Eileen Harris. The circumstances surrounding that fact are an entirely different matter with implications on another case that I would think the prosecutor would wish to pursue." Terry shoots a sideways glance at Devoe then pauses, thinking. He must give it his all now or never. There is no better way to quell the tide of doubt than with a strong blitz of the naked truth. "This case has been unusual from the beginning in that my client never veered from his account that the dead woman was not the woman he had met and known in the jury box. Also, many of the jurors seemed to agree, but weren't sure enough, especially after the media blitz. This made my defense of this man incredibly difficult since I couldn't present the truth my client wished to present because we had nothing concrete to back up that claim, especially in the face of such certain assertions and assumptions on her jury service from the other side. I chose to suppress that for obvious evidentiary reasons. Also, because this is all so inextricably tied to Senator Claxton, a very powerful man in our midst, our burden was that much greater. This brings up the veracity of the Senator's trial as well as his behavior and complicity in what happened to Ms. Harris. With all due respect, your honor, we were in a tenuous position from all sides. I hope that this evidence will prevent further injustice in all this."

Devoe finishes reading the documents on Claxton and Sofia and reviews Terry's summation. He looks at the judge. Terry notices that Devoe remains speechless.

"Can you get any of the other jurors from the Senator's trial to take a look at this photograph and sign statements of doubt surrounding Ms. Harris' participation?" the judge asks.

"Yes, your honor. I believe we can," Terry offers.

"Go to it and since the jury still hasn't reached a verdict, I'll instruct them to break and call them into court in the morning. I want those statements before 9 a.m."

"Yes, your honor."

* * *

Stephen wants to go with Terry to visit some of the jurors from the Claxton trial, but Terry refuses to let him. Instead, he allows Janet to accompany him while Stephen resigns to picking up the kids and taking them, along with Rob and Michelle, to dinner.

Terry opts to focus on the jurors he found the most accommodating to him the first time. Janet and he are armed with already prepared affidavits. Their first stop is Melita Colt. Loud music and voices spill out from her apartment. Terry and Janet approach the open front door and party in progress. The tattooed, pierced and party set is in full swing. A young woman, cigarette in hand, twirls to the music between two muscular young men completely oblivious to Terry as he steps through the threshold, and she slams into him. “Woah…hey...sorry,” she says and continues her gyrating.

Terry, with Janet right behind him, looks around then turns to a guy wearing a wife–beater and a bandana and asks, “I’m looking for Melita Colt. Is she here?”

“Melita?!” He yells over the music.

“Yeah!”

“Over there, man.” He points to an alcove where Terry spots Melita hovering over a bong with several others and walks over to the young woman.

As soon as Melita spots Terry coming toward them, she stands up and tries to block him from the bong, grabbing his arm and directing him away from the alcove. “Looking for me?”

“Yes, actually.”

“My friend’s borrowing my apartment for a party, so...”

“Don’t worry, I don’t care about that. Can we go somewhere and talk?” Terry suggests. Melita unhappily leads him out of the apartment and down the hall. Janet follows. “This won’t take long,” Terry reassures her. They settle onto a dirty, makeshift bench near the exit. Janet remains standing.

Terry pulls out the photo of Sofia as Eileen Harris and the one of the real Eileen Harris. “Can you tell me again which of these women was the one you remember on the jury?”

“This one.” Melita points to Sofia without hesitation and both Terry and Janet smile.

By the end of the night, they complete their task of obtaining sworn statements from Melita and three of the other jurors, Mike, Ted and Laura.

47

W*omen are a strange and erratic breed*, George muses. Everything had been executed perfectly, failure was never an option with him, and he can't understand Sofia's behavior lately. She knows very well he had to get back to the business of cleaning up any doubts his arrest had caused and begin re–building his power base in Washington.

Growing power in this city takes a delicacy, a commitment and a giant set of balls. It also requires immediate and in–person spin with other Senators, lobbyists, publicists and even aides. Purchasing loyalty and people is an art and there's always a price.

Sofia feigned a headache last night and said she would come by today. Claxton left early this morning and tried calling her, but she ignored his calls. He may need to schedule a weekend away to keep her pacified, in lieu of that overwhelming vacation she keeps suggesting, until he arranges his next steps. The time has come to distance himself from Benjamin Mining. Sofia might understand, thinking he will include her in his life or maybe even some other ventures; however, she too may be a liability for the long haul. He can't be on record as being intimately involved with a shareholder from that company, let alone a family member. And with her unpredictable behavior lately, you never know where the quicksand will turn up. Best to distance himself from *anything* associated with this murder incident. He will have to begin slowly and find a way to make her think it's her idea.

Claxton's car pulls up to his residence and he gets out without a word to his driver. He tries Sofia's number again. Straight to voice mail. Probably on her way over right now. His phone rings as soon as he enters the house. Alton.

"Yeah?" George answers.

"Judge Ramen just sent word for the jurors to appear in her court in the morning," Alton informs him.

"Verdict in?"

"It doesn't look like it. Could be further instruction."

"Is that a problem?"

"Probably not. Just wanted to keep you in the loop."

Claxton hangs up and his back goes up. He smells a rat, and his mind tries to recall any signs of trouble along the way. What could have changed in the last few days? He rips off his tie and pours himself a drink. As he caps off the decanter, he notices the envelope propped up on his desk. Foreboding encroaches. 'George' reads the addressee, in her handwriting. Yesterday, he may have welcomed her departure, thinking it best that she decide to leave on her own, but today after the call from Alton, something warns him that this might be a complication. He tears open the envelope.

'*Dear George,*

You and I have been through some incredible times together and even though I will never forget those moments of connection, I wonder if you will even remember me in a heartfelt way years from now. If your thoughts will drift to memories of a time we thought our future would be filled with togetherness. I believe we made a great team, but I've come to realize something different. When I'm by your side I feel emptiness around me, and life feels too treacherous. Yes, even for me. I grow weary thinking of the journey ahead with you, knowing you are not a man that wishes to share the road in the way I had hoped. You are not finished. I don't know when it will ever be enough for you. We must go our separate ways. Don't worry. We cannot allow our secrets to enslave us. I will keep yours and I will not cross your path again. I will keep moving.

Yours in memory, Sofia'

Unease descends on Claxton. Sofia wouldn't simply leave without...Claxton immediately leaps to his computer and begins accessing his accounts. She knows of two of his accounts that are associated with their deals, the Isle of Man and the Cayman accounts. But she would have to have the passwords and all document information to gain access. His mind races as he replays moments of conversation and places where Sofia may have gotten her hands on some of these facts and figures. He had been careful, moving information, regularly changing passwords and keeping most items in his safe.

He knows better than to trust anyone, especially after being married to Cynthia. Sofia only had access to his safe on the night of Joel's murder, and only out of necessity to remove the flash drive containing information on dealings that would raise red flags with the DA if found. He had other account information, but he made sure that even if she had seen it, she wouldn't be able to put it together with the specific account. He changed the code to the safe the next day and the only thing he hadn't changed were the codes to the Cayman account. He'd been a little busy trying to make sure he didn't go to jail and felt it best to let sleeping dogs lie. The screen loads and reflects the Cayman account balance of just over $20Million. Claxton sits back in his chair and stares at the image. Sofia took a chunk but didn't clean him out. Why? This fact should make him happy, but he knows better. Something is off. She's up to something. But what?

48

Sofia stands by the large window overlooking the planes. She loves First Class lounges, where she can choose to seclude herself from the teaming masses in the terminals and contemplate the transition from one place to another, from one experience to another. This will be a more complete change for her. She has chosen Argentina as her destination for beginning a new life. Sofia Arden travelling as Ann Hoffman would become Sofia Moreno once in her new town. She feels comfortable with that name – partially her own and partially borrowed – a good way to integrate who she had been with whom she hoped to become. She sips her club soda and goes to sit back down in the leather chair. She had given Stephen's side all the pieces they need to ensure his acquittal. Her remorse lies only in the fear and extremely difficult months she'd put Stephen through, but not in choosing him. It has been four and a half months since the end of George's trial and all that has happened. In a way it seems like no time has passed, and in another way, it feels like a lifetime ago. Strange to think how her time with Stephen and being away from the rest of the world brought her back to a place of hope. She doesn't want to lose that again. She can't. She has a new mission.

George has read her letter by now and knows that she took some of the money. Sofia laughs. He would have taken it all and is probably trying to figure out why she didn't. She knows the information that will get Stephen released will be used to re–arrest George, so perhaps part of her decision stems from the guilt of putting him through that. But knowing George and his love of strategy and proclivity for maneuvering, she feels certain that he will find a way out yet again. Perhaps he may have to give up politics, but certainly he will re–invent himself with a different type of power position. Whatever life he chooses for himself, she wishes him well. She's choosing a life where scheming, hiding, manipulation and hurting people isn't the norm. I n her mind this is progress.

George had said, "Progress is essential to the survival of the mind." When she questioned him about their submitting false documents to the regulatory agencies and essentially allowing her company to poison the environment, he replied, "The only question lies in what you deem to call progress. This will probably create other agencies or companies to clean up the mess, creating more jobs of a different kind." To George, progress meant amassing more money, and she had put aside her own disturbed feelings for that same quest. No more. Now she has another to consider.

Sofia places her hand on her belly. A new life. Not just her own. She wants to create a place of love and safety in her new circumstances. She wants to create what she had seen was possible.

49

"Due to new evidence and pending further investigation, we move for dismissal without prejudice in the case of the People v Stephen Reeves," Devoe announces, standing before the court. Only Terry notices the discomfort in the prosecutor's stance. No DA likes to think they almost prosecuted an innocent man and with such vengeance.

"Motion granted," Judge Ramen says and turns to the jurors. "Thank you for your service ladies and gentlemen. You are dismissed."

Stephen observes the surprise on the jurors' faces and empathizes. Most of them avert their gaze. He can see that some of them look genuinely distraught. Eileen's parents seem genuinely shocked and distressed. Their grief and exhaustion overwhelm them onceagain.

Relief washes over Stephen realizing the battle is over. For a man who had spent no time in a courtroom throughout his life until this past year, to then spending months in a courtroom experiencing so many sides of the system, he held up quite well to the casual observer. To those who know him, the scars are many. As he turns to look at Janet, a different feeling takes over. Now he will have to confront the long–term impact his actions have had on those he loves and figure out how to put his life back together. In a different sort of way, another battle is just beginning. Janet's smile tugs at his heart, wishing he could keep it growing. As they all stand up, Janet hugs both Stephen and Terry before they make their way out of the courtroom. Michelle gives Stephen a warm smile and her daughter a tight squeeze. Rob too hugs his brother in more of an embrace than Stephen can ever remember receiving from him. Stephen wonders if he can hope for more hugs in the days to come.

"We should celebrate," Terry says. "The prosecution has a big mess on its hands, but you should be done with this. For good."

"Let's grab an early lunch," Janet suggests as Terry moves to fend off reporters.

"Give me a minute," Stephen says. He moves past them and toward the door to the jury deliberations room. He looks in, surveying it – much like the one he spent all those days in with Eileen and Charlie and Mike and Marge. A cleaning lady is on her way out. "I have to lock up," she tells him, motioning for him to step away. He notices that she's holding a half empty bag of trash in her hand.

"Is that the trash from in there?" he asks her. She nods, eyeing him suspiciously. "I'm sorry to bother you, but I think I may have dropped my good pen in there. May I take a look?"

"It's just trash," she says as she hands him the bag and walks off, shaking her head.

Stephen looks through the empty soda cans and crumpled sheets of paper and wrappers. He spots a folded sheet of paper that reads: 8 – guilty/ 4 – undecided – a large X covers the preceding words and then below it reads: 10 – Guilty / 2 – undecided. Stephen shivers and crumples the page up in his hand and puts it back into the bag. So many of them thought him guilty.

"Stephen, come on bro," Rob calls from down the hall.

"Coming," he says as he drops the bag into a large trash can at the end of the hallway.

"Are you okay?" Janet asks as he walks up.

Stephen looks at his wife and embraces what he recognizes as a second chance. "Better than okay. I'm a lucky man," he says. Janet so badly wants to enjoy this moment and to not think ahead. She opts to do just that. Michelle smiles at her daughter, encouragingly.

Terry asks Ellen to join them for their celebratory lunch and Janet calls Kathy. A weight has been lifted and they need to acknowledge their efforts in bringing the truth to light. Terry beams with relief of a job finally concluded and Stephen's face releases some of its strain. The Stephen Reeves' family and defense team convene at the Lawfully Wetted Bar to punctuate the end of this ordeal. Ellen is relaxed as Kathy jokingly says to Janet, "Boy, am I looking for some serious days off."

"Terry, man, I can't thank you enough," Stephen says as he looks at his friend with genuine warmth, then he looks at everyone at the table. "All of you are responsible for this outcome. You've all been here for us, and I can't tell you how grateful I am."

"This was by far the largest team effort ever and you all know it," Terry chimes in. "Now, I don't know about the rest of you, but this really made me realize how lucky we are to have each other. I think I might be just a bit dependent on all of you. I mean every case from now on will pale in comparison and where would I go for a home cooked meal? Ellen, that includes you. Thanks for all you do. You're the best paralegal out there."

"And friend," Janet adds. She knows Terry is lobbying to ensure that she and Stephen stay together, and she lets him. The three of them have been through a lifetime together.

"No matter what would've happened, we never would have stopped, you know that, right?" Terry adds, looking at Stephen.

"I know, I know. You guys are the best. I think I might actually sleep tonight," Stephen says and instinctively looks at Janet for a moment, then quickly looks away.

"I'm just glad I will still be in the good graces of Mark and Emily. I made them a promise that I wouldn't let you go to jail, and I must admit, for a day or two, I was sweating it," Terry says.

"*You* were sweating?" Stephen responds.

"Let's focus on the positive here," Janet interjects and turns to Stephen. "I think you should pick them up from school today and tell them."

"Why don't you both go," Michelle injects. "I'm sure I can get Rob to help me with a few errands."

"Absolutely, madam. I am at your service."

The relief felt at the table is palpable. The good feelings created as a result of the morning's announcement cannot be squelched and to an outsider, the gathering appears light and animated. Rob orders a bottle of champagne from the only two options, neither of which is top shelf. "Merely for a toast," he assures them, "I assure you no one will get pissed on just a sip."

50

A barrage of conflicting emotions sweeps through Janet. Stephen will not go to prison and for the most part this nightmare is finally over. The key phrase being 'for the most part.' Now there is no trial to attend, no evidence to uncover, no continuous stream of concerns to overcome. There remains only the two of them, their family and friends, and the remnants of the life they had known. The past couple of hours at lunch were a reminder of the good things in their life. Of the connection between them. Of what they have created together. The thought of dismantling their life, the life they'd spent two decades building, paralyzes her. But the thought of just picking up and continuing without making some major shift exists in a time and place that's no longer available to her. If they are to remain in their marriage, a new relationship will need to be formed. A rebirth of sorts, that will allow for the past year's events to be acknowledged, accepted, and then placed aside. This will not be easy. If she hadn't spent these past months processing all of the events and trying to help Stephen get to the greater truth, she's not sure if she could ever go back to him. If she would be able to put the image of him making love to Sofia out of her mind long enough to not want to keep punishing him for it. This is the question before her. Can she grow to love him again in a way that is new and that can move past his infidelity?

She and Stephen ride to the school side by side, neither knowing what to say. Janet wants the kids to sense a victory without tension and for all of them to be able to enjoy this evening. They all deserve that. One evening of normalcy as a family. To bring up the subject of the state of their relationship would surely destroy all hope of an evening with no tension. She chooses to focus on the moment and on the anticipation of Mark and Emily's faces once they hear the news. "We should all go out to a movie then to dinner tonight," she says to Stephen, thinking a movie would be a great way for all for all of them to share in something without risking too much conversation that could prove awkward, if not volatile. There would be enough opportunity for that atdinner.

"Great idea." Stephen's mind swims with questions, but he knows to put them aside for the rest of this day and night and to simply enjoy the victory. He will have to find a way to create a new life with his family. He can feel that Janet is open to making it work, but that it will be up to him to create the blueprint for the opportunity. He's familiar with blueprints and he will do whatever it takes to make this one magnificent.

After picking up Emily and Mark from school and the initial rounds of 'yes this is really over' and 'life can resume normally now,' Stephen announces, "We're going to make one stop before we go home."

"Where?" Emily asks.

"You'll see."

"Are you taking us to the observatory?" Mark asks.

"Only you would like that, dork. Mom, where are we going?"

"I don't know either, Em," Janet answers, giving Stephen a curious look.

During the entire drive, no matter how hard the kids press, Stephen refuses to divulge his destination. When they pull up to the Georgetown University campus, Stephen parks and leads them to Healy Hall and into the Riggs Library. It's been a long time since either Janet or Stephen had returned to their campus and both are brought back to a special time in their lives.

The library is occupied by students doing research, homework or reading.

Stephen leads his family through the stacks of books. Finally, Janet asks, "Stephen, why are we here?"

"Give me one second…." Stephen says as he keeps moving through the library looking for a specific section. He stops at the literature aisle and announces, "This is it." He leads them into the middle of the empty aisle.

"What is it?" Emily asks confused as Mark looks at the titles on the shelves and adds, "These are not books on real things."

"What this is, is this is the place where I first told your mother I loved her." Stephen announces as he turns to Janet and looks into her eyes. He reaches over and takes her hand. Janet's mind travels to a million places at the touch of Stephen's hand on hers, but she lets it be, feeling the warmth of a touch she hasn't allowed herself to feel for a very long time.

Mark seems a bit disappointed, "Oh," but Emily smacks him on the arm and looks at her parents, waiting to see what will happen.

"I knew I loved you right here, eighteen years ago, Janet Ellis," Stephen begins, "And I love you even more eighteen years later as Janet Reeves."

Janet can't stop the tears from coming and cascading down her face. Stephen brushes them from her cheeks and continues, "I will do everything in my power to make this right again. Thank you for being my partner." He motions for Emily and Mark to come closer, and he hugs them into the fold. He looks up at his wife, "I love you. Always have."

Janet fights through a barrage of emotion and finds her way to this place and this time and the love around her, "Always will," she whispers.

51

In the short time George Claxton has lived in his townhouse he has grown fond of it. The imported Indian silk that makes up the drapes in his bedroom and the antique Balinese dresser remind him that his taste, much like his reach, extends beyond borders. He takes the photo of his two daughters in the Tiffany frame as well as the silver framed photo of himself in the Alps with Hans Adam II, the Prince of Liechtenstein, wraps them in a cashmere scarf and places the bundle in a half–packed suitcase. He places the nearly empty Baccarat whiskey decanter next to the laptop on the small desk near the window and looks out at the morning light and the way it softly illuminates the grounds and brickwork below.

One must separate oneself from the herd for so many reasons, he reminds himself. *First, to gain power. Second, to garner momentum and to build a following. Third, to have a voice that people notice. You can talk all you want, but if no one's listening, what difference does it make? It's an ugly game. Almost makes you detest the human beast – so full of fear and cowardice. That's what sets him apart. He has balls. A large, monumental set of steel balls. No one can ever call him a coward. Even so, where does it all lead anyway? We strive for things – achievements, money, fame, accolades – and for what? A moment here and there of misguided satisfaction from something that doesn't really matter. A height that others envy, only to be taken away by some bumbling moron. We tell ourselves stories that it matters, that we're doing something good.*

Building something. Something better than average. That we will be remembered. But why does being remembered matter? If we're being remembered, we're dead, so why would it matter to us? The sad and sick truth is that you can't get there without compromise. Compromise of your soul that is. We tell ourselves that purely, generously and ethically, whatever those words mean, is how we're going to do it, but then we begin to realize that one person's ethics is another's blasphemy and we're stuck. We're in over our head in what we must do, so we push on. After all, what some consider heinous crimes are to others salvation. Seeing that is disturbing, sure, but it's the way it is.

Some say family is everything. Where are they when they think you're not who they want you to be? Under the nearest rock feigning ignorance or shock, that's where. But they sure are there, right by your side, when you're at the top. They're there soaking up the adoration by association, the extra money, the invitations into circles they would never otherwise grace by their meager selves. Life – it's a fucking game of shame. A game that you sometimes lose, because some nutbag decides that it's his turn. It's not that he's any nobler than you, or more ethical. Quite the contrary. He's even sleazier because he is ignorant of what it took for you to get there. Life, it's merely a gateway to death. Some of them want to kill you, but they have to catch you first.

* * *

As police cars descend upon the home of George Claxton, John Alton jumps out of his car to beat them to the front door. He tries calling Claxon on his cell for the third time in the past hour, but George refuses to pick up. Alton had texted him that it was urgent, but still nothing. The high–priced defense lawyer had already relayed to George what happened on the Reeves' trial and the evidence that came out about Sofia. They discussed several possible scenarios, but none of them were what George wanted to hear. Unfortunately, his political career is over, because now the prosecution has a reason to retry him for the Joel Christiansen murder and, with the additional evidence, the outcome doesn't look promising. George does not do well with bad news and Alton is concerned, especially after getting a call from the prosecutor that they would be bringing Claxton in for immediate questioning.

Alton rings the bell and pounds on the front door. No answer. His security detail is questioned, but claims that as far he knows, the Senator is inside his house. A couple of officers make their way around the side of the house and to the back as Elliott Mann, flanked by two more uniforms, arrives at the front door and stands next to Alton.

"We know he's in there, John," Mann announces. "One of our cars saw him pull into the garage a couple of hours ago and he didn't leave."

"You've had him under surveillance?" Alton asks.

"Only since this morning. Under the circumstances, we thought it prudent." The two men stare each other down, then Mann begins incessantly ringing the doorbell. "Senator Claxton, open up! Police!"

Alton chimes in, yelling through the door, "George, you have to open the door. I'm already working on it. Don't make it worse."

"We'll have to break the door down." Mann motions for the officers to step in. Two uniformed policemen step forward with a ram and break down the front door.

Mann, Alton, and the officers enter the house and begin going through, room by room.

"George!" Alton yells, heading for the study. It's empty.

As the men make their way through thc house, they find every room devoid of life. In the master bedroom, the drawers and closet have been emptied. On the small desk by the window sits a laptop with a paused video visible on its screen. Alton walks over and hits play. The scene comes to life. It's a younger George Claxton giving his speech to the small crowd those many years ago. "You cut that one little corner that one little time and it will build and build and build into the maelstrom we're in now. I'm here to get us out of it…How you do anything is how you do everything! Back It Up! Thank you!" Alton shuts the computer. Senator George Claxton is in the wind.

ACKNOWLEDGMENTS

The creation of every book has a story of its own. This story began an as idea when I was on jury duty and completed its cycle after my daughter's input on the screenplay version.

I am grateful to everyone who has participated in this journey beginning with the early incarnations of the story, and support from Davis Entertainment, Picturemaker Productions, and Mark Teitelbaum, along with Mark Vancil and Dennis Quaid. This story got a second wind with Mike Burkenbine, Zach Lasry, and Gerry Santos before I turned it into this novel.

Thank you to those who encouraged me to complete this book, including Allison Montgomery, David Rothmiller, and Tanya Buckley. And most of all, this book would not have been completed without the input and push from Geoff Payne and Arianna Lasry.

I'd like to thank all the readers out there. You are the reason we write. Reading is an incredible way to explore, learn and connect, and I sincerely hope you enjoyed the experience. Independently published books rely on you to spread the word. If you enjoyed your time through these pages, please tell your friends and post a review. Thank you!

Aleks

Made in the USA
Monee, IL
01 July 2022

1608c504-636a-4c99-9e9c-6cba886e34ffR01